Rage and Retribution

Also by Tony Read

Innocence is No Defence

Death in Dark Waters

A Proper Country Funeral

Murder Must be Witnessed

Death Stands on Guard

Death Takes Revenge

The Perfect Candidate

The above novels feature Detective Inspector Mark Hobson and his wife Helena, and the stories are set against the backdrop of the stunning scenery of The Peak District National Park.

Insatiable

A crime thriller without detectives in which an ordinary man is driven to commit murder, and the terrible consequences that flow from one drunken moment of rage.

Well Versed (or maybe not)

A short book of serious and comic poems.

Rage and Retribution

Tony Read

Copyright © 2024 Tony Read

All rights reserved, including the right to reproduce this book, or portions thereof in any form. No part of this text may be reproduced, transmitted, downloaded, decompiled, reverse engineered, or stored, in any form or introduced into any information storage and retrieval system, in any form or by any means, whether electronic or mechanical without the express written permission of the author.

This is a work of fiction. Names and characters are the product of the author's imagination and any resemblance to actual persons, living or dead, is entirely coincidental.

The views expressed in this work are solely those of the author and do not necessarily reflect the views of the publisher, and the publisher hereby disclaims any responsibility for them.

ISBN: 978-1-917293-95-2

Dedication

As with all my books, this book is dedicated to my wife Shirley and to my sons John and Paul. I am forever grateful for the love and support they give me in all aspects of my life.

This book is also dedicated to the many other family members and friends who have encouraged me to keep on writing.

In particular, I want to thank my good friend Dr Graham Brodie who has painstakingly read through the text of this novel correcting many typing and grammatical errors that the original manuscript contained. I also want to thank my friend Nicola Bremner who, with meticulous attention to detail, also greatly assisted me with this process.

Prologue

The corpse was that of an adult female, probably no more than forty years old. Her face had once been beautiful but now showed the first visible signs of decay. The labels inside her clothing spoke of high end expensive couture, but her coat and shoes were splattered with mud, and a substance, that could only be blood, stained much of her upper body. A red rose made of silk had been folded into her right hand; and pinned to her chest was a page ripped from a book of poetry; a sonnet to love; perhaps the most romantic lines of verse Shakespeare ever wrote.

    She lay just yards away from a well used footpath, hidden from view by dense foliage and overhanging branches. Probably hundreds of ramblers had walked past this spot oblivious to the nearby presence of death. Doubtless one day she would have been found when the stench of rotting flesh started to pollute the clean air, and scavenging animals had attacked her remains leaving their debris scattered across the ground, making identification of the deceased a nightmare for investigating police officers; but her killer had wanted no such outcome. It was as if he had a need for her body to be discovered while the symbols of love that adorned it were still in place knowing that they would ensure there would be widespread publicity for this unhappy find. An anonymous telephone call to the local police station made from a pay as you go mobile phone was all that was needed. Clear directions had been given; an officer had been sent to check out the story, and had discovered to his horror that the call was not a hoax. So begins a murder inquiry led by Detective Chief Inspector Hobson of the Derbyshire Constabulary.

CHAPTER ONE

Tuesday September 10th 2013-Feelings of frustration, conversations with "The Grim Reaper", and a totally unexpected development.

It was Sod's law. The decision of Detective Chief Inspector Mark Hobson to postpone a routine dental appointment so that he could spend a carefree day with his lovely wife Helena amidst the stunning scenery of the Lake District had come back to bite him. He had woken up this morning with a raging toothache, which the ingestion of super-strength painkillers had done little to suppress.

Worse had then followed. His long planned meeting with Detective Chief Superintendent Stanley Hardy, the head of the Peak District CID to discuss administrative changes within the department, and for which he had spent many hours preparing, had had to be postponed without notice because Hardy had flu. This had soured his mood still further, but up until the moment of the discovery of a body in the Goyt Valley was made known to him he had had at least the consolation of a dinner date that evening with close friends to look forward to. Now everything was in tatters. Muttering expletives Hobson snatched his coat from the peg behind his office door, and in a state of ill-concealed displeasure he set in train a murder inquiry, and in a far from happy state of mind made his way to the scene of the crime.

The footpath near to where the body lay had been closed to public access, and police and other emergency vehicles had taken over a small car park a couple of hundred yards away from the place where it rested. Already parked up was the VW Golf owned by Dr Gerald Grimshawe, the forensic pathologist for the High Peak, and when he saw it the DCI's mood lightened appreciably. His encounters with the grumpy but brilliant police surgeon were always stimulating. The "Grim

Reaper", as he was universally known by disrespectful police officers, was not an easy man to talk to but he was never dull or banal. Sparring verbally with him was always enjoyable: his temper much improved by the prospect of the encounter Hobson set off purposefully to climb the steep hill which led to where the body lay.

The going was tough. When he reached the scene of the crime he was breathless; Doc Grimshawe had obviously found it daunting; even several minutes after reaching the summit his face still had the appearance of a grilled tomato, and his snorting and gasping for breath reminded Hobson of the bellowing of a stag at rut.

"Afternoon Doc" he said, "It's a great day for a bit of mountaineering; what have we got here then?"

"Well to my mind it's a dead woman" snapped Grimshawe; "Jesus Hobbo didn't they teach you anything at detective school?"

"They taught me not to banter with a police surgeon when he's sweating like a pig and on a very short fuse" replied Hobson; "I'd better go and stand out of harm's way while you carry out your initial examination. Have you any idea how long that might take?"

"It will take as long as it takes" responded the Grim Reaper. "Why is everyone so ffing impatient these days; just make sure none of your lads in blue don't wander into the restricted area while I'm working; brains the size of peanuts and boots the size of packing cases some of 'em. If they represent the best that modern law enforcement can offer then we're all bound for Hell on a handcart that's all I can say"; and still chuntering, the portly pathologist turned his back on the detective chief inspector; and with much wheezing and muttering struggled to squeeze himself into his sterile white boiler suit.

A period of enforced idleness for the waiting PC's, PSSO's and the other personnel now at the scene followed; nobody could begin their tasks until Doc Grimshawe gave the all clear. The ambulance crew could only sit and wait; the body could not be touched until the Grim Reaper said that it could be removed from the scene for further detailed examination elsewhere.

It was during this time of frustrating inactivity that DCI Hobson was joined by Detective Sergeant Peter Bennett; the lanky DS was his usual irreverent self.

"I hate hanging around doing bugger all" he announced to nobody in particular; "do you think the Doc's dozed off in the afternoon sun Gov? Maybe if I lob a few pine cones in his direction we might get some sign of movement."

"Patience Peter, patience" responded Hobson, "he'll be done soon enough", and as if in response to his prediction Grimshawe emerged from the gazebo which had been placed over the body to deliver his initial findings to the waiting detectives.

"You can tell the ambulance crew they can take her to the mortuary" he grunted; "and yonder gaggle of aliens" he said pointing at the PSSO's in their overalls "can begin crawling around on their hands and knees whenever the fancy takes them. It's an interesting one this Hobbo. I fancy you and your lads will have a lot of work to do to get a result. She's got a load of blood on her coat, which to begin with I thought might have seeped through the fabric but she hasn't got any puncture wounds so far as I can discover. She does have finger bruises to her neck and throat so she was throttled to death, and I'm almost sure she was killed here. In my view it would have taken an unusually strong man to drag or carry a body to this spot and potentially it would have been quite a risky thing to do. I'm not a detective, but it's distinctly possible that she was forced to walk up the hill at gun or knife point, but surely if that was the case then at some stage she would have tried to make a run for it; and if she had broken free and then been caught, the weapon her attacker had with him would have been used in anger; but that hasn't happened."

"Could it be that you're right about the weapon, but the struggle only happened here when the killer grabbed her throat" asked Hobson; "suppose she managed to snatch the weapon from him and stab him; might not that explain the bloodstains on the coat?"

"It might" agreed the Grim Reaper; "but I don't think that was the case. The amount of blood on the coat is significant; a person bleeding profusely might well finish an attack he had started before seeking medical attention for himself, but would he take the time to place a love token in the victim's hand and pin a piece of romantic verse to her chest? I don't think so. And there's something else I've yet to tell you about. The victim has a diamond and sapphire ring on her wedding finger, but it hasn't passed the knuckle because it's too small. I think that whoever killed her tried to force the ring onto her finger after she was dead, there is evidence of rubbing along its entire length, but why someone would attempt to do that I can't imagine; but you're the detective my friend, it's up to you to figure it all out.

"The only other thing I can tell you at this point is that my wife would give her eye teeth to wear the clothes this woman is wearing. I reckon that with the coat, boots and designer jeans she has on you're probably looking at a retail value well in excess of £5000. You mention the labels to Helena when you get home; my bet is she'll tell you that I'm being very conservative in my estimate."

"You probably are" laughed Hobson, "and Helena will certainly know if you're anywhere near the mark; but if you're correct about the blood not belonging to the victim or her attacker it begs the question who could it belong to. Is it possible that she might have had a nosebleed brought on by extreme anxiety? If that was the case then the blood could be hers, even though there are no wounds."

"Possible but unlikely" responded Grimshawe. "If she'd have done that I would have expected to find traces of snot and mucus around her mouth and down her chin. There aren't any so I don't think there is much mileage in that theory, I'll know for sure when the blood is tested. I'm buggering off now before I succumb to altitude sickness. I'll let you have a full report within the next twenty four hours" and with that the Grim Reaper trundled out of view and at the same time the ambulance crew arrived with a stretcher to carry away the remains of the once beautiful woman.

DS Bennett turned to DCI Hobson. "The Doc's right about one thing Gov" he said; "this case ain't going to be easy to get a result on."

"Murder seldom is" replied Hobson; "but if we get the basics right we will get there. Once we know who she is we can discover how she lived her life, who she loved, who she loathed, who she associated with, who she avoided; and from that we may find motive, and once we have motive we're a long way down the road towards solving the case."

"Do you know I might just about have fathomed all that myself Gov" laughed DS Bennett, "but you're right of course. First thing I'll do when I get back to the nick is trawl through the missing person reports. If we get no joy there then I suppose our next step will be to get local and national media involved in an appeal to the general public for help. Also if her clothing is as exclusive as the Doc thinks it might be then potentially only a limited number of retail outlets will stock such items, and if we can discover the shops that do we may pick up a trail from one of them."

"We might indeed" agreed Hobson, you get on with all that, and, flu or not, I'll go and brief Stan Hardy on developments. That may be about as much as we can hope to achieve today; tomorrow will be when the hard graft really starts."

"So no nasty surprises this evening then Gov?"

"I don't think so" replied his boss, but in that respect DCI Hobson turned out to be mistaken. It was after his conversation with very much under the weather Detective Chief Superintendent had concluded, and as he was contemplating leaving the office for the night that he received the phone call from the Grim Reaper.

"I've got some news for you Hobbo" he announced. "The blood on the coat has been tested, and I'm absolutely gobsmacked. Brace yourself for a shock Mate. I'm one hundred and ten per cent certain that it isn't human."

CHAPTER TWO

Wednesday 11th September 2013- A blazing vehicle, a case of animal cruelty, and several conflicting theories.

The 999 call was received at the fire station at a little before 11 pm. A vehicle was on fire. The cause could have been an electrical malfunction, but such incidents generally occurred during the hours of daylight. A call at this time of night usually had a different explanation. More often than not it turned out that a cheap family car, not in the first flush of youth, had been stolen from one of the sink estates in South Yorkshire or Greater Manchester and driven for the hell of it by some boneheaded cretin, before being torched by the thief in the belief that this would destroy incriminating fingerprint or DNA evidence. It was a sad fact of life that very few of these people were ever caught by the police.

Potentially a blazing vehicle presented a real danger to the fire crew who attended the scene, but the Derbyshire Fire Service, like their compatriots elsewhere were trained to deal with such a situation. Such occurrences were unfortunately not rare; incidents like this happened several times a year. It said much about the society we live in; but fire fighters aren't philosophers; their job is to deal with the problems anti-social youth throws at them not to analyse them.

The expectation had been that a Ford Fiesta, Vauxhall Corsa, or any other bog standard car not protected by a burglar alarm, immobiliser, or any other electronic safeguard would be the target of the vandal, but this expectation couldn't have been more wrong.

What the fire crews saw when they arrived at the lay-by on Long Hill overlooking the Fernilee reservoir was a luxury car in flames. A top of the range Bentley Continental was burning ferociously. At any minute the fuel tank could explode. The heat was intense. Fire had spread to a clump of small trees that partially screened the lay-by from the road. Maximum care would be needed to bring this blaze under control.

It took time, and a great deal of professionalism for the flames to be extinguished, but only then was the extent of the destruction fully apparent. A dream car, an iconic vehicle, which had cost more to buy then the average three bed-roomed house had been turned into molten scrap. A limousine, which from its registration plate was no more than a few weeks old had been incinerated. This was no ordinary taking without consent; there had to be more to this extreme act of destruction than that.

"Not human!" Helena gasped in amazement; "you're not telling me she was abducted by aliens. It sounds like a plot line from E.T. How could this poor woman be covered in blood which isn't human?"

"No, she wasn't attacked by visitors from the Planet Zog" laughed Hobson; like most police officers he discussed bizarre aspects of a case with his spouse knowing that those conversations would not go further, but he never showed her witness statements or revealed sensitive information or shared any intimate details about any individual with his lovely wife.

"So far as the Doc can tell, he thinks the blood is that of a dog. He believes that the animal was stabbed to death, perhaps in front of the victim's face as she lay dying, and then held over her chest as it bled to death which does make me wonder why she herself wasn't killed with a knife as her murderer clearly had possession of a blade if the Doc's theory is correct. It probably means that somewhere in the woods its body is rapidly decomposing. It's going to be a nice job for the lads in the morning trying to find it, but it could be important, if the animal has been chipped then we should be able to trace the owner.

"There are other weird things about the case too" he added, and Mark then told Helena about the love poem, the red rose made of silk, and the little ring apparently forced onto her wedding finger.

"It looks to me like the killer could have been rejected at some time by the victim" said Helena, "and in death, after he has killed her, in his mind he has consummated, and maybe even legitimised a relationship that never existed in life."

"It's a theory, and a good one too" replied Mark, "but I have an alternative one. I think it's possible that the murderer is rubbing a rival's face in the dirt by sending out a message "she was precious to you but you couldn't protect her. I took her. I had her, and in her final moments she wore my ring".

"It sounds melodramatic I know, but everything about this case is melodramatic. My biggest worry is that somewhere a person incandescent with rage is planning a tit for tat reprisal. That fear is compounded by the fact that I don't think money would be an object. I think this person could well afford to pay people shed loads of cash to do his dirty work for him", and DCI Hobson then elaborated as to why he felt this way.

"The dead woman was wearing very expensive clothing" he said, "Doc Grimshawe thought that what she was dressed in probably cost several thousand pounds. He said to ask you as you would probably know"; he then listed the brand labels of the items she had on.

"He's not wrong" replied Helena. I love the boots. The coat is mega expensive, but it wouldn't do for me. It's too showy, too ostentatious. It's a "Look at me" garment; it's the type of fashion a very rich WAG might wear."

"I've checked the register of missing persons and unearthed sweet F A;" Detective Sergeant Peter Bennett was explain to his boss Mark Hobson the results of his endeavours. "A woman who disappeared from her home in Hartlepool twelve days ago looked promising but when I read further I discovered she was of mixed race, which our dead lady certainly isn't: another woman who went missing from a hospice two years ago could have fitted the bill but as she had been diagnosed with terminal cancer and given just three months to live the odds are that she is pushing up the daisies somewhere so I discounted her from the equation. It's down to you now Gov; I assume you'll be issuing a description to the media, and enlisting their help to identify the body."

"Spot on there" replied Hobson, "I'm going to telephone Stan Hardy as soon as our conversation is over, and by lunchtime the wheels will be in motion. While I'm doing that can you get the lads looking for retail outlets that sell the sort of expensive stuff our victim was clad in. We also need to get a search team back in the woods today to look for a dead dog", and Hobson then explained to his incredulous DS that the blood found on the victim's coat was of the canine, and not the human variety.

"It's a bit of a long shot" he admitted, "the carcass could have been thrown into the reservoir, and if it was I doubt we will ever find it; or he might have collected the remains in a plastic sack to dispose of them elsewhere but my gut feeling is he didn't do that. I think getting rid of its body might have been an afterthought so my hunch is that it is still probably somewhere nearby.

"Jesus Christ what's the world coming to" exclaimed Bennett; "this case gets stranger by the minute. A woman dressed in clothes that make Kate Middleton look like a poor relation is butchered on our patch; a pet dog is sacrificed to make some bizarre point or other, and overnight the sort of car only a millionaire can afford is turned into a burned out wreck"; the DS then told his boss about the discovery of the blazing vehicle on Long Hill.

"It's a top of the range job Gov, less than two months old, yet its theft was not reported to the police. The owner is a chap called Alexei Andropov, who I'm sure you've heard of. He's got his finger in all sorts of pies. GMP say he's a Russian Oligarch, and as bent as a nine bob note, but there is no hard evidence to back that up. He claims to be an agent for a number of high profile Premier League footballers; and if he is then that alone guarantees he's worth a bob or two. He certainly lives the lifestyle of the mega rich. Three years ago he bought a nice little farmstead somewhere between Macclesfield and Alderley Edge, razed it to the ground and built a monstrosity in stainless steel and glass to replace it which is now home to his wife, possibly also a mistress, he is reputed to be a womaniser; and maybe one or two children, although there is some doubt about that. When he was questioned by Cheshire Police about why he hadn't reported the taking of his luxury motor vehicle he said that he had been too busy doing other stuff. Can you imagine that Gov, too busy to find the time to report the theft of a car worth well over a quarter of million quid; it stinks Gov it really does."

"It reeks to high Heaven "agreed Hobson "It's clearly not true; there are so many things about this claim that bother me. As I understand it he is alleging some kind of opportunist theft, but he lives in the middle of nowhere so passing villains are probably thin on the ground, and how could the average little scroat who routinely nicks cars take that kind of vehicle? You'd need more than half a tennis ball, a coat hanger and a house brick to get away with your prize. Without the right key or codes, even if you smash your way inside you're going nowhere, and the burglar alarm would be waking up half the county; so how could an opportunist thief get his hands on such information?

"He's lying through his back teeth Pete, he knows or suspects who took that car; and if he does, my big worry is that he is already plotting his own revenge; and here's what really bugs me. Do you think it could be possible that our murder and this burned out car are in some way connected?"

"They could be Gov" replied the detective sergeant. "Both scream of money. Might the victim be one of Andropov's women, maybe somebody he once loved, maybe somebody he had killed because she cheated on him, but inwardly still wanted; that could explain the rose, the poetry, and the ring?"

"It would" agreed Hobson, "but in that case why would he set fire to his own luxury vehicle? The car was destroyed many hours after the body was found; there would be no reason to wreck it, so I don't buy that as an explanation."

"Well how's this as an alternative explanation Gov? Suppose our dead lady was a person who regularly used the car. Suppose somebody kidnapped her at knife point, or simply persuaded her to drive him somewhere intending all the time to kill her and thereby send a message to Andropov that nothing and no one was sacred, and that every evil under the Sun was possible, and there were no lengths that would not be gone to if he got in their way."

"I like that as a theory" said Hobson, "even though it does sound a bit farfetched: do you think the killing of the dog falls into that category too?"

"It might do" murmured Bennett, "but if that was the intent why not leave the remains of the animal alongside the body of the woman for greater impact?"

"I can't answer that" replied Hobson, "but maybe things will become clearer with time. I've just got one final thought for the moment. I think the destruction of the car has to involve at least two people. I don't think whoever ignited the petrol would then have casually wandered off down the road. It must be at least three miles before he would reach civilisation. A walker at that time of night could be noticed by passing motorists, and that would be a risk. I think a second vehicle must have been on hand to assist the get-away."

"Unless he parked another car in the lay-by earlier in the day; which would mean that no other person would need to be involved."

"But a car left in a lay-by unattended for several hours might be at risk of vandalism" countered the DCI, "I don't think he would have taken that chance."

"You're probably right Gov" conceded DS Bennett, "you're probably completely right."

CHAPTER THREE

Mid-January 1999. A plane journey to a new life, and memories of growing up

It was cold when the plane landed at Manchester International Airport. Sleet had fallen intermittently throughout the evening making the world seem grey and waterlogged. In the Peak District of Derbyshire and along the Pennine Chain wet snow covered the hilltops; the Cat and Fiddle, the Snake Pass and the Woodhead were all closed. It was a different world there; it was a different world that Sasha was arriving into too, and she had so many mixed emotions.

The tall blonde young woman who had left Minsk wrapped in a long fur coat to protect her from the bitter chill had spent most of the flight trying to come to terms with the decision she had made. Most of her friends said she was mad, though some had praised her courage and her sense of adventure. Her parents had tried to dissuade her; they thought she was making a terrible mistake to leave her homeland and settle in a country she had never visited before. They wondered how she would cope with the language, even though she had graduated from the University of Minsk with a good degree in English, and if not completely fluent in every aspect of the tongue, she was totally able to converse with English speakers and make herself understood.

What had attracted her to Manchester? Manchester was so different from Minsk. Minsk was one of the oldest cities in Europe, although much of it had been re-built after the Second World War. It had almost one thousand years of history; Manchester by comparison had less than two hundred. Minsk was a capital city, Manchester just a regional hub, and it had a much smaller population. If she was honest she might have admitted to herself at least, that the destination she had just arrived at meant very little to her. London was the place that excited her. London was where she longed to spend time. London was the land of opportunity, but he lived near Manchester, and that was everything. In any event he had promised that they would make frequent trips to Chelsea, Mayfair, and the West End so that she could see and do all the things she had always fantasised about doing.

She had always been a dreamer. When she was a little girl her nickname had been Alyonka (*the heroine of a centuries old folk tale about a little girl who saved her brothers from being turned into swans*), and perhaps that had set her apart from other children. Maybe that was why when she was in her early teens, and a very pretty adolescent she had attracted the attention of Dimitri, the son of the school's headmaster, and three years her senior. Older girls had thrown themselves at him, in the main to no avail, but she had kept herself to herself, perhaps waiting for her Prince Charming to arrive on a milk white steed; and this had increased his fascination with her even more.

When she was only fourteen he had sent her a portrait he had painted of her, copied from a photograph which had been taken at a festival at which all the young girls wore national costume and had their hair bedecked with Spring flowers. Her parents thought it was a lovely gesture, her elder sister had been green with envy, and for a while thereafter had been quite horrid to her. She had been uncertain how to react. She was flattered, of course she was, but was this intended as a route map for a journey that inevitably led to marriage, domesticity and kids; if it was, then that was not what she wanted at all.

Shortly after this he had asked her to go to the cinema with him, and she had been too shy and too polite to say "no"; and at the end of term dance he had eyes only for her; and they had danced together as the whole school looked on; and in everyone's opinion they had become an item. Older girls had been really bitchy after that, but despite that fact she had started to revel in the status this presumed relationship gave her; maybe it could be after all a passport to a new and exciting life.

For her fifteenth birthday he had given her a pendant shaped like a heart made of silver and mounted with a blood red garnet. Her mother said it was the prettiest necklace she had ever seen but warned her to be careful because boys often expected "rewards" for their gifts. She had listened and heeded the warning: not being putty in his hands had excited his interest even more.

When she was nearly sixteen she had met his friend Alexei for the first time. He was the son of a semi-literate policeman, and he was everything that Dimitri was not. He was big, and rough, and arrogant; not the stuff of dreams; but had had a strong animal magnetism, and a whiff of danger that excited her. How Alexei and Dimitri had met she didn't know, but there were rumours that Dimitri's parents had been under secret police surveillance, and that they might have been warned off attending a gathering of liberal-minded intellectuals which had been raided, and from which many arrests had followed. If Alexei's father had seen the chance to make a little extra money maybe it was possible that his son had been the bearer of "interesting news", and that Dimitri's parents had been "grateful" for the information they had received. For whatever reason, for a while thereafter both young men had seemed inseparable, if unlikely, companions.

As she tried to consolidate her thoughts at 30,000 feet she remembered with a shudder the day of her sixteenth birthday, and the dramatic consequences which had followed on from it.

It had started with presents, and family hugs, and a big bunch of flowers had arrived from Dimitri. The scent of the roses had been exquisite, and she had been overwhelmed. If he wanted to ask her to become his steady girlfriend she had decided to say "yes."

It had been just after 7pm when he arrived at the house. He'd looked thoughtful, and flustered and unsure. His conversations with her sister and her parents had been stilted and disjointed; when they finally left the room he had seized his chance. He had started to address her in faltering tones, and then produced from his pocket a small box and began to earnestly entreat her to become his fiancé

It was at that moment that there had been a loud bang. The door to the living room had been flung open, and in had stormed Alexei, his face contorted with rage.

He had snatched the box which contained a small engagement ring from Dimitri's hand, and then waving it in his face had shouted "You stole this ring from my grandma's house while she was on her deathbed, and now you're trying to deceive Sasha into becoming your sweetheart."

The effect of this outburst had been cataclysmic. She remembered how the colour had drained from Dimitri's face, and how the shouting and upheaval had caused both her parents to come running back into the room. She recalled her excruciating embarrassment watching Dimitri try to deny Alexei's allegations and claim that it was in fact Alexei who had taken the ring and then sold it to him so that he could propose to her. Alexei had laughed contemptuously and called Dimitri several unprintable names.

Her father had been incandescent. He ordered Dimitri out of the house, never to return again, and he had left in tears, still protesting his innocence. Her mother had grabbed the bunch of roses from the vase, where they had held pride of place and hurled them at his back as he retreated. Her mum and dad then profusely apologised to Alexei, and promised that news of Dimitri's treachery would be spread far and wide. Alexei in return then apologised for making a scene, and then he had offered his heartfelt condolences to her.

"I thought he was my friend" he had exclaimed, "but he is jackal, and he has abused both our trusts", he squeezed her hand gently, and told her quietly that he was sure that she would soon find someone new.

That was the last she ever saw of Dimitri. It was said that his parents packed him off to live with an elderly relative in Ukraine, and that his name was never mentioned again in their household. Rumours occasionally emerged that he had become embroiled with the Russian mafia which usually elicited the response "well he would do wouldn't he." Sometimes it was alleged that he had become wealthy on dirty money, but no one knew for certain, and nobody cared.

She hadn't seen much of Alexei after that incident either. In the two weeks immediately after the explosive events of her birthday she recalled spotting him a couple of times on the street at a distance, but that was all. He too then disappeared off the radar. Her parents learned from an acquaintance of theirs that he had told his son that his grandmother had left him a little money in her will.

"Not a king's ransom" he had said, "but enough to travel to Western Europe to seek my fortune" so he had departed Belarus to look for lucrative work in the capitalist west.

With the removal of both Dimitri and Alexei from the scene, she recollected with a shudder how tense her last two years at school had been. Some of her fellow pupils blamed her for Dimitri's downfall. She had been subjected to snide comments and aggressive behaviour, and she had received hate mail, some of which was really vile. During this period she abandoned any form of social life, preferring the safety of her own home; but this had meant that she had devoted more time to study, so she had qualified to go to university, with excellent exam results.

At university she had thrived. Her tormentors from school were no more. She was with intelligent youngsters like herself; and over the next three years had made many friends, but she had never entered into a serious relationship with any of the boys she met socially. Inside she was still a dreamer. She wanted more than they could offer, and she had a conviction that if she waited long enough then sometime, in some way that she could not predict, what she longed for would finally arrive.

Time had slipped by without a breakthrough. She recalled her false starts and dashed hopes. The TV producer who had told her that she was gorgeous and that she would be a natural in front of the camera had turned out to be the maker of low budget sex videos. Fortunately, after a few moments of euphoria, common sense had kicked in, and she had looked at the man's sordid credentials, and not liked what she had seen.

There had been other near misses too, which wormed their way back into her brain as she tried to grab a moment's sleep; sometimes the temptation had been great, but always in the end reason had prevailed, and she had averted disaster.

Then one morning, in her twenty fourth year, she found a note that had been hand delivered to her parents house. It was addressed simply "To Sasha", and it caused her momentarily to panic. Recollecting the hate mail she had received in her teens she recoiled from the envelope as if it was a Cobra waiting to spit its venom; then she steeled herself, grabbed it from the mat, and with hands trembling ripped it open. She was amazed by what she read.

CHAPTER FOUR

Thursday 12th September 2013-A search for evidence, an appeal for information, picking up the gauntlet, and a small but vital clue

Overnight the weather had turned damp; low cloud masked the hilltops, and the kind of relentless drizzle that drenches to the bone was falling from a leaden sky. It was not the best of days for a search team to operate. Detective Chief Inspector Hobson was glad that he personally would not have to be involved. He imagined some of the PSSO's would be muttering under their breath "all this for a f***ing dead dog", and wishing that they were warm inside drinking tea, and reading the back pages of the daily newspapers. When searching for the body of a child or a missing adult it was different. There was a passion, a sense of urgency to get a result; the same was not true when the object of the search was a decaying animal, but the job had to be done; and if the rotting carcass lay within the search area Hobson was sure it would be found.

 A swathe of land on either side of the track the murderer must have followed had to be painstakingly examined. It was believed that the killer would not have wanted to keep possession of the dead or dying dog any longer than was absolutely necessary so it was thought that the spot nearest to where the murder victim's body was found offered the most potential. If a search of that area proved negative then the whole length of the track would need to be investigated. Initially a range of 50 yards either side of it would fall within the search area, this was because common sense suggested that the killer would want to make haste back to his vehicle at the bottom of the hill, and to rid himself of all incriminating evidence as quickly as he could. Even Geoff Capes could not have flung a small animal more than seventy or eighty feet, and in any event simply hurling an object into the woods was risky. Suppose it landed high up in a tree, out of reach of recovery, it might be very visible, but nothing could be done to remedy the situation. Hobson was pretty sure that the butchered animal would instead have been secreted in thick undergrowth where it would be completely hidden from view. Detective Chief Superintendent Hardy had agreed with this analysis; but he had added a note of caution.

"Don't forget badgers" he said; "contrary to what some people maintain they'll eat fucking anything; if one of them has sniffed out the remains they could have been dragged anywhere in the woods to a place where it felt safe to devour its prey."

"I'll remember that Sir," replied the DCI; "I just hope that doesn't turn out to have been the case."

The fact that the body of a woman had been found in woodland in rural Derbyshire was finally becoming national news. Details of the discovery were only just being released, and of course not every detail was being disclosed. The press release authorised by Detective Chief Superintendent Hardy contained a description of the deceased, five feet eight inches tall, slim build, naturally blonde hair, believed to be between thirty five to forty years old. It also listed the clothing she was wearing (including colour and brand labels) and it finished by stating that it was not thought the victim had been dead for more than seventy two hours when the body was found. No mention was made of the canine blood on the coat, nor the red rose, nor the love poem; the fact that a ring had been forced onto her finger was also omitted; although some or all of this information might be the subject of a further press release at a later date. The current press release ended with an appeal for anyone who thought they might know who the deceased was to contact the police, and likewise anybody who believed they had seen a woman who matched the description of the murder victim in the last fourteen days to contact Derbyshire Constabulary, or their local police station, stating where, and under what circumstances the sighting had taken place. As yet no link was being suggested between the deceased and the burned out Bentley, but if a connection could be established, that would change; for the moment though the general public had no inkling that these two events might have a common thread.

The destruction of the luxury car was however widely known. All the daily papers carried photographs of the wreck. Wanton vandalism on an epic scale was big news; a dream car turned into a charred shell excited readers' interest; it also gave several of the tabloids a chance to wring their hands and moralise about the sanctity of ownership, and the evil of taking other people's property without consent.

"Except it isn't that" Hobson had said to Helena over the breakfast table, "it ceased to be TWOC the moment the torch was put to the car; it became theft, and theft on a grand scale; and I should imagine if anyone is ever arrested for this incident the CPS will also advise a further charge of causing criminal damage by fire, or even arson with intent to endanger life or being reckless as to whether life is endangered. If the petrol tank had exploded, people, most likely fire-fighters, could have been killed; and no judge worth his salt would ever pass a lenient sentence in those circumstances."

When he heard the appeal for information on the lunchtime news it confirmed everything that he had suspected. Deep down he had always feared the worst; deep down had had known that there could only be one outcome. Now he knew for sure that she was dead. He had been a fool, he had given her too much freedom and that had been a fatal mistake. Rage boiled within him; very soon molten anger would spew from him spreading hatred across the Earth. Had the police published a picture of the dead woman with the red rose and the love poem still in place he would have exploded with fury; if they had made public the facts about the ring he would have been incandescent. The loss of the girl was hard enough to bear; the fact that her killer had left behind him a triumphant message of victory would have been intolerable. Even without this knowledge he vowed he would have his revenge. There would be bloody, brutal, total war. Like would be repaid with like, but on a grander scale. Horror would be heaped upon horror. The man who had killed his woman had thrown down a gauntlet, he was picking that gauntlet up, and his response would be swift.

But in one respect her death had given him an escape route out of a difficulty he had created for himself. His account of how his car went missing was not credible, he had always known that; and although he despised the police, and had contempt for their ability, the fact that he had told them a story which even they would dismiss as garbage now bothered him. They would want to speak to him to "clarify" certain details such as where exactly his car was when it was stolen, why the burglar alarm on it was not set, and how, in his opinion, could anyone not in possession of a set of keys, manage to drive the vehicle away?

He decided that he would come clean; or at least that he would appear to do so. He resolved that he would straight way contact Derbyshire Constabulary to inform them that a friend, who had been staying with him, had recently gone missing. He would reveal that an argument had taken place between this person and his wife, and that he thought she had taken the car to put distance between herself and his irate spouse. He would admit than when he received the initial phone call about the burned out vehicle he panicked and told a pack of lies to protect the lady concerned. He would be tearful and remorseful and apologetic; and he would tell them her true identity, and answer any questions they asked about her: some of these answers would be factually correct; others would be less so. Realising that he had to compose himself before making the telephone call he walked into his home office, locked the door, and started to map out exactly what he would say.

The search had so far lasted for five hours. To date the remains of one rabbit, probably killed by a fox, and one wood pigeon, cause of death unknown, had been discovered. Of a dead dog there was as yet no trace. The searchers crawling through the undergrowth on their hands and knees were becoming dispirited.

"Has Hobbo ever considered the possibility that the wretched animal could have been butchered somewhere miles away from here and that its blood was collected in bowl and then decanted into a bottle for later use" moaned one man? "I'm waterlogged, worn out, and not to put too fine a point on it really, really pissed off."

"So no change there then" said a colleague, and everybody laughed, lightening the mood; then out of the corner of his eye he spotted something utterly unremarkable, and completely out of place.

There had been three phone calls to the police from members of the public who thought that they might have seen the woman described in the appeal for information within the last seven days. One placed her at a train station in Shropshire, a second related to a cafe in Carlisle, and a third had her shopping for cosmetics at Manchester's Arndale Centre. All of these reports would be looked into, but none seemed to offer much hope of a positive result; which was not great news.

The fact that the search for the dead dog had so far drawn a blank wasn't great news either. Detective Chief Inspector Mark Hobson was beginning to wonder if he had been wrong to assume that the animal had been killed on site; it was at this moment of self-doubt that Detective Sergeant Peter Bennett strode into his boss's office.

"We've had a bit of a development Gov" he announced; "I thought you might just want to hear about it".

"And what is this development Pete?" asked Hobson. "Don't keep me hanging on like a Muppet; put me out of my misery; just tell me what it is that you know and I don't."

"Well one of the lads crawling about in the woods found this" replied the DS, and he produced a clear plastic bag containing a small piece of card. "It's a parking ticket from a Pay and Display car park. If it had been at the bottom of the hill among all the other detritus laying there he probably wouldn't have batted an eyelid, but nearer the top it seemed a bit out of place. It couldn't have been carried there by the wind; it has to have been dropped by someone, probably inadvertently; maybe when pulling something out of a pocket; but here's the thing: the vehicle registration number on the ticket is the same as the one allocated to the burned out Bentley."

"Bloody brilliant!" exclaimed Hobson; "to my mind the parking ticket being found so close to the body indicates a clear connection between our victim and the wrecked car. I still want the lads to keep looking for the dog, but it's now no longer vital that they find it. I think our next step should be to talk to Andropov at length; he knows a hell of a lot more than he's letting on at present. Contact him immediately and tell him we need to speak to him urgently this afternoon, and don't take no for an answer."

"No need to Gov" said Bennett looking smug. "Andropov himself telephoned here not more than half an hour ago. He sounded contrite. He admitted that the account he gave to Cheshire police about his car going missing was a load of balls. Now he's saying he wants to set the record right; more importantly though he says he thinks he knows who our victim is; and that if he is allowed to do so, he's pretty confident that he can identify the body."

"Better and better" exclaimed Hobson; "let's go and grab a bit of lunch, and then prepare ourselves for our meeting with the duplicitous Mr Andropov."
"

CHAPTER FIVE

Minsk 1996.- An unexpected letter, "dubious infatuation or dangerous obsession", a night of revelations and an unwanted telephone call.

"My dear lovely Sasha,
 It is eight years since we last met, and I suspect that you thought never to hear from me again. Much has happened in that time, but throughout that period even if you never for a moment wondered about me, I have constantly wondered about you. In my mind I can still see the look of shock and disbelief on your face when you discovered Dimitri was a thief, and that he had tried to gain your affection by giving you a ring he had stolen from an old lady as she lay dying. I added to your distress that night by showing real anger, appalled by what a boy who claimed to be my friend had done. For that I apologise, but I take comfort in the fact that I saved you from being seduced by a heartless villain.
 I never spoke to you again about that fateful day, and within weeks I left the city of my birth to seek my fortune in the capitalist West; and I believe I have succeeded in that aim. I know that you stayed close to your roots and that you have evolved from a pretty teenage girl into a ravishingly beautiful woman. I have been told about your time at university, and I have followed, with great interest everything you have done since then. I asked friends to watch over you. If you had been unwise enough to fall for the lies of that producer of pornographic filth they would have stepped in to protect you; but I should never have doubted you; your innate common sense prevailed, as deep down I always thought it would.
 I have frequently thought about contacting you, but the time never seemed quite right. Now it does. I am back in Minsk for a few days and I long to meet with you again.

I have reserved a table for two at the Kuhmistr for 7 pm tonight. Put on your finest dress, and please God a happy face. There is so much I need to tell you, some good, some less so; but unlike Dimitri I will always be honest with you. I count the seconds until then; don't dash my hopes; if you fail to turn up I am sure it will destroy me.
See you tonight beautiful lady,
Alexei.

She was amazed; many conflicting thoughts hurtled through her brain.

Was the letter actually from Alexei at all? She didn't know. She had never seen his handwriting. Suppose it was a horrible prank to humiliate her? She had received hate mail before; that had ceased to arrive a long time ago, but perhaps the dislike that had led to the written abuse hadn't withered and died, maybe it had just remained dormant; and now, for some reason, was being resurrected. What if somebody intended to photograph her waiting dejectedly for a boy who never came, and then mock her stupidity on social media? That would be intolerable.

But even if the letter was from Alexei, which she thought was probably more likely, there were things within it that made her feel distinctly uncomfortable. He had been Dimitri's friend that was all. He and she had never been close, but he claimed to have always been thinking about her; and, more scary than that, he admitted that he had had people secretly watching over her and reporting back to him on her transformation from girl to woman. That was unnerving. It was almost as if she had been under surveillance by the secret police. The wise thing to do would be to stay well away from him. And yet...........

And yet, although the letter could be a sign of dubious infatuation or even dangerous obsession, it had a warmth and tenderness about it too. It felt romantic. It excited her. It offered her the chance to meet and talk to a person who was different from every other boy she had met. He swore in the letter he would be truthful, and the fact that he was prepared to concede that not everything about his life had been good might be evidence of that claim. Surely meeting him just the once in a public place could do no harm, and to dine at one of the best restaurants in the city was an enticing prospect. She made up her mind. She would be on her guard, but she would keep the tantalising dinner date.

So it was that shortly after 7 pm Sasha ventured out onto the street to date a man she barely knew. Her afternoon had seen many mood swings. Despite her resolve to meet Alexei, there had been several times she had almost changed her mind and decided to stay at home, but the sense of intrigue, and the lure of the Kuhmistr had been too strong and had driven her forward. Now there could be no turning back; it would be an act of cowardice if she did, and something that would haunt her for the rest of her life if her courage failed her at this late stage. She kept telling herself that this was a one-off occasion, nothing more than that, and that to meet with Alexei and learn from him how life was really lived in the West would be enthralling.

She fastened her coat tightly against the evening chill. Underneath she was wearing a dress of pale blue silk decorated with silver thread. She had a dress that was prettier than this one; her mum and dad said that she looked like a princess in it; but that was the point. She didn't want to look like Cinderella at the ball. She didn't want to appear too girly. The dress she had chosen was more sophisticated, more classically elegant; and it gave her a feeling of being in control. It would turn heads, she knew that; she hoped Alexei would like it, but in her mind this dinner date had to be a meeting of equals. She might choose to agree with every suggestion he made, but she might not, wearing the dress gave her the confidence to be herself, and not someone overawed, or easily dominated by her companion.

Another thought struck her as she neared the restaurant. It was this. She had changed a lot in the last eight years; Alexei must have done the same. Suppose she arrived at her destination and there was a queue of people waiting outside; would she recognise him? He might have dyed his hair, he might have grown a beard; or put on, or lost weight. She could easily walk past him without giving him a second glance.

She need not have worried however. The instance she laid eyes on him she recognised him, even though his hair was streaked blonde and his body was more muscular (as a result she later discovered of frequent visits to a very exclusive gym).

He also now sported fashionable designer stubble, and had the aura of a man brimming with self-confidence; this impression was re-enforced by the extremely expensive suit he was wearing, and the Rolex watch that adorned his left wrist. To any teenage girl who gazed upon him he looked an icon of style and sophistication; to Sasha it looked a bit too much like attention seeking, but maybe in the last decade of the twentieth century, being in the limelight was the only way to get ahead.

He identified her immediately he saw her. He strode purposely towards her, and before she could say a word, or even draw breath he had flung his arms around her, as if he was greeting a well-loved partner after a long absence, and kissed her passionately on the lips. Such was the ardency of his greeting it totally overwhelmed her. She couldn't help herself she flinched, and tried to extricate herself from his grasp.

Immediately he realised that he had gone too far. Instantly he begged her forgiveness, and entreated her not to be put off by his error of judgement. So sincere did his apology sound it resonated with her and quickly overcame her moment of unease.

"That was crass, stupid, and totally unacceptable" he stammered. "I've dreamt about this moment for so long, and then when it comes I totally fuck it up" then he stopped in mid flow, apparently embarrassed by the swear word he had just used. His aura of self-confidence vanished in a flash; he looked like a schoolboy trying to explain some misdeed to an angry parent; Sasha could do nothing else but laugh.

"Apology accepted" she exclaimed; "now for Heaven's sake Alexei can we just go inside and eat; my teeth are chattering, and my feet feel like blocks of ice" and totally unexpectedly roles seemed to become reversed, and it was she who was the more confident person.

Inside the restaurant it became a meeting of equals. Sasha listened graciously to advice he gave about the menu, but then made her own unfettered choices. He praised her for selecting well, and not simply picking the most expensive meal on the carte, which he said a lot of English girls would have done if somebody else was paying for the food.

For most of the time thereafter it was Alexei who did the talking. He told her about arriving in London not knowing anybody, but with an address to go to which his father had arranged. During the day he had worked at a car wash supervising low paid unskilled migrant workers who toiled for a pittance to clean and valet the cars of the wealthy and at night he explained, through his own efforts, he had found employment in a bar in Soho. There he said he had met an alcoholic journalist who had taken a fancy to him, and she had given him expensive gifts in return for sex. "I closed my eyes and thought of you" he confessed; "it was the only way I could perform adequately" and then he added that he now felt ashamed of his behaviour.

"Yet" he admitted, "I do have cause to be grateful to her because through her I met a Premier League footballer from Belarus who became a friend, and I helped him negotiate an eye-watering new contract with his club. Because of that success word spread, and other very well known foreign footballers then enlisted my aid to renegotiate their contracts, and through them I became rich. I then started to mix with other rich people from many walks of life (he didn't explain who they were or what they did) and many and various doors began to open for me.

"I represented something different you see Sasha. I wasn't bound by their rules or constrained by their no-go areas. I was a pit-bull among poodles. I could get things done which others could not. People saw in me strength and power; that was what intrigued them. The professional footballers I represented knew that I wouldn't sell them short. What I promised I delivered; and all the time my reputation grew.

"About three and a half years ago I moved to Manchester because Manchester is a football mad city and a place where all forms of life co-exist; rich and poor, high-life and low-life, greed and compassion; hope and fear. It is a dangerous and exciting city, more suited to a kid from Belarus than the seat of privilege which is London City" and at that point Alexei paused his monologue and drank deeply from his glass of wine.

Sasha didn't know what to think. The more she had heard the more amazed she had become. The man who sat opposite to her thrilled her and appalled her in equal measure; and yet he had a sense of desperation about him too.

"You say you thought about me when I graduated Alexei" she said, "so why didn't you write to me then? Why leave until now to contact me?

He took another deep drink of wine and became very serious.

"I was going to Sash" he said, "but two people who I trusted, and who I saw as Guardian Angels keeping you safe lied to me for reasons I do not know; although I suspect dirty money was the cause.

"They told me Dimitri had returned to Minsk a rich man and that he had won your heart with his wealth and power. I believed them to my eternal shame. I was so angry, so gutted, that I shut my mind to your existence. Then when I was half cut in a bar a girl came on to me and we had a night of drunken sex. She became pregnant. I felt trapped. You may find this incredible; I did the decent thing and married her. It was the worst mistake I ever made. She is nothing but a whore. She attracts men like jam attracts wasps, but for the sake of our son I stuck with her. Then I discovered that I had been misled, and that Dimitri was still in Ukraine, and that you and he had never been together. I was overwhelmed by joy and by despair. I thought through my actions that I had lost you forever. Then my "loving wife" went off with a very well known professional footballer I had represented, and she is now suing for divorce alleging mental cruelty. I want rid of her but I will not consent because she now wants half my fortune. I know in time she will settle for a lesser sum and then I will be free, although the custody of my son will be a battle. Seeing an end to my unhappy marriage in sight I finally picked up the courage to meet with you and to tell you the whole unvarnished truth. I think about you every day my sweet girl, and I do hope one day to make you mine, but I know that day is not today, and you will need time to make up your mind. All I ask is that after I leave here tonight you will let me write to you........." then at that moment his mobile phone rang.

A look of anger flashed across his face followed closely by a look of concern.

"Damn it" he exclaimed! "I'm so sorry Sash. Please excuse me, I have to take this call," and he stood up and left the table and stepped out into the street where he could have privacy. Ten minutes later he returned.

"I'm afraid something's big come up Sash" he said. "I've paid our bill and booked a taxi to take you home safely. I wish this evening hadn't got to end like this. I'll write to you next week to explain, and my hope is that you will write back to me. In the meantime have this, and occasionally please think of me," and he pressed into her hand a single red rose which had the most beautiful fragrance she had ever smelt, and then he was gone.

CHAPTER SIX

Thursday 12th September 2013 continued- A body is identified, an explanation is discounted, information is revealed, and a struggle to control emotions.

"We're in the wrong job Gov. I thought that maybe having had his dream car put to the torch Andropov might have needed to hitch a lift here on the back of a tow truck, but not a bit of it. He's just parked a brand new Porsche in the space reserved for Stan Hardy. I'm going to make damn sure he gets a ticket when he leaves this building" and Detective Sergeant Bennett then launched into a diatribe about arrogant oligarchs and filthy rich wheeler-dealers of all generic types.

"What make you think he'll be leaving this building today" asked DCI Hobson? "He's got a hell of a lot of explaining to do before he does that; but for the moment we treat him with kid gloves. He says he believes he knows who our murder victim might be, and discovering her identity has to be our top priority. If he can tell us who she is, and if the information checks out, then we turn our attention to the lies he told Cheshire police about the car. What he says then could amount to an admission that he obstructed the police, or even attempted to pervert the course of justice, which might lead to him being locked up; but if either we, or the CPS decide that he can leave this nick today then you can have your fun; but not until then. Now smarten yourself up, paste a polite smile on your face, and let's go and listen to what Mr Andropov wants to tell us."

The initial conversation took place in a small office adjacent to the enquiry desk. Hobson introduced himself and Detective Sergeant Bennett to Andropov and then asked if he was correct in understanding that he was in possession of information which might help the police identify the body of a woman found strangled in the upper Goyt Valley.

Andropov nodded his head. "I would not be here if I did not" he replied; "there is nothing else about this place that would tempt me to give up my time to come here and talk to people like you" Hobson saw the hackles rise at the back of Pete Bennett's neck and shot him a warning glance.

"I appreciate that Mr Andropov" he responded; "and I am grateful for your assistance. Please tell me why it is you think you might know the lady currently resting in the mortuary next door to this building"

"Well somebody who has been staying at my house has disappeared. She had a furious row with my wife, who is a very difficult woman. She blamed Anastasia; her full name is Anastasia Maria Karpovich; for the loss of her little dog Greta, which wasn't fair because I think it just wandered off by itself. Anyway Anastasia protested that the disappearance was nothing to do with her, and the two women spent the next half hour screaming at each other. In the end Anastasia could stand it no longer. She took one of my cars from the garage and drove off in it. That was about a week ago. I have heard nothing from her since, then the Cheshire police telephoned my home late at night to tell me my car had been found burned out in a lay-by in Derbyshire."

"I see" said Hobson with interest. "Would you be willing to walk across to the mortuary with me to see if you can identify the body we have there?"

"Of course" said Andropov; I am not squeamish, I won't faint, or run from the room if it turns out to be Anastasia."

And he didn't do either of those things; but when he confirmed that the body was indeed that of Miss Karpovich Hobson noticed his fist clench momentarily and a look of rage for an instant flash across his face; "and" said Detective Sergeant Bennett later, "I'm sure the bugger did wipe away a tear."

Identification now complete; and personal information noted down; the Derbyshire officers, after recording exact details of times and dates; and obtaining from the witness an account of the deceased routines when she stayed with him, turned their attention to the matter of the stolen car; and at this point Hobson warned the mega rich "tycoon" that his answers to questions would be written down and that his replies could be used in evidence against him. The reaction of Andropov was a text book example of self control. Resentment burned within him, but he nodded meekly, and through gritted teeth stated that he expected nothing less.

The account that he gave painted him as a caring man trying to protect a good friend. He accepted that what he had done had been wrong, but what would any decent man have done in the circumstances? He hadn't reported the taking of the car by Anastasia because he believed that she had been seriously provoked by his wife; and in any event he had reasoned that it would only be a matter of time before she returned the vehicle; he also hadn't wanted her to get into any trouble with the police. He claimed that when he received the phone call he panicked, and that trying desperately to keep Anastasia's involvement a secret he had made up a story which he now accepted was full of holes. When bluntly accused of telling a tissue of lies by DS Bennett he acknowledged that that was the truth. Watching his face and his body language DCI Hobson felt sure that the last thing the man in front of him would do was panic. He didn't voice his opinion.

If he wants to portray himself as Sir Galahad striving to protect a damsel in distress let him get on with it he thought, *while he's talking there's always a chance that something useful may slip out; if he clams up we add nothing to our store of knowledge.*

Asked why he had now decided to come clean he responded angrily that that was obvious. Anastasia had been brutally murdered; he could do nothing to save her now. All he wanted was for the animal who had killed her to be caught and imprisoned for the vile crime he had committed. The fury seemed real; but could the two officers be in the presence of a consummate actor? Neither DCI Hobson nor DS Bennett could really tell.

At this point Hobson decided to take a gamble. Switching the subject to the killing of Anastasia he revealed to Andropov that the police had a theory that her killer may not have been a complete stranger, but rather somebody she had known at one time or another in her lifetime. Andropov looked amazed. The Detective Chief Inspector then asked him if Anastasia had any enemies that he knew of, or people who might wish her harm. He responded by shaking his head violently.

"Only perhaps my wife sometimes" he blurted out, "and my wife may be many things, but she is not a killer. Everybody who met Anastasia loved her. Why do you think someone may have secretly hated her? It's impossible. I don't believe it."

Hobson didn't respond immediately, then he asked a question that seemed entirely unrelated to everything that had gone before.

"Mr Andropov, this may sound a little odd, but have you ever read anything written by William Shakespeare?"

The sheer irrelevance of the inquiry enraged the witness.

"I'm talking to you about a blameless woman who has been murdered and you start asking me about a dead playwright. This makes no sense. Why would I want to talk about fucking Shakespeare at a time like this?"

"I'll take that as a no then" replied Hobson. "The reason I asked you that question Mr Andropov was that whoever killed Miss Karpovich certainly had access to a book of his works because he tore a page from it and pinned one of his romantic poems to her chest after she was dead. He also pressed a red rose made of silk into her hand, and have you ever seen this before?" and he produced from inside his jacket pocket a small self-seal plastic bag that contained the ring that had been removed from the dead woman's finger.

"Have you seen it before" he asked. "The pathologist who examined Miss Karpovich's body found this little ring forced onto her wedding finger. We think that the killer was making some sort of statement by this bizarre act."

Andropov's face turned crimson, he started to shake; to the watching police officers it seemed as if grief and fury were battling for supremacy, but then he overcame his emotions and became cold and unresponsive; and despite being pushed hard on the point by both detectives he maintained that he had never seen the ring before, and did not have the faintest idea who could have placed it and the love tokens on to the body of the deceased.

He's lying through his back teeth thought Hobson, *but even the Russian secret police couldn't make him talk; of that I have no doubt. He has a person in mind, and there will be a reckoning; but at present all we can do is monitor his every move to see what develops.*

There was little point in further conversation. Andropov was told that the police would seek advice from the CPS to ascertain if it was in the public interest to prosecute him for obstructing their inquiry, but that at this stage there would be no charges. It was not thought necessary to bail him pending that advice. DS Bennett then escorted him from the building, and took great delight in pointing out that there was now a fixed penalty notice attached to his car; and that if he wanted to avoid such tickets in the future he should accept that rules applied to him as well as to other people. The "oligarch" reacted petulantly and muttered darkly about the appalling attitude of the British Police.

"I wouldn't trust you lot to find a stray cat" he snapped. "After she finally accepted that Sasha hadn't abducted the useless animal, my wife became convinced that it must have been stolen by a third party for the purpose of ransom, or perhaps just because it was wearing the stupidly expensive collar she had bought for it and she wanted to report the matter to the police. I told her it would be a waste of time and that you lot wouldn't be interested. The events of today just show how right I was." He climbed into his vehicle and slammed the door, alarming the jackdaws perching in a nearby tree; and drove out of the police station yard at a highly unnecessary speed.

CHAPTER SEVEN

A building restored to its former glory, reporting to the head of CID, and a visitor to the police station bearing an "unusual gift".

For more than thirty years prior to the commencement of the twenty first century Moor Top Grange had been a farmstead in decline. The impressive stone house, built in the reign of Queen Anne, had started to wither and die. Paint had peeled from the windows; broken glass in many of the farm buildings had not been replaced; iron pins holding metal downspouts in place had rusted leaving brown stains down the facade of the main house; and water had probably seeped into the attic through cracks in some of the roof slates. It was a great pity. Everybody who saw the magnificent building in its current condition said so. It had such commanding views, such high status credentials. Why didn't the old man who lived there as a virtual recluse, do something about it? His family had inhabited the dwelling for at least six generations, and by repute had always been regarded as wealthy. He looked and dressed like a tramp. He spent nothing on himself, and took frugality to the Nth degree. Somewhere surely he had vast sums of money stashed away, but if he had, preserving the family home so that it could be passed onto the next generation was not one of his priorities

But in truth the assumption of riches was seriously misplaced. The old man had lost his money by making a series of rash and ill-advised investments in dubious stocks and shares; and because of his rashness and his pig-headedness neither his son nor his daughter now spoke to him; the last thing they wanted was to return to live in not so splendid isolation in a draughty, cold, unhappy house.

The old man died suddenly in his bed having suffered a massive stroke. It was ten days before anybody found him. His children were not distressed by his passing. Within a week they had brought in a house-clearance firm to rid out most of his possessions, but some genuine antiques were carefully excluded from the package, and these were later sold for a tidy sum. The house was placed on the open market even before his sparsely attended funeral could take place.

As soon as the "For Sale" signs went up rumours began to spread. The one that most people believed was that a very well known professional footballer wanted to buy the property. This caused much excitement locally, and a degree of trepidation. What would such a person do to the property? Could he be trusted to respect its history; or would it be turned into a parody of its former self? Even if the house was a listed building, and nobody was quite sure whether it was or was not, could somebody with the right amount of cash, and the right people pleading his cause drive a coach and horses through planning restrictions? A vanity project to one man's ego could have been on the cards; but fortunately that did not turn out to be the case. The house and the land were sold by auction, and the footballer did attend with a small army of supporters in tow. Their presence boosted the numbers in the room, and the footballer did make a substantial offer for the property, but he was out bid. By whom nobody in the room knew, but it was later revealed that the purchaser was a" foreigner".

The same worries that had emerged when it was thought that the house might be modified to suit the fashion of the Premier League now resurfaced, local people fearing that the new owner would have little empathy with the homestead and its surroundings; but these fears turned out to be misplaced. Very carefully, and at considerable expense, using the best materials available, and the finest craftsmen the house and outbuildings were restored to their former glory. It was wonderful to see the place happy and vibrant again, and the gardens surrounding the dwelling immaculate and well cared for.

The stone built shippon was converted into a fabulous, state of the art stable block, and very soon a number of fine thoroughbred young horses were housed within it. It transpired that the daughter of the new owner was a keen, and very able, young horsewoman, and very soon she was taking part in local and national events with a considerable degree of success. Of the owner himself, not a lot was seen but people who met him said that he was very nice, and he turned out to be a generous supporter of local charities. It was in that capacity that Helena Hobson and Jackie Nadin first came into contact with him. They were both keen supporters of their local hospice, and somebody suggested to them that the new owner of Moor Top Grange might be willing to donate a prize for a fund raising event they were organising. With more than a little trepidation the two friends had approached him and asked for his help. Helena later told Mark that he had been "utterly charming" and more than willing to assist their cause, and since that meeting prizes had been donated by him to every fund raising event they had held, and twice yearly, a cheque for a four figure sum, was also forthcoming.

If only everybody was as generous as him thought Jackie, *all our financial worries would be over,* but in the real world genuine philanthropists were remarkably thin on the ground.

The only complaint that was sometimes voiced about Mr Zalenkov was that he didn't employ many local people in his household; instead preferring people who came from the land of his birth. None of these people seemed to have any desire to mix with the local population; having a limited understanding of English was clearly a problem, but some effort to integrate would have been greatly appreciated. Despite this one point of criticism however it was universally acknowledged that the farm was in a far better place than it would have been if it had been subjected to the questionable tastes of professional sportsmen and their attendant "Wags."

"We now know that Miss Anastasia Karpovich has been resident in the United Kingdom for in excess of ten years, apart from brief returns periodically to her home state of Belarus. Most of the time she seems to have lived with Alexei Andropov at his luxury pad in Cheshire, but it's possible she has also resided elsewhere. We believe she made regular visits to London, and may even have had the use of an apartment there, but about her life in the Smoke, if it existed, we currently know nothing" Detective Chief Inspector Hobson was updating

Detective Chief Superintendent Stanley Hardy with the latest developments in the Goyt Valley murder case.

"Overnight Pete Bennett has browsed the internet and found a number of photographs of Andropov attending public events. In almost all of the photographs he is accompanied by one of two females. Pete has identified one of these two females as his wife, and the other is clearly our murder victim. So far he has unearthed twenty seven such photographs; now what do you think the ratio between the two women is?"

"I don't know Mark, maybe 80-20 in the wife's favour."

"Spot on Sir" replied Hobson, "except that you've got the roles reversed. Miss Karpovich is far more visible, and it is she who accompanies Andropov to the most high profile gatherings. I think that tells us a lot about how our East European "Mr Big" felt about both ladies."

"I agree" said Hardy. "It's hardly indicative of a happy marriage, so here's a thought, is it remotely possible that a spurned wife might have hired a contract killer to get rid of a hated rival?"

"It's certainly worth looking into Sir, and it could well be the case, but there are aspects about that theory that bothers me."

"And what are they Mark?" asked Hardy.

"It's this" replied the DCI. "My gut feeling is that the victim must have known the killer, at least to some extent. We've discounted the possibility that she was killed elsewhere and that her body was dragged or carried up the hill to the place where it was found, and I don't think she was pulled struggling to the place of execution. I'm pretty convinced that she made the ascent voluntarily, completely unaware of what her companion intended to do, which implies to me that she must have to a degree trusted him, and that one way or another he must have persuaded her to accompany him of her own free will."

"Any ideas about how he might have done that?"

"Well, she wasn't dressed for hiking in the Derbyshire hills, so I can rule out a pre-planned ten mile ramble. There could be any number of reasons of course, but my bet is she thought she would discover something of value secreted at the location she was being taken to. Whether that was something of intrinsic worth, or whether it was perhaps something she feared might do her harm in the wrong hands I can't say; but without a worthwhile prize at the end of the journey I can't see how an intelligent woman, dressed in designer clothing could have been persuaded to scramble though the woods to arrive at the spot where she was then murdered."

"Interesting thoughts Mark, interesting thoughts;" responded Hardy. "I like your reasoning, but uncovering proof to back it up will be a nightmare. You'll have to question Andropov again of course, and that won't be easy, and as regards his wife I hold out very little hope that she will co-operate with you; and I bet you a pound to a penny that all his domestic staff will have been warned to keep silent. I don't envy you your job at all; I fear that this case has got "unsolved crime" written all over it; but maybe that's just the after effects of flu having a moan. You've got a good team working with you; if anyone can pull a rabbit out of a hat, you've got a better chance than most of doing so."

"Thank you Sir" responded Hobson. "I hope you will be feeling better soon. I'll not take up any more of your time. I've just been pinged by Pete Bennett; I think there may have been a development."

And in that belief he was correct.DS Bennett gleefully informed him that a local scout leader had just left the nick.

"He caused a right furore at the Inquiry Desk" he said. "He had a dustbin bag with him and it stank. When he opened it up it contained a dead dog, a French Bulldog with its throat cut and covered in maggots. It was wearing a red leather collar studded with small diamonds. He'd taken his troop out for a romp through the woods, and one of his lads found it near the reservoir. He thought he'd better bring the carcass to us; and he was asking if there might be a reward. The Desk Sergeant took his details and told him that we'd keep him informed. There is a name tag on the collar. The dog's name was Greta; there's also a contact phone number. It looks like we've found Mrs Andropov's pet pooch; maybe this will make her a little bit more willing to talk to us."

"Let's hope so Pete," replied Hobson, "let's bloody well hope so."

CHAPTER EIGHT

Minsk 1996 continued- A time to think, a disturbing letter, and a carefully worded reply.

It had been such a sudden end to the evening. One minute Alexei had been expressing his love for her and revealing details of his unhappy marriage, which had filled her with so many conflicting emotions, then he was gone, and she was sitting in a taxi trying to come to terms with everything that had just occurred.

The man who claimed he thought of her constantly had confessed he had a wife and child, and in one sense blamed her for that situation. A drunken dalliance with an English girl which had happened he said because he mistakenly believed she was lost to him forever. His spies had misled him, they had fed him false information, but in truth he had no right to have collected any information about her at all. This was covert surveillance, and perhaps evidence of controlling behaviour, and this fact alone should have been enough to wipe him from her mind forever, but she had sensed that his pain was real, and Sasha felt that indirectly his "messed up" life was down to her. And could a life, which in many ways was so successful, be described as "messed up" at all? He had come so far in such a short space of time; from rags to riches, a person of note in his adopted country. He held, or at least seemed to hold the keys to the good life in his grasp; anybody would be a fool just to dismiss him out of hand.

She wondered what it was that had called him away from the restaurant so urgently. It was obviously something important that needed immediate attention, and not something that could be delegated to a third party. Sasha started to speculate on what the cause might have been, and to her great unease concluded that something more than money was involved, although cash she felt might be part of the equation.

Alexei was such a mysterious figure; there was a tangible sense of danger about him, there always had been. Suppose something had gone horribly wrong. Suppose it involved a threat to liberty, or even life. One thing was clear as her mind went into overdrive in the back of the taxi, anybody close to him would not lack excitement. A small part of her thrilled at that idea; she didn't know what she would do next, and she certainly wasn't going to ask anybody for advice. All she could do was wait to see if Alexei would keep his promise to write to her, and then make a decision how to proceed.

It was actually nine days before the letter arrived. Sasha had just started to believe Alexei had had a change of heart, and inwardly perhaps to have a feeling of relief that this was so when the post was delivered to her door. When asked by her mother, who had picked up the envelope from the floor who could be writing to her from the United Kingdom she lied and told her it was probably a friend from university. She didn't open the letter immediately, but instead left it until she could be alone to read his words in privacy. Later she told her parents that her friend had been complaining about the English weather, but had been bowled over by the fashion outlets and trendy boutiques. They accepted her explanation as true, and her father bemoaned the fact that in a foreign country like England, with so much history and so many iconic buildings, all her friend could do was think about pretty frocks.

The letter, when she read it, had very different content.

My dear, enchanting Sasha,
   I'm so very sorry our evening ended so abruptly last week. There was so much more that I wanted to say, but an event occurred that could have had fatal consequences, and damaged irreparably more than one person's life. I cannot go into detail; I promise you that it's better for you if you do not know, but I had to act quickly to save a life and prevent a catastrophe from happening. I caught the first available flight to London Heathrow, and fortunately I was able to avert disaster. All through my flight back home I thought about you, and I cursed the fact that I could not be with you.

When I arrived back at my house, tired and exhausted having spoken to so many people in my efforts to solve a problem, I had intended to write to you straight away, but I discovered to my utter dismay that my wife had returned. Her affair with the footballer was over; he had found the attractions of a young actress with an hour glass figure, and a beer glass brain, too strong to resist. My wife is out; she is yesterday's news so far as he is concerned, so she has moved herself back into her bedroom, and has spent the whole of the past seven days wallowing in self-pity, and spitting bile every time she opens her mouth. I want her to go, but I cannot throw her out for the sake of our son; but I promise you this situation will not last. If she will be sensible about our divorce then matters will be resolved; but she is so different from you in every respect that I cannot be confident of a speedy outcome. For the moment it is impossible to talk to her, but for now we have to co-exist. There is so much beauty just outside my window which one day I hope to show to you, but she taints everything. I dream sometimes of pushing her from a high cliff into a pit of fire, and I wake up rejoicing, then I hear a sound from her bedroom and the dream is shattered; but one day it will come true and you will be beside me.

Write back to me my sweet girl. Tell me of your dreams and daydreams and your secret desires. If you think of me only one hundredth of the time I think of you then I will fill many of your waking thoughts.

Your truest, and most devoted friend,
Alexei.

Her hand was shaking as she put the letter down. The intensity of its tone alarmed her. There was so much to comprehend. This man, this married man, confessed that he dreamt of seeing his wife dead, indeed of being the cause of her destruction. Maybe he had never really loved her, but he must have been attracted to her. If love could turn to loathing once it could do so again. Surely the wise thing to do was to sever all contact with him?

But maybe his feelings for her were on an altogether different level. Maybe in his eyes she was his one true love. If that was so it would be cruel to crush his hopes completely. Never had Sasha felt more confused, more unsettled, and more indecisive.

Other aspects of the letter worried her too. She knew he was rich because he had told her so; she knew he associated with very wealthy footballers, but even if one of them had met with a problem would the issue be a matter of life and death as he had claimed; she thought probably not; yet strangely she implicitly accepted the truth of that claim. He had said cryptically that there were some aspects of his life which must remain secret, because revealing them to her might put her at risk. A professional sportsman was unlikely to present a danger to third parties,. Was it possible that there were things that Alexei did which brought him into contact with men of violence? Was his world one which ignored the ordinary rules of life? He had always exuded a sense of danger; and now, richer, more sophisticated, more mature, that sense of danger seemed even stronger. Heart and head pulled her in different directions. What she did next could affect the rest of her life. Perhaps the best thing to do at this moment was "to seek further and better information" as she had once heard a lawyer friend of her father say. She decided that she would reply to the letter, but not in a way which would commit her to any course of action.

After much deliberation she wrote to Alexei.

Dear Alexei,

Thank you for your letter; it only arrived today; I had started to wonder if it ever would.

There are things contained in it which surprise and trouble me. You tell me that your wife has returned, and describe in detail how badly she has behaved throughout last week. This is obviously annoying, but you say you dream that she is dead, and that this makes you feel happy. You even dream about killing her yourself, and that is not good. Whatever you feel for her she is a human being, and the mother of your son. It is wrong to wish misfortune on another person. For your sake you must put away these terrible thoughts; hatred in the end devours all those who feel it.

You also tell me that when you were called away from the restaurant, ending our dinner date so abruptly, it turned out to be a matter of life and death. That is an expression people frequently use, and more often than not it is gross exaggeration, but you claim that in this case it was not so. I know so little about your new life, but the world you have told me about seems no place for such extremes. You tell me specifically that there are things which it is better for me not to know for my own good. This is alarming Alexei. What are you involved in which could cause danger if revealed to the wider world. I do not want to pry into your private life, but if there is any chance of us becoming really close I cannot be kept totally in the dark.

Perhaps for now it would be better if we corresponded only occasionally; after all, there is so much that needs to be sorted out. You tempt me by telling me that there is a beautiful world just beyond the confines of your house, and express a hope that one day you can show that world to me. I share that hope, but I think a lot needs to be resolved before anything can happen. You are an attractive, charismatic man, and I feel such excitement in your company; but I need the complications in your life to be sorted out before I can consider a deeper relationship with you.

Write to me again in a month's time to let me know if anything has changed. In the meantime I will think of you sometimes, as you have asked, but not for many hours every day.

Yours affectionately,
Sasha.

CHAPTER NINE

Saturday 14th September 2013-A visit to "Fort Knox", a meeting with an embittered wife, and two new theories

The first thing that struck DCI Hobson and DS Bennett when they arrived at the property was the height of the perimeter fence and the size and construction of the entrance gate. Many people had wondered how planning permission could have been granted for such industrial size barriers to be erected in a Green Belt area, but those who bothered to check found that they had been approved. Local residents were sure that money had talked, but nothing could be proved. Some of these people now referred to the farmstead as " Fort Knox" or "Guantanemo Bay" but there was nothing anybody could do to change the mindset of the owner to persuade him that something a little less overpowering would be a more suitable choice.

The next thing that became clear to the two police officers was the fact that the country road that they had driven down was narrow, the grass verge in places non-existent. There was nowhere to safely park up a vehicle, so the claim that Andropov made initially, which he later retracted, that his Bentley must have been stumbled upon by an opportunist thief, was patently untrue. No sane person would have left a high value car partially blocking the road, and at high risk of being damaged by any passing tractor or van as it tried to squeeze a way past this obstruction. The only sensible place for such a car to be would be inside the farm yard, and there it would not have been visible to the outside world.

The third thing the officers noticed was that on several buildings which overlooked the farmyard CCTV cameras had been placed; it looked like the chances of anybody getting beyond the perimeter fence unseen were virtually zero.

The last things that took their attention were the brightly coloured signs which screamed out warnings to "Beware of the Dog".

Little Greta, the French Bulldog must have been an incredibly ferocious beast thought Hobson, unless of course these notices relate to other Guard Dogs, and this deduction soon proved to have been well-founded.

What was abundantly clear from everything they saw before them was that Andropov took the security of his property and of his person very seriously.

He has much to hide thought Hobson, *he has very much to hide.*

There was an intercom attached to the gate so Mark Hobson instructed DS Bennett to press the buzzer to announce their arrival at their destination, and confirm that they were expected by Mrs Andropov.

From somewhere within a button was pressed; the main gate slowly swung open, and the two Derbyshire officers and their vehicle were permitted to enter the farm yard. Watching them silently, chained to their kennels were two large German Shepherds. The presence of the young man who had emerged from the house to greet the policemen was enough to ensure there was no noise; DCI Hobson felt sure that but for his presence the situation would be very different

"Come this way please" he said, with a strong East European accent, as Hobson and Bennett got out of their vehicle; "Mrs Andropov is expecting you", and gesturing for them to follow him he led them towards the glass front door of the main house.

It was not to his taste, but it was impressive. It was an eye-catching, in your face celebration of modernism; anyone permitted to enter the inner sanctum could not fail to be overwhelmed by the extravagance on show. DS Bennett muttered under his breath about disparity of riches and the sin of ostentation, but he kept his opinions to himself as he and his superior officer were escorted into a large and airy open plan sitting room to meet the lady of the house.

She was seated in a red leather armchair; her face was grim, an aura of resentment hung over her; this was not an auspicious start. The wife of Alexei Andropov clearly did not see the Derbyshire detectives as welcome guests. She looked exactly like the photographs Hobson and Bennett had seen of her on the internet. She was heavily made up, and wearing clothes that might have come straight from the catwalk, but when she spoke her voice was pure Cockney. It was as if the two officers were in the presence of some high profile reality TV starlet. Personal feelings should never enter into the equation, but Hobson felt an instant antipathy towards the woman they had come to interview.

She gestured towards a large sofa, and with no apparent enthusiasm invited both men to sit down, then she rang a bell, and a few moments later the young man who had showed them into the house re-appeared. Without sounding remotely hospitable she asked whether her "guests" would like tea or coffee to drink. Both opted for coffee. It probably wouldn't help, but in the past experience had shown that the informality of a chat over a cuppa was sometimes the most effective way of learning useful little bits of information.

From within the briefcase he was carrying DCI Hobson produced the ornate dog collar sealed in an exhibits bag and asked her if this was the one that she had purchased for her pampered pet. She almost snatched the bag out of his hand and for a second, until warned not to do so, she seemed ready to rip open the bag to get her hands on the object contained within it.

"You can't do that I'm afraid" said Hobson forcefully, "the collar has still to be examined for fingerprints. I just need you to confirm this is the collar that your little dog was wearing when it went missing. I also have a photograph of the animal which is currently lying inside a freezer back at the police station. Is that animal Greta?", and this he also produced from the briefcase at his side.

Mrs Andropov took one look at the picture and started to sob. "She was such a beautiful dog" she wailed; "she used to beg for food and I used to tickle her chin and then give her doggie chocolate treats; and now she's dead" and for several minutes she became distraught.

I bet she wouldn't be as emotional if it was her husband thought Mark, *this is way over the top; it's not natural to show this amount of grief for a mere animal.*

Slowly, and treading carefully so as not to unsettle the woman further, the detective chief inspector gradually switched the conversation to the disappearance of Anastasia Karpovich, and the fact that the police had been told that there had been a fierce argument between herself and the murder victim on the day the victim drove hurriedly away from the property never to be seen again alive.

"Of course there bloody was" she replied. "I'm sure she was behind Greta's disappearance, but my so called husband, more fool him, believed she could do no wrong. He invited her here to stay for the first time more than ten years ago; she took advantage of his misplaced generosity; and from that moment on she wrapped him around her little pinkie. I warned him she was a trouble maker, but he stopped listening to common sense a long time ago. We live our separate lives. He can go to hell so far as I'm concerned and take whoever he wants to with him. She took him for a fool time and time again, and laughed at his stupidity.

"I told her that I knew she was a thief and that she had kidnapped Greta to extort money out of me. She called me a spiteful old witch. I said if she didn't get out of my sight that very moment then I would scratch her fucking eyes out. That fucking scared her; I knew she had no fucking bottle. She nearly shat herself. She ran from the room and jumped into the car I use and drove out of the yard like Stirling fucking Moss. She could have taken any of Alexei's cars, but she chose that one just to spite me. And by the way Inspector the coat she was wearing when you found her was my coat; I'd left in on the back seat of the vehicle by mistake; so you can see she wasn't averse to nicking other people's property. If she was still alive I'd demand you charged her with robbery, but she's ffing dead, and, unlike my husband I won't shed a single tear for her. Good riddance to bad rubbish, call it like it is, that's what I always say."

"You have strong views" commented Hobson. "You paint a very different picture of the deceased to that depicted by your husband. To your knowledge are there others who feel the same way about Miss Karpovich as you do?"

"For sure" answered the embittered wife; "there are many people who saw through the deception to view the real person underneath;" but when she was pressed to provide details the request was met with near stony silence. The hitherto talkative Mrs A became monosyllabic and imprecise. She maintained her claim was true, but despite this assertion, she couldn't, or wouldn't provide the police with a single name. Impasse had been reached. There seemed no worthwhile point in prolonging the interview. The detectives clarified the exact date and time the "witness" admitted the argument took place, and her answers dove-tailed with what Andropov himself had already said, and also with the findings of Doc Grimshawe; so, after politely thanking her for seeing them the officers left the farm and commenced their return journey to Buxton Police Station.

When they were able to speak freely Bennett turned to Mark Hobson and said: "That's some angry woman. I wouldn't put any fucking thing past her. She's got access to bags of money; maybe she spent a bit of it to enlist somebody's help to get rid of a hatred rival, and also to rub her husband's nose into the dirt."

"It's possible Pete," agreed Hobson, "I'm certainly not ruling out Mrs Andropov as a suspect."

"Good" grunted the detective sergeant; "but while we're engaging in conjecture I've just had another thought come to me which might also be worth considering. We know, because of what we have just been told, that Mrs Andropov was a regular user of the Bentley, and we now also know that Miss Karpovich was wearing a coat belonging to her when she was killed. Is it remotely possible that this could have been a case of mistaken identity and that the murderer believed his victim was Mrs A, a woman he had been paid to get rid of?"

"Now there's a thought indeed Peter" said Hobson; "and one that is definitely worth a second glance; I'll have a think about it when I get home and maybe run it past Helena when the kids have gone to bed."

"And while you're doing that Gov, have a look around your living room and see how many kid's toys and games you can count; and then compare that with the number of such things we saw in that house today. There were none. Whether it had once been inhabited by two or three assorted children, as GMP led us to believe may have been the case, I don't know, but I can say with total certainty there aren't any children there now, and my guess would be that there haven't been any there for a very, very long time."

So later, as he had promised he would, Mark Hobson discussed Peter Bennett's mistaken identity theory with his wife Helena. She agreed that it was viable, but then she added "but I thought from things you have said earlier that you and Pete believed that the victim accompanied her killer up the hill voluntarily; could a man who believed he was dealing with another person persuade the wrong person to go willingly with him?"

"I don't know" admitted Mark, "but its best we keep all options open for now. It's a different world that people like Andropov inhabit, and one in which anything can happen. I'll tell you one thing though; he's paranoid about his own security"; and then he described to Helena all the steps the man had taken to create an impregnable fortress in a quiet Cheshire backwater.

"It's so over the top, so out of place, it's got no empathy with the surrounding countryside; but maybe that's something we should expect if rich foreigners acquire quintessentially English rural properties."

"Not a bit of it" responded Helena. "Jackie and I were invited to meet Natasha Zalenkov today at Moor Top Grange, and that place is stunning; the work that has been done there is superb, and so in keeping with the character of the house. Our hostess was charming, and her dad was too. And you should see the stable block; they've got three fantastic young horses in there, and one adorable foal. Jackie said Alice would love to see it, and I piped up that David would love to see it too, so we've been invited back up there on Saturday morning so that the children can have a conducted tour of the farm, and make friends with the little foal."

CHAPTER TEN

Monday 16th September 2013- a battle plan, a letter written in a different century, and a "delightful day"

His plan of campaign was complete. War had been declared upon him; violence had been unleashed; an innocent person had died; and he had been wounded by her fate. Now it was time to fight back, and to fight back in a way which would overwhelm his enemy. The response had to be more terrible than the attack; the loss caused had to be greater; the suffering more acute. He would make his Nemesis regret forever the day he had decided to initiate conflict between them.

From the outset he had been convinced that the perpetrator could only be one man, but he had needed to be sure; and if it was who he suspected it was he had had to find out where he operated from and then learn all he could about that place, and the people routinely to be found there. This had taken time, and all the while there had been one person who had taken great delight in belittling everything he did, and who would only be too pleased to see him fail. The day would come when he would address the problems that she caused him, but for now that day could wait; his first priority had to be revenge.

It was clear he would need help, but that wasn't a problem. He knew people who had no moral compasses except money, who would do anything they were asked to do, if the price was right; indeed he had employed them in the past from time to time. He also knew enough about them to ensure that they would never betray him because to do so would reap destruction upon themselves in a terrible and terrifying way. The "where" and the "how" were now set in stone, the only issue still to be resolved was the "when", and before that was decided he had one more decision to make. Was it better for the intended victim to be engaged in battle from the first moment of the attack, or would it cause him more distress if he was absent at the time, believing his "citadel" to be safe and secure, only to return to find tragedy and devastation. He concluded that the blame he would heap upon himself for not being there to try to do something to save the innocent from Armageddon would be eternal and unbearable. He decided that what he must do was somehow to discover the day to day movements of his enemy and select a date when he would not be home, or engineer a reason why he would be miles away from his base when it was raided.

Exactly four weeks to the day after she had asked Alexei to limit his correspondence with her, and perhaps write once a month at most, and only when he had made some progress in sorting out his complicated personal life, the letter landed on her doormat. He had paid for delivery to be expedited; if she had been more analytical Sasha might have been perturbed about how literally he had taken her at her word. He was clearly a man who would push boundaries; he had complied with her instructions, but only just.

The letter read as follows:-

My dear sweet Sasha,
I have done as you asked and let four weeks slip by without writing to you, although I have thought about you every day, and not to put pen to paper before now has been hard.
Your letter, although at times it saddened me was full of goodness. When I told you that I dream of killing the wretched woman who is my wife, albeit in name only, you scolded me and said that I should not think evil thoughts, and that people who do are contaminated by the hatred they feel.
I am not like you. I do see a world that can be hostile, dangerous, and unfeeling, but for the last four weeks I have tried to view life through your eyes, and I have not risen to the bait when she has provoked me. The result of my forbearance has been that a sort of uneasy truce now exists between us. Whether this can lead to a more amicable split is doubtful; but it is early days yet, so there is a chance that may occur. If it

does, and if the right arrangements can be made for me to have access to my son (you see I am not without a father's feelings), it could clear the way for you to travel to England to spend time with me here. There is so much I want to show you, magnificent architecture, awe-inspiring history, fabulous concerts, and unbelievably expensive shops. When you come it will blow your mind; perhaps like me, you will never want to leave.

You also asked me about the life I lead, and whether I exaggerated when I told you in the restaurant that a matter of life or death had arisen which I had to deal with personally. That was probably an over-dramatic thing to say, but at the time I could take no chances. I am not trying to over glamorise my life. Mostly I am a middle man, a facilitator, a person, who as the Americans say, plays hard ball on behalf of others.

My fortune, such as it is, mostly comes from the commission I get when I have negotiated a ridiculously lucrative contract for a foreign footballer playing for one of the big clubs in the Premier League. Without me, many of them would be tongue-tied, and a push over for their clubs to deal with. With me on their side it is a different story, and that has made me rich, but nothing to compare with the wealth of some of the men outside football I now deal with. I sort out problems for them if they occur; I lay down the law if I have to. If I am asked to ensure obstacles are not put in the way of a businessman or a dealer achieving what he needs to achieve I do it. Sometimes I have to appear to be tough to make my point; but it is all an act, I swear to you. It might have been different if I had never met you, but you bring out in me the very best of what I am. In many ways I see myself as protector of those who employ me. If you are ever in trouble Sash, which I know you will never be; I will be aware, and I will be there for you; the knight in shining armour that you always dreamed about.

I will write to you again, exactly one month from today and update you with my progress on the route to fulfilment.

Till then be happy,
XXX
Alexei

"It was fabulous Darling. Natasha was wonderful; David and Alice just loved it. The foal is gorgeous, and the horses are stunning. The only drawback so far as Jackie and Alan are concerned is that Alice now wants a pony. I think they will face an uphill struggle to persuade her that it really isn't a good idea just at the moment. Fortunately David is still mad keen on becoming a professional footballer; so we're spared that ordeal."

"Thank God" murmured Mark Hobson with feeling. "I can just about cope with cleaning up after Lucy's rabbits; mopping up the calling cards of an incontinent stallion would be way beyond my powers."

"You'd leave it to me to do" laughed Helena; "but if we had a bigger place I wouldn't be against the idea. Everything about the animals was stupendous, and the way they are looked after is superb. I'm certain that there can't be a better stable block anywhere in the country than the one we looked at again in more depth today with Natasha. It isn't flashy, it isn't in your face opulence, it is just a well-designed, practical, quality, set up, but yet totally in character with the age and ethos of the building.

"After Natasha had given us the "grand tour" she arranged for Alice and David to be taken around the whole farm by one of the young men who work for her dad. She's only eighteen, but she's got so much natural charm. She showed Jackie and me some of the trophies, medals and commendations that she's won. She wasn't showing off; it was just a young woman happy with her lot wanting to share her involvement with people she thought might be interested.

"Then, while the kids were still occupied looking at livestock, Natasha invited us into the house for a coffee. We've been in before of course, but this time she took us into a side room where she and her dad go to relax. It was lovely. There was a warm fire, a choice of several comfortable armchairs, a coffee table, some really nice paintings on the wall; it felt so homely. Her dad was already in there, reading a book. We've met him a few times, but never in such an informal setting, and he was very much at his ease.

"Natasha's eighteen, her dad must be in his early forties, but he looks younger. He's a generous man, and highly intelligent, but for all that I wouldn't want to fall out with him. He's definitely compassionate, otherwise he wouldn't have supported us like he has done in the past, but I suspect like everyone he has his own issues, and he is most certainly not weak. There was a photograph of a young woman on a sideboard, and Natasha said that was her mum. Jackie asked where her mum was now, and Natasha told her she was dead, and Jackie was embarrassed about having asked the question. She started to apologise, but her dad interrupted the apology, and said there was no need; then he opened up a little and obviously wanted to talk about his wife. He said that he had met her when he was young, and in a very bad place. He had fallen out with his family and become an outcast. He felt he was without blame, and he bitterly resented what had happened to him, and that he could see no point to his life. He didn't tell us what it was he had done which had led to the break up, but he did say that at the time of the meeting he was sleeping on the street. One night he noticed a pretty young girl who appeared to be lost wandering down the road. Then, a group of youths emerged from the shadows and surrounded her, and tried to snatch the bag she was carrying. She clung onto it. They pushed her to the ground, but she wouldn't let go. One of the lads kicked her. That was more than he could stomach. He weighed in to help her and the youths fled. The girl was badly shaken up so he walked her to her home; and in return for his bravery was offered a bed for the night.

"To cut a long story short, her family helped him find accommodation and a job, and gradually a romance blossomed. Eventually, with the blessing of her family, they were married. He said that they were very happy and he forgot his former life. His wife became pregnant with Natasha, which thrilled them both, but sadly she died in childbirth. From that moment on all the responsibility for child rearing fell on him, but her family helped a great deal. He was so touched by their support that he asked if he could change his surname to become one of them. They agreed, and from that moment on treated him as the son they never had. When his father-in-law died he left much of his property to him, hence his ability to buy Moor Top Grange.

"We felt it was a sad but lovely story. Natasha and her dad are so close. I think without her he would be distraught. I also think there is still deep anger inside him about the events that made him an exile, but as long as he has his daughter I'm sure he keeps his feelings under control. I like him a lot Mark, I'm sure you would do to. Before we left he suggested that perhaps Jackie and I, with our respective spouses, might like to go to the Grange for a meal. I said that was a lovely idea, so my Love someday soon it will be necessary for you to smarten yourself up, put on your glad rags, and accompany me on a trip to see how the other half lives."

"I don't like wearing glad rags" retorted Mark a little huffily. "Can't I just wear a nice T-shirt and jeans, if I've got to wear a suit I'll feel like I do at Crown Court just before I'm about to be cross examined by some toffee nosed, jumped up little barrister."

"Treat it as a rehearsal for Lizzie's wedding next month" laughed Helena. "I'm the matron of honour, Lucy's one of the bridesmaids, and she's so excited about walking behind the bride. They'll be photographs after the ceremony. Lizzie wants to see pictures of family groups as well as more traditional wedding snaps. With Lucy and me dressed up to the nines, how will it look if you stand next to us looking like a poor man's Worzel Gummidge. You're lucky you don't have to wear a top hat and tails so console yourself with that thought, and treat our visit to see Mr Zalenkov and his daughter as a practice for the main event."

"I will" said Mark defeated "I'll do my best to grin and bear it."

CHAPTER ELEVEN

Wednesday 18th September 2013, Some CCTV evidence is discovered, a brutal murder is remembered, and plans for extreme retribution are finalised.

"Two bits of interesting news, Gov." Detective Sergeant Peter Bennett was telling DCI Hobson about some recent developments that had taken place in the Anastasia Karpovich murder investigation.

"The Bentley was caught on a CCTV camera driving through Adlington three days before the discovery of the body. The security camera scans the driveway of large private house. The owner and his family have been cruising in the Caribbean for the last fortnight. They only returned home yesterday, and they didn't check the tapes until this morning, hence the delay in uncovering this evidence. The video doesn't show much; you certainly can't identify people in the car, but it looks like there are two, or just possibly three, individuals inside it. The driver appears to be male, but even that isn't 100% sure. What it does show is the car pulling partially off road, maybe because the driver wants to make, or answer a call on his mobile phone. It remains in situ for about four minutes then it is driven off As it does so there is a reasonable view of the rear number plate; and when the tech boys enhanced it became clear that we are looking at the correct vehicle. Significantly nobody attempted to leave the vehicle which, if there were only two people inside the car, which was probably the case, could suggest that the front seat passenger was not desperate to make a bid for freedom. If that passenger was Anastasia, and if she was an unwilling occupant of the vehicle, then this short stop could have given her an ideal opportunity to escape."

"Is there no chance that the tech boys could enhance the images still further to give us a view of the driver's face" asked Hobson? DS Bennett shook his head

"'Fraid not Gov, the best thing they can do is give us a rear view of a man's head, and a vague silhouette of somebody in the passenger seat. It's not brilliant for identification purposes, but it's the best we're going to get."

"What time of day was this" asked Hobson?

"Shortly after 6-30 pm" answered Bennett; "that's part of the problem. The sun was low in the sky and shining more or less directly into the lens of the camera. Everything is blurred to some degree. In many ways the tech boys have worked miracles to give us as much as we actually get. The only bit of luck that we had was that the sun went behind a cloud just before the car was driven off, that's why we got a decent view of the rear number plate as the car swung back onto the road.

"Point taken" responded Hobson. "So what's your other bit of news Pete?"

"Do you remember about ten years ago the murder of a suspected drug dealer who lived in a posh house on the outskirts of Knutsford. I can't recall his name for the moment, but it will come to me; but I remember that the villains who killed him were called Steer and Warden. They forced their way into his home, tortured him to make him reveal where he had stashed a shed load of Cocaine, then they bundled him into the boot of his own car which they then drove to a National Trust car park just outside Alderley Edge. There they set fire to the vehicle. They told him what they were going to do before they did it; he knew what his fate would be. The poor sod was burned alive. Purely by chance they were stopped a few miles away from the scene by a passing police vehicle because the car they were in was nicked. There was enough circumstantial evidence to hold them in custody, but the case wasn't that great. However Cheshire Police had a brainwave. They engineered it so that the killers were banged up with a local small time villain, and they boasted to him what they'd done. He grassed them up in return for the promise of a lesser sentence, and they were both convicted: without his evidence it would have been a very different story; but here's the thing. I've just had a phone call from one of the detective's involved in that case. He can't say that everything Steer and Warden told the informer is the gospel truth; they probably bull-shitted a lot to boost their self-importance, but they bragged that but for being stopped by the police they were contracted to commit a second murder on the same night. This time the unnamed victim was to be a woman, and the person who wanted her dead was her husband. They didn't say who he was, and they didn't state explicitly that the same man had paid them to commit both murders, but that has to be a distinct possibility. They were planning to do both jobs on the same night because they were all fired up to commit murder and, more mundanely, because both intended victims lived in the same geographical area. The DC who phoned me wanted to let me know that Andropov lives slap bang in the middle of that area. The Cheshire Police know, as we do, that he hates his wife. They suspect that she was the intended second victim that night, and that Andropov was the paymaster for both projected jobs. It could be mere coincidence of course, but to my mind the common thread of the theft and destruction of two very expensive motor cars is significant. Maybe Andropov decided to have another go, and sadly for Miss Karpovich it was a case of mistaken identity. I think the killing of the dog adds credence to this theory. Mrs Andropov was clearly besotted with the wretched animal; perhaps it was butchered in front of the woman the killer believed to be her to increase her level of anguish. That could explain a great deal."

"It might indeed" responded Hobson; "and as I've said before, I'm more than happy to run with the idea, but there are things that don't fit the pattern. If Alexei has arranged a contract killing, only the wrong victim was selected by the killer, why would the killer have been instructed to place the rose in her hand and fix the poem to her chest? That has to be something that he was ordered to do, not something he dreamed up by himself; and most importantly why would Alexei tell him to force an engagement ring, which he must have given him, onto her wedding finger?"

"I don't know Gov" responded Bennett, "unless Andropov was thinking "You didn't want me, you wanted to break free, but now you're tied to me for all eternity. I won. You lost. You should never have fought against me".

He had already come to this conclusion, but the more he thought about it, the more he became convinced that the shock of returning to a place that seemed impregnable to find it wholly or partially destroyed would be immense; and if the life of someone he cared for had been snuffed out, or irreparably damaged, the despair would be a thousand times worse. The problem he faced was how to engineer a situation in which the property would be unprotected; somehow he needed to discover the plans of the man he believed responsible for cold blooded murder and blatant triumphalism. The forces of law and order when they wanted to uncover a criminal's intentions got answers by tapping phones, or covert surveillance, or by hacking a computer, or maybe by doing all three of these things; but of course he didn't have their resources.

What could he do? A person acting alone could possibly arrange an invitation to some event which might succeed in tempting the recipient to attend; but no response could be guaranteed; and in any case he could not for the life of him think of what such an event might be then, out of the blue, two snippets of news in a local paper gave him the answer. The first was a piece about an Awards Dinner to be held at a prestigious and very expensive restaurant near Baslow; the second was a publicity announcement in respect of a horse show to be held at Chatsworth the day following this. "Early to bed and early to rise" would be watchword of anybody competing in this event. He had his answer; now all he needed to do was acquire the services of the people he required to help him carry out his plan.

He knew exactly where to look. There were places in the city, too many places, where absolutely anything could be purchased at a price; including men's' souls; but he wanted more than just thugs and vandals with a ruthless streak and zero concept of morality. The people he entrusted this job to had to have brains. The people he employed had to be able to follow orders. They had to know how to react if problems arose. They had to know how to keep their mouths shut, and not brag to every little scroat within earshot if they got half cut. The people he employed had to be trusted never to reveal details of their employer; even if placed under intolerable pressure by the forces of law and order if they were ever arrested. Such people were rare, but they did exist. One thing was certain though they would not come cheap but fortunately, in his case, money wasn't a consideration.

A man less confident than he, a man not steeped in hatred, might have hesitated for a moment to ask himself what might happen next if his plan went ahead. He was clear that his response to the provocation and humiliation he had received had to be proportionately greater than the original deeds. This was a dreadful thought, and the strategy carried enormous risk. It would be so terrible that it could lead to the mental disintegration of his hated rival; that would be the ultimate triumph; but it might spark even greater retaliation against his own life and property. He was acutely aware of that. He and his house and possessions were well guarded now; the circumstances that had led to his security being breached could not occur again, but in the future he would have to do even more to protect himself and everything he valued from catastrophic attack.

And should that come he would answer it with even more ferocity. There would only ever be one winner. He refused to let doubt or fear divert him from his purpose.

Everything was now set. He knew exactly what he wanted to see done. He knew precisely when his plan should be carried out. All he needed to do now was enlist his troops, and this was a task he now set about with vigour.

CHAPTER TWELVE

Wednesday 18th September 2013 continued, Updating the DCS, thoughts about mobile phones, and a theory about fingerprints

"It's a bit like wading through treacle Sir;" Mark Hobson was explaining to Detective Chief Superintendent Hardy the limited progress that had been made in the Anastasia Karpovich case; "but we now have some tenuous evidence to support the theory you put forward that this murder could be a contract killing that went wrong, and was in fact a case of mistaken identity.

"As you know Alexei Andropov has got his fingers in all sorts of pies. He makes a legitimate fortune out of being an agent for elite footballers, although I'm sure Pete Bennett would dispute the term "legitimate." He is also strongly suspected of having links with the Russian mafia. The SFO (Serious Fraud Office) believe he is into money laundering on a grand scale, and the Regional Crime Squad is of the same opinion. The money he is suspected of handling is mainly the proceeds of drug dealing and people trafficking, plus some of the other nasty little trades super criminals are routinely involved in."

Hobson then went on to explain in detail why it was he felt that Anastasia might not have been the intended victim, and outlined to his senior officer the theory Detective Sergeant Peter Bennett had postulated not more than sixty minutes earlier. He particularly emphasised the role played by the police informant.

"He was absolutely pivotal Sir" he said; "because of his evidence two men are now serving life sentences with a direction that they should remain in custody for at least thirty years before being considered for release. But here's the thing Sir; while they were bragging about butchering the drug dealer they also boasted that they had had another murder planned for the same evening. The reason they had chosen to kill two people on the same night was proximity. The second intended victim lived only a short distance away from the spot where the drug dealer was incinerated. They joked that the second person they were contracted to erase from the register of the residents on Planet Earth was female; an unwanted encumbrance for the unnamed man who was paying their wages. They also bragged about how they would have sexually abused her before doing the deed they had been paid to do. Her identity was never specifically mentioned, but the thing is Alexei Andropov's house is less than five miles away from the spot where the drug dealer died. I think his wife was the intended target; his affections, assuming he is capable of having any, obviously lay elsewhere. All this happened a long time ago of course, but is it possible that he has recently decided to have another go at removing an obstacle to his future plans, and the hit man simply cocked up and got the wrong woman; although there are some problems with this theory as I have already outlined before?

"Because there maybe some mileage in this line of thought I did get Pete Bennett to telephone Cheshire Police a short while ago to talk to them about their murder inquiry and they told him something that might be of value. The petty criminal who grassed up the assassins is still living locally, and has apparently largely put his past behind him. They think, probably for a small sweetener, he would be willing to talk to us. I may need to make a claim on petty cash in order to enlist his help. Anyway Pete Bennett and I plan to visit him later today to see if he can tell us anything more about the conversations he had with the killers. It's a long shot, but I'm sure it's worth the trip, and if he can tell us anything new that could relate to Andropov then our journey will have been worthwhile. After we have done that we intend to visit a coffee house in Alderley Edge, and a cafe in Wilmslow which we know Miss Karpovich used to frequent. It's possible one or the other of these places might have CCTV evidence which could be useful; and even if they don't we're hoping to learn from staff if she regularly met with people there; and if she did get some useful descriptions of the people concerned. If we end up being able to identify individuals we intend to speak to them as a top priority. It is distinctly possible that she may have regarded one of these as a close confidante, and shared her hopes, fears and aspirations with that person. If we can discover these it could open the floodgates to whole new lines of inquiry.

"There's more to be done too. When Anastasia's body was found she had nothing on her person to aid identification. A woman like her would surely have had a mobile phone. We did ask Andropov if that was the case, and he confirmed that that was so, but he was adamant that she always carried it with her so we presumed that the killer must have taken and disposed of it, which is very likely to be correct. The thought that has been going through my mind for some time now is whether she might have had another mobile phone which she used for her most intimate and personal messages. Drug dealers and career criminals often use cheap "pay as you go" phones for nefarious purposes and then quietly dump them when they think it is advisable to do so. I'm not suggesting for a moment that Miss Karpovich falls into that category but she could have picked up a few bad habits while living with Andropov. The problem is that although we could ask for permission to search Anastasia's bedroom for such an item, there is little we can do if that is declined. We don't as yet have enough evidence against Andropov to prove he has participated in the crimes we are investigating, so it is unlikely that we could successfully apply for a search warrant to enter his house. The other related thought that I have is that a sophisticated, intelligent woman like Anastasia, for whom money doesn't appear to have been an issue, very probably frequently updated her phone when a more high-tech model became available. If she did this it is likely she swapped SIM cards over so that a record of the calls she had made and received would be encoded on her new phone. She probably also copied over texts and photographs to retain access to them, but her old phone would also retain this information. It is perfectly possible that she may have kept one or more of these phones as backup in case the one she was using was stolen or permanently damaged in some way. If she did it's possible that Andropov might be willing to hand over such phones to us if he could be persuaded that they represented no threat to him. We wouldn't have the call logs of course, but we would have photographs and text messages to work through, and that could be extremely useful. Our Eastern European friend might simply tell us to take a running jump; I'm well aware of that, but we don't lose anything at all by asking."

"We don't" responded Hardy; "but personally I wouldn't hold my breath. I don't expect one ounce of co-operation from that quarter."

And Hardy wasn't the only person to feel this way. Another person who was highly sceptical about the chances of getting any worthwhile help from Alexei Andropov was Detective Sergeant Peter Bennett who believed the émigré from Belarus to be as crooked as a bent corkscrew, with no redeeming features, but he did at least accept that circumstances might prove him wrong, although he prefaced that remark with the comment "but pigs might fly." Bennett did however have two pieces of Information to share with DCI Hobson before they set out on their trip to interview the man Cheshire Police now believed had put his active criminal career on hold.

The first piece of news was not unexpected. Bennett was able to confirm that the blood taken from the body of the dead dog in the police station freezer matched exactly the blood found on the coat being worn by Anastasia when her body was discovered.

"Which means" he said to Hobson, "that Andropov's wife could be correct in alleging that Miss Karpovich did take the dog, either deliberately to cause trouble, or inadvertently if it was inside the Bentley when she drove off. I personally don't buy that because the "lovely" Mrs A was so totally besotted with the animal that she would never have left it unattended in the back of a car, and in any event a person would have to have been oblivious to almost everything not to notice it when he or she entered the vehicle, even if the dratted animal was asleep."

"You might be right" accepted the DCI, "but I can think of another explanation. Suppose the person who killed Anastasia had previously stolen the dog, and maybe in some way used it as an inducement for her to accompany him, perhaps by persuading her that he needed her help to recover it, and by doing this she could improve her ice cold relationship with Andropov's wife."

"Possibly" murmured Bennett, "very possibly. Perhaps we may know more by the time our day is done today.

The second piece of news was then explained by the detective sergeant.

"This just might be a break through Gov" he said; "the fancy dog collar has been checked for fingerprints, and some partial prints have been recovered. They're on the underside of the strap, and interestingly they relate to two different people. The ones nearest the buckle offer the most potential; the others, which are more central could have been left by the scout leader when he picked up the dog's body. We're hoping to get a set of elimination prints from him later today, and the answer then should become clear, but if they aren't his that does give us a second string to our bow.

"The ones nearest the buckle are inverted, and are more likely to have been left by the killer. From what Mrs Andropov said, the silly little creature was often stroked under its chin by her before she gave it a treat. I think the murderer did the same thing, then grabbed the collar and snatched the animal up into the air prior to slitting its throat just below the spot where his hand was. It's only a theory of course, but it may have some mileage because the dog was used to such pampering, but whether it develops into anything more concrete only time will tell."

"Let's hope it does Pete" said Hobson. "We're chronically short of physical evidence at present; something tangible and indisputable would be enormously beneficial to this investigation."

CHAPTER THIRTEEN

September 1996--January 1999:-a collection of letters; conflicting emotions; promises kept and promises broken; and a big decision is finally made.

Why she kept the letters he wrote she wasn't really sure; maybe it was because she needed to understand Alexei, and to rationalise what she truly felt about him. The trouble was she felt differently every time she received a letter.

A collection of thirty-one hand written epistles now filled the folder that was secreted in the bottom drawer of the small chest she used as a bedside table, and which was home to her jewellery box, her toiletries, and her most expensive perfumes and cosmetics. Periodically she would open up the folder and pick out a note at random to see if anything made more sense than it had done before; usually nothing did. Twenty seven letters covering a period of twenty seven months; Alexei had been assiduous in his correspondence; that in itself was a worry. He seemed to have to do everything according to routine. She would have been happier if occasionally he had missed a month because something else had been on his mind, but he had never done so. The last things he seemed capable of, at least so far as she was concerned, was human frailty. He had promised that he would write to her every four weeks, (which was not strictly speaking every month as she had suggested), and by hook or by crook he seemed determined to keep that promise.

There were four other letters too in Sasha's collection. In one sense they weren't letters at all because these were notes written inside Christmas and Birthday cards. These cards had always accompanied generous gifts of jewellery which had clearly cost a lot of money. Sasha's favourite piece was something Alexei said was Blue John stone set into a heart shaped pendant made of 18 carat gold. She had worn this on a night out with friends, and they had all admired it. Her mother had commented on how lovely it looked. She had asked where it came from. Sasha told her that she had seen it in a catalogue and purchased the jewellery on line. Her mum had warned not to be too reckless with her spending, but had added that she had shown "remarkably good taste." Later in the privacy of her own room she had opened up her cache of letters and re-read the note that had been written on a sheet of paper inside the birthday card which had accompanied the gift.

Alexei had been at his most charming.

"Dear Sasha" he wrote,

Have a very, very happy birthday. I hope you like the little gift I have sent you. It is a simple thing, but I believe it will be dazzling when you wear it around your beautiful neck. The world is in need of all the beauty it can get. This month so much that is vile and repugnant has filled the papers here. Stories of human misery have made the headlines. I suppose I feel so affected by this sadness because I am unhappy too, and the one person who could alleviate my pain is a thousand miles away in a distant land. My son has been ill, and I have been too busy to look after him properly, and my wife she does not care. I think the infection he has contracted came from a chance meeting with other children. His little life is generally lonely; it is not right that a small child should be so often on his own. I realised something needed to be done, and that I was the only person who could do it. Through my work with the footballers I represent I meet some very attractive young mothers, and I thought that if I invited a few of them to my house with their offspring those children would be company for my son.

My wife laughed at the idea, but told me to go ahead if I wanted to, so for three weekends my house was filled with laughter and happy toddlers. My son adored the company; my wife did not; she shut herself away for the whole time and never showed her face. Then my little boy became ill. He caught Measles and also Whooping Cough. My wife would not go near him, even though he cried for her, because she claimed he was contagious. It was so pathetic; he looked so lost and so unhappy, and I realised that when he is better I will have to act to make his future brighter.

One of the footballers' wives is desperate to have a child, but she cannot conceive. She doted on my son Leo when she came to my house. I have made the heart-breaking decision that it would be better for him to be brought up in a home where he is truly loved by both his parents, and where he can interact with children of his own age. I have therefore taken steps for him to be adopted by this unhappy lady, and I have made her feel fulfilled. If you had been my wife I would never have had to make this choice. It is only by thinking of you now that I manage to avoid sinking into a pit of depression. You alone give me hope that one day my world will be better.

Wear the pendant often my angel, and when you do think of me.

I am forever yours,
Alexei

Re-reading this letter again brought tears to her eyes. Every time she did so it was the same. That a father should have to give up his only son because of an uncaring wife and mother was tragic. Her heart had filled with sympathy when she read the note for the first time. She had immediately written back to tell him of her sorrow, and how desperately sad it was that he had to surrender the custody of his child to another. She had assured him that the one bright spark of hope was that the little boy would be looked after and cared for by somebody who truly loved him; and she finished her note by adding that since Leo's future was assured surely now was the time he could firmly tell the cold-hearted bitch who he had married out of a sense of duty, to get out of his life forever. She ended her note by thanking him for the lovely present he had sent her, and telling him how much she liked it; and then repeated her fervent wish that he could finally rid himself of the person who had caused him so much pain.

It was a surprise therefore when she received his next letter.

My dear Sasha he said,

I am so very glad that you like the gift. You looked stunning when you wore it on your night out with friends. I am only sorry that I could not have been there myself to see the impact that you made upon all around you.

My little boy Leo has now gone I boxed up all his toys so that they could go with him to his new home, although I kept a little stuffed teddy bear to remind me of him always. He will I have no doubt be showered with presents by his new mum. I shed many tears, my wife not one. Your assessment of her as a "cold-hearted bitch could not be more accurate, and it is totally understandable that you feel it is time for me to kick her out onto the streets, but I am afraid it is not that simple.

I have to confess my sweet girl that until now I have not been entirely honest with you. I haven't lied to you, but neither have I told you the entire truth.

The night I had sex with my wife I was, as I have said before, sad, lonely, and depressed; and very far from sober. I hadn't spoken to her before, but I knew who she was, and I knew that she had lots of money. I was in need of cash, and somehow I thought that intimacy with her might help me acquire the money I needed to pay creditors and put my life back on track. I am not proud of myself, but the plan worked. Her family helped me re-finance my life; but at a cost. If I force her out onto the street they will reclaim every penny that they lent me, and probably a great deal more; and if they do that I will face financial ruin. If she makes a personal choice to leave that would be a different matter, but she rejoices in tormenting me, so I do not think she will be departing any time soon, There is in the future a step I could take to resolve this mess once and for all, but it is very risky, and now is not the time for such a gamble.

For the moment my wife and I must continue to live in the same house, but already we lead separate lives, and apart from a few occasions when, for various reasons we need to be seen together, we are mostly invisible to each other

I am sorry not to have been frank with you before, but I feared you would despise me. Your good opinion is what I treasure most.

Please forgive me and tell me I have not lost your love forever.
A thousand, thousand apologies,
Alexei

This letter aroused different emotions in Sasha. It was disturbing from the outset. Had Alexei written "I'm sure you must have looked lovely when you wore the pendant" it would not have caused her any concern, but to state that "she looked lovely" as an absolute fact worried her. Had he once again had people watching over her, and maybe secretly taking photographs on their mobile phones and sending them to him? She didn't know. It was a possibility, and a possibility that should never have existed.

Disturbing as this thought was however, it was not the thing about this letter that caused her most disquiet. Alexei's admission that the woman he claimed to have met by chance and with whom he had had a one night stand resulting in her becoming pregnant was in fact known to him; at least to the extent that he was aware she was very rich; was devastating. From the outset he had seen her as a solution to his financial difficulties. This was cold, calculating, and ruthless, and Sasha felt appalled by his willingness to use people for his own ends. Alexei had always had his dark side, and against her better judgement his dark side had caused within her a flutter of excitement; perhaps it still did. He had been different from all the other boys she knew. The boy had become a man; but deep inside he was still the same person.

What seemed beyond doubt was his unwavering infatuation with her. The contrition expressed in the letter appeared to be genuine; his plea for forgiveness heartfelt. It was this fact alone that had persuaded her to reply to this letter. What she wrote was not easy reading. She told him how angry she was that he had allowed himself to exploit another human being with a view to financial gain, and advised him, for his own sake, never to be so manipulative again. "This time" she said, "I forgive you, but there must be no more such episodes otherwise our friendship is at an end". She had finished the note by saying that "men have to earn the affection of others, they cannot buy it", and she told him to send her no more expensive gifts. She had thought about adding a postscript to the letter seeking to clarify what the "risky step" he might take in the future to put an end to his sham marriage might be, but decided that it was better not to know. After she had posted the letter she regretted her cowardice in not asking that question.

There were many other letters too, but the ones that followed her ultimatum that there could be no more forgiveness if he repeated his bad behaviour had gradually become lighter in tone. They contained more that was inconsequential, and more light-hearted, and seemed to signify a man at peace with himself. The "war" with his wife seemed to abate over time. If he talked about her it was now only in passing; and both parties seemed to be content to lead separate live. Sometimes Alexei mentioned his son, and the news was always encouraging, and occasionally he touched upon his business activities which appeared to be going from strength to strength. The one unchanging thread which ran through all his letters was the strength of feeling he expressed for her, but sometimes now in a funny, self-deprecating manner. More and more Sasha had felt herself warming to Alexei; and beginning to consider a trip to the United Kingdom; then the final letter arrived.

My dear sweet Sasha,

I fear this letter will make me appear boastful, which I know I should not be, but you will see from the photocopy of the newspaper article which I have enclosed that probably, for the first time in my life I have done something which other people have praised me for. It is written in English of course, but I know you will be able to read it without difficulty. The photograph of me isn't that great, but that doesn't matter. What matters is that I was there when a serious accident took place. For a few seconds I stared at it open-mouthed, then, in my head, as clear as day I heard your voice telling me that I must do something to help. Had I not heard your voice I might have remained an onlooker, but I couldn't ignore your plea. To my mind at least it is you rather than me who is the true hero.

At this point Sasha put down the letter and picked up the copy of the newspaper article that had been enclosed with it. Alexei was right, the photograph did not flatter, but it was unmistakably him. The text recounted the fact that the driver of the car, a man in his early seventies had suffered a heart attack at the wheel, lost control of his vehicle, and had collided with a parked van causing substantial damage. It related how a passing motorist Mr Alexei Andropov had seen the accident take place. He had stopped his car and ran across to the damaged vehicle and tried to open the driver's door to drag out the man and his hysterical passenger. Petrol was leaking from both vehicles, and the engine of the car was still running; at any second there could have been a catastrophic fire. At first Mr Andropov had not been able to gain access to the vehicle, but had eventually persuaded the panicking passenger to press the door release. Risking his own life he had lent into the vehicle and pulled the unconscious driver from his seat, after he had struggled to release his seat belt, and dragged him to the other side of the road to safety. He had then returned to the car to rescue the old lady, the man's wife, from the vehicle. Seconds after he had done this the car had burst into flames; had the two occupants still been inside they would certainly have perished.

The article concluded with comments from a local police inspector and the chief Fire Officer stating how brave Mr Andropov had been, and informing the readers of the paper that he would receive a special commendation for his actions.

It was at this moment that Sasha finally decided she would do as Alexei had so often entreated, and join him at his home in rural England.

CHAPTER FOURTEEN

Wednesday 18th September 2013- later in the day

The council estate where Wes Steele lived was not regarded by local people with great affection. There were some streets where it was obvious that many of the houses had been purchased from Macclesfield Borough Council by their occupants, and these were the ones where solar panels and modern PVC windows vied with each other for attention. Many of these former council houses no longer had front gardens, and instead had neatly tarmaced or paved areas where multiple vehicles could be parked. Almost all were maintained to a high standard, and it was agreed by most people that here was an OK place to call home.

There were other streets where the urge to become home owners had not been so paramount, possibly because these properties were tenanted by people with less well paid jobs, or maybe because they were too set in their ways to contemplate change, but, with the odd exception these streets were generally neat enough, with a decent level of community pride.

Finally there were streets like the one Mr Steele, the man who Detective Chief Inspector Hobson and Detective Sergeant Bennett were about to call on, had his home.

The first thing that struck anybody about Wes's address was the creaking gate that clung to its post by a single hinge and swung dementedly open and closed if there was the slightest breath of wind.

The next thing that caught the eye was the battered old refrigerator which at some time long past had been unceremoniously ejected from the house. The door had been ripped off, maybe in a fit of pique, and was now wedged between the main body of the fridge and the garden fence. Dirty water and rotting leaves now filled the carcass of the electrical appliance, and it was obvious from the grass growing up around it that this defunct example of 20th Century technology had laid where it rested for a considerable period of time. The sad thing was that this house was not a carbuncle amid crown jewels, most properties on the cul-de-sac were the same; shabby and uncared for, and in need of a monumental amount of TLC. This was clearly not a street populated by well to do super criminals, unless of course it was an elaborate hoax to fool the authorities into believing that the dregs of society eked out a miserable existence there when in fact many of the movers and shakers of the underworld were concealed behind these grim facades: not for one second did DCI Hobson and DS Bennett believe that to be the case. When the man they had come to see opened the door to them his appearance immediately confirmed that their initial judgement had been entirely correct.

Steele was a big man, probably six foot five inches tall and weighing in excess of twenty stone. At one time he must have been fit, but not anymore; his upper arms were flabby, and his belly hung over his belt like melting snow in a gutter just prior to a catastrophic fall to the earth below.

DCI Hobson showed him his warrant card and politely asked if he and his colleague, who he then introduced, could take up a few moments of his time to have a chat with them. Some groundwork had already been done. It had been explained to him in a telephone conversation with an officer from Cheshire Constabulary that two Derbyshire officers wanted to come and talk to him and that if he co-operated with them it could be to his advantage. Steele wasn't expecting a life-changing cash bonanza for his help, but the possibility of a few quid, or a decent bottle of Scotch had been enough to persuade him to agree to the interview. He was never-the-less uneasy about the presence of the two detectives outside his house.

"Get inside here" he hissed "before anyone sees you. Folk round here can spot fucking coppers a mile away and it will do my reputation no good at all if I'm seen chopsing to the likes of you."

Hobson and Bennett did as instructed. The inside of the house was just as depressing as the exterior. Wes Steele may have been a career criminal; he certainly had a long record for petty crime, and he had done time for Burglary and Assault Occasioning Actual Bodily Harm; but he clearly hadn't prospered. Anybody who thought he had made a good living from his illegal activities was sadly delusional.

It quickly became apparent that Wes himself fell into this unfortunate category.

"All the coppers in town used to know me" he said proudly. "They warned probationers to steer clear of me because I was a reet handful, "Steele by name and Steele by nature" they used to say (which was true, except that if that comment had ever been written down the second spelling of his surname would have been *steal* and he would have been categorised as a pain in the arse rather than Public Enemy no.1) "They don't do that now cos I don't do bad things no more"; and Wes then went on to complain about his arthritic hip, his two wonky knees, and his poorly controlled Type 2 Diabetes. It was clear his Damascene conversion to the paths of righteousness owned everything to his decline in health, and nothing at all to do with a genuine change of heart.

"Yeah you were a big man in those days Mr Steele" said Hobson, massaging the pathetic ex-con's ego, "but the biggest thing you did, and what made you a hero in a lot of people's eyes was to stand up to two sadistic killers and ensure that they were put behind bars".

"They were all mouth and bullshit" scoffed Wes, "but evil little bastards; they deserved everything they got. They burned a poor sod alive you know, and they were going to do the same to some woman after they'd finished having their way with her, the dirty little buggers."

Wes then went on to recount, in graphic detail everything that Steer and Warden had said to him in the prison cell. The problem Hobson and Bennett had was keeping him focussed on the points that really mattered; and the conversation lasted much longer than they had anticipated; but by the end of it they had learned three interesting things:-

Although they had never named names, or disclosed any specific details about their employer, both men had joked that at one time or another they feared that they might be paid in roubles rather than good old pounds, shillings, and pence.

They said that their employer had described the intended female victim as a "slag" and given them carte blanche to fuck her as many times as they wanted to before finally ending her life.

In addition to the substantial cash payment they had been promised tickets to the Cup Final, and other significant football matches as little bonuses for a job well done..

Both officers knew that none of this could be regarded as evidence that could be used in court. Wesley Steele was not a man to win the hearts and minds of any jury; and in any event what he said was all hearsay. The Cheshire police had been able to track down hard evidence to support their case against Warden and Steele for the Alderley Edge murder, such as the exact place where a roll of razor wire used to make a ligature to strangle their victim had been disposed of, but there was nothing concrete to confirm the story that a second murder had been contemplated. Never-the-less what Steele had said confirmed in the minds of Hobson and Bennett that their suspicions about Alexei Andropov were well founded. They were now sure he was behind the killing of the drug dealer, and convinced that he had plotted to have his wife murdered on the same day by the same killers. More and more it was beginning to look like the murder of Anastasia Karpovich was a case of history repeating itself, but with the twist that this time the wrong victim had perished.

It was significantly after 3 pm when the Derbyshire officers said their goodbyes to Wes. The £20 note and the bottle of inexpensive Scotch they left behind them meant that he was a happy man. *Never* thought Detective Sergeant Bennett *has a "super-criminal" been so cheaply bought.*

The next item on their itinerary that day was a visit to the coffee shop in Alderley Edge which had been one of Anastasia's favourite places to relax. Time was now at a premium for the Derbyshire officers if they were going to fit into the rest of the day all that they hoped to achieve. The distance they had to travel was approximately six miles; with DS Bennett driving it took just under ten minutes for them to reach their destination. It was perhaps fortunate that there were no police speed traps in operation that day but as Pete Bennett often used to say "fortune favours the brave."

The coffee house was all that they expected it to be. It was ultra smart, and very expensive, totally in keeping with the ambience of a village that thought itself a cut or three above its neighbours. It was regularly frequented by the girlfriends of very rich footballers, and the partners and spouses of stockbrokers, company directors, and members of the legal and medical professions.

The manageress; a woman in her early sixties who dressed like a person half that age, and indeed could be taken as such if you accepted her jet black hair as natural, and ignored the bags under her eyes which the heavy use of make up only partially camouflaged; clearly regarded the arrival of the two detectives as an inconvenience; but, after a brief conversation, she was at least willing to let the officers leave with CCTV tapes that covered the last thirty days.

"But I want them back quickly" she said, "we re-use the tapes time and again, and I need to have them returned to me by the weekend." When she was shown a photograph of Anastasia she did confirm that she had been a regular customer, and stated, that as far as she could recall, she was generally alone, but she conceded that there were probably times when she had been accompanied. This account was largely supported by other members of staff, although a bright young sixteen year old waitress did recall three occasions when she had been accompanied by the same man, who she described as being in his early twenties, with reddish brown hair, and for some reason, and she wasn't really sure why, she believed may have been foreign. She told Hobson and Bennett that she didn't think that the tapes they were taking away would show him because she believed that it was about six weeks ago that he last came to the shop.

The cafe in Wilmslow was not dissimilar to the coffee shop in Alderley Edge in that it catered for the same class of people, but it was less pretentious and more welcoming to customers who were not lucky enough to have six figure salaries or drive cars only Middle Eastern royalty could afford.

The owner was an attractive woman in her late forties with a bubbly personality, and a knack of putting people at their ease. She was more than happy to talk to Hobson and Bennett and to take time to fully answer the questions they had for her. There was a problem however; this cafe did not have any CCTV cameras.

"I didn't want my customers to feel that they were being spied upon "she said; "we never have any trouble in here so I had them taken out about three years ago." She readily confirmed when shown a photograph of her that Anastasia had been a frequent and popular visitor; she was also able to tell the Derbyshire officers that there were many occasions when she was joined by friends; one lady in particular stood out.

"She's still a regular customer" she said. "I don't know her name or address, but if you like next time she comes in I will ask her to contact you straight away."

It was the best Hobson and Bennett could hope for, and with that offer of help duly obtained they left the cafe after thanking the owner for her invaluable assistance.

The only thing left on the agenda for that day was to make contact with Andropov to see if he would be willing to allow the police to search Anastasia's bedroom to look for discarded mobile phones. A telephone call was made, but there was little hope of a positive response; but in that both detectives were mistaken. The answer Andropov gave was "yes, but not today, and only at a time when he could be present to ensure nothing untoward took place".

"He's a cheeky bugger suspecting us of skulduggery" complained Bennett, "he needs to brought down a peg or three; I reckon if we told his wife some of the stuff Wes told us, she'd be champing at the bit to help us nail him."

"Not ethical Pete" said Hobson "and potentially very dangerous. If she tried to settle scores her own way we'd be in for the high jump. For the moment at least, what Wes told us has to be a closely guarded secret so far as the lovely Mrs A is concerned.

CHAPTER FIFTEEN

Events of the 18th and 19th September 2013- a feast fit for a Tsar, a day filled with anticipation, a glimpse of evil, a useful meeting, and an interesting development.

The invite to dine with Vitali and Natasha Zalenkov had come much sooner than anticipated, and had necessitated some last minute changes of plans for Helena and for Mark, but it had all been worthwhile. The evening at Moor Top Grange had been wonderful, and the food had been amazing. Canapés stuffed with Caviar and Foie Gras; Venison cooked in red wine and herbs; and an assortment of mouth-watering desserts. Later, on their way home Helena had commented "I could get used to dining like that." Mark had quickly responded that "she shouldn't hold her breath as having a meal like the one they had just eaten, on a regular basis, would bankrupt them within the year" but he did whole-heartedly agree that the food had been a delight.

And it wasn't just the food that had made the evening so enjoyable. Natasha and her dad Vitali had been wonderful hosts. Vitali had been relaxed and attentive, particularly to Helena, and had asked her so many questions about her life, and shown genuine interest in her children and her family history. With Mark his queries had been about his job as a detective chief inspector, and how he reconciled the responsibilities of being a husband and father with the at times dangerous and stressful day to day existence of a senior police officer. From another person's lips it could have become tedious, or excessively inquisitive, but Vitali seemed to know precisely when to back off, and the conversation was punctuated with light-hearted comments, and tales about Natasha when she was little and his hopes for her future, and also about how much he loved England and his beautiful home. He spoke a lot about the family who had taken him in when he was destitute, and whose surname he now so proudly bore; of his life before that time he said absolutely nothing.

That period of his life is a closed book thought Mark; *the memories are still red raw, if he were to talk about it now he would find it exceedingly painful.*

When Natasha had her moments in the spotlight she talked about her love of horses and how she hoped to do well at this weekend's Chatsworth horse trials, and how glad she was that David and Alice had enjoyed their visit to the stable, and what nice children they were; which sent her approval ratings sky high in Helena's eyes.

The conversation switched to the Grange itself. Vitali was happy to talk about the very considerable amount of thought that had gone onto every stage of the restoration process. With another man this could easily have descended into boasting, but from his lips the enthusiasm he had for the task, and the detailed accounts that he gave about how he sourced the highest quality materials he could to complete the refurbishment made fascinating listening. He was justly proud of what he had achieved, and he happily admitted that he was overjoyed that tomorrow night he would be receiving an award for his efforts voted for by people whose knowledge he respected and admired.

"I will be so happy" he said; "for a man like me to receive an honour like this is amazing. I will share my joy with the world."

"And he will too" teased Natasha, "he really will"; and everyone laughed at Vitali's obvious delight.

DCI Hobson was late for work, and because he was generally so punctual that fact was noticed.

"Someone had a good night last night" joked DS Peter Bennett; "I don't know, partying into the wee small hours at your age; next thing you know you'll be going to all night raves, and strutting your stuff on the dance floor until the break of dawn."

"Helena and I had great night thank you Pete" replied Hobson, "but I'll have you know we were home shortly after 11pm, and tucked up in bed with our Horlicks well before midnight; but it was bloody brilliant Peter"; and Mark then described to the envious detective sergeant the superb meal he and his wife had so much enjoyed.

"Why is it always those at the top of life's ladder who get the lollipops" complained the disgruntled junior officer; but then deciding that there had been enough banter for the present he explained to his boss the real reason he had come to speak with him.

"I got a phone call less than half an hour ago Gov" he announced; "It was from a woman called Jennifer Drake; she's the person Anastasia used to meet in the cafe in Wilmslow. She was phoning us because the nice lady who owns the cafe was as good as her word and had asked her to contact us as soon as she could. I told her that I'd have a quick chat with my boss then call her straight back to fix up a meeting. She sounds very pleasant, and she's happy to come to Buxton because she's got friends who live in Burbage so she'll combine a trip to see us with a visit to see them."

"That's great"" responded Hobson; "if she could make it this afternoon round about 3pm that would be ideal"

"I'll try and set something up" said Bennett. "How about if we take her up to the canteen and chat to her there, it will be very quiet at that time, but it will make things more informal, and that should put her at her ease."

"A good idea" agreed Hobson. "Let's do that. Fingers crossed Miss Drake will be able to shed some light on the private life of Anastasia Karpovich."

For very different reasons Vitali and Natasha Zalenkov were finding it hard to feel relaxed. Natasha was acutely aware of just how much needed to be done to get herself and her young horse Yuri ready for tomorrow's show at Chatsworth. Everything had to be perfect Hours of patient grooming lay ahead, and every bit of tack had to be cleaned and polished and ready to impress. Second best was not an option. If she wanted to win, and she wanted to win very much, she and her horse had to look immaculate; and that was just the beginning. Her state of mind had to be right. She had to feel confident. She needed to be mentally and physically alert. While her father was drinking champagne, and being praised by the great and the good for his excellent taste, she planned to be tucked up in bed by 10 pm trying as best she could to get a good night's sleep.

Her dad was also feeling nervous. He had a speech to write and then to learn. He didn't want to use notes unless he absolutely had to. It might have taken hours to create, and still more time to rehearse, but he wanted his address to sound spontaneous, and that would be no easy task. The man he was now, the man who had wealth and power could do this; the person whose life had changed forever in a single night could not have done so. The boy banished from his home city in disgrace would have been mute; the enormity of the task would have overwhelmed him; but he was sure he could rise to the challenge. The invisible spectre of the youth he once had been watched over him; for now he was oblivious to its presence, but whether that would remain to be the case was by no means certain.

They had been given their task, and half the cash they would ultimately receive had been paid up front; now all they had to do was wait, and waiting wasn't easy. The enormity of what they were about to do didn't faze them for a moment. Nothing mattered in life except money. They had no no-go areas. Compassion and pity were emotions that had always eluded them. Most villains had some scruples, most villains had lines they would not cross, but they did not. They were prepared to do anything that was asked of them, no matter how cruel, or heartless, or sickening that might be: that was why they were rated so highly in their specialist field; and the reason they did not come cheap. They looked at their watches, it was nearly half past two, in another eight hours they would be reeking the sort of havoc only men with strong stomachs could unleash. In the meantime they allowed themselves a single glass of beer, and shared jokes about death and total destruction; and recalled episodes of rape and murder they had been involved in. These were not nice men; but in fairness they would never have professed to be so.

Mark Hobson had let the Inquiry Desk know he was expecting a visitor, and had instructed the Desk Sergeant to let him know the moment Jennifer Drake walked through the police station door so that he could meet and greet her without delay; and these instructions were followed to the letter. It was only after the DCI's visitor had left the foyer accompanied by the Detective Chief Inspector that the young constable who had spoken to her started to rack his brains, trying to work out where he had seen her before. A lot of people who saw Ms Drake on public transport or on the street had the same conviction that she was somehow familiar, but they, like the worried officer, were usually entirely mistaken.

She was a handsome woman in her early forties, but looking much younger. She had an attractive, intelligent face; her naturally auburn hair was sleek and shiny; her clothes expensive but understated; in many people's eyes she appeared to be the epitome of good taste. The common misconception was that this lady was perhaps a BBC regional newscaster, or the presenters of some current affairs programme that they never watched. None of this was true. Jennifer was a qualified accountant by profession who had given up work when she became pregnant in her late thirties, and who now devoted her life looking after her two small children. Her husband was a senior partner in a prestigious law firm, he brought home the dosh, and anybody looking at Jennifer could tell in an instant that there was plenty of dosh to survive on. She was also, as DCI Hobson was about to discover, a good friend of Anastasia Karpovich, and quite devastated by her brutal murder.

Over coffee, seated in armchairs in a quiet corner of the canteen Jenny explained that she had first met Anastasia seven years ago at a party hosted by one of her husband's professional colleagues. On this occasion she had been invited to attend the event together with the man the organiser thought to be her partner, Alexei Andropov. He had dropped out at the last minute, but she had thought it impolite not to honour the invitation so she attended, but she had been alone and sometimes isolated. Jenny had taken her under her wing, and they had chatted off and on throughout the evening. By the end of the night Jenny had learned that whatever Alexei may have believed to be the case he and Anastasia were not partners in any normal understanding of the concept; although they did cohabit: by this time the two women had also become friends, and from that night on had met frequently in cafes and coffee shops "to put the world to rights."

"Mostly" she confessed, "the conversation was inconsequential", but sometimes Anastasia had talked about aspects of her life before she came to England, She told Mark that the thing that seemed to have made a lasting impression on her friend was an occasion when a young man tried to propose to her using a stolen engagement ring. This episode she explained had made Anastasia wary of accepting things at face value and needing proof of integrity before allowing relationships to develop. She also informed Mark that the one thing she believed Anastasia now regretted above all else was when a few years later she learned from a third party that tragedy had come into this young man's life she had posted on the Internet a comment that "everybody gets their just deserts" effectively blaming his bad character for his own misfortune.

This revelation interested Hobson. It could be the basis of motive, albeit from way back, so he wrote down all the details that Jenny could recall: and there were other things too that appeared to offer potential. Jenny told him that over the course of the last few months Anastasia had developed a keen interest in local history which seemed strange. She had asked her how she could access back copies of the local newspaper from a dozen or so years ago; and Jenny had said this would not be difficult, and had given her practical guidance on how to go about the task.

After their conversation was complete, and Jennifer Drake had left the police station Hobson turned to DS Bennett and said:

"We need to discover the story Anastasia was trying to unearth. I may well be wide of the mark here, but my guts tell me that this somehow links into the murder we are investigating."

CHAPTER SIXTEEN

A wicked Samaritan, vile and despicable behaviour, the destruction of two worlds, and a vow to bring justice

She was exhausted, but she was ready; she had done all that she could do; now all she wanted to do was to sleep. Her dad had promised her that he would be quiet as a mouse when he returned from his expensive night out and that Josef (the youth who was tonight acting as a driver) would be so too. Her alarm was set for 6-30 am, tomorrow would be an early start. As her head hit the pillow she worried that she would struggle to drift into the land of dreams, but not a bit of it; as soon as she closed her eyes she was in deep slumber; it was only just after 9 pm.

The thunder roared like heavy artillery, lightening ripped the clouds asunder; in her mind she could hear the wailing of lost souls; then slowly, resentfully, she emerged from her apocalyptic dream to discover she wasn't dreaming at all. Somebody was pounding on the front door with his fist. A male voice was bellowing "Fire! Fire!" looking out of her window towards the stable block she could see smoke and flames. The building was on fire; her beloved horses were in deadly danger.

Leaping out of bed she threw on a T-shirt and a pair of jeans, and sliding her feet into the boots she had so carefully polished for the equestrian show she ran down the stairs and rushed to the front door which she flung wide open in her anxiety. A man who she had never seen before took a step back, surprised by the force with which the door had been opened. Had she not been in a state of blind panic she might have wondered how he had managed to gain access to the farmyard.

"I saw the blaze as I was driving past" he gasped."I.ve dialled 999. The fire brigade will be here very soon, and they'll soon have things under control." The silence of the night was shattered by the frantic whinnying of the terrified animals trapped inside the stable. If she had been capable of clear thought Natasha would have realised the there should also have been the snarling and growling of angry guard dogs but their silence failed to register; her mind was fully focussed on getting the horses out of the burning building.

"Too late" screamed Natasha, "too late. We have to act now. Help me, please, please help me to get the horses out. If we stand by and do nothing they will die.

The man looked hesitant, but then seemed to find courage. "OK" he said, "but just you remember that a human life is worth more than that of any animal; if the roof starts to creek, or is in imminent danger of collapse then we both get out quickly: do you understand?"

Natasha nodded. She was already half way to the stables. The stranger who was risking his own life to help her was close on her heels. Out of the corner of her eye, for a fraction of a second she thought she caught a glimpse of another figure, but it disappeared in an instance and she told herself that it had just been a shadow, and the product of a distraught mind.

Ten more steps and she was at the stable door. Without a moment's hesitation she drew back the bolt and entered the burning building to try to remove the first horse.

"If I can get it to the door" she shouted "you grab its halter and lead it towards the paddock while I bring the next one out." The man did not reply. Instead the stable door slammed shut, and Natasha distinctly heard the bolt being drawn, preventing her from getting out. She was trapped in a blazing inferno with no means of escape. Why her Good Samaritan had turned into her Nemesis she didn't know. She was terrified and on the verge of hysteria. Outside the man who had locked her in the burning building gave a thumb up sign to his mate, who then casually lit the petrol bomb he was carrying, and as nonchalantly as if he was taking an evening stroll approached the house and tossed the burning missile into the hallway of the building.

The food had been excellent, but nothing less than excellent would have been good enough given the price the guests were paying for their meals. The venue oozed class; that was why it had been picked to host the event; but anything less than 5 Star plus would have been unacceptable ; but in truth, superb as the dinner and the service had been, it was not these factors that thrilled Vitali so completely.

It wasn't the praise he had received that had so moved him, although there had been plenty of that both in the formal speeches, and more tellingly in the individual conversations he had had with so many people when everyone was gathered together for champagne cocktails before the main event. He had "made his mark"; umpteen people had told him that. In a world where money talked, but often in a course and vulgar voice, he had demonstrated restraint and good taste, and an empathy with the history and character of the building he had rescued from decline and with the hills and valleys that surrounded it. He had been asked where he had sourced his materials, and how he had found the craftsmen with the skills to renovate the centuries old farmstead in such a stunning way. The unspoken question on the lips of many of the persons he spoke to, the one which they wanted to ask but knew it would be improper to do so, was how come a foreigner from a little known country on the edge of Mother Russia had had the foresight to achieve what had been achieved when that outcome seemed entirely beyond the capability of all the native born sons of John Bull, whose only plans seemed to have been total or partial demolition followed by reconstruction according to dubious twenty first century taste. He had savoured these compliments like good wine, and had felt drunk on the admiration that engulfed him, and that had certainly massively affected his mood; but it wasn't this that made him feel so euphoric. It was the belief that now he could finally draw a line above his early life; and put behind him every action he had taken he wished he hadn't, and erase from his memory every unkind thought he had ever had. It was the feeling of acceptance; it was the feeling of totally belonging, the feeling of a new beginning that now overwhelmed him. When he returned home he would tell Natasha how wonderful the world was now and how brightly the future beckoned; but not tonight; tonight she needed her rest. He hoped her day tomorrow would be as gratifying as his day today had been: then his mobile phone rang.

The fires had both been brought under control by the time DCI Hobson arrived at Moor Top Grange. He had been looking forward to an early night, but as the senior detective on call a report of a serious case of arson had to be attended to, so he had immediately made his way over to the crime scene. What he saw confirmed that he had been right to do so. One wing of the house had been badly damaged, but the bulk of the building still stood. It was however certain that many of the stunning interiors and the beautiful items of furniture contained within them would have been ruined by the thousands of gallons of water that had been pumped into the building to put out the fire.

The stable block had suffered far more; it was now little more than a shell. The roof had collapsed minutes after the first fire crew arrived. Of the horses inside it now only one remained; two had died in the inferno the building had become; and one, although rescued by the firemen had such horrific injuries that it had to be put down by a vet; the beautiful little foal that David and Alice had fallen in love with had also sadly perished. Also found to have suffered a sudden and violent end were the three guard dogs, all of which had been shot at close range by someone with a pistol.

Natasha had been found unconscious behind the stable door. She had been badly burned and had sustained life-changing injuries; but it was believed she would survive, although her life would never be the same again. She was already being rushed by ambulance to a hospital in Stockport by the time Hobson turned up on site. She had apparently briefly regained consciousness when being tended to by the paramedics, and had cried out that she had been locked inside the burning structure. The fire crew later confirmed that the stable door had been bolted shut when they first tried to gain entry to the building.

That she was alive at all was in itself a miracle. A local farmer who lived on the other side of the valley, about a mile away from the Grange had seen a red glow in the sky, which had quickly become a fireball. He had immediately dialled 999 to report the blaze and then jumped straight into his car and driven to the Grange to see if he could render any assistance. He had nearly had a head on collision with a car being driven at speed away from the burning buildings. Later, seated in an armchair in his own home, he was able to tell the police that the vehicle he had seen was a dark blue Toyota (model unknown) which he believed may have contained two people. Its headlights had been on main beam, and he had be dazzled by them so the little he could say about the occupants was based on the fraction of a second that he had to glance inside the car as it swept by him. He could not give even the vaguest description of the men inside, and he did not see the registration plate so he could not assist the police in that regard. He did think the presence of the car highly suspect, and immediately wondered if it was somehow connected to the fire; a view that DCI Hobson later fully endorsed.

The Chief Fire Officer, when the police questioned him was able to state categorically that the fire in the house and the fire in the stable block had been started deliberately. An accelerant, almost certainly petrol had been used. He was 100% certain that the police had two cases of arson to investigate. What was also clear, given the claim by Natasha that she been deliberately locked inside a burning building (a fact verified by the firemen at the scene), was that this was also a case of attempted murder. DCI Hobson was almost overwhelmed by pity and by anger. Only a day ago he had been a guest of the owner of this farmhouse, and he and his wife Helena had been charmed by him and his lovely daughter. Now she was undergoing emergency treatment in hospital, her innocent life, her hopes, her good looks all in jeopardy. This was no run of the mill attempted murder; this was cruel beyond comprehension. How men could be so evil to commit such an atrocity beggared belief. Hobson made a vow to himself that he would hunt down whoever was responsible and bring those persons to justice; and not just the thugs who did the deed; the person who had paid them their money and given them their instructions had to face justice too. What had happened tonight was sheer evil; whatever it took, there would be a reckoning.

CHAPTER SEVENTEEN

Destruction on a scale undreamt of, a life in peril, an unquenchable desire for vengeance, and a search into the past for no apparent reason

He was in a state of anxiety. With the telephone call everything had changed. His mood of euphoria vanished, his hopes for the future disappeared; in an instance his world had turned bitter; all he wanted to do now was flee from the luxury restaurant and the coterie of admirers whose approval he had bathed in only moments before.

He garbled a barely coherent apology. He explained that an emergency had arisen at home and that he had to leave immediately. He asked if his certificate, which he had not yet been awarded to him, could be posted to him instead; then, to the consternation of his hosts, after extricating Josef from the adjoining bar, forcing him to leave untouched the expensive bar snack he had just ordered; and inwardly cursing the day he accepted this invitation, he left.

Once in the car he implored Josef to make all possible speed to get him back home as quickly as possible.

"Getting there fast is all that matters" he screamed as Josef momentarily slowed to allow an on-coming HGV to pass a parked van. "Own the bloody road Josef" he bellowed, "for God's sake own the bloody road."

Throughout the interminable journey back to his house he was in turmoil. If he had been a religious man Vitali would have prayed to God that things might not be as bad as he feared they would be, but God did not exist. God was a myth, created by the deluded to fill a psychological need, a crutch to support the inadequate; there was no point in trying to enlist the aid of a being, who supposedly dwelt somewhere above the clouds surrounded by sycophants playing golden harps, to be his saviour.

He needed to be rational. The phone call he received had been brief; he knew that there had been a fire at the Grange, and that Natasha had been taken to hospital, but that was all. Perhaps he was over dramatising, perhaps his daughter was only slightly harmed; maybe he was panicking too much; and then as the car neared its destination, instantaneously he knew that his worst fears came nowhere near to doing justice to the scene of utter devastation that now confronted him. In the course of just a few hours his beautiful home had been partially wrecked. One day, if he had the stomach and the willpower maybe it could be restored for a second time to its former glory, but for now, it was impossible to live in and he had effectively been rendered homeless.

And the stable block had fared far worse. It was just a smouldering ruin, nothing could be done to save that; and thorough bred animals conservatively valued at over eighty thousand pounds had perished; but as appalling as this was, all this was insignificant when weighed against the fate of his daughter. Natasha was not going to be released from hospital any time soon. Natasha was lying on an operating table as surgeons battled to save her life. If they failed then something pure; something money could never buy; something irreplaceable; would be lost forever.

The rage within him threatened to engulf the world. The person who had commissioned this crime would live to regret this day, of that he was sure. Pain and suffering; and a lifetime of abject misery would be the price exacted for this heinous deed. He was certain he knew who had paid the piper, but he would not act until there was not a shadow of doubt left in his mind; then, and only then, the monster who had sought to take from him the most precious thing in his life would reap the whirlwind.

Helena cried when Mark told her what had happened. As a policeman's wife she was used to hearing stories about "man's inhumanity to man" but this felt different. It was almost as if the violence had entered the everyday world she inhabited A little more than twenty four hours earlier she and Mark had dined with the young woman who had been so cruelly used. This felt personal; it felt tragic; and far too close to home. Her mood mirrored that of her husband when he left for work; and that was a mood he could not easily shake off. It was a very sombre detective chief inspector who later that day met with Detective Chief Superintendent Stanley Hardy to explain to the Divisional Head of CID the dramatic events that had occurred overnight.

"So this is another example of serious arson in which the victim is of East European origin; are these two cases linked? If they are then a very disturbing trend seems to be developing involving wanton destruction on a grand scale, and a callous disregard for human life. It's only by sheer luck, and the timely intervention of a good neighbour, that Miss Zalenkov wasn't killed. Has somebody got a vendetta against wealthy immigrants? We need to get this one cleared up quickly Mark before things escalate out of hand and we get kicked from pillar to post by the tabloid press. We have to make damn certain that that doesn't happen."

"We're doing our best Sir," replied Hobson. "Yes I do believe that the two cases of arson are linked; and also the murder of Anastasia Karpovich ; and we're doing all that we can to discover what that link is; and if we are able to then I think we will be well on the way to solving all these crimes." DCI Hobson then went on to explain to DCS Hardy the steps that had already been taken to piece together the individual fragments of evidence the police currently possessed into a coherent whole.

"I think that in ways we don't yet know the early lives of Anastasia Karpovich, Alexei Andropov and Vitali Zalenkov are somehow intertwined" he said, "and I have a strong feeling that it is Anastasia who is pivotal to the whole case. We obviously know that she co-habited with Andropov for many years, although according to her friend Jennifer Drake she did not see herself as his partner, and Miss Drake believes that whatever the relationship was between them it had recently significantly cooled. In any event Andropov has a wife; who not to put too fine a point on it is a complete bitch. She also hated Anastasia, which would not have made for a relaxed "ménage-a-trois"; her possible involvement in Anastasia's murder is one line of inquiry that we are already following up; as you already know Sir. We also understand from Miss Drake that Anastasia in the weeks before her death seemed suddenly to have developed an interest in local history, at least to the extent that she wanted to search back numbers of local newspapers to find a story reported in them a dozen or so years ago. I've got Pete Bennett pulling out all the stops to uncover what that story was because I'm convinced it does have a bearing on this case. In addition to all of this we plan to visit Andropov's home later today to search Anastasia's bedroom for any old mobile phones she may have hung on to for back up in the hope that there might be photographs or texts stored upon them which could assist our investigation.

"When the doctors tell us she is fit to be interviewed then we will obviously talk to Natasha. This has to be handled with great care. She has met me, so I intend to be the one who speaks to her, and I intend to take Sue Graham (*a trained Victim Support officer*) with me. It may take a long time to get anything useful from her; and I'll be guided by the medical staff the whole time. If she gets distressed then I'll have to back off, but I'm hoping that over time I will be able to gently tease an account of what happened out of her; and crucially perhaps a description of the man who locked her inside the burning building.

"I'm pretty well convinced that this was a professional hit, and that the men who set fire to the stable block and then lured Natasha into it are hired assassins. They almost certainly come from outside Derbyshire, most likely Greater Manchester or Sheffield, or perhaps even further afield. We're already talking to GMP and South Yorkshire Police, and we have approached the Serious and Organised Crime Squad for help. There has to be intelligence somewhere which will assist us. The bastards who did what they did to an innocent eighteen year old girl, and the evil sod who paid them for doing so, want locking up forever; and I swear to God that I'll not rest until that has happened": so ended Mark Hobson's lengthy conversation with the head of North Derbyshire CID.

The phone call that Jamie Edwards had just received from Detective Sergeant Peter Bennett of the Derbyshire Constabulary had come completely out of the blue. He remembered Anastasia Karpovich, of course he did, no red-blooded male with an eye for beauty could forget such a person; and he knew, as anyone who read the papers, or watched local news programmes on TV knew, that she was dead; but not for one second had he thought that her three visits to the offices of the Macclesfield Advertiser, where he was employed as a junior admin assistant, would be of the least interest to the police.

Detective Sergeant Bennett asked him if Miss Karpovich had ever attended the premises where he worked, and he had confirmed that she had done so on three separate occasions. In total she had spent several hours there searching through back numbers of the paper looking for a particular news story. The back numbers were now all on micro-film, and he had shown her how to scroll down through the pages to look for the information she required; which he told DS Bennett that she had initially found quite hard. He also mentioned to the officer that although it was not unusual for members of the public to call in and look for news stories, mostly they knew in advance what they wanted to find, and could indicate which edition of the paper they wanted to search. Such visits were generally of short duration. Anastasia had shown a doggedness and a determination to find what she was looking for which was rare. He didn't say this to the police, but if he was honest with himself he was glad that had been the case: he had liked looking at the beautiful woman who had brought a touch of glamour into his sometimes humdrum existence.

Eventually on the third occasion she had found what she had been seeking. She had asked if she could have a photocopy of the article, which he had provided. When DS Bennett asked if the police could be faxed a copy of that article he readily agreed. The report he had photocopied dated back to late 1998. It told the story of how a local man named Samuel Postles had heroically rescued an elderly couple from a crashed vehicle moments before it burst into flames. When he asked Miss Karpovich if Mr Postles, or any of his family were known to her he had been surprised when she told him that that was not the case. He said as much to DS Bennett, and DS Bennett had agreed with him that this was very strange.

"What Anastasia said to the lad at the Macclesfield Advertiser was absolutely true Gov. While you were having your never-ending conversation with Stan I was busy looking up Samuel Postles' address, and then I gave him a call. He couldn't have been more helpful. He is one hundred per cent certain that he has never met, or even seen Anastasia in the flesh. He told me that he definitely would have remembered catching sight of a woman like her, and he was adamant that none of his family had ever had any contact with her either, which I totally accept. I then started to wonder if maybe Anastasia was in some way connected to the old couple he saved, but Sam thought that unlikely as they were just passing through the Peak District with no local ties: and in any event it's possible she wasn't even in the country when the accident occurred."

"You're probably correct Pete", agreed DCI Hobson; "but if Anastasia has no personal involvement with Mr Postles or his family, and the same is true in respect of the old couple he rescued why the hell did she search so diligently for this particular news report?"

"I don't know Gov" responded DS Bennett, "but finding that story was clearly important to her; all we have to do is figure out why."

"Which will not be easy" murmured Hobson; "but perhaps something might come to us as we drive over to Andropov's house later today to search for discarded mobile phones."

"No longer any need to go" announced Bennett; "Andropov himself made a flying visit to the police station not more than half an hour ago. He brought with him two mobile phones in self-seal plastic bags. He said he just happened to be passing so he thought he'd save us a journey, but then he let it slip that he'd been getting a load of ear ache from his wife who had had a mega strop at the thought of policemen crawling all over the house."

"That's just bullshit "responded the DCI angrily, "but at least we've got the phones, although how much stuff will have been wiped from the memories before they were handed over is anybody's guess."

"It is Gov, but it is what it is, and you never know for all his arrogance, the cocky bastard may have overlooked something vital."

"We can but hope Peter" said Hobson; "We can but flipping well hope."

CHAPTER EIGHTEEN

Anguish and anger, truth versus lies, crimes and punishment, and planning a terrible revenge

Was it love or hatred that had made him who he was? Almost certainly it was both, but had there not been in his life events that had dragged him from the peak of happiness to the depths of despair would he still be the same person? He didn't know the answer. What he did know was that he was sick with worry about his child. Her health and her beauty could be gone forever, and if that was the case would she feel she had nothing left to live for? The sadness and the distress one terrible night had caused would be unbearable; and even if the doctors and the plastic surgeons could save her looks, and in time she could regain her physical fitness how would she cope with the knowledge that somebody had tried to kill her in a most terrifying and heartless way, and had deliberately at the same time destroyed her hopes and ambitions by cruelly slaying the young animals who could have been her passport to a glittering sporting future? Vitali could not see how she could ever get over their loss. Her mental anguish would never go away, and every hour of every day he would have to watch his daughter suffer.

He remembered when he was a teenager seeing a young girl who enchanted him. She had taken over his mind and possessed his dreams, and had done so without the slightest intention of doing so. Her innocence and her beauty had been captivating. Many years later he had seen the identical qualities in his daughter, and he knew that young men looked at her in the same way that he had looked at Sasha. He recalled how he could not hide his desire for her, and how a "friend" had encouraged him to reveal his feelings, and had even helped him buy a ring. "It was a fine ring" he said, "one that he was able to purchase at a good price", and because this "friend" claimed to know more about girls than he did, and understand the things that turned them on he had handed a sizeable chunk of his savings to him so that he could acquire the pretty piece of jewellery.

He recalled how nervous he had been on the day he planned to reveal to Sasha how much he cared for her and the thrill he had experienced when he offered her the ring and she had smiled so sweetly when she gazed upon it, then there had been an explosion of noise; and in a single second his "friend" had become the devil incarnate, and his mortal enemy.

He had been stunned. In vain he tried to explain that Alexei was lying; that the ring had been bought and paid for; that his feelings were real, and that this was a travesty; a product of Alexei's warped and evil mind; but words hadn't come easily; and he had not been believed. Sasha had recoiled from his touch; her parents had thrown him out of the house, and thereafter they, and Alexei, and even Sasha herself had trashed his reputation in the city of Minsk.

A good liar is far more credible than a poor teller of the truth; tongues wagged; doors were shut in his face; people laughed; people jeered; even his parents disowned him; he had felt suicidal, but had been too scared to do the deed. It had been a black, black time; and undoubtedly it had changed him as a person. He had become angry, and bitter, and terribly alone. Once, just before he left Belarus for ever a stray dog had tried to snatch a piece of bread from his grasp. He had hit it with a brick and then tossed its body into a refuse skip. This act would formerly have made him feel sick; now alarmingly it made him laugh.

He had quit the country of his birth in the dead of night under a dark, dark shadow, hating the people he had once loved, yet perversely still longing for Sasha who had completely expunged him from her mind, and he had spent weeks in a strange land on the edge of desperation. Then, as he had told Detective Chief Inspector Hobson and his wife, he had been saved by the chance encounter he had had with a pretty girl in need of protection, and by the subsequent gratitude and affection of her family. The blackness had disappeared; maybe not completely; but well hidden; and he had been happy. To marry for love was something most people aspired to; he had done that and a whole new world had opened up for him; then, just at the moment when he thought his life would be made complete by the arrival of a baby his wife had tragically died in childbirth. Once more it seemed that Fate was conspiring to make his life unbearable.

The unconditional love of an infant and the steadfast support of his wife's family had brought him back from the abyss, and gradually the scars had healed. For the first time in years he had respect and status, and the bad times in his life had become distant memories, shut away in a closed corner of his mind, forgotten, but not totally obliterated; and although he didn't know it, capable of resurrection if his life once again turned sour.

The move to the United Kingdom had been a decision he had come to after his parents-in-law had died. He now possessed their fortune, willingly gifted to him by them, but the cause of some friction and envy among their distant blood relatives. He could do without the resentment, and in any event he had believed England to be a land of opportunity for a young girl with Natasha's looks and ability so he had settled here to fulfil a dream. Where was that dream now? Struggling for life in a hospital bed and buried under tons of rubble and burnt fragments of timber; no dream could survive such an onslaught. And who was responsible for this? The person who had tried to ruin his life many years ago had now tried to do so again; and if Natasha died, or became a disfigured cripple he would have succeeded. Vitali did not know that this would be the case, and hoped with every fibre of his body that it would not be so, but the very thought that this could happen made him shake with anger. Why Alexei, who, all those years ago he had believed to be a soul mate had acted as he did he could only guess, probably to try to gain Sasha for himself, or maybe he just liked destroying peoples' hopes, but he now believed him to be the embodiment of evil. He had to be punished. He had to suffer for the rest of his life. The violence he had commissioned would rebound on him tenfold. How could any human being be so heartless? Not for one second did Vitali place his own character under the microscope when he asked this question. Instead he telephoned the hospital. He was told it could be hours before Natasha came out of theatre. The person he spoke to said it would be better to wait at home for a phone call telling him she was now on a ward rather than coming down immediately and pacing around the waiting room unsettling other people with his anxiety. He wanted to scream that he no longer had a home, but he managed to control this urge; and trying not to think about what the next news from the hospital could be if the surgeons failed in their work, he instead began to plan how he would have vengeance.

What happened to Alexei had to be appalling. It had to involve the infliction of pain. His loathing for his enemy knew no bounds. The man had to be beaten; he had to be tortured, and also mutilated; and made to live the rest of his life a grotesque figure of ridicule; but that was nowhere near enough. He wanted to hear him beg for a bullet to be put into his brain, or a knife plunged into his heart to put him out of his misery; and he wanted to deny him that request. A quick death was not an option; a long life of suffering had to be the outcome.

And even this was insufficient; if this was all Alexei would not be universally reviled. Alexei had started their battle with a lie; it needed to end with another; but what should that lie be; and then on that awful, unforgettable night the answer came to him. Alexei needed to be accused and convicted of a crime he had not committed; a crime so bad that it would guarantee a sentence of life imprisonment without parole; a crime so heinous that he would be placed on permanent suicide watch by the prison authorities."Don't ever let the bastard escape justice by taking his own life" would be the instruction; and the prison warders would be zealous in making sure that that did not happen.

His crime had to involve the destruction of innocent lives. It had to be seen as an assault on the fabric of the state. For a moment Vitali fantasised about a murderous attack upon a high profile figure, perhaps a member of the Royal Family or his or her offspring; but even with all the money at his disposal that would be virtually impossible to arrange, and it would be even harder to frame an innocent man for the outrage. An attack on a primary school, or a church congregation, or a hospital ward, as appallingly happened so frequently in the USA, would be a little easier to stage, although finding a person to pull the trigger would be difficult; and to be the person who had caused such a sickening crime to be committed would make him an even worse villain than Alexei; it would also bring tragedy into too many ordinary peoples' lives.

But to select just one man and his immediate family would limit the spread of grief; but who should that person be; then the plan crystallised. To kill a high ranking copper and those closest to him that would fit the brief. He knew such a person, and he knew that he had a beautiful wife and very photogenic children. To be wrongly convicted of their murder would guarantee the result for Alexei that he most craved. As yet this was only an idea in embryonic form; much needed to be done before it could become reality. He had to seek out the right assassin to carry out the attack; he had to research exactly how evidence could be planted so that Alexei was incriminated for this crime. He believed that the fingerprints and the DNA of an individual could be left at a crime scene or on a weapon without that person ever having been there or ever touching an individual item. He would have to spend many hours and maybe days looking for inspiration. As he waited for the telephone call from the hospital to arrive he opened up his lap top, and for the moment at least, his thoughts were no longer on Natasha.

CHAPTER NINETEEN

Patience and pity, a thought-provoking conversation, a shadowy figure, and planning to sow seeds of unease

The news that awaited Detective Chief Inspector Hobson when he arrived at his desk the next morning was that Natasha Zalenkov was now on an intensive care ward. Currently she was heavily sedated. It was remotely possible that by the evening she might be fit to be interviewed, although the doctor to whom he had spoken thought this unlikely.

"Better chance tomorrow" he said; but even that prospect could in no way be guaranteed.

Hobson felt frustrated, but he understood; Natasha's physical and mental well-being was paramount.

"The poor kid's been through Hell" he later said to Peter Bennett; "she may never come to terms with what happened to her last night. God knows what she will be feeling when she finally wakes up. We have to be patient; it's all we can be in these circumstances."

But the fact that the police couldn't yet interview Natasha didn't mean there was nothing they could do. There was so much that needed to be attended to. The search for the dark blue Toyota spotted by the local farmer who rushed to help Natasha was still in its infancy. Hours and hours of checking CCTV cameras within a five mile radius of the farm had to be undertaken. It was more likely than not that the police would draw a blank, but there was a one per cent chance they could get lucky; and if they did that could be a game changer. SSO's (Scientific Support Officers) were beginning to pick their way through the debris of the stable block in their search for clues, and they would in due course subject the house to similar examination. Hopes were not high but they did exist; one fingerprint might be all that was needed, or one tiny fragment of DNA.

There were other lines of enquiry which were on-going too. The report of Sam Postles's heroism had to be a piece in the jigsaw. Mark Hobson read and re-read the newspaper article to try to discover if anything had been overlooked, but he could find nothing. There appeared to be no connection whatsoever between Anastasia Karpovich and the event described in it, but it was this report she had so diligently searched for; there had to be a reason why.

Sam Postles doesn't know thought Mark; *and the one person who does know the answer is dead and can't help me anymore; it's a long shot but maybe there is somebody else who can. I need to speak to Jennifer Drake; it's just possible she may be able to shed a little light on Anastasia's reasons for searching for this newspaper article.* He picked up his phone and dialled her number, she answered after the third ring. Somehow that spoke volumes about the person Jennifer was; honest, straight forward, direct. If the world was populated with more people like Jenny thought Mark it would be a less chaotic, more rational, more caring place. He apologised for the early call, and asked if it was a convenient time to chat. She indicated that it was, so the DCI then explained the reason for the phone call.

In answer to the direct question as to whether Anastasia had ever explained the reason why the article she was looking for had such significance for her she replied that she had not. She added that if her friend had been searching for something that related to a person or persons she cared about she was sure she would have said so, so she discounted any historic or recent friendship towards any of the people mentioned in the article. She went on to say that she was fairly confident that for Anastasia the actual story was a side issue. She pondered if the page of print was what really mattered, and Mark Hobson found himself believing that she could be right. She then asked a question, which once spoken, seemed to throw a shaft of light onto the whole conundrum.

"Sasha wasn't a very happy person in the weeks before her death" she said. "She told me that her relationship with Alexei was at an all time low. Then she added that she now believed that the last twelve years of her life had been based on a lie. What that lie was she never told me Mr Hobson, but in my mind it has to have something to do with Alexei Andropov. My feeling is that the article she was looking for in some way or another gave her the truth she was seeking. Can you see any merit in this line of thought?"

He could; and Mark Hobson responded that in his eyes it had a great deal of merit indeed. He concluded the phone call by thanking Jennifer profusely for all her help. A whole new line of inquiry had opened up; there was however still a mountain to climb. On the face of it the report in the paper was a factual account of a tragedy being averted. There seemed to be nothing about it at all that could be contentious. How possession of this story would help Anastasia Karpovich expose a lie was unclear. The only person who would know how that could be was Andropov himself; and as sure as eggs were eggs he would not be bending over backwards to help the police understand how this was so.

The two mobile phones that Alexei Andropov claimed had belonged to Anastasia had now been examined; neither had proved to be a source of vital information. In both the SIM card had been removed. Data relating to calls made and received, which could have been enormously helpful no longer existed. It was as DS Bennett thought it would be, but it was still disappointing. A limited number of text messages sent and the replies these had generated remained on the phones' memories, and these had now been examined. On one phone they covered a period in late 2007, on the other they related to Spring 2012. None of these messages seemed to shed any light on the crimes the police were investigating. DS Bennett was certain that Andropov had deleted anything that he thought might incriminate him before bringing the phones to the police station.

Both of these phones did contain photographs. Almost without exception these were of scenic locations of lakes, and hills, and wild countryside; although some were of people. There were two "selfies" of Sasha and Jennifer Drake, and three other people who were clearly known to Anastasia; but of course there was nothing to indicate who these people were. DS Bennett assumed that they must be friends of Anastasia. If their identity could be established it would be worthwhile talking to them. He wondered if Jennifer might know them. He made a mental note to suggest to DCI Hobson when he spoke to him later that morning that he should once again ask for Miss Drake's help. It was only after he had more or less concluded that these three photographs were the only one with any potential to be useful that he glanced again at the two "selfies" of Jennifer and Anastasia. Both had been taken in Spring 2012, and clearly at two different locations, with no apparent link except, when he peered closely at them again there was a male figure in the background, largely out of focus, who seemed to DS Bennett to be the same person. He could be mistaken of course, but that might become clearer if the photographs could be enlarged and subjected to microscopic examination; it could be pure coincidence; although the odds against this man happening to be in the same place and at the same time by chance, when the places seemed to be utterly unconnected, and maybe many miles apart had to be astronomically high; or it could be that this man was spying on one or other of the two women for a reason that was probably malign: it was this explanation that Detective Sergeant Bennett found to be most convincing.

"And my bet is that the person he was most interested in was Anastasia" he later told Mark Hobson. "It's hard to tell from the photographs at present how old the chap is, but I have a feeling he is young, which makes it likely he was acting on the instructions of another person, and reporting back his findings to him or her. All we have to do Gov is work out who that person could be."

"How about Andropov for starters" suggested Hobson? "We know that Anastasia felt herself to have been deceived by somebody, and in my view that is likely to be Alexei; her animosity towards him could have given him a reason to keep tabs on her."

"It could Gov" agreed Bennett; "and if he thought she was being disloyal, or doing something that put his way of life under threat then that could have been the prelude to him commissioning something that would be to her detriment."

"Like murder" queried DCI Hobson?

"Like murder" responded Peter Bennett; "do you think it's time we started rattling the cocky bastard's cage a wee bit to see if we can engineer a response?"

And how should we go about that Peter" asked Hobson? "If you've got any bright ideas let's hear them now. I do agree with you that the more unsettled we can make him feel the more liable he will be to make mistakes."

"Well if he thought that somebody was talking to us behind his back that might faze him" suggested DS Bennett, particularly if that person was somebody who he knows would bad mouth him to all and sundry given half a chance. The delectable Mrs Andropov falls into that category. If we go and talk to her, even if she tries to convince us that her husband is the Archangel Gabriel, which she won't; he'll believe that she has done her upmost to drop him into the proverbial; and you never know we might actually persuade her to do the dirty on him. If we could in some way convince her that he was trashing her reputation whenever an opportunity arose she'd probably delight in revealing to us every nasty little secret she has ever known about him."

"Agreed" responded Hobson; "but that might be easier said than done. Is there any evidence at all to support such a contention?"

"Well there might be" conjectured Bennett. "Over the years he has attended a lot of publicity events connected with Premier League football, usually unaccompanied, but in the early years he was sometimes seen with Anastasia, probably because he knew that with her there would be photographs in the press. This hasn't happened so much recently, possibly because she got fed up of being used as eye candy; but over the last decade the number of times his wife was with him can be counted on the fingers of one hand. I think he feels her presence would cramp his style. I'm sure I read a report of one of these events from way back when he cracked a couple of jokes about his spouse. I believe he had his audience rolling in the aisles; if the ever patient Mrs A had been present then I have no doubt she would have done a first rate impression of Queen Victoria sucking a lemon. I doubt if this sort of behaviour was a one off; maybe if we trawl through old press cuttings and search for any video footage that may exist on You Tube we will find other examples of him mocking her. If we do, and then we compile a composite record of what we have unearthed and show that to his wife she might take it very badly. Nothing is guaranteed of course, but if you think it is worth a shot I'll get the lads to have a ferret around the archives."

"It's worth a shot" said Hobson. "Nothing ventured nothing gained; we certainly won't find anything out by sitting around waiting for answers to fall into our laps. You go and crack the whip downstairs. While you do that I'll scan the three photographs from Anastasia's phone and then give Jennifer Drake a call; she'll know immediately if she can put names to faces. If she can then we'll have leads to follow up; if she can't we will have to work out another way of discovering who they are."

CHAPTER TWENTY

Selecting a killer; the flawed nature of mankind; wealth, power, and greed; tender true love and all-consuming hatred; and sucking upon citrus fruit

A bomb taped to the underside of a car; a bomb made of Semtex such as the IRA used to use in Northern Ireland to deadly effect; a bomb that wiped out an entire family; if a bomb like that was detonated with tragic results, the appalling consequences of such a brutal attack on innocent lives would cause disgust, revulsion and anger on a seismic scale. Anybody convicted of involvement in such a gross crime could expect no mercy; to be kicked, to be beaten, to be spat on by prisoners and prison warders alike; every hour of every day made a living hell; that was the outcome he wanted for his enemy; but he found himself unable to contemplate sanctioning something so appalling. The very thought of children being blown to bits was as abhorrent to him as it was to any sane person on the planet; he would not countenance this; there had to be another way.

There were Islamic extremists who could commit murder in the name of religion, and readily sacrifice their own lives in the deluded belief that doing so brought them closer to their God, but he wanted nothing to do with such unhinged zealots; in any event he would have to invent a credible lie to secure their co-operation to attack a particular individual. It would not be difficult to concoct a story that would excite their wrath; believing that someone had burned the Koran, or urinated upon it as American GI's had allegedly done to cause distress to captive followers of Bin Laden would send them apoplectic, but such a myth would need to be supported by evidence, and so far as he knew, there was absolutely none to give credence to such a claim.

There were home grown men of violence lurking under the radar in many English cities, and almost universally their hatred of the police would be extreme; but, for the most part, except for the nutters and the psychopaths, who were to be avoided at all costs, killing women and children was a step too far. Many of these men were Union Jack waving anti-immigration activists; they would not react well to a non-British national planning to kill a white English family in cold blood.

But there were other men for whom human life was cheap. He remembered the blackest days of his life; he remembered sleeping rough in shop doorways fearing that tonight the secret police would come and that he would be removed from the street like a piece of stinking dog dirt and disposed of with the same degree of contempt as any foul smelling bit of trash would be eradicated from existence. Not all of these clandestine officers who ruthlessly acted to suppress "enemies of the state" were mindless thugs, some were clever, and street-wise, and utterly terrifying. Nor were such men restricted to the land of his birth; most states in Eastern Europe had their secret police, but one country stood head and shoulders above the rest when it came to state sponsored terror. As yet the people of the United Kingdom did not see Russia as a rogue state, but given time he was sure that situation would change. Rumours already circulated that Vladimir Putin had his own private army of mercenaries who operated outside the law and exterminated his potential enemies both at home and abroad. The men who carried out the crimes sanctioned by the "Supreme Leader" were ultimate professionals, and he suspected that some of these men were embedded in the fabric of many of the major cities of Europe and further afield. The English and the Americans called them "sleepers", other nations had other names for them; what Vladimir called them nobody knew, it might be "Heroes of the Republic" for all he could guess. Finding such a person would be hard, but easier for him than the agents of MI 6 because he still had contacts in Belarus who could help him. If he could locate such an individual then he felt sure that for the right price, and a promise that nothing he asked him to do would adversely affect his ability to carry out his primary tasks, as and when required to do so, a plan could be put together to see a clinical execution of a man and his family who were to be the reason for the universal hatred his enemy would have to endure.

He convinced himself that such a man could kill without inflicting pain. In the hands of a true expert death would be instantaneous, and until the first shot there would be no fear. It was certain that thereafter there would be terror and pandemonium; but not for the sustained period that his daughter had had to suffer, at least not for the other victims, because within seconds they would be dead. The trauma suffered by anyone else present at the murderous attack would be deep and long lasting, which was sad but could not be helped; and the anxiety they experienced would make the news media scream loudly for vengeance.

There were other advantages too in using an elite member of a secret mercenary group to be his hit man. Undoubtedly such a person would be skilled in creating a false narrative while concealing the truth. How many "enemies" of Mother Russia had been dispatched on the orders of "Mad Vlad" as one day he was sure the world's press would christen the stony faced little billionaire, who now ruled what remained of the USSR, was anybody's guess. The answer was probably hundreds, if not thousands; yet in the vast majority of cases the sudden demise of most of these victims had been wrongly categorised as accidents by the civil authorities of the towns and cities where these murders had occurred. If anyone could frame his enemy for a monstrous crime he had not committed such a man could; but it would be at a high price. One worry he had was that all these "loyal protectors" of the diminutive despot who gave them their orders might be too scared that their involvement in a little capitalist free enterprise would come to their commander's ears to take up the challenge. His belief was that he could convince them that "he who must be obeyed" would actually applaud their initiative, although no doubt demanding a share of the substantial payment that had been received for himself to add to his already overflowing coffers.

There was one other worry which was his greatest fear. He was planning to do all this to pay back the man who had heaped terror and violence on his lovely daughter. If he did not love her so much he would not feel such hatred; but what would she feel for him if she ever found out that he had caused the vilest of crimes to be committed in her name. He would tell her, which would be true, that his love for her was pure, and tender, and eternal. He would say she made the world exist, and that everything about him that might be deemed good, and decent, and caring existed because of her, and that she was responsible for creating within him the good man he had so often tried to be. He would confess however that there was a side to his character that was tainted, and angry, and cruel. He would add that this battle between good and evil was fought in the minds of every person who had ever lived. He had not planned to be this way; it was something he had no control over; perhaps all men were deeply flawed. Even as he had these thoughts he realised that she would not accept this explanation and that she would be deeply hurt when she discovered what he had done. She was a sweet innocent in a hospital bed; he couldn't change the way he was. If he did nothing his hatred for his enemy would gnaw at his brain until it destroyed him. He made a solemn promise to himself that she must never find out. If this terrible plan he was about to set in train remained forever hidden, and if she could be restored to full health and beauty, which was his dearest wish, then maybe nursing her back to health, being with her every minute of every day, might in the future drive the dark side of his character into exile forever and ever. It was with this feeling of hope that Vitali sat by his phone and mentally planned what words he would say to Natasha when he was permitted to see her in her hospital bed. His eyes filled with tears; she was his angel, and he would ensure that she knew how much she was adored by everyone who truly knew her.

It was perhaps significant. Two CCTV cameras in Glossop had captured a dark blue Toyota car travelling through the town three hours after the fire at Moor Top Grange had been started. The police could not be certain that this was the vehicle they were looking for as the description they had of the car that had been seen near the burning building was very vague; but it was being driven at speed towards Greater Manchester which was where DCI Hobson suspected that the men who had committed the crimes of arson and attempted murder had probably come from. There was a problem however. Using logic Hobson assumed that once the buildings were ablaze the offenders would want to put distance between themselves and the crime scene as quickly as possible.

Dump the car, torch it if necessary; and slip back into their lair that is what he thought their mindset would be, but if that was so then the times of these sightings should have been two and a half hours earlier. Had the men pulled up somewhere not far away from the Grange to watch like voyeurs the result of their actions? He thought this unlikely. He wondered if perhaps they had visited their paymaster to receive full recompense for the cruel handiwork they had undertaken before bolting for cover in the inner city rabbit warren that was Greater Manchester; DCI Hobson believed this was a much more credible scenario; although why they had then retraced their steps instead of heading back to base another way was a mystery. Perhaps they had indeed decided to take a peek at the scene of the fire to confirm in their own minds that everything had been done to their employer's complete satisfaction in case he ever tried to argue otherwise. *These men are bastards* he thought; *while they are at liberty nobody is safe. They have to be brought to justice; I will be failing in my duty if I fail to do this.* It was at this moment of introspection that he was joined by Detective Sergeant Bennett.

"I thought you might like to know Gov that we've made a bit of progress in respect of Andropov's public comments about his "adoring wife". So far we've found six instances on You Tube when he's poked fun at her. Les Dawson he ain't; he doesn't actually have his audience rolling in the aisles but what he says is pretty unflattering and I guarantee the lovely Mrs A will definitely not be amused by them. I think that probably there are still a few more one-liners to be uncovered, we'll know more by the end of the day. Sometime when you've got a moment it might be worth you having a quick glance at what we've discovered so far. I think there's enough to needle the woman into playing ball with us, but it's obviously your call. Whatever you say goes; and if you think nothing would be gained by confronting her with this evidence of her husband's contempt, then so be it."

"I'll do that Pete" replied Hobson, "and if I can see some potential in approaching her then maybe later today or perhaps tomorrow we should have a trip out to try and bring a bit of humour into her sad self-obsessed little life."

CHAPTER TWENTY ONE

Papering the walls with banknotes, a helpful telephone call, a distressing telephone call, feelings of intense anger, and a strange sense of humour

The bottle of whiskey was empty. Three blue movies had been watched. Jokes had been told that even these men would not have voiced in public, but they were on a high; they had done what had been asked of them; they were way too pumped up to sleep; and of course they had counted, and re-counted the money they had been given. Fifty thousand pounds each, in cash; enough bank notes to fill two suitcases; or paper in their entirety the walls of the room in which they sat; or cover the wages paid to a star Premier League footballer for almost a week; or the salary of an educated professional man for a whole year. It was a strange world, full of distorted values; but they didn't care. For the moment they were rich; for the moment they could spend; but natural cunning told them that they must be careful not to attract too much attention to themselves; and if, and when, the money ran out there was always another job to look forward to. Buoyed up by feelings of invincibility; and with dreams of riches still to come; and not at all upset by the whinnying of hysterical animals, and the screams of a terrified teenager, which sometimes rattled around their heads, at an hour well after dawn had broken these two *gallant gentlemen* finally succumbed to the call of sleep.

Before joining Peter Bennett to go through the on-line stuff he had unearthed which showed Alexei Andropov being bitchy about his unloved wife, Mark Hobson telephoned Jennifer Drake. He had intended to make this call much earlier, but he had been sidetracked by a phone call from Detective Chief Superintendent Hardy asking for a progress report on the investigation into the arson and attempted murder at the home of Vitali Zalenkov. The photographs discovered on Anastasia's phone had now been scanned and it would be the work of a moment to forward copies to Jenny for her to examine. When she answered the call she was her usual cooperative self. She was more than happy for Mark to send her the information he possessed immediately, and she promised that she would look at the E-mail as soon as it arrived and telephone him straight back with an answer if she could give one. Unsurprisingly she was true to her word. Less than five minutes after putting the phone down and sending the scan it rang again; Hobson answered the call without delay.

"The woman with fair hair is Penelope Kenyon" she said. "She lives in Alderley Edge and I think Anastasia met her about three years ago. The other woman with short dark hair is Liz Allman. She lives not far from me and I see her most days taking her dog for a walk. She's known Anastasia for about eight months. I know both Penny and Liz were her friends, but whether they were so close that she revealed personal secrets to them I can't say, but you can find out by asking them can't you Mark? As regards the youth in the background I'm afraid I can't help you. He's so indistinct, but he doesn't look remotely like anyone I have ever seen before; and I'm sure as I can be that he hasn't been following me."

Mark thanked her for her assistance. Names had been added to two pieces of the jigsaw. In all likelihood neither lady would be able to shed new light on Anastasia Karpovich's quest for knowledge; but perhaps that was being pessimistic; all would become clear after these women had been spoken to. It was as he was waiting for a computer search of the electoral register to be completed to ascertain the addresses and contact telephone numbers of the two potential witnesses that DS Bennett once again entered his office.

"I've just been chatting to the lads searching for evidence up at the Grange" he announced. "Nothing major to report so far. There are one or two footprints which have been photographed, and one was deep enough to enable a cast to be made but, like as not, these will relate to the fire crews who attended the scene. They are all a fair distance away from the stable block;

anything left close by has been trampled into oblivion by firefighters boots or washed away by their hoses. It is now certain that the fire in stables was started using petrol, and that seems to have been poured on straw at several places within the building. The fire inside the house was started by a petrol bomb being thrown into the house as we suspected would be the case. It begs the question why the same M.O wasn't used in the house as in the stables; that would have ensured a more complete destruction of the building. My thought is that with the stables already alight, and with the fire maybe attracting the attention of neighbours they didn't want to hang around. In any event, if murder was part of the plan, the intended victim was trapped elsewhere; nothing that occurred in the house could have put her in greater danger."

"I think that has to be right Peter" said Hobson. "I doubt we are going to learn much more about what happened at Moor Top Grange until we speak to Natasha, and the way things are looking at the moment I don't believe we'll be able to do that anytime soon."

"Her feet and legs are badly burned; she'll need skin grafts and plastic surgery; her upper body has more minor burns ; and her face is bruised and scratched but is otherwise uninjured. She is likely to need physiotherapy to regain full mobility, and she may never recover a complete range of movements. All these injuries are however treatable, and the long term prognosis is to a degree hopeful. My immediate worry is for the short term. Natasha has inhaled a lot of smoke, and almost certainly also particles of ash and red hot fibres. These could cause damage to her internal organs, particularly her lungs and her kidneys. If these organs become diseased then her auto immune system may go into overdrive to produce antibodies to fight the infection. I have to tell you that in these circumstances Sepsis is a real risk, and I'm sure you know Mr Zalenkov how dangerous that could be. I wish I could give you better news, but I cannot mislead you over possible consequences. We are doing everything we can to save Natasha, but the next few days could be critical. You can visit her later today, but in controlled conditions. To know that you are there besides her may give her hope, and her state of mind could be crucial at a time like this."

She could die, she could struggle to walk again; she would always have the physical scars to remind her of the night her world was destroyed. She had talent, she had dreamed of being an Olympic champion; she had hoped to compete in equestrian events at the highest level, and that ambition had been a realistic one .Where was that dream now: Incinerated in a hate fuelled bonfire in a single night. It was a tragedy; a tragedy born of malice, a tragedy written in blood by a vindictive monster; and she wasn't even the intended victim; He knew that his daughter had been attacked to cause him pain. His daughter was suffering so that he would feel anguish. The hatred deep inside him erupted once again. Those who destroy a world of hope should see their worlds destroyed in turn for the wrong that they had done. As he had been waiting for an update from the hospital and considering the dreadful step he had been planning his resolve had begun to falter; but not anymore. The plan would be carried out and he would have his revenge. It was sad innocent lives had to be taken, but that was exactly what his enemy had attempted to do in his insane desire to destroy him.

"It won't be today now Pete." DCI Hobson was explaining to his detective sergeant that the doctors treating Natasha Zalenkov had confirmed that she was in a critical condition and that they were worried that her health could deteriorate further. "Only her father is permitted to be with her at the moment" he said. "I completely understand why that is so, but it's still frustrating; Natasha may be able to tell us what the person who pushed her into a burning stable looked like; she might also be able to say if he had an accent; she might even be able to pick him out from albums of suspects, and all that now has to be put on hold."

"It was ever thus" responded DS Bennett sympathetically; "but at least we now have time to concentrate on other things. While you're here Gov take a quick butchers at the stuff we've now unearthed on Alexei Andropov."

There were now eight short videos circulating on You Tube covering a period of several years. The quality of some was poor, but it was clear from listening to Andropov speaking that he had no great affection for his spouse.

"He doesn't get it does he Gov" said Bennett after his boss had viewed the videos; "doesn't he know that a joke is supposed to be funny? If he'd have told these stories with a twinkle in his eye and a lilt in his voice people might have roared with laughter because they would have known he didn't mean the things he said, but it sounds to me that he's just venting his spleen. Why she stays with him is anybody's guess."

"It has to be financial in some way" suggested Hobson, "but it's not just money because she's well off in her own right; I think she sticks around to spite him. I certainly got that impression when we last spoke to her. In many ways they are both as bad as each other. If she hasn't seen this stuff before there will be a reaction; our problem is how to present the information to her. She's not a fan of the police; if we phone up to try to arrange a meeting she'll probably tell us to "piss off"; so have you any thoughts about how we can persuade her to have a chat with us?"

"Well maybe if she thought she could be at risk she might talk to us. I appreciate that we can't reveal our sources, nor can we specifically point a finger towards any one person, but if I tell her we have received some information that makes us concerned about her welfare, and try to convince her that it would be in her best interest to co-operate with us to keep from harm she might be willing to meet with us again. We could also tell her that we believe that Anastasia was spied upon by an unknown male before her death, and that there is a possibility that she was also being covertly observed; that could do the trick. We obviously can't overplay our hand but we could divulge that one theory about Anastasia's murder is that it was a case of mistaken identity; which would be true. That might put her on her guard which would be in her best interest. If we then show her the photographs from Anastasia's phone she'll know that we aren't trying to con her, and if she thinks she recognises the man as somebody her husband had dealings with she might then assist us. It's not normal procedure Gov, and if anything goes wrong our heads will roll, but in my book it's worth a gamble. Do you think it is worth giving it a go?"

"It's worth a gamble Pete, but it will need your silver tongue to get her to agree to a meeting; and here's a thought for you. Andropov has got a number of employees keeping his precious pile looking immaculate; it's just possible one of them could be the male in Anastasia's photograph. If that is the case, and we are very lucky, we could catch sight of the fellow ourselves, which could mean that even if Mrs A is profoundly unhelpful, our visit will have been worthwhile."

"Don't hold your breath Gov" responded DS Bennett; "the chances are pretty slim; but we could just get lucky, and that would indeed be a giant leap forward in this investigation."

CHAPTER TWENTY TWO

A perfect place for a wedding, an apoplectic detective sergeant, some thoughts about St Thomas A Beckett, and a "carnivore" named Karlos

"You will absolutely love it Helena. Alan and I went there to a wedding eighteen months ago and it was fabulous. We didn't stay there of course, unlike you and Mark will do, but we enjoyed every minute of the day. The food was to die for, and the venue was perfect. You'll have a fabulous time the week after next when you go there. There's plenty for the kids to do as well. There's a small swimming pool, and adventure playground and a games room; they'll be in their element; the only trouble is they won't want to leave." Jackie Nadin was extolling to her friend Helena the virtues of Summerford Hall, a plush, and very expensive, hotel and wedding venue.

"The grounds are absolutely superb" she continued. "Rolling lawns gently slope down towards a lake. If the weather is fine and warm the marriage ceremony will be held outdoors. There is a beautiful little temple on a small man-made island, and that's where the vows are exchanged and the marriage is solemnized. It makes for the most glorious wedding videos: do you know what the long term forecast is for the next ten days?"

"According to the BBC's mid-range forecast it's set fair" replied Helena, "'which probably means that it will be blowing a gale, with none stop sleet and everybody will need to wear thermals" and both friends laughed at the ludicrous picture this suggestion made in their minds.

"Well if the weather is bad there is a beautiful Assembly Room on the ground floor which is also licensed to hold weddings. Rain or shine it will be lovely. Do you know whereabouts in the hotel you will be sleeping?"

"At the front" replied Helena. "I've seen photographs of our bedroom on their website and the room looks very opulent. I've told Mark he's not to leave footprints on the furniture or sticky fingerprints on the wall mirrors, and I've read the Riot Act to Christopher, David and Lucy too. They've got a bedroom on the other side of the corridor which isn't as grand as ours but it's still one or two notches up on their rooms at home. Lucy is absolutely looking forward to being a bridesmaid, it will be the grandest event she's ever been to; and, if I'm honest Jackie, I'm very much looking forward to it too."

"You enjoy the moment Kid" retorted Jackie smiling, "a weekend in the spotlight every now and again is no bad thing, and I bet you'll be the most glamorous Matron of Honour the hotel has ever seen."

"Oh shut up" laughed Helena, "you're making me blush, but it will be nice for Mark and me and the kids to have a couple of nights away from the stresses of day to day life. This latest case Mark is dealing with is really getting to him; he needs a break from work if only for a few hours."

"You all do" said Jackie sympathetically; "enjoy the pomp and circumstance, and then when the loving couple are finally hitched and the evening meal is over, and the kids are at last asleep, you and Mark strut your stuff at the disco, get plastered on Prosecco, and at a time too ungodly to mention, finally wend your merry ways to bed."

"It took half an hour Gov, but she finally agreed to see us. We should feel honoured. She's allocated us a twenty minute slot this afternoon between saying goodbye to her home manicurist and departing with her freshly varnished fingernails to visit her personal trainer named Freddie." The contempt in Peter Bennett's voice was clear to hear. "She's a God awful woman" he pronounced in exasperation: "come the Glorious Revolution people like her will find their heads on spikes or be condemned to cleaning out latrines for the rest of their worthless little lives."

"Easy does it Pete" laughed Hobson, "you'll give yourself an apoplectic fit; but well done. Now go and get everything we need to show her copied onto a CD and then come back up here for a coffee and a chat as we plan the best way to conduct our interview with the "lovely" Mrs A."

DS Bennett did as he was told. Twenty minutes later he was back with Detective Chief Inspector Hobson and the two of them then mapped out in their heads the approach they would take with the conceited, difficult woman who was the wife of the man who seemed pivotal to their investigation into the death of Anastasia Karpovich.

After some discussion it was agreed as anticipated that the main emphasis of the visit had to be the concerns the police had about safety and security. Both officers thought it likely that Mrs Andropov would accept, albeit reluctantly, that there were obvious similarities between herself and the murdered Anastasia. They were of similar age; they both had the same coloured hair, although the way it was styled was somewhat different. They were also both slim and of average height; if someone who did not know them personally had been told to look for an attractive blonde woman wearing a very particular coat, and to single that person out as a target, then it was easy to see how a mistake might have been made. There was some debate about whether, without revealing any sources, disclosure should be made of the incident ten years earlier when a deadly attack had been planned upon an unknown female, who might have been her, had been prevented by police action. In the end DCI Hobson decided that this was a step too far and that no mention should be made of this particular incident.

Only after this aspect of the case had been fully aired did the DCI think the matter of her husband's unflattering comments should be broached. Mark Hobson wondered if he could suggest that the police were worried that somebody who had heard these unfunny jokes, and seen Alexei's obvious dissatisfaction with the state of his marriage; in order to ingratiate himself with a very wealthy man, might be planning to take it upon himself to rid the frustrated husband of an unwanted encumbrance. If Mrs A had been of a more cerebral nature Hobson added that he might have tried to draw a parallel between her situation and that of St Thomas-Beckett, but he doubted that the lady had even heard about "Murder in the

Cathedral" so instead he proposed that the police should keep things simple.

"I agree entirely" concurred DS Bennett; "we should just show her the clips from YouTube and let her make of them what she will. My bet is she'll be spitting feathers by the end of our little piece of comic entertainment. If she does react in that way then we should ask her outright why she has stuck so long to a man who wants nothing whatsoever to do with her, and my bet is we might get some very interesting answers. It would be then I would show her the photographs from Anastasia's phone and ask her bluntly if she has ever seen our mystery "spy" before. If she thinks she has then I guarantee she'll tell us; and if she does then we will be one step nearer to solving at least part of this whole wretched case."

"I agree Peter" said Hobson, "but let's take nothing for granted. Let us instead go and grab a bite to eat then, suitably refreshed, set off on our journey to meet with a very difficult lady."

The family whose surname he had proudly adopted and from whom he had inherited his wealth had been clever, and hard working, and clear sighted. Nobody had given them their success, they had earned it, and he was sure they had not let ambition rob them of their innate decency; and yet........They had prospered in a city where the secret police were ruthless; they had made their money in a country in which the state took no prisoners. To survive in such circumstances they had followed the party line; they had not, at least publicly, endorsed any move towards a more liberal regime, and he supposed that from time to time they must have oiled the wheels of commerce with a well placed cash payment to obtain a favourable outcome. Because they were not seen as trouble makers the powers that be had left them alone to carry on making money, although no doubt expecting a cut; and how many petty bureaucrats had had their palms greased in the process was anybody's guess. Vaguely he remembered snippets of occasional conversations his father-in-law had had with third parties at times of trouble. If a problem needed sorting one name would be whispered. It was only if there was a difficulty that this was so; during good times when life was easy he was never referred to. Whether this person was still alive he didn't know, but he needed to find out. If he was, as he now suspected, somebody who upon instruction had bought off persons who might become dangerous, or even, in the last resort, arranged altogether more final solutions for those not swayed by money then he was the answer to his prayers. Such a man would surely have his fingers in many pies, and potentially even access to some of the files the secret police possessed relating to nefarious operations that had been carried out both at home and abroad. If he could remember who this person was, and if he could devise some way of making contact with him then, in return for an eye watering amount of cash this man might be prepared to act as his agent and recruit for him the skilled professional killer he would need to put into practice his unspeakably cruel plan. He racked his brain to try to remember a name, or any small detail that might help him locate this individual then, just as he was beginning to think it never would, it came to him. Not a full name, not an address, or a location, or a place of work but a nickname "Karlos" once christened "Karlos the carnivore" by an unknown individual in a conversation with his adopted dad. He wondered if that name might still be whispered on the street by ordinary people as a warning to children not to misbehave. There were still members of the Zalenkov family living in their home city; surely one of them might be able to furnish him with the information that he needed. By telephoning, or texting, or e-mailing he might soon get an answer. Ignoring the hour of night he set about bombarding the relatives he knew with urgent pleas for information.

CHAPTER TWENTY THREE

A "spoilt little princess", dogs that howl with anger, signs of real emotion, a pre-nuptial agreement, a possible solution to a puzzle, and a feeling of unease

Her fingernails were pink and shiny, as was her lip gloss; her eye shadow was silver grey and her skin was chestnut brown, its colour owing everything to the spray can, and nothing to the golden rays of the sun; to Mark Hobson she looked like an automaton, skilfully assembled in some beautician's salon, a piece of modern art reflecting the fashions of the moment, and utterly, utterly false. It was a pity. Beneath the make-up, the fake tan and the sparkly lipstick there was a face that was naturally quite pretty, although the sulky expression that she habitually wore would have detracted from the overall impression. As she had been on the last occasion that they had met Mrs Andropov was dressed to the height of fashion, but she would not stay dressed as she was for long. Soon no doubt she would be itching to change into leisure gear before departing to see her personal trainer. What she might wear then was anybody's guess *maybe designer ski pants and a T-shirt from the House of Gucci covered in sequins;* for a brief moment in his head Mark Hobson heard the voice of Glen Campbell singing *"Like a Rhinestone Cowboy." Everything about this woman is calculated to make an impact* he mused. He wondered what the real woman was like underneath all the powder and paint; he suspected that somewhere hidden behind the glitz was an insecure, inadequate individual tormented by frequent bouts of anxiety.

Before they had finally set off on their journey to meet Andropov's wife Hobson had instructed DS Bennett to find out as much as he could about the lady's early life, and it was what this search had revealed that had caused him to think this way. What Bennett had unearthed had been informative. Chloe Tiffany Andropov nee Coxford turned out to be the only daughter of Elvis Leonard Coxford, (otherwise known as Fat Lennie), who owned a number of betting shops in the East End of London. Hobson recalled that somebody had once told him that there was no such thing as a poor bookmaker, but if there was Fat Lennie was not the exception that proved the rule. Flamboyant in the extreme he was famed for wearing excessive amounts of gold jewellery and driving expensive motor cars. It was said that at one time he had owned a Porsche for every day of the week, a claim he never sought to deny. All of his vehicles were brightly coloured; there seemed to be no doubt that his daughter had inherited her father's genes when it came to matters of taste and self-restraint.

His "Little Princess" had been hugely over-indulged as a child. He had thrust her into the limelight on every conceivable occasion. DS Bennett had not yet discovered this, but several local newspapers held in their archives dozens of pictures of the doting father's "pride and joy" from toddler, to teenager, to young woman who had been pictured at the forefront of public events over a period in excess of two decades. By the time she was in her mid-twenties she had become somebody who was recognised in clubs and bars as the rich daughter of the man who had made a fortune out of gambling, drove flash cars at speed, and frequented the best restaurants in town. Fat Lennie believed he had given his daughter everything she ever wanted, (except perhaps a good example to follow), and he was pleased. He had created a person in his own image; he was totally unable to see how much he had damaged a young woman's life.

On arriving at their destination the first thing both Derbyshire officers had noticed was that existing security measures had been ramped up to new heights. Additional CCTV cameras were clearly visible, and probably many more had been concealed to give blanket coverage of the whole of the farmstead. When they were admitted inside the perimeter fence by the same youth who had greeted them on their first visit, and who was definitely not the mysterious man in Anastasia's photographs, it was immediately apparent that two more guard dogs had been acquired, and this time not even the presence of Andropov's employee could silence them. Fierce and ferocious they howled with anger. For now they were restrained by stout chains, at night Hobson suspected that they were allowed to roam free.

And God help anyone who wanders into their domain then thought Hobson, *the injuries they could inflict if unchecked would be appalling.*

The youth noticed the looks of concern on Hobson and Bennett's faces.

"Don't worry" he said mockingly, "their bark is much worse than their bite, and in any event they have been fed today, the postman arrived early this morning", and he laughed at his heavy handed attempt at humour.

The two officers were led into the house and taken to the same large room where they had met Mrs Andropov before. Andropov himself was not at home, but no doubt would view the day's security tapes on his return. If DCI Hobson had wanted his visit to remain secret there would be zero chance of that happening; fortunately however that outcome was the exact opposite of what he actually desired.

Mrs Andropov was seated in an armchair. She did not get up to greet the two officers; instead she made a point of looking at her watch.

"I've got just twenty minutes before I have to go and get changed" she said "so let's just get on with things. He" she said, pointing at DS Bennett while talking to Hobson, "fed me some bullshit about me being in danger. I suspect that was just a cock and bull story he dreamt up so that you had an excuse to come and see me. So let's cut out all the crap and you tell me why the police have come up with this totally half-baked idea."

"It was something you said to us about the coat when you accused Anastasia of being a thief" replied Mark. "The more we thought about it afterwards, the more we wondered if Miss Karpovich's murder might be a case of mistaken identity. In many ways she looked a lot like you." Chloe shook her head and pulled a face but Hobson continued. "She was blonde like you are, she was of similar height and weight, and I think there was only a couple of years difference in your ages; I'm not trying to alarm you, I'm just stating a possibility; but murder when there has been mistaken identity is a lot more common than you might think. My sergeant discovered by chance a video of your husband posted on You-Tube in which he makes jokes at your expense, and since then he has found several other examples of him making derogatory remarks about you. He's got a CD in his brief case that we can play to you if you don't believe what we are telling you. Now I'm not suggesting that your husband has been anything other than boorish, but we do think it is possible that somebody watching or listening to these digs at you may have assumed that you are a person he wishes did not exist, and may have decided to solve a problem for him in the hope that he would be generously rewarded for his actions."

Chloe's face turned crimson. "Has he by God!" she screamed. "Give me the bloody CD, and snatching it out of DS Bennett's hand she placed it straight into a lap top that sat on a table beside her, and immediately started to view the clips Peter Bennett had unearthed.

To say that she was not amused would be a gross understatement. Looking at her face, and inwardly smiling at her annoyance Detective Sergeant Bennett felt totally vindicated. "The bastard" she kept exclaiming "the total, total bastard!"

At a point near the end of the CD the servant who had shown them into the house put his head around the door to advise his master's wife that if she wished to keep her appointment with "Mr Freddie" she had better begin to get ready. Hobson was sure that the man was following orders and that this was a pre-arranged strategy to bring the police interview to a close.

"Bugger Freddie" screamed Chloe, "tell him I'm not meeting him today", and in less than polite terms then suggested that the flabbergasted lackey should quickly vacate the room.

"He'll pay for this" she said coldly. "Well two can play at that game; I know plenty of stuff about him that he wants to keep secret."

"Like what" asked Hobson gently?

"Like how he conned that silly little bitch from Belarus to come over here. He told her he was a hero" she snorted, "he hasn't got a heroic bone in his body, but she believed him. He sent her proof of his bravery; it wouldn't have fooled a five year old but she fell for it hook, line and sinker."

"Do you know what that so called proof was" inquired the DCI.

Chloe shook her head.

"I just know he was terribly smug when he'd done it" she explained. "I could have smacked his face; and then on top of all that he told her a pack of lies about our son. He roughed out a first version of the letter he was going to send which he chucked in the bin; I saw it lying there and I read it; I could have killed him then."

"What did he tell her" asked DS Bennett?"

"He told her that I was a dreadful mum" she replied resentfully. "He made out that he was a loving father, but the truth is he couldn't have cared less about Leo. He said he married me when I became pregnant to do the honourable thing, but he only married me for my dad's money. In the end I felt life was so bad for Leo that I gave him up for adoption. He wasn't even present on the day I handed my little boy, his only son, to his new mummy" and for the first and only time Mark Hobson saw evidence of tenderness, and genuine tears.

"So why do you stay with him "questioned DS Bennett intrigued; "surely you could divorce him for mental cruelty?"

"And lose 90% of his entire estate" laughed Chloe. "My Dad insisted he entered into a pre-nuptial agreement before he would lend him a penny. If he divorced me he would lose practically everything he owns. If I walk away from the marriage I would only get the amount of money that my Dad lent him to bail him out of a financial black hole; that's chicken feed in today's terms. I ain't stupid Mr Hobson; that would be playing straight into his hands."

It's also a motive for murder thought Mark, but he didn't specifically voice his concern. He did however advise Mrs Andropov to be watchful at all times, and that if anything occurred which caused her alarm she should contact the police without delay.

The meeting was now virtually at an end. The only thing left to do was to show Chloe the photographs taken from Anastasia's phone, and ask her if she had ever seen the mystery man in the pictures. She looked carefully at the images and shook her head. She was adamant that whoever the man was, he was not somebody she had ever laid eyes on before.

"It was a useful visit Love", Mark Hobson was explaining to Helena the outcome of his trip into Cheshire to speak with Chloe Andropov.

"Pete and I now believe we know how Anastasia was persuaded to come to the UK. According to Chloe Anastasia thought her husband had done something heroic. We know that in the weeks before her death she had become obsessed with finding a particular story in the local papers. From what we learned from a chap at the offices of the Macclesfield Advertiser the discovery of the report on the bravery of Sam Postles was her "eureka" moment. We now think Andropov copied that report from the paper, inserted into it a photograph of himself rather than Sam, and changed references in it to replace Sam's personal details with his own; in other words Anastasia was deceived by a piece of false evidence into coming here by a very devious and cunning villain. Chloe is also convinced that Andropov told Anastasia a sob story about his son's adoption. She was in tears when she talked about this episode; it was the only time we witnessed genuine emotion in her during the whole of our visit."

"Poor woman" murmured Helena. "If Andropov used false stories about his little boy to lure another woman to become part of his household then that is contemptible; but it does show how much he wanted Anastasia to come to him, and that fact must have been very distressing for his wife."

"Maybe, maybe not" replied Mark; "I'm not so sure. She could have walked out on him at any time, but money is more important to her than anything else", and he told Helena about the pre-nuptial contract that had been negotiated, then he added playfully "do you think Lizzie and her intended might have entered into a similar agreement?"

Helena prodded him in the ribs and laughed. "No" she said sternly; "It's strictly a love match, and it's going to be such a beautiful wedding. Lucy and I tried on our bridesmaids dresses for the first time, they fitted perfectly. She looked so lovely Sweetheart, but in one sense I felt sad. When Jackie and I chatted with Natasha on our second visit to the farm I told her about Lucy being a bridesmaid at a posh wedding. She said she was sure she would look stunning and she asked me if I could send her a photograph of her in her finery, which I promised I would do, but I can't do that now can I ? It's so sad"; and trying not to cry she brushed away an embryonic tear, and, with difficulty, held her emotions in check.

"It is Love" responded Mark, holding her hand tightly, and gently he tried to lead her thoughts away from such an unhappy place.

"Talking of photographs" he said, "the one area where we have had no success at all is discovering who the mystery man might be who appears in the background of Anastasia's "selfies", and trying to distract his wife from dwelling on Natasha's injuries he produced copies of both photographs for her to look at.

She studied them carefully for a little while and then said; "I'm sure I have seen him somewhere before, but only for a moment or two. I'm racking my brain to think where that could have been, but I can't for the life of me remember at the moment. It will come to me Sweetheart, I'm sure of that, but I am afraid it may take time."

"Then so be it" said Hobson. Inside he suppressed excitement that a vital clue might soon be solved, but he also felt unease. If this man had for some reason been watching his wife it could not have been for any well-meant reason.

CHAPTER TWENTY FOUR

A day of rage, an evening of uncertainty, a night time conversation during which an assassin's needs are considered, a price is put on human life, and a contract is agreed

He had been at the hospital for most of the day. Natasha had mainly been sedated, but occasionally she had drifted into consciousness, and then the look of panic and confusion in her eyes had made him want to cry. He had said "you're going to be alright my precious", and "I'm here for you Sweetheart" and "try to sleep again little one, tomorrow you will feel better," and sometimes the words had appeared to calm her, but mostly he supposed that they were empty noise, a meaningless jangle of sound rattling around inside her head. Never had he felt more useless, more helpless; more distraught. At times he had wanted to scream, to bang his head against the wall, to smash his fist into the face of the first person that he saw; and if that person had been the man responsible for Natasha's plight he would have ripped him limb from limb, and rejoiced at the agony he was inflicting.

How he drove back from the hospital to the caravan where he was now forced to sleep without having an accident was a miracle; and how he stopped himself drinking himself into a stupor in his grief he did not know, but the overwhelming need to respond to any phone call from the hospital if his daughter's condition worsened kept him sober. Because his mind was in such a bad place he found himself unable to concentrate on anything remotely technical so he had forced himself to try to sleep. He had struggled to do so, but finally after about two hours of trying he had fallen into uneasy slumber, but at the very moment he could have succumbed completely to tiredness his mobile phone rang. It was now well past midnight. Nobody telephoned at that hour of the morning unless it was bad news. Cold sweat trickled down his face. With his hands shaking in trepidation, he answered the call.

It was not the hospital. He did not hear the calm voice of a health professional bringing him news; instead he heard a very different voice; a voice that sent a chill down his spine; a guttural voice that sounded like a metal rasp being scraped over rusty iron; a voice that oozed menace. Transfixed he listened to the words it uttered. The man spoke in English, but with a strong Eastern European accent.

"Vitali Zalenkov " he said; "I hear you have need of my services."

Somehow the message had got through. Somehow a man feared throughout Crimea had learned of his desire. There were still many obstacles to overcome, not least the price to be paid, but if these could be resolved a plan conceived in the darkest recesses of his mind could soon become reality. Perhaps there was a God after all; a snarling, terrible, destructive being who from on high had seen his hunger for vengeance and decided, for his own amusement, for the time being at least to indulge this puny little Earthling.

"Karlos" he whispered quietly, "is it you?"

"Who else would it be" answered the voice. "I am told you need my help, which I may be prepared to give you. I make no promises however. Tell me what you wish to be done so I can then decide if I might be willing to undertake the tasks you wish to see performed."

The words tumbled from his lips. Once he had started to talk he couldn't stop. He told Karlos how the man he hated had paid men to set fire to his home and outbuildings and that their actions had caused nearly one million pounds worth of damage; how this attack upon his property had also destroyed valuable livestock; and how, much worse than all of this they had inflicted terrible injuries on his daughter who might yet die as a direct and intended result of their actions. His enduring hatred of the man who had ordered all this to be done was clear. Karlos was convinced. There would be no change of heart, no backing out; no quibble over price no matter the amount charged for services rendered. This would be a good deal from his point of view; a money spinner; a cash cow. He could not lose; in his hand he held all the aces

"So what exactly do you want me to undertake" he asked. "How is this man who has done you so much wrong to be punished for his misdeeds?"

"He has to suffer for the rest of his life" responded Vitali coldly. "I wish him to be dragged from his home in the dead of night, or lifted from a street where he feels safe, and thrown like trash into a foul stinking van. I want him to be taken to a dark, dank cellar, and there I want him to be kicked, beaten and tortured. Cut off his fingers or his balls if that amuses you; or pox mark his skin with cigarette burns; but he must not be killed; even if he begs for his life to be ended. All of this brutality must be filmed so that I can have the pleasure of watching him suffer whenever the fancy takes me; but this is just a small part of the price he must pay."

"You want a lot" murmured Karlos quietly, "but all this can be done exactly as you require, but you tell me this terrible fate is not enough. What more do you want to see happen?"

"I want him to rot in gaol for the rest of his life convicted of a crime, but one that he had no part in; a crime so unspeakable that he will be hated by everyone for the rest of his hopefully long unhappy life." Vitali then outlined the terrible offence he wanted to see his enemy wrongly accused of.

"It has to be seen as an attack on the British way of life; an act of terrorism born out of fanatical hatred; an act so abhorrent that it seems impossible to believe that a man could be so cruel. I have a target in mind. I see a man, a senior police officer gunned down in front of many on-lookers, and his wife and children also killed in cold blood; an attractive family slain without mercy, and on a day which should have been joyous. The sense of outrage at such a crime would be enormous; a person convicted of planning such brutality would be beyond redemption."

Karlos listened without emotion. "You are bad my friend, maybe even mad; we are made of the same stuff you and I, but what you want can happen: now is there anything more I need to know?"

We are not made of the same stuff thought Vitali. *I have been loved. There is a person lying on a hospital bed who means the world to me. You love only money. I know real love* but it was that love which was driving him to commission acts of unspeakable horror.

Replying to Karlos's query he said, "Yes there is more. The person who carries out this attack must be a skilled assassin; it is imperative he is expert in the art of murder and a master of his trade. I like the people who have to die, I do not want them to suffer; I wish their deaths to be as quick and painless as they can possibly be. They have not wronged me; I bear them no ill-will; but there is still more. The person I need has to be a master of deception. A false trail of evidence must be created, realistic enough to convince the police and a court of law that the prisoner in the dock masterminded this crime. I have searched the Internet, and I have read that fingerprints can be planted, as can DNA, and that other evidence can be created to support a prosecution such as messages of hate emanating from the accused, and even false affinity to a fundamentalist cause. Do you know of anyone capable enough to do all of these things?"

"You ask a lot" responded Karlos, "there is somebody, but I warn you he will demand a high price for his services; I fear the re-building of your home may have to be put on hold. If he and I consent to work for you the insurance payment you receive should just be sufficient to meet our needs. Tomorrow I will send you details of how to make payment. I will require an immediate sum of two hundred thousand English pounds to cover initial outlay, and a further seven hundred and fifty thousand pounds must follow no later than seven days from today. I never negotiate on price, take it or leave it my friend, the choice is yours: It's make your mind up time Vitali. Tell me now what your decision will be?"

"The money will be sent tomorrow" he replied, "providing I have your assurance that things can be done quickly. Very soon the perfect opportunity will arise, I know this because of things my daughter has said to me in conversation; there may not be another occasion so suitable for many months to come."

"You ask still more" murmured Karlos;"by rights I should add another fifty thousand to your bill, but I am a generous man at heart and so will not do so. When I have received the cash and it is safely in a bank account shortly thereafter you will get a phone call from a man you will never see, and who you will only ever know by the code name Mikel. You will need to be prepared when this phone call comes. Mikel will want precise details of time and place; he will need the name and address of the man whose kidnapping and assault he has to arrange; and be warned he will expect you to be thorough. There will be no second chances. He will demand to be told much about this individual, and not necessarily only obvious stuff; if you cannot give him the answers he requires then he will conclude that you are unreliable; and he will not act for you if he comes to that conclusion.

"He will also need to know many details about the family you want to see sacrificed to achieve your goal. Research everything you can about them. Be ready to give a detailed description of the man and the woman you want him to kill; and to a lesser extent the children also; although he will know them when he observes them with their parents. There must be no room for error, to select the wrong targets would be a disaster; and also a deplorable waste of ammunition", and Karlos laughed as he uttered these words.

He is a man without feeling thought Vitali, *a man who can joke about tragedy, without any regard for human life is a demon; to think I am driven to enlist the help of such a being. It is your fault Alexei; none of these things would have to happen if you had not declared unjust war upon my daughter.*

CHAPTER TWENTY FIVE

A suspect is named, an unfaithful wife, a medical update, preparing for interrogation, and a readiness to die for love

Detective Sergeant Bennett had arrived early at his desk. He had slept poorly because of a stiff shoulder. Ibuprofen had ultimately relieved the discomfort, but it could not give him back the three hours of sleep he had lost before the drug took effect. He was now kicking himself for not making the effort to go downstairs and take the pills when he felt the first twinge, but what was done was done, and he could not turn back the clock. It meant that he was far from being bright eyed and bushy-tailed, and quite unlike his usual ebullient self. His boss Mark Hobson was not due for another two hours; a small part of him resented the DCI's latitude. It was as he was grumbling to himself about the unfairness of life that the phone on Hobson's desk rang; he was tempted to ignore it, but shaking himself out of his lethargy he did what was required of him.

The caller was an officer from Greater Manchester police who introduced himself as Detective Constable Tony Charles. Peter Bennett explained that DCI Hobson wasn't expected for another couple of hours and asked if he could take a message; DC Charles was happy to allow the DS to be his intermediary.

"It's just a bit of news that my boss thought your Governor might find interesting" he said. "That dark blue Toyota that Derbyshire Police were interested in which was dumped on our patch may have been left there by a piece of Belarusian pond life called Vlodomir Petrov; we think this because Petrov was spotted on a CCTV camera only a couple of hundred yards away from the car. There is no physical evidence to link him to the vehicle, but we do know that he is a very dangerous man, often used by drug dealers to extort money from their pathetically addicted clients. Pushing a young girl into a burning building would be right up his street; and burning down a luxury home would be a joke to him. There is some intelligence to suggest that he has links with a group of mercenary killers who operate out of Crimea. We can't prove any of this of course, otherwise the bastard would be behind bars, but we are watching him; and if we do discover any evidence to link him with your crimes, your DCI will be the first to know. The only other thing we need to tell you is that the word on the street is that in the last couple of days Petrov has been spending big: he could have won the lottery of course, but the smart money is on the probability that he has been paid recently for some nasty little job he has just completed."

DS Bennett thanked DC Charles for the information, which he promised he would acquaint DCI Hobson with as soon as he entered the office, and the conversation ended with the detective sergeant writing down a contact number in case Hobson himself wanted to clarify anything with the GMP officer. It was just after he had placed this note on his boss's desk, and at the very moment he had picked up his mug to make himself a drink of tea that the DCI's phone rang again. Stifling an expression of annoyance he replaced the mug on his desk and answered the phone again. Maybe another piece of helpful news was about to fall into his lap. If he could be the bearer of even more glad tidings when his gaffer finally deigned to appear it would be brilliant; but this time he was to be disappointed.

The caller was Jennifer Drake. She was bright, breezy and positive as usual, and it was a pleasure to talk to her, but this time what she was about to reveal to the police did not in any way further their investigation into the death of Anastasia. She told Pete that last evening, quite by chance, she had bumped into Liz Allman (*one of the new friends of Anastasia*) out walking her dog, and as they were very near to her home she had invited her in for a coffee and had then shown her the scan of the photograph DCI Hobson had sent to her. Jenny said that Liz had looked at the scan very carefully for a long time and then stated that she was absolutely certain she had never seen the man before. During the subsequent chat the two women then had Liz mentioned that Penelope Kenyon (*the lady in the second photograph on Anastasia's mobile*) had recently left her husband following a domestic argument, and gone to live with an unnamed man with whom she had been having an affair. The whereabouts of the couple was currently unknown, so, for the immediate future, the chances of getting any information out of her which might assist the police were non-existent. This was not great to hear, but sometimes a door fully closed was better than one left tantalisingly ajar. Peter Bennett thanked Jenny for the update; and after exchanging pleasantries the telephone conversation then ceased.

Hardly had the call ended when DCI Hobson's phone rang yet again.

The boss is a very popular guy this morning thought Bennett, *every Tom, Dick and Harry on the planet wants to talk to him today. Can't a man get a moment's peace*; and a little peevishly he picked up the receiver for the third time in less than half an hour.

This time the man with information to impart desired only to leave a brief message. He sounded harassed. The last thing he wanted to do was engage in idle chatter. In the background Bennett could hear another phone demanding attention, and he visualised an over-stretched, under manned office, with one poor admin assistant trying to cope with the pressure of multiple enquiries. The caller didn't give a name, he didn't need to. He said he was part of the patient liaison team at the hospital where Natasha Zalenkov was being cared for. He informed DS Bennett that her condition had improved somewhat overnight and that the doctor treating her now believed she might be strong enough to talk to the police later in the afternoon.

Three bits of news to pass on thought Bennett, *one good, one bad, and one somewhere in between; a mixed bag*, but overall he felt it was likely that DCI Hobson would be reasonably happy with the way the Karpovich murder inquiry had progressed that morning.

He knew where Alexei lived, of course he did; on two occasions he had observed his house from afar, and just the once he had gained access to the farmyard. The security had been tight then; since the murder of Anastasia and the destruction of the Bentley Continental he was sure it would be tighter still. No doubt a team of men equipped with sledgehammers and wrecking bars could break through the barrier fence within minutes, but such an attack would not be silent; in the time it took to gain entry Alexei could perhaps flee the property unseen, or call the emergency services, or lock himself inside a secure strong room which could not be broken into except by using explosives, or heavy duty cutting equipment. It was obvious therefore that to abduct his enemy from his fortress home would not be at all feasible.

The alternative to a raid on the house had to be for Alexei to be snatched from a public place where he felt at ease. To do this Mikel would need to discover his regular haunts. It might cost more, but he would ask him when he telephoned to begin his surveillance of his Nemesis straight away. If he was as good as Karlos suggested he was then this should not be a problem, and very soon he would then work out where the best place to seize Alexei would be. And the time to act was crucial. Alexei had to be taken prisoner before the murders at the wedding took place. If it could appear to the police investigating these grotesque crimes that he had gone to ground to avoid possible arrest, that would be the very best impression that could be created. In his mind's eye everything was clear. Vitali felt confident that he could answer any questions Mikel might ask about the man who was to be framed for committing an unspeakable crime and about the offence he was to be falsely accused of, so he turned his thoughts to the most terrifying aspect of his plan.

As regards the murders at the wedding venue he felt less sure. He knew the address where Helena lived with her husband because that was noted down in an address book. She had written to him to ask for a donation to help her local hospice. He had written back enclosing a cheque, and after that his support had been enlisted whenever a fund raising event was being held. He had been pleased to help, and subsequently Helena had visited his home several times. He thought she was beautiful, and clever, and sweet natured; it was such a pity that she had to die.

He knew the date of the big wedding she was going to because Natasha had mentioned it in the course of conversation; it was the same date as her mother's birthday; but he couldn't recall the place where the marriage ceremony was going to be performed. He was by no means certain that it had ever been referred to at all, but if it had the details hadn't stuck, and that was a problem. The simple way to find out was to telephone Helena about the hospice and then make reference to the wedding in casual conversation; but now was not the time to do so. With Natasha still in hospital; and with his emotions still red raw following the attack on his home, the last thing anyone would do would be phone up a casual acquaintance for a jolly natter about a wedding. He couldn't think of a way forward. Maybe Mikel might have an idea. If somehow Lucy could be asked the question the excited little girl might readily reply; that could be an option; but how to initiate the conversation was anybody's guess.

He Googled a few smart wedding venues just to see if any might leap from the screen with a shout of "mia culpa" but of course not one did. There were so many sites available. At least though he could tell Mikel he had tried, and not sought to shift every aspect of the planning onto his shoulders. He had also made time to trawl through on-line editions of *The Buxton Advertiser* to find out what he could about DCI Hobson. He discovered a story of love and self-sacrifice when he read of an incident in which Mark Hobson had been to prepared to end his own life in a most dramatic and public fashion to try to save his wife from a dreadful fate. That event had made the national news, although he had never before been aware of it. Here was something to tell Mikel; it also confirmed in his mind the belief that the fact of both their deaths would be front page news: tabloids and broadsheets alike would cover this tragic story in great depth. He could not have chosen better, only the assassination of a leading politician, or the attempted murder of a senior member of the Royal Family would be more newsworthy. The anger the general public felt would be extreme; the demand that the person responsible for this cold-blooded slaughter of the innocents be brought to justice intense; the pressure on the police to make an arrest immense; he could not wish for more; he almost felt a twinge of sympathy for the man who would be unjustly accused of masterminding this crime, but then he remembered every bad thing Alexei had ever done to him, and his face broke into an unkind smile.

He could do no more. At any moment he might get the call from Karlos instructing him where to send the two hundred thousand pounds. As soon as that call came, and the details had been received and understood, he would transfer the cash electronically into whatever account he specified, and shortly after that he expected to receive a spine chilling call from the very dangerous Mikel

The wheels would then be in motion; the juggernaut of Revenge would have commenced its irreversible journey; from that point onwards there would be no turning back. The sword of Damocles hung by a thread over Alexei's head; very, very soon the blade would fall.

CHAPTER TWENTY SIX

Traffic jams and wedding plans, a hospital visit, a watchful nurse, happy and unhappy thoughts, and a softly spoken assassin.

Detective Inspector Mark Hobson was audibly chuntering as he arrived at the office twenty minutes late.

"Bloody traffic coming into Buxton was horrendous. The road works on Fairfield Road are a nightmare. Over one hundred yards coned off, one small hole in the road, not a soul to be seen actually doing anything, and they say they will be in place for the next two months."

"Should have been in earlier Gov and avoided the rush hour" said DS Bennett a little disrespectfully, "I sailed through them at 7 am this morning."

"I had things to do Pete" responded Hobson; "Helena said I must try on my best suit before I left for work to see if it still fits me."

"And does it" asked Bennett, anticipating the reply he would get?"

"No it bloomin' well doesn't" answered Mark Hobson gloomily. "I can get in it, but Helena says it doesn't look right. She's already seen a suit on the John Lewis website that she thinks would be ideal. Four hundred quid for a Jacket and trousers, my first car cost a hell of a sight less than that."

"And beer was three halfpence a pint, and you could have a good night out for ten bob" laughed Bennett. "It's the way of the world; and you wouldn't want to look penny-pinching at a posh wedding would you Gov? But putting all thoughts of genteel celebrations aside for the moment, I've got a couple of bits of news that I think will interest you." Detective Sergeant Bennett then told his boss about the various telephone calls he had received that morning.

"This character Petrov sounds promising" said Hobson. "Give the detective constable you spoke to earlier today a call to see if he can let us have a photograph of him, or at the very least a pretty detailed description we can work with. If Natasha is well enough to answer specific questions about the events leading up to her being locked inside a burning building, she might just be robust enough to look at a picture of a possible suspect. It all depends on what the doctors have to say; I can't push her too hard; it's likely that today she will only be able to answer a few very basic questions."

Natasha was lying on her bed. Her eyes were open, but whether she was truly awake was uncertain. She was in a room by herself. Detective Chief Inspector Hobson had been told that he could only spend a few moments with her; and that if she started to become distressed the interview would have to cease. A nurse was watching through the glass panel in the door, she would intervene if the patient showed any signs of anxiety. Hobson had been required to wear a face mask to reduce the risk that he might inadvertently infect Natasha with any germs he might be carrying, and he had been rigorously questioned about his current state of health before the interview was permitted. All this was by no means ideal, but it was the best he was going to get. He had with him a photograph of Petrov which DS Bennett had been able to obtain. It had been taken from distance and was not pin sharp, but it would have to do. He also had a description of the suspect-five feet nine inches tall, dark hair, well built, with a small birth mark below his left ear which was not easy to spot. It could have been more detailed, but that was all GMP could tell him; the worry was that this description could probably cover a quarter of men in the UK (apart from the birthmark), and if Natasha described her attacker in similar terms that by itself would not put Petrov in the frame for the callous and brutal assault.

Slowly it appeared to dawn on Natasha that there was another person in the room. The presence of a stranger, his face partly covered by a surgical mask seemed to alarm her; if her fear continued to grow the interview would be over before it had begun.

"Natasha please don't be afraid" said the DCI gently, "it's me Mark Hobson, I'm Helena's husband and Lucy's dad. We met at your father's house a few days ago. I'm here to help you; and to try to put the man who did all the horrible things that have happened to you behind bars. It won't take very long I promise you, but are you willing to let me ask you one or two questions? I promise you I will be as brief as I can be; and if you want me to stop at any time just tell me, and we'll call a halt to the conversation we are having."

His voice was soft; his manner gentle; those criminals who had faced the senior detective across the table in an interview room would not have believed he could be so tender. Natasha turned her face towards him and a little of her alarm evaporated.

"I remember" she whispered hesitantly, "it seems so long ago" and there were tears in her eyes as she recalled that dinner party, "we all had such a good time" and it seemed to strike Natasha that that occasion might be the last happy memory she would ever have. There was now a real danger that there would be an outpouring of emotion, and that the nurse on watch outside the bedroom would intervene and that the interview would be terminated before it had really commenced.

Trying to give the unhappy girl some reassurance, and wishing that he could hold her hand and remove his face mask Mark Hobson said quietly; "we did Love, we really did, but there will be good times in the future. You will get better, I know you will, and you'll have your whole life ahead of you; and if we can lock up the man who did such terrible things to you, life will feel a whole lot safer" and then for a second he hesitated. A memory from many years before sprang into his mind, a memory of seeing Helena in a hospital bed after she had been injured in a car bomb attack that had killed her wealthy employer. She had feared for the future, she had worried that her looks would be irreparably damaged, and he had given her reasons to hope. That was the moment he thought that he had begun to fall in love, and just for an instance Hobson himself almost succumbed to his own emotions, but he controlled himself.

"Help me catch the monster who did such wicked things to you Natasha" he said; "in a few words just tell me what happened on the dreadful night of the fire?"

"I was alone in the house" she replied; "It all seems so unreal. My dad was out at a function. I had such a big day ahead of me. I was tired; I'd spent all day getting ready for Chatsworth. I knew I needed to be at my best, so I had gone to bed early. I think I must have dozed off then I heard shouting and a banging at the door. I thought I was dreaming then gradually I came to. I saw a strange light outside; I looked out of my bedroom window and saw flames, then I think a heard a voice shouting "fire."I realised something was horribly wrong. I threw on a T-shirt and a pair of jeans. The banging and the shouting got louder. I flung the door open. There was a man on the doorstep, and for the first time I could see clearly the stables were on fire. My first thought was the horses. I had to try and save them. The man said he had dialled 999 and that the fire brigade would be here soon. I said "there's no time, there's no time" and I begged him to help me. He kept saying that I shouldn't put my life at risk but I was adamant. He wasn't happy but he agreed but he insisted I shouldn't put myself in danger, and that horses or no horses, if the building started to creak then we must abandon all our attempts to save the animals. He seemed so nice, my saviour, my Good Samaritan, but then as soon as I entered the building he slammed the door behind me and locked me inside" and with that thought the tears in her eyes welled up once more.

"I know this is hard" said Hobson, "and I won't keep asking you questions for much longer, but what do you remember about the man? Was he tall? Was he short? What colour was his hair? Did he speak with an accent? Did he have tattoos, or any unusual physical features?"

"He had dark hair" replied Natasha, "and a deep voice with an accent that did not sound to be local. I don't remember any tattoos or anything like that; and to the best of my recollection he was about the same height and weight as you are."

So not Petrov thought Hobson despondently. *I did so hope there would be a* positive *ID.* He showed Natasha the photograph, just in case she might be mistaken about the stature, but there was not the slightest hint of recognition. The nurse was now peering into the room and tapping the dial on her watch. It was time to go. Hobson thanked Natasha for being so helpful and stood up to leave, then, almost as an afterthought he asked her if there was anything else she wished to add.

"I think I imagined this" she said, "but as I was running down to the stables I thought I saw the shadow of a man near to the garage about fifty yards away from me. It was only there for a moment. I'm sure it was nothing, but at the time I thought that a second person could be in the farmyard. That's all I can tell you Mr Hobson, now all I want to do is sleep" and Natasha closed her eyes and turned her head away from the Derbyshire officer.

The phone call was short and to the point, but that was all it needed to be. He knew how much Karlos would require as a down payment, he just needed the details of the bank account the money would be transferred into. Not that it would stay there for long. Vitali was sure that within minutes of being received the cash would be moved into another bank account, and then moved on again several more times. Tracing the money would not be easy. Should the police ever try to discover where the money that had left his account had finally ended up, the task would be fraught with difficulty.

He wondered at what stage Karlos would contact Mikel to let him know that the first instalment of the cash had been paid; he assumed he would act swiftly. At any moment his telephone might ring again, and this time when he answered it he would be talking to a cold blooded killer who was going to assassinate an innocent family, and destroy Alexei's life by framing him for this unspeakable crime.

He could feel his anxiety level rising. Despite paying two hundred thousand pounds, an agreement was still not a done deal. Karlos had said that Mikel would only take on the task if he was satisfied that his "client" could be trusted not to panic, or to undergo a last minute dramatic change of heart; he also had to be confident and well informed; a muddle-headed scatterbrain would not be accepted, and would lose any money paid up front in the twinkling of an eye. These were tense moments, and the longer he waited for a call the more unsettled he became. When his telephone failed to ring for the next two hours Vitali became more and more convinced that he had been conned.

Finally it burst into life. Trying to stay calm, even though his hand was shaking, he picked up the receiver. The voice on the other end of the line was quite unlike anything he had expected. It was soft and well-modulated, and for some bizarre reason sounded a little bit like his grandmother, but with a hint of steel that could not be missed.

"Vitali" it said confidently, "I am Mikel, I hear you wish to employ me."

CHAPTER TWENTY SEVEN

A possible sighting, a conversation with a cold-blooded killer, thoughts of extreme violence, financial blackmail, and a small but significant find

"It was worth the visit Pete", DCI Mark Hobson was telling DS Bennett about his meeting with Natasha Zalenkov at the hospital. "She's still very shaken up of course, and not surprisingly she isn't absolutely clear on everything, but I'm pretty sure that most of what she told me is more or less accurate"; and Hobson then explained to the detective sergeant the account that came from Natasha's lips.

"The man who locked her in the stable is definitely not Petrov. She looked at the photograph and didn't recognise him and, unless the description you got from GMP is widely inaccurate the description she gave of her attacker was significantly at odds with the information we have on file; which was a bit dispiriting ; but then in her very last comment to me she said something which might be highly significant." The detective chief inspector then told DS Bennett about Natasha's belief that a second man could also have been inside the farmyard.

"I think we always suspected that might have been the case because the CCTV photographs of the blue Toyota opened up that possibility, but we couldn't be sure. Natasha thinks she glimpsed a figure standing near the garage, that's a fair distance away from the stables, and I doubt if the SSO's paid too much attention to that area. I'm going to send a team back in today to see what they can find. There may be nothing of course, but they might just stumble upon something that could turn out to be vitally important.

"There's another thing too Pete. Later on today we should receive news that a Home Office pathologist has had an opportunity to examine the dead guard dogs. We know exactly what killed them, we don't need to know anything more about the animals themselves, unless they were jam packed with a virus that could exterminate half the planet, but we do need to take possession of the bullets that ended their ferocious little lives. Once we have these we can determine the exact nature of the weapon that killed them, and if we ever have a suspect firmly in the frame, and if we were to find such a firearm in his possession that would be pretty conclusive evidence that that person played a very active part in the arson at Moor Top Grange, and that attempted murder of Natasha Zalenkov.

This was the phone call he had been waiting for. A one word answer would have been sufficient; a simple "yes" was all that was necessary, but for a second Vitali was tongue tied. This was not a good start; and all the while inside his head he could hear Karlos warning him that Mikel did not suffer fools gladly, and that if he was not sure that the person in need of his services was dependable he would refuse to become involved in any scheme dreamt up by such a being.

"Did you not hear me? I need an answer. Do you, or do you not want my help?" The voice was still soft but the impatience was obvious; he might only have seconds before the phone went dead. This time he had to speak. Words now tumbled from his lips at a volume that was far louder than necessary. Vitali responded "yes Mikel, I do, I do; I need you to perform a very important task for me."

"I am not deaf Vitali, there is no need to shout. Tell me immediately exactly what you want me to do."

"Has not Karlos already told you; I explained everything in great detail to him?"

"He has, but that is not the point. I need to hear your proposal from your lips. We are wasting time Vitali, and time is money; so let me hear the details of your plan."

So Vitali told him everything. He told him how and why he hated Alexei, and how deep that hatred was. He told him about his lovely daughter and his beautiful house, and how in the course of just one night, his home had been partially destroyed, and the life of his child had been ruined. He told him about his desire for revenge, and the physical and psychological pain he wanted to inflict on his enemy. He explained why he had chosen one particular family to be sacrificed to achieve his aim; and he revealed in as much detail as he could everything he knew about the family he wished to see slain. He admitted that there were gaps in his knowledge, that the time scale was tight, and that Mikel would not have long to prepare for the fateful day. He confessed that there were outstanding difficulties in that he didn't yet know the venue where murder would take place, and then he fell silent. He felt exhausted; he waited to hear Mikel's response: everything could depend on what he said next.

"You make things difficult" he remarked, "and you give me so little time. To work out where and when to snatch Alexei from the street will take careful planning, and to find somewhere to imprison him may not be straight forward, however once he is in my custody the rest of your desires will be easy to fulfil. If he is as bad a man as you claim him to be I will enjoy inventing ways to make him squeal. The assassination at the wedding is a much bigger operation. It would be simpler if this could take place on the steps of a local church. To shoot a bride and groom as they left the building would be relatively straight forward, and the sense of outrage would be just as great; could not your plan be changed to allow me to pick a random a wedding to disrupt?"

Vitali shook his head vigorously, a spontaneous but pointless gesture because Mikel could not see his reaction.

"No, It has to be as I have outlined it" he insisted; "the victim needs to be of the establishment, an employee of the state. The cold-blooded killing of a senior police officer and his family will feel like a monstrous act of terrorism, and the state will show no mercy to anyone thought to be responsible for causing it to happen. If Alexei is convicted of such a crime he will be daily mistreated by prison warders and inmates alike. It has to be as I have set out. I cannot change my mind Mikel: the plan must go ahead unaltered."

"If that is your demand, then so be it; but I will require additional funds because the risk is greater."

"And how much will that be" asked Vitali angrily? I am paying nearly one million pounds to you already; many people might say that was already extortionate."

"Get rid of the word "nearly" responded Mikel. "Call it a cool one million quid as the English might say; either we have a deal at this price, or our conversation ends now. You know from what Karlos has already told you that I never negotiate,"

"We have a deal, my needs to see this plan carried out transcend everything, even financial blackmail, but there are still problems to overcome. I do not know exactly where the wedding which holds the key to everything is to be held, and I know not how to find out. I can't simply pick up the phone and ask the detective or his wife where it will be; that would look suspicious, particularly as my daughter remains in hospital, and her future is far from certain: a loving father would not telephone casual acquaintances in these circumstances to inquire about their social calendar."

"I was told you were intelligent" murmured Mikel in exasperation; "was I misinformed. Use your brain Vitali. I believe that recently the husband and wife were guests at your table, and that the evening was a pleasant one; is this not correct?"

"It is" replied Vitali, "they were good company; the night was enjoyed by all."

"And has the detective visited your daughter in hospital to try to advance his criminal investigation"

"He has" replied Vitali, "and his behaviour towards Natasha was exemplary."

"Well there you go then" sighed Mikel, as if he was talking to a five year old; "telephone his home, speak to his wife, and tell her that the doctors treating Natasha want her to concentrate on pleasant things. Ask her if the wedding venue has a website that you can log onto so that you can copy all the promotional pictures they use to promote their business. She will be only too pleased to help. She will think that anything she can do to make Natasha smile is worthwhile. Do this as soon as our conversation ends, and then when you have the link wait by your phone until I call you again to get the details. This is important; we do not have the luxury of time at our disposal.

"There is one other thing to bear in mind. You and Natasha are seen as victims, there is widespread sympathy for your plight. When the assassination of the detective and his family has taken place, and after the trial of Alexei is over and he has been branded a monster, before he is sentenced you can add to his woes by going public, and revealing to the tabloid press how kind the detective was to Natasha, and how distraught his killing has made you both feel. It turns the screw; it gives you the chance to heap a bit more agony on Alexei, and maybe even to add a few more years onto his sentence. If you look for them Vitali, there are always ways to make a bad situation worse; and that my brother I'm sure will please you."

I will never be your brother thought Vitali, *but the thought of twisting the knife does please me very much.*

"There is just one more thought before this little chat ends" said Mikel. "You have told me that you and Alexei have been enemies for decades, but for a long time you co-existed without open warfare. You have listed all the things that Alexei has done to you; you have not told me of anything you have already done to him. Is there anything I need to know?"

Vitali hesitated. Some things were better left unsaid, some actions were better unrevealed: "my conscience in all of this is clear." he protested.

"And pigs might fly" murmured Mikel coldly; "but I will not press the point; but if at any time I find your secrecy puts this whole venture at risk Vitali I will be gone; as sure as the sun will set tonight Vitali, as sure as darkness follows daylight."

The biggest clues are often found in the smallest, most insignificant looking objects; a fact well known to police officers and pathologists the world over. A single strand of human hair might be all that is necessary to send a man to gaol, a minute speck of blood almost invisible to the naked eye can lead to a villain being locked up for decades behind steel bars. Potentially such a clue was discovered when the search team returned to Moor Top Grange. Nestling on the ground right next to the stone built garage was a cigarette end. It might be nothing of course, that would not be known until it had been examined in the laboratory, but it might contain traces of DNA. That DNA could belong to one of the men who worked regularly for Vitali Zalenkov and have absolutely no evidential value, but it could be the DNA of a man who had lit a petrol bomb and casually thrown it into a magnificent house; that same man might also have possessed the weapon which had silenced forever three angry guard dogs. DCI Hobson felt a shiver of excitement when he was told of the find. This might be a big leap forward; with every fibre of his body he hoped that this would be the case.

CHAPTER TWENTY EIGHT

A hysterical woman, an unexpected request for help, kindness and compassion, the "The Temple of Diana," and a degree of contingency planning

Despite the strong advice he had given to Chloe Andropov that she should telephone the police if she had any concerns about her personal safety Mark Hobson had believed that it was unlikely that she would make such a call, so it was a bolt from the blue when his office telephone rang and the switchboard operator informed him that a Mrs Andropov was on the line demanding to speak with the DCI as a matter of urgency, and asking him if he wanted to take the call. Hobson replied that he would, and seconds later he was talking to a very disturbed woman who seemed to be on the edge of hysteria. In the background the detective chief inspector could hear multiple voices and the clinking of glasses; the upside was that Chloe was in a crowded place, and maybe safe from immediate harm; the downside was that she was obviously in a busy pub, and although it was only a little after 1pm she was already slurring her words, and clearly affected by drink; it was also very possible that she had taken other substances which might in part account for her highly unstable state.

"Good day Mrs Andropov" he said, "you sound very upset; what has happened to cause you to make this call?"

"He's got somebody spying on me" cried Chloe, "I know he fucking has. He thinks I don't see things, but I fucking do. I know he's got it in for me; he wants rid of me, he's made that very clear. I ain't going to give him that satisfaction though. I want him stopped. I want you to lock him up and throw away the fucking key."

"Is the person who has been spying on you watching you now Mrs Andropov? If you feel you are in any danger you must dial 999 straight away and a local police car will be with you in minutes."

"No he's gone now" snorted Chloe. "I thought I saw him stood outside on the pavement peering at me, but maybe it weren't him at all, but I have seen him staring at me and watching my every move; and one time he had something in his hand, and maybe it was a gun, I don't know;" and then just at that moment there was a burst of raucous laughter. It was unconnected with anything Chloe had said; maybe an Englishman, an Irishman and a Scotsman had just walked into the bar, but the noise was disconcerting, and for a second Hobson had feared that something dramatic had just occurred, but it quickly had become apparent that that was not the case.

"Mrs Andropov" he said, I think we need to talk about all this in detail. Can I come and visit you later today. You say that you are not being watched at the moment, so now might be a good time to go home; but can I ask you how you got to the place where you are because I worry that you might be too upset to drive safely." He could have said "I think you're pissed, or too drugged up to get behind the wheel of a car" but he felt that if Chloe could get back home safely by means other than driving it was better not to antagonise her.

"You may be right" she sniffed. "It would suit his purposes just fine if I wrapped the car around a tree and ended up on a stone slab in some sodding mortuary. I'll get a taxi in a few minutes when I've finished my Prosecco. I'll be back at the farm by three: make sure you are too. I don't want to be sat twiddling my thumbs for a couple of hours waiting until some copper can be bothered to turn up."

"I'll be there" said Hobson, with forced politeness, "pen and paper in hand, and you can then tell me all about the man who has caused you such anxiety. I'll see you then; we'll get to the bottom of this Mrs Andropov, you have my word on that."

Helena was on the point of going out when the telephone rang. She had had a busy but frustrating morning. The Tesco shop had been a nightmare. The store had been extremely busy. There had been long queues at all the checkouts, card readers had malfunctioned, and then to cap it all, a befuddled lady, of mature years, had managed to reverse her unnecessarily large Range Rover into Helena's parked car causing minor damage to both vehicles. Details had been exchanged. The woman had been very apologetic and had become distressed. For twenty minutes Helena had tried to calm her down saying "accidents will happen", "the insurance will cover it", and "nobody's hurt, and there's no real harm done". Her schedule for the rest of the day had been badly affected. She was already late for a planned meeting with Jackie. She was sorely tempted just to ignore the phone, but she did the responsible thing and responded to its strident demands. The voice on the other end of the line was familiar and totally unexpected. If Vitali Zalenkov wanted to speak to her at this time, with everything he was going through at present, it had to be important.

"Helena" he said, "I'm sorry to bother you. Have you got time to talk? I need your help; it's for Natasha."

"I've got all the time in the world" replied Helena. "You know Vitali that anything I can do to aid Natasha I will gladly do; so tell me straight away what you need."

He sounded emotional, which moved Helena greatly. He explained that his daughter was a little stronger, but that the doctors were concerned because she was so depressed.

"They want her to think about happy things, but not joyous days from her past because inevitably she will make comparisons in her mind between how good things were then and how bad they are now, which could make her feel worse. Somehow they want her to focus on events to look forward to. I've struggled to think of ideas, but one thing I wondered was that if we talked about the wedding venue where Lucy is to be a bridesmaid that would please her. She's a lovely girl Helena, and her excitement was infectious; Natasha was so full of smiles at Lucy's pure pleasure. I thought therefore that if you could perhaps let me have the web address of the venue where Lucy is going to take centre stage I could copy some photographs from it, and maybe there might be videos too; and after the event is over maybe you could even let me have a copy of the actual wedding video with Lucy doing her stuff."

"Of course, of course" responded Helena. "It's all happening at Summerford Hall, it's a gorgeous Georgian country house in

Cheshire. If you Google it you'll find hundreds of pictures, and dozens of reviews, and of course we'll get an extra copy of the wedding video for you to keep; and I'll get Lucy to make Natasha a get well card; and if there is anything else I can do please don't hesitate to let me know."

"You are very kind" said Vitali, and Helena thought she detected a note of sadness in his voice: "you're a good person Helena; the world would be a much better place if there were more people like you in it; and a lot worse place if you weren't here."

"I'm going nowhere" she replied sweetly, "and I'll always be here if you need a chat, or think of anything at all I can possibly help you with."

There was a silence, followed by what sounded like a stifled sigh, then, as if he was a person struggling to find the right words, he replied "that's so kind Helena, so very, very kind" and at that point the conversation ended.

The pictures of Summerford Hall were encouraging. As soon as Mikel logged on to the website he became sure that everything Vitali wanted to see happen could be accomplished

It was clear that the hotel was no more than one hundred yards away from a large lake, and that in the lake had been created a small man-made island upon which a Grecian temple had been erected probably at, or shortly after, the hotel was built. Access to this island was over an ornate bridge designed by a contemporary of Capability Brown's, and constructed out white marble, imported at great expense from Italy. Inside the temple could be seen a small number of white painted wicker chairs, and placed centrally in front of a lectern decorated with flowers were two other chairs painted gold in which, at the appropriate time, brides and grooms would sit. All this was clearly visible from the hotel. When a wedding was to take place many more chairs were placed on a flat area of lawn adjoining the lake for friends, family, and invited guests to sit in to watch the wedding ceremony. Perhaps it was a bit too romantic, maybe a little Disneyesque, but the hotel was selling happy ever after dreams, and nobody had ever asked for a more austere approach to be adopted in their particular case.

It was also clear that after the marriage had been solemnized that here was the place where the majority of the wedding photographs would be taken. Dozens of newly married couples had been pictured there; to begin with by themselves, then with their retinue; then the size of the group would usually expand to include parents, grandparents, and other close relatives. Often it seemed that after the formal photographs of the bridal party had been completed family groups would take their turn to stand before "The Temple of Diana" to record their presence at the event. Mikel anticipated that the family he was hired to destroy would follow this tradition, so here was where he envisaged slaughter would take place. For a man with his particular high level skills to fire off a volley of deadly shots would take only seconds; the first body would still be in free fall when the next victim succumbed to his lethal aim. Only when the carnage was complete would people really realise what a terrible tragedy had occurred. There would be panic and pandemonium; and in the chaos and confusion that followed an ice-cold killer could slip away unseen. The only unknown factor was the weather. The ten day forecast was good; with a cynicism that came naturally to him Mikel started to figure out what he would need to do if it rained.

He knew that inside the hotel was a large assembly room where weddings took place if rain lashed the outside walls and wind threatened to topple the tallest tress. To commit mass murder inside the building and escape unseen would be much harder, but he was the ultimate professional, and the greater the challenge, the more he rose to his task. A visit to the hotel was essential: there had to be vantage points from which a sniper could carry out his work; all he had to do was to find them. He also needed to familiarise himself with exits, and entrances, and back passages, and quiet nooks and crannies, so that he could properly plan his escape. Mikel always worked to the rule of three; If not A, then perhaps B, and if B was not an option then he could resort to option C.

There was another potential advantage in visiting the hotel. At one time Vitali had toyed with the idea that Alexei should be abducted immediately after the shooting to make it look as if he was hiding from the police; but that had made little sense. To be seized a day or two before the murders was clearly a better course of action and one which he had ultimately persuaded Vitali to follow. He had stressed that by doing this it would allow more time for physical and mental torture to be heaped upon Alexei, but it would also open up an option of planting his fingerprints on objects that could be left at the hotel. It would not be unheard of for a guest to remove a monogrammed water glass as a keepsake, or to idly pick up and put down various items in a bedroom. When he stayed overnight at the hotel a few days before the attack a glass or a water jug could be removed; and if a note of apology claiming it had been accidentally broken, and the cost of a replacement was left where it once stood, nobody would bat an eyelid. This would mean that if he chose to, and he could see any benefit in doing so, that on the day of the murders, these items, which he would have forced Alexei to handle under threat of further physical abuse could be substituted for items currently in the bedroom. It was a contingency plan, but one worth having; Mikel was a great believer in contingency plans.

There remained the problem of how to enter a front facing bedroom of the hotel on the day of the shooting if the wedding was to take place outdoors. Inevitably all the doors would be locked, so to do so secretly, and without leaving tell tale signs of a break in, for the average sneak thief would be difficult; but for Mikel with his links to espionage this was not a problem. Key cards could be cloned; in the hands of an expert this task was not a hard one. Mikel knew of such an expert; Mikel knew lots of clever and unscrupulous people; that was one reason why he was so good at his job.

CHAPTER TWENTY NINE

An insecure "Fort Knox;" a lack of hospitality; passwords, revelations, lies; and an invisible hotel guest

It was a little before 3 pm when Hobson arrived at "Chez Andropov." He had expected the main gate to be barred and bolted, and anticipated that he would have problems gaining entry into the farmyard. A paranoid Chloe could easily have lowered the portcullis and raised the drawbridge to prevent anyone coming within one hundred metres of the house, but to his amazement the gate was wide open; a whole bus load of ne'er-do-wells could have made their way onto the property without let or hindrance. This was not good; there was nobody at all to be seen. For a moment the DCI worried that although he was early for his appointment he was already too late for it to have any purpose. If Chloe had arrived home to find an attacker already waiting for her she could be laying somewhere in a pool of blood, and he would be rightly condemned for not doing more to ensure a vulnerable woman's safety.

Fortunately however that fear was groundless; the silence of the farmyard was shattered by Chloe's dulcet tones.

"You're late" she wailed. "What time do you call this? You said that you'd be here by three."

"Actually it is two minutes to three" replied Hobson testily; "but let's not quibble about a couple of minutes. You're here, I'm here; you've got a lot you need to tell me, so shall we both just go inside and sit down then you can explain to me in detail exactly what has been happening to you over the past few days.

The logic of the suggestion seemed to register, so, in a far from gracious manner Alexei Andropov's disgruntled wife, with a curt "well get a move on then." gestured for the DCI to join her inside the twenty first homage to modernism which was his in your face, look at me aren't I rich, ain't it cool, concrete and glass unlovely home.

A million pounds to build thought Hobson, *with a life expectancy of maybe no more than fifty years before it is razed to the ground to be replaced by the next salute to transient fashion* but very wisely he kept his thoughts about cutting edge architecture to himself.

"I'm right with you Mrs Andropov. It's strangely quiet here at the moment, and the gate is wide open. Are you here on your own? Where is everybody? Last time I was here it was like gaining entry to GCHQ. With you having been spied on I thought I'd have the Devil's own job just getting into the farmyard; why are things so different this time?"

"He's away" snorted Chloe petulantly; "he's always fucking away these days, and he's taken Ivan and Nikita with him for some reason, and Sergei is a useless little pillock. I told him to lock the gates but he just messed about so I just let him know what a waste of space he was, and he stormed off in a strop, taking the dogs with him. He's hiding somewhere out of sight, but he'll be watching every move we make, and he'll report straight back to his master, the useless little turd."

Given the mood she's in thought Hobson, *this interview is unlikely to go well, but there's a chance she may let something slip which she wouldn't do if she was a bit more rational; we can but live in hopes.*

He entered the house and followed Chloe into the same room where he and DS Bennett had met her previously. It was far from tidy. Magazines were strewn across the floor, each probably discarded after a few seconds when terminal boredom set in. Nobody today had tried to clear up the mess Chloe had caused. Hobson breathed an inward sigh of relief that his own wife Helena was the exact antithesis of this self-centred, self-obsessed, resentful woman.

There was no offer of hospitality; nobody was on hand to make coffee; which was probably all to the good. Detective Chief Inspector Hobson sat down in a chair and took out a notebook and pen.

It was a long rambling account. The description of the suspect tended to alter as the story progressed. Estimates of height and weight were forever changing; details of skin tones and hair colour were far from consistent; Chloe was extremely vague when she tried to describe his face, which she claimed not to have seen clearly, yet at the same time she alleged that he had fixed her with a cruel, threatening stare. At one stage DCI Hobson actually queried if there could have been two people spying on her, but he was met with a look of incredulity and a blanket denial that that was the case. The amount of alcohol she had drank that day was obviously a factor in her less than convincing testimony; but despite her tendency to assume and invent crucial details Hobson felt that underneath everything more than a grain of truth lay concealed.

"So if we agree that you are being watched Mrs Andropov" he said; "have you any idea why that might be?"

Chloe looked at him as if he was an educationally-challenged five year old.

"Because he ordered it "she replied derisively. "I've read his e-mails. I ain't daft; he doesn't know it, but I've got his passwords. He doesn't always take his laptop with him. He thinks I'm too thick to do anything but watch porn and buy stuff on line, but I can do a hell of a lot more than that", and she gave a triumphant little giggle as she said these words.

Now Hobson was really interested.

"How do you know his passwords" he asked? "You're not a secret computer hacker are you?"

"He's got a little notebook with all his passwords in it. He dropped it once. I found it when he was out. I copied all the stuff he had in it then put it back where it was. He still doesn't know that I did that, but every now and again I take a peep at his E-mails; he sends out some pretty creepy stuff" and Chloe grinned like the proverbial Cheshire Cat, pleased as punch at her own cleverness.

"And what is that password" asked Hobson with his pen poised?

"I ain't telling nobody that" she said; "it's my secret; I'm never going to tell anyone."

"If I'm going to try to help you, you've got to help me. I need to know about these E-mails; I have to be able to see them for myself."

His request was met with a vigorous shaking of the head.

"I can't let you do that" cried Chloe adamantly; "anyway they will have been deleted by now; he never keeps nothing on his laptop for long, unlike the sad little cow he lusted after for more than twenty years."

"You had access to Anastasia's computer too" exclaimed the DCI in amazement

"Yes" shouted Chloe exultantly; "She never deleted nothing, and some of the stuff she kept was nasty. She wasn't as sweet as she pretended to be either. She said some horrible things on line about a former boyfriend."

"Like what" asked Hobson intrigued? This did not sound like the person Jennifer Drake, and other people had described; personally he trusted their judgement a great deal more than he did that of the lippy, embittered woman mouthing off in front of him.

"Somebody close to him died in an accident or something. I don't flipping know, but she posted that it was probably his fault, and that bad things happen to bad people. She also sent out other horrible E-mails slagging him off" she cackled; "only she didn't do that; I did it for her; and I did it good. Even if the whole world thought she was lovely I made sure that there was one person who felt differently. She was a parasite living well off my husband's stupidity. Somebody had to set the record straight;" and she howled like a demented hyena. At that point, although Hobson wanted to discover what had been said, he realised that given the mood she was in, further conversation with this woman would be a waste of time; but despite all his misgivings, which had proved well-founded, something really important had been uncovered by this interview.

Midweek at Summerford Hall was sometimes quiet, although at the height of the wedding season marriage ceremonies were daily events, and invariably during this period the hotel would be full to capacity. This week was not such a week. The next big wedding was not until Saturday. Rooms were available; and if they were, it was not unusual for them to be snapped up by couples who had been married there wanting to re-visit the scene of their nuptials, and celebrate in the hotel's renowned restaurant an anniversary of their wedding day. Single travellers wanting to break a journey for an overnight stay were a rarity, the price of the room alone a deterrent to all but the most well heeled of voyageurs. So when "Mr Robinson" from Greater Manchester telephoned to book a room for just one night it was unusual.

He arrived precisely at the time he said he would do so, which was not something many of the guests at the hotel managed to achieve, a non-descript unimpressive little man with plastered down hair and horn-rimmed glasses; and he asked if he could have dinner brought to his room rather than sample an a-la carte meal in the luxury dining room. The staff paid him very little attention: couples trying to recapture a precious moment in their lives often ordered champagne; and sometimes drank more than was sensible; but frequently they were easy to manipulate, and so generous with their tips: it was very quickly decided that there was no point whatsoever in buttering up a man who preferred the isolation of his own company to intermingling with fellow human beings.

The tone of his visit had been set the moment he entered the foyer. He had spoken no more than was necessary to the hotel receptionist when he checked in, just giving her the basic details she required. He had declined the offer of help with his luggage, (a single suitcase of modest proportions that had seen better days) preferring to have it under his control the whole time.

The lengths some people will go to to avoid putting their hands in their pockets thought the receptionist, *it's as though he sees this place as a den of thieves, and he's got the Crown Jewels secreted in that battered old portmanteau.* She rapidly decided that he was not worth the effort of a second look; in no time at all she would be hard pushed to recall a single thing about his appearance.

Unlike the receptionist, in the privacy of his bedroom "Mr Robinson" remembered every detail of the hotel he had seen so far. Carefully he placed his case upon the bed. He opened it and removed from it the stock of a rifle, then, with the skill that comes from years of practice he laid the other parts of the gun beside it, and quickly and efficiently fully assembled the weapon. He had no intention of using the firearm that day but he wanted to feel it in his hand, and to look through its telescopic sight to the place where slaughter would take place to make certain nothing would impede his aim. He knew that once an assassin had failed in his task because he ignored a weather vane on the apex of a roof which had reacted to a sudden gust of wind at the precise moment he pulled the trigger and rotated to shield the intended victim from a speeding bullet; he was determined he would never make such a basic error.

Fortunately however there was no such difficulty to overcome in this case. If he was able to fire from any of the second floor bedrooms of the hotel he would have a clear view. It would take five seconds to end five lives: if he had been a philosopher "Mr Robinson" might have mused about the fragility of human existence.

Satisfied that if the wedding took place outdoors his contract could be easily fulfilled he turned his thoughts about what he would need to do if the weather drove everybody indoors, and then beyond all that to work out how to slip away unseen.

After he had eaten in his bedroom, the guest in room 204 surprised some members of the hotel staff, who had expected him to stay locked away all evening, by emerging from his chamber and taking a long leisurely walk around the grounds. If anybody had been remotely interested, but nobody was, they might have noticed how competitively little time was spent looking at the facade of the splendid Georgian building, and how much time disproportionately was spent looking at its rear.

"It takes all sorts" somebody might have commented, but in many ways he was already invisible to the hotel's employees; there was no advantage to them in watching what he did,

He did pay a visit to the ornate Assembly Room, which was something guests in the hotel often did. He studied the entrances and the exits, including the position of doors that said "private" and "staff only", and he wandered up into the Minstrel's Gallery at the far end of the room to look down on the vista from above. Then, when he had taken everything in, he returned to his bedroom and was not seen again that night.

Next morning he breakfasted early, and then he checked out. When his room was later cleaned by the chambermaid she noticed that some of the fliers promoting local places of interest were missing, the stock of sachets of coffee had been depleted, although there was no obvious sign that any coffee had been drunk; and a monogrammed water glass had also disappeared.

Some people she thought in her Slovakian brain, *they will take anything,* but she replaced the glass from the supply the hotel had in store, and then moved on to another room to continue her cleaning duties.

CHAPTER THIRTY

Death down a dark alley, a positive DNA result, the power of "Prosecco and praise", exchanges of information, and hopes raised and hopes dashed

The shooting of a man with a criminal record in Moss Side was not front page news, not even in Manchester. Individuals could be killed sometimes just for giving a dirty look; loss of face was paramount; a small humiliation could lead to a huge over-reaction. Life was cheap there, and the cost of causing death was even cheaper.

The body had been found in a narrow alley at the back of a grotty pub well known to Greater Manchester Police. Generally speaking they gave it a wide berth. Uniformed officers would be met with open hostility if ever they entered the premises: undercover officers took their lives in their hands if they dared to mingle with the regular drinkers in search of information. Not long ago a mature student researching the causes of urban deprivation had made the mistake of taking out a notebook and pen whilst seated near the bar. He had been mistaken for a CID officer. His notebook had been snatched from his grasp; his fingers had been broken when a pint pot was smashed down on his hand; and he had been bodily ejected from the pub with a verbal warning about what would happen to him if he was ever seen inside the establishment again.

The dead man had been shot four times. The pathologist thought the first bullet had entered his heart and that death had been instantaneous, but two more bullets had been fired into his upper body; it was believed that he was well and truly dead when the fourth bullet entered his brain. Whoever had killed him had taken no chances; life had been dramatically extinguished. A not very nice man had come to a sudden, violent end; and few people would mourn his passing. There would of course be a police investigation, but the chances of a successful outcome were small; people in Moss side with an interest in self-preservation didn't talk to the cops; they kept their knowledge to themselves; it was that kind of place.

The confirmation that DNA had been found on the cigarette butt was not front page news either, but to Detective Sergeant Peter Bennett it felt like it should have been. A positive result had been obtained, a match had been found with DNA on the police data base; it was as DCI Hobson hoped it would be; the DNA was that of Leonid Petrov, the man seen close to the spot where the dark blue Toyota was abandoned. He would have a lot of explaining to do, but his chances of persuading a jury that he was not involved in the fire at Moor Top Grange were miniscule. Much hard work still lay ahead, but if they did everything by the book, and avoided making any mistakes that would give Petrov a legal loophole, convictions for arson and for attempted murder would be the final outcome. Detective Chief Inspector Hobson was going to be very pleased indeed.

In the car park at the back of the Kebab shop in Rusholme more than two dozen men had assembled. Word had gone out that HE needed help; like Victorian labourers in need of work they had gathered. If HE had a job for some of them to do they had to be there; not to answer his demand for assistance would incur his anger; and to incur his anger was a very dangerous thing to do.

"Mr Robinson's" departure from Summerford Hall had been no more noteworthy than his arrival. No pleasantries were exchanged with the staff, so as far as they were concerned his visit to the hotel of less than eighteen hours duration was instantly forgettable. Nothing about him was engrained upon their memories; unlike many more sociable guests; not a thing, except maybe in some cases his horn rimmed spectacles, had registered with them. He had become an invisible non-entity; "Mr Robinson" much preferred it that way.

Here though it was very different. The man they had come to meet had impact. When he arrived at the car park every eye turned towards him; a hush immediately descended on the crowd. The contrast between its attitude and that of the hotel staff was immense; had the crowd but known it the difference between his appearance here and at Summerford Hall was also immense. His hair was no longer plastered to his head; his cold blue eyes were laser sharp; the horn rimmed spectacles had been consigned to history; it was hard to believe that this was the same man; which was of course exactly the outcome that was desired.

He studied the disparate group of men carefully, his eyes flitting from one person to another; only the roughest hardest looking of them met his criteria.

"You, you and you" he said, touching three men on their shoulders "stay here; the rest of you can all go"; and the crowd dispersed. Away from the car park individuals who had not been chosen voiced their discontent, but not a word of protest was uttered in the presence of the man who had commanded their attendance in the dirty, dismal parking lot hidden away behind the scruffy fast food restaurant.

For Mikel, a.k.a. "Mr Robinson" and many other aliases there was satisfaction. He had his team of "heavy lifters", he had the manpower he needed to put into action the final part of Vitali Zalenkov's plan. He now knew how the abduction of Alexei would take place: (a tipsy Chloe Andropov would talk to any half way decent looking young male if he bought her sparkling wine and complimented her on her appearance) Whether her claims about being spied upon by agents of her husband were true he did not know; what he did know was that as soon as Vitali had paid him money he had mentally identified the uncaring wife as a potential unwitting ally. He had had her watched. He had instructed the man charged with the task of keeping tabs on her to ingratiate himself with her when the moment was right. He had done this; praise and Prosecco had worked wonders. He had discovered she had access to her husband's computer, which was manna from Heaven. He had made Chloe feel like a sex goddess; and she had been putty in his hands; there was nothing she would not do for such an admirer. The world he knew was filled with people who had inflated ideas about their own worth, he was just glad that Chloe was one of them.

As well as knowing from where to snatch Alexei, he also knew where he would hold him captive. The boarded up Victorian house in Ancoats that nobody wanted would make an ideal prison. In the damp cellar, where rats and cockroaches reigned supreme his unwilling "guest" would be beaten, and abused, and totally humiliated. The thought of the torture he would inflict made him smile, and when he smiled Mikel became the Devil incarnate.

When DCI Hobson arrived back at the police station the first person he bumped into was Detective Chief Superintendent Hardy who was returning from a meeting with the Deputy Chief Constable. Pleasantries were exchanged and Hardy then asked if there had been any new developments in the Karpovich and Zalenkov inquiries since they last talked. When Hobson indicated that he thought there might have been he invited Mark to join him in his office to update him fully on the latest state of play.

In Mr Hardy's office Mark recounted his meeting with Chloe Andropov."

"She would be a nightmare witness in court. I don't think for a moment that a jury would believe she had much credibility, but I've got a gut feeling that quite a lot of what she told me does have a basis in fact. She'd been drinking of course, and her descriptions of the man who had been watching her were all over the place; at times it was as if she was describing at least two different people."

"Maybe she was" murmured Hardy; "have you thought about that possibility Mark?"

"I have Sir" said Mark, "and I queried that with her, but she was adamant that that wasn't the case; and to be honest if she was being spied upon it would make more sense for one person to do it to get the best idea of her routines, if she had any, but it is possible that the task was split between two persons for one reason or another."

"Or that for reasons we don't know more than one person was interested in her movements" suggested Hardy; "I don't think that's likely but let's keep all options open at this stage; but none of this is evidence of a breakthrough, and you seemed very excited about something when we spoke to each other downstairs in the foyer."

"I am Sir" replied Hobson. "I now know that Chloe was able to access her husband's E-mails, and thus was aware to some extent of his future plans. I also know, because she gloated about this, that she had access to Anastasia's E-mails, but more than that she actually sent out poisonous E-mails in Anastasia's name to one particular individual. We don't yet know who that individual was, but I think for the first time we can maybe see a motive for her murder; and that in my view is a major step in the right direction."

"I think it is Mark" agreed Hardy, "I really think it is."

His boss was grinning when he entered the CID office. Detective Sergeant Bennett smiled when he saw him come into the room; in a few minutes, after he had imparted the news he had to give he felt sure the grin on DCI Hobson's face would grow to epic proportions.

"You're looking pretty pleased with yourself Gov" he said, "but I suppose spending time with the "delectable" Chloe is good for the soul." The grin turned into a grimace.

"She's a cow Pete, as you very well know, and would try the patience of a saint; time spent with her is purgatory, but at least today I think the experience has been worthwhile"; and the DCI then shared with his DS the information he had already divulged to Detective Chief Superintendent Hardy.

"That's bloody good news" said Bennett: "if Chloe wrote some really hurtful stuff in the name of Anastasia then it's easy to see how a grieving man's mind could be filled with hatred: and whilst we're talking good news I've got a bit more of the stuff which I think will make your day"; and DS Bennett then told his boss about the positive DNA result.

"We've got the bastard" exclaimed Hobson! "Leonid Petrov was at Moor Top Grange; he won't be able to wriggle out of this; and now we know he was there we can ask GMP what they have on file about any of his known associates; if we're lucky they may come up with a few names and photographs, and then there's a chance that Natasha may recognise someone from the pictures as the man who locked her inside a burning building. Our top priority has to be to contact them and update them with this development. Get on to it straight away will you Peter. If Leonid Petrov is in a police cell by tonight I'll crack open the champagne. I bet a pound to a penny that in the end, when facing decades in gaol he'll whistle like a canary to try and shave a few years off his sentence."

"I'm on it Gov" replied Bennett, and then he left the room, to make a very important phone call.

Less than ten minutes later he was back; the air of optimism had disappeared; Hobson could tell immediately that the news was not going to be good.

"What's the matter Pete" he asked; "you look like a man who has just lost a million bucks; tell me why this dramatic change of mood?"

"It's Petrov Gov" responded Bennett. "We won't be interviewing him any time soon; his body was found last night in a back alley in Manchester; he'd been shot four times. Unless we can communicate with him using a Ouija board, we won't be getting any useful information out of him."

CHAPTER THIRTY ONE

An effective way to skin a cat, expletives and expletives, a high status vehicle and one fit only for the crusher; and setting out on an "adventure".

Alexei Andropov allowed himself a moment of self-congratulation. At long last he could see a glimmer of hope. He wanted nothing more than to be rid of his wife; he had wanted that from the moment they were married; in truth he had never wanted her at all; nor had he wanted the son she had born him; but he had definitely wanted her money, or more accurately some of her father's money to which she had access. She had turned out to be his financial saviour and the destroyer of his day to day life. Even in the eyes of Alexei, a man with no moral compass, her behaviour was routinely appalling. Every day he wished she would go away for the sake of his sanity; but she never did. The pre-nuptial agreement her overbearing, pompous father had forced him to sign as a condition of giving him money meant that he couldn't walk away from her otherwise he would lose everything ; but if she bailed out of the union then that was a different matter.

Several years ago, when she had been at her most annoying, and he had had a passion for the beautiful creature he had lusted after for more than a decade he had devised a permanent solution to his problem, but the intervention, by chance, of a roving police car had put an abrupt end to his scheme, and for a while he had fretted that he would find himself in police custody. The villains he had employed, whose trade was death had remained silent; but at a cost. They were banged to rights for the murder of a drug dealer; they would serve long sentences; they could not benefit from his cash directly, but they insisted members of their families should receive substantial and totally unmerited windfalls. Because of this near catastrophe he had never sanctioned another attempt on his partner's life: and for the moment at least, with the death of Anastasia, and the dramatic events at Moor Top Grange, the time was not right to try again; but he had thought of another way to persuade the dreadful Chloe to flee the nest. He had hired an unscrupulous private detective to spy on her and to make a record of all the places she most liked visiting, and where she felt most at home. That list was now complete. The next step was to spread vile rumours about his "better half" and to make sure that these were both credible and widely known. He had also got the detective to secretly film his wife when she was making a fool of herself. Very soon he was convinced, when her antics were made public, she would become persona non grata at every place she wanted to be. Even Chloe could feel despair, he knew that was true, he had seen evidence of that when their son was put up for adoption. She would at some stage tell him to "go to Hell" and run home to daddy, and when that happened that was job done. She would have walked out on him, and he would not have broken the terms of the detested pre-nuptial agreement. He believed that to some degree his plan was already working. He knew that she was jittery, that the fear that something nasty might happen to her was already affecting her behaviour. Sergei, his loyal informer had told him about the state she was in when she cut short her afternoon out and arrived home in a taxi. He had let him know every little detail. She had called out the police, that wasn't good; he didn't like detectives visiting his home, but in this instance it had its merits. The pressure was getting to her. If she was vilified in places where she felt safe, and ostracised by the people she wanted to be with that would unsettle her still further. If she was publicly harangued when she was out; if her car was vandalised when it was left unattended; scratched with keys, daubed with sickening graffiti, or smeared with human excrement that would bring home the message that the world hated her, and that only a place far away from her usual haunts was safe. All of these things could be arranged; and although it would be suspected that he was behind these occurrences; and that his behaviour amounted to harassment or constructive desertion he would ensure that nothing could ever be proved.

As the English sometimes weirdly exclaimed "there was more than one way to skin a cat"; and Alexei was sure that he had found a very inventive one. His thoughts turned to his schedule for today; it was going to be a busy one; the highlight would be lunch with a high-profile Premier League footballer at an exclusive restaurant in the centre of Manchester. He toyed with the idea of getting Boris to chauffeur him to the venue but decided against it; Boris would be better employed doing other things. He would drive himself; this was primarily a business meeting; he had to keep his wits about him so he would not be drinking heavily; if he took himself to the venue he had complete freedom to decide when to leave, and where to go next; there wouldn't be any tiresome waiting about; he could do anything he wanted to do after the meeting was over without having to rely on anybody else.

The string of expletives that fell from Hobson's lips would have made a fishwife blush; if Helena had been present she would have taken him to task for using such bad language, but she would also have understood his anger and his frustration. Had the positive DNA result come just one day earlier there would have been a good chance that Petrov could have been arrested before Fate armed with a handgun had decided to play his deadly little end game.

"It's a crap discovery" agreed DS Bennett; his own reaction when he heard the news had made Hobson's outburst sound like sophisticated chatter at a vicarage tea party; but he had now calmed down; "but all may not be lost Gov; who knows what GMP may find when they search Petrov's flat?"

"They're not going to find a letter saying *"Dear Mr Petrov, Please will you go to Moor Top Grange in Derbyshire, burn the stable block to the ground and then kill the beautiful 18 year old girl who lives at that address. I will make it very much worth your while. Yours most sincerely* followed by a clear and unequivocal signature are they Pete? I doubt if they will find anything at all to link Petrov with any other individual."

"Perhaps not" agreed Bennett, "but they might find other things. They could find the firearm that killed the dogs at the Grange, or maybe some ammunition identical to the bullets which were recovered from there; they might discover bank statements which show hefty payments into a bank account; and if he has a lap top there could be interesting E-mails on it; something decent could still turn up."

"I wish I had your optimism Pete" responded Hobson despondently, "but you could be right; it's still early days. I suppose he could have slipped up somewhere; and if he has we have to make damn sure we discover how that was."

The car was sleek and stylish, and it oozed class. His first thought had been to take the bright red Porsche which he loved to drive, but as the meeting he was about to attend was at a large city centre hotel where bankers, and lawyers, and company chief executives held working lunches he had decided that the top of the range BMW which he had recently purchased was a better choice for the job in hand. It was a performance vehicle in its own right, but it was also spacious and comfortable to travel in; and it had all the technology any man in his right mind could ever wish for. Above all of this however it screamed of wealth and power; only the richest of people could afford a vehicle of this quality. He climbed into the driver's seat, switched on the ignition, and the car purred into life; as soon as the roads were wide enough he would make it roar; the thought of the power he would unleash made him smile: the kid from Minsk had done well; very, very well indeed.

Only two more bends lay ahead followed by a narrow but straight stretch of road and then he could turn onto an A road. Mentally he was already putting his foot hard down on the accelerator then, as he exited the last corner, he saw in front of him a dirty off-white coloured Transit van; it was crawling forward at the pace of a comatose snail, It was belching smoke, and fit only for the crusher. The driver was clearly struggling to keep it moving; then it juddered to a halt blocking the carriageway. Twenty yards further on was a field gateway; if it could make that distance it could pull partially off the roadway; and Alexei and his BMW could squeeze past--- just. It had to be obvious to the cretin driving the vehicle that this was the thing to do. Loudly he sounded the BMW's horn. There was no response. Alexei sounded the horn again, louder and more stridently than on the first occasion, but again nothing happened. The brain dead idiot in the driver's seat didn't do a thing: some people did not have an ounce of common sense. Realising that sounding the horn alone would not achieve anything; and brimming over with frustration and annoyance Alexei jumped out of the car and strode angrily to the van to remonstrate with the driver. He gestured for him to wind his window down; the driver seemed to be in a daze and did nothing. Perhaps he was drunk, or drugged up on some illegal substance, or maybe he had had a stroke; none of this mattered; all he had to do was move the sodding vehicle a few feet then he could stay where he was until he rotted. With his temper now at boiling point Alexei yanked open the driver's door. It was at that moment that he felt the gun prodding him in the back. He had not heard the rear door of the van open; he had not seen the big man with a firearm climb out of the vehicle; and he had not anticipated that the van driver would suddenly leap into life and smash his fist hard into his face. One second he was standing up ready for confrontation with a buffoon; the next minute he was laid flat on his back, his face covered in blood, a heavy boot pressing down upon his chest, and a gun pointing threateningly at his temple.

He was in a state of shock, gripped by a blind panic. His initial thought was that he was being robbed; his first impulse was to scream "take the car, take my wallet, but for the love of God please don't hurt me anymore;" but when he uttered his first sound the foot exerted even greater pressure on his body. The pain was unbearable; any second now he was sure that his ribs would crack under the strain; the strangled plea became a cry of anguish.

"Shut the fuck up" his assailant bellowed at him; "now listen carefully to me. In just a minute I'm going to take a step back. When I do get off your arse and stand up; and don't even think about trying to run away; because if you do you'll have no fucking kneecaps left" and to emphasise the point he waved the gun in front of Alexei's face.

Terrified he did as he was told. When he was upright a third man who had appeared out of nowhere grabbed his arms and forced them behind his back; a cable tie was placed around them, and drawn so tight it cut into his wrists. Unable to control himself he cried out in pain; his hair was grabbed; his head was pulled back; a piece of rag was rammed into his mouth; the smell and the sticky texture of the cloth made him want to vomit.

"That's what you get for being a twat" said the man unsympathetically as he bent down to wrap a second cable tie around his ankle. Trussed up like a chicken in a butcher's shop he was now helpless; movement was impossible; bodily he was lifted into the air and then thrown into the back of the van like a sack of potatoes.

"You're going on a bit of an adventure now Mate" announced one of his captors; "have a good trip", and the vehicle started to move without any of the apparent difficulties it had exhibited before.

After it had set off, two of the men who had been left behind, pleased with their success, climbed into the BMW and followed the van down the road. This luxury car was part of their reward for a job well done. By the end of the afternoon it would already be inside a shipping container hidden beneath bags of unwanted clothing; by the end of the evening the container would be on the quayside awaiting loading on to a ship bound for Southern Africa. A lot of money would soon change hands; the lion's share would go to Mikel, but four figure sums would filter down to the men at the coal face. Not a penny would be deducted from Vitali's bill; this car was a perk of the job, and not anything that the men who had carried it out felt he had any right to have a share in.

CHAPTER THIRTY TWO

A beautiful dress, a fistful of banknotes, a collection of names and photographs, and a terrifying journey finally comes to an end.

"You look absolutely gorgeous Helena; the dress is beautiful; it's so elegant: if I was the bride I wouldn't let you anywhere near the wedding ceremony; every eye will be on you; I'd be green with jealousy; I'd see to it that you were locked away in a dark room until the ceremony was over. Every woman in the place will be thinking secretly *I wish I could look like her*"; Jackie Nadin was in raptures about the appearance of her best friend who was showing her the dress she would wear in a couple of days time at the big wedding she would soon be attending.

"Oh shut up "said Helena, "you're making me blush, but the dress does look lovely doesn't it? I think it really is pretty."

"It's fabulous, it's stunning Helena; it's the nicest dress I've ever seen at a wedding, but it looks so good because the woman wearing it looks so great. Mark will think himself the luckiest guy on the planet, and the envy of every other man in the room. I just hope he steps up to the plate too."

"He will Jackie" laughed Helena, "I persuaded him to buy a new jacket and trousers from John Lewis's; he moaned about the price, but secretly I think he's very pleased; and before you ask, Lucy and the boys will look fantastic too. When we were in John Lewis's I bought a really nice silver photograph frame. I'm going to make sure that we have several pictures taken of us as a family, and the best one of them will go into that frame which will then have pride of place on the mantelpiece for everyone to see."

"That's the stuff Girl" said Jackie; "I'd do exactly the same thing; it will be a lovely memory of a fabulous day; and a record of how the kids once looked when they start dressing like punks and dyeing their hair purple in a few years time" and she and Helena collapsed into a fit of giggles at the thought of Christopher, Lucy and David doing a pretty decent impression of the Sex Pistols when the years of teenage rebellion kicked in.

"No gun, no bullets, no bank statements, no E-mails," Detective Sergeant Peter Bennett was reporting back to his boss the bad tidings, but despite the search for all these items drawing a complete blank the detective sergeant was in a surprisingly upbeat mood.

"So none of the things you speculated might be found in Petrov's apartment were there then Pete; I would have expected you to slink into here with a face like a wet Monday afternoon yet you are almost annoyingly chipper my friend; so come on, spill the beans; tell me why you've still got that big grin on your face?"

"Twelve thousand pounds in cash", responded the DS; "mainly £20 notes, some are brand new, some are used notes. GMP haven't yet had a result, but they feel there is a good chance fingerprints may be found on some of the bank notes they have recovered. The used notes may be problematic because they are likely to have been handled by many individuals, but the new notes could be a different story; we need to get lucky only once and it could become a whole new ball game."

"I think we'd need more than just one print to persuade the CPS that that was sufficient evidence that one individual had given the whole bundle of notes to Petrov" said Hobson, "but this could be significant I agree with you there. The twelve thousand pounds does surprise me a bit though; I would have thought Petrov would have demanded a lot more than that to do what he did."

"Maybe he did Gov" replied Bennett; "he could well have squirreled away a large amount of cash in some bank account, or stashed some away in a secret hiding place a long way from his bedroom; and if Greater Manchester Police keep looking they may find it. This could just be money he wanted easy access to. GMP told me that he was an inveterate gambler;

perhaps this cash was simply his kitty to fund his visits to the casino."

"Maybe" murmured Hobson, "maybe; we'll have to wait and see what GMP come up with; but you're still grinning like a Cheshire Cat Pete; is there something else I need to know?"

"There is Gov. During the conversation I had about the money I was also given a list of names of Petrov's associates: and literally moments before I came to see you I received an E-mail with a number of photographs attached to it. A couple of them are a bit ropey, but most are pretty clear. I think that there is a good chance that if one of them is of the man who locked Natasha inside the stable she will be able to recognise him."

"Now that is good news exclaimed Hobson; "that is very good news indeed."

The inside of the van was filthy and it stank, of what Alexei couldn't tell; it was an oily, chemical, disgusting smell, a bit like rotting domestic waste. Never in his life had he felt so wretched. He was terrified that at any moment he would be sick and that he would choke on his own vomit because the dirty rag still tightly wedged inside his mouth meant that nothing that rose from his stomach could be expelled through his lips. What germs were impregnated in that nasty piece of cloth he had no means of knowing, what debilitating sickness might lie ahead he could only guess. Half an hour ago the world would have looked upon a rich man in his Armani suit and envied him but the world would not envy the pathetic specimen of humanity he had become. His suit, which had cost more than a luxury holiday for four in the Caribbean, was covered in grease and grime and fit only for the refuse bin; dried blood was caked upon his face; his wrists were horribly swollen; and every time the van went over a bump his head banged against the side of the vehicle. Alexei suspected that the driver was doing everything he could to make the journey as uncomfortable as it could possibly be; and in that assumption he was entirely correct; the driver made sure he never missed a pothole, and that he always threw the vehicle into every bend that he came to.

The concept of time disappeared; already Alexei felt that he had been a prisoner for decades; the nightmare journey he was on seemed endless: he wanted it to cease, but at the same time he was dreading what would happen to him when it did. The one thing that was certain was it would not be good; the dampness between his legs was symptomatic of how much he feared what the outcome might be.

The speed of travel of the van gradually changed; forward motion was less fluid; there was more stopping and starting, probably caused by traffic lights changing to red; and more ninety degree turns indicative that the vehicle was weaving its way through side streets to reach its intended destination. The background traffic noise was less obvious too; perhaps a sign that it had entered an area where few motorists chose to drive; and then suddenly the Transit came to an abrupt halt. Voices could now be heard outside, loud rough voices, sometimes uttering crude obscenities; then all of a sudden, light flooded into the vehicle.

"Let's get the cunt out of here" he heard one man shout; "and let's be quick about it, we don't want any nosey bastard clocking what we're doing. I'll get the front door unlocked then you two can drag him out of the van and straight into the house, the sooner the sad fucker is inside the better it will be for us all."

A large man with an unshaven face and an overall scruffy appearance climbed into the van. He grabbed Alexei's feet and dragged him as if he was a rolled up carpet towards the back door; his head scraped along the floor; the man could have been removing a dead pig from the back of a knackers' wagon for all the concern he showed for his prisoner. At that moment Alexei would have given his entire fortune to be rendered unconscious and to remain in a state of suspended animation until this nightmare was over, but his brain kept screaming at him that this could never be.

He was yanked out of the vehicle. For a moment he feared that his head would be allowed to hit the roadway with a sickening thud and that he would suffer a fractured skull from the impact, but just when he thought that this was about to happen, and the trickle of urine in his pants had become a flood, another pair of hands grabbed his shirt collar, and he was carried horizontally into a dark and dingy Victorian house.

The place smelled of damp, it was obvious that no one had lived in this crumbling edifice for a considerable period of time.

"Get him on his feet and into the sodding cellar" said the man who appeared to be in charge, "and don't stand for any nonsense; if he's the least bit difficult then kick him down the sodding steps."

"Will do" said one of the other men; "and if he tries to piss me about my foot will hit his arse so fast that he'll think he's been struck by an Exocet missile."

The cable ties were removed from his legs and arms, and he was permitted to pull the horrid piece of rag from his mouth. Even though the air was stale he breathed in deeply; to be able to inhale and exhale without impediment was such a relief; he opened his mouth to speak but the big man shook his head.

"Not a fucking sound" he ordered. "You'll talk when I say you can talk and not before; now get down them fucking stairs straight away; your luxury apartment awaits you below"

The steps down into the cellar were narrow and uneven, and the smell of damp grew even stronger; you wouldn't keep a dog down there, let alone a human being but he couldn't argue for fear of physical violence; in abject misery he descended into the depths below.

At the foot of the stairs the main cellar was home to assorted bits of rusty metal and broken pieces of furniture long since abandoned to the woodlice and cockroaches that had made them their home, but there was a smaller room with a substantial door secured by a hasp and padlock. It was into this cellar that Alexei was directed. It was dimly illuminated by a battery powered lantern, and it contained a rickety chair, an uncomfortable looking camp bed and a bucket.

"This is your home now Mate" laughed the big man; "until you end up a guest of Her Majesty in a high security gaol. Make the most of it. We'll give you a little time to settle in and then we'll come and play a few games with you. Something to look forward to eh?" and the door was banged shut leaving Alexei alone with time to think; not surprisingly all of his thoughts were bad.

CHAPTER THIRTY THREE

A cryptic message, an assortment of villains, a grinning Macaque, and recognising the face of a would-be killer

The cryptic message left on Vitali's voice mail said simply "it is done"; it did not specify what the "it" was; it didn't need to; those three little words told him that the man he most hated in the world was now in the hands of his employee; for the first time in days he felt a sense of exhilaration. Soon the piece by piece destruction of his enemy would begin. The person who ultimately the police would arrest for a grave crime he had not committed would be nothing like the arrogant, boastful, untouchable human being they had encountered before. Broken and humiliated he might try to protest his innocence, but he would not impress. A jury would judge him to be a hypocrite, a charlatan, a man attempting to attract their pity, but it would not work. If Mikel did his job well, if he was meticulous in laying a false trail of evidence that lead straight back to Alexei there would be no escape for him. Convicted of procuring the murder of a whole family there would be no mercy. The judge would condemn him in the strongest possible terms; a whole life sentence would be guaranteed. How the mighty would have fallen. Vitali allowed himself a rare smile. Over the next few days he expected to receive reports of Alexei's mental and physical deterioration from his captors, and to see on video tape his anguish and hear his cries of pain. It was pay-back time. The man who had caused so much damage at his home, and such harm to his lovely daughter would now suffer in return; and that, reasoned Vitali, was exactly how it should be.

"They're a motley crew Gov. Petrov certainly knew how to pick his friends; low life from near and far; a Serbian deadbeat, a thug from Belarus, a drug dealer from Afghanistan; and various home grown villains from Greater Manchester. All of them have got form; none of them have got any redeeming features; and taken all in all they are the sort of people who give the underworld a very bad name" Detective Sergeant Peter Bennett then read out the list of names and descriptions Derbyshire Police had been given by the Greater Manchester force.

"As you say not an Archangel Gabriel amongst them" commented Hobson; "I reckon that we have some likely candidates here. Natasha told us her assailant had a deep voice, and an accent that didn't sound local. Whether she meant local to the Peak District or local to the UK I don't know. I don't think it's likely that he had a markedly foreign accent, so any potential suspect who isn't fluent in English is probably a non-starter; but someone speaking pure Manc, or English with only a trace of accent is a very different story. It may well become clearer if I am able to visit her this afternoon. If she can point a finger at any particular individual then hopefully by tonight we may have somebody in custody."

"That's what we thought might happen with Petrov" said DS Bennett a little warily "I don't think lightening can strike twice in the same place, but you never know."

"Don't depress me Pete "groaned Hobson; "let's take it step by step. Will you contact the hospital to see if I can visit Natasha this afternoon; and if I can then I'll give her dad a ring just to keep him fully in the picture."

It might have been an hour; it might have been a lifetime since he had been left alone to wonder about his fate; and many times during that period he had thought he had heard footsteps on the stairs and he had been consumed by fear, only for the sound to fade away to nothing, but this time there was no doubt. Heavy boots slammed down upon stone steps and then crunched across the cellar floor to his prison cell. Any second now the men who had abducted him would enter the room and then his torment would begin. What they had in mind for him he would soon discover. They had left him to stew in his own fear; they had told him that when they returned they would play games with him. In a very real sense they had already started to do so. The time he had been left alone had been time to imagine what those games would be; and terrible thought after terrible thought had already attacked his sanity. Now the waiting was over. The door to the cell was flung open, and two ugly, callous, brutal men, grinning like Barberry apes entered the room; one of them was carrying a length of rope and a cordless drill; the other held in his hands a state of the art Smart phone and a notebook and pen. Alexei backed away from them in mortal dread; if the cellar walls had been less robust they might have crumbled under the pressure he exerted upon them in his panic, but the brickwork held firm; there was nowhere he could go.

The man with the drill and the rope placed them down upon the bed, took two steps towards him, then he seized him roughly by the arms and dragged him back into the centre of the room. Even though he was a big man his struggles were futile; his assailant was built like an ox. Alexei found himself being forced down onto the chair, and with the confidence of somebody who had done this many times before the man lashed his arms and legs to the seat. He could still squirm, he could still wriggle, he could still shake with fear; but that was all he could do. He could not raise a hand to protect his face, he could not scrunch himself up into a ball to shield his stomach from a blow; every part of him was vulnerable. The smiling Macaque looked down upon his prisoner.

"Cheer up Alexei" he said, "It's going to be a fun evening. Let the games begin."

"Yes. There should be no problem in you visiting Natasha later on today. The usual caveats apply. She is still in a very depressed and vulnerable state so you can't stay with her for too long; and if she starts to find the experience upsetting the doctor will require you to bring the interview to a close. If she wants to have her father or a nurse present that should be allowed, and the request is that you treat her as gently as you possibly can" Detective Sergeant Bennett was explaining to his boss the result of his phone call to the hospital.

"Understood Pete" replied Hobson, "I'll treat her with kid gloves. Can you go and put the photographs and descriptions into an easy to use pack for me to take with me; while you do that I'll telephone Vitali to keep him in the picture and let him know that if he wants to sit in with his daughter that is perfectly OK by me."

And DCI Hobson was as good as his word; and so a couple of hours later, taking with him the pack of photographs and descriptions DS Bennett had prepared for him the detective chief inspector set off on his journey to meet Natasha. He felt full of optimism. Providing he could keep the girl relaxed, providing he could keep her mind on the job in hand rather than focussing on the wicked events which were the reason for his visit; and providing Vitali, or some well-intentioned nurse, didn't throw an unintended spanner in the works he was hopeful that he might come away with a result. If he did he would know a would-be murderer's name, he would know his face, and very soon thereafter he could hope to meet with that man in person, and the process of bringing him to justice would begin.

When he arrived at the hospital he was permitted to go straight to a small room where Natasha and her dad were already present. She looked anxious and unhappy, and the extent of her injuries was clearly visible, but perhaps she was a little less fragile than she had seemed before. Mark tried to put her at her ease. He explained that all she needed to do was to look at each photograph he showed her carefully to see if she could recognise the man who had first alerted her to the fire in the stable. As gently as he could he asked her not to think about the horror of that evening but instead simply try to recall everything she could about his face. Vitali also urged his daughter to close her mind to what had been done, and remember only the man's appearance; and so, with the support of her father, Natasha started to examine the photographs that were placed before her. She took her time, which was exactly what was needed, and she shook her head when examining the first three images. When she looked at the fourth photograph she visibly shuddered; the colour drained from her face; her hand started to shake; Hobson was sure she was holding in her hand the likeness of the man who had tried to murder her. She let it slip to the floor with a cry "It's him, it's him!" and then she started to sob. He had his man. Quietly the DCI thanked the beautiful but damaged young woman for her invaluable assistance. He thought it better not to mention at this time that at some stage in the near future she might have to view a video identity parade, but before he left the hospital he did inform Vitali that this was a distinct possibility and to seek his support if this course of action did become necessary. The next step though was now clear. Josef Kosygin. A twenty eight year old bouncer from Wythenshawe, known to be a member of one of the notorious Moss Side gangs; with a reputation for violence, but surprisingly few criminal convictions would soon be getting an unwelcome visit from the police. Hobson didn't imagine for one second that when the heavy hand of the law landed on his shoulder he would have a "mea culpa" moment and confess his sins; vehement denials or stony silence would be his response to police questioning; at least in the beginning; but maybe later, possibly much later, as the police case developed that situation could change. All in all though he felt satisfied; things had turned out about as well as he could possibly have hoped

CHAPTER THIRTY FOUR

The rules of the game, pin cushions and dentistry, two heart-warming letters, a change of plan, and a frustrating vanishing act

"We're going to play a little game of "fact or fib", the oversized ape was enjoying himself; he was smiling the most disconcerting smile Alexei had ever seen, and he kept pressing the on switch on the cordless drill, only for a few seconds at a time, but the noise it emitted when it burst into life made Alexei shake with fear.

"The rules of the game are very simple" added his laughing tormentor; "I will ask you a series of questions. If you answer truthfully my friend will note down what you say in his little book and you can add your signature when we untie you to confirm that that is a fact; but if you tell a lie nothing will be noted down on paper and instead you will have to pay a forfeit: can you guess what that forfeit might be?" and he activated the drill again, this time letting it run for a good ten seconds before switching it off again.

"Now let's start with something easy. Is your name Alexei Andropov, and are you a dishonest cunt from Belarus who is as bent as a nine bob note?"

Alexei did not reply, but instinctively shook his head in response to the question. The drill exploded into life and the grinning colossus grabbed a handful of his hair with one hand, pulled his head back, and then held the whirling drill bit a millimetre away from his cheek.

"Wrong response Alexei", he said; "silence isn't a fucking option, so I will ask you again, are you Alexei Andropov the dishonest cunt from Belarus, and this time I need an answer otherwise I will have to start turning your body into a fucking pin cushion. Now speak up and give me a proper response."

"I am "shrieked Alexei, "I am; just keep that drill away from me; I'll answer any question you want to ask."

"Wise move my friend, wise move," laughed his inquisitor, "but that was a simple question to deal with. Now I am going to ask you some more detailed questions, and to them I'm going to need some very detailed answers. If I think you are telling me the whole truth I won't need to practice my needlework, but if I think you are trying to bullshit me, or fob me off with a load of rubbish then you know what to expect. I may even have to try my hand at dentistry, which could be fun; and for the second time in only a few minutes he held the rotating drill bit close to Alexei's face, but this time he motioned as if he was about to jab it into his expensively whitened immaculately presented teeth, and he kept up this charade for nearly a minute before finally tiring of his little game and letting the drill fall silent. Alexei had thought that after his "accident" when he was dragged from the van his body had been totally drained of piss; the last sixty seconds proved conclusively that he was wrong.

"Oh you are a messy person" chided his gaoler, as if he was talking to an incontinent three year old; "if your friends in high places could see you now, what would they think?" and he, and his unprepossessing companion succumbed to a bout of unsympathetic laughter.

"But enough of this hilarity" chortled his mate, after a few minutes of mirth, "we need to be cracking on" and he suggested to his power tool wielding associate that perhaps cross-examination of the prisoner might begin with an attempt to discover what dealings he had had with a man found dead in a back alley with four bullets in his body.

The envelope was a little bigger than a standard letter size. The handwriting on the front of it was neat and clear; the sort of script the GPO; would wholeheartedly approve of; Vitali did not know anyone who wrote in such a fashion. It was a personal letter, obviously not junk mail, and it was addressed to him. He opened it with a degree of interest. Inside the envelope he discovered a carefully crafted epistle, and also a second envelope addressed to Natasha; the writing on this envelope was in a different, less confident hand. He perused the letter that had been addressed to him. He was surprised to discover it had been written by Helena Hobson: he was deeply moved by what she said. The letter read as follows:-

Dear Vitali,

I hope you don't mind me writing to you at this time; you have so much on your plate to think about at the moment, but I wanted to let you know that you and Natasha are forever in our thoughts and prayers. The news I get from my husband Mark is that Natasha is slowly recovering from her ordeal, but that she is still very shaken by the terrible events that happened at the Grange. I am writing to tell you that the way she feels at the moment is only natural. Years ago I was injured when a car bomb exploded near me killing my boss, and injuring me in the blast. When I lay on my hospital bed I thought my life was over; I was frightened that I would bear the scars of that dreadful day forever; and that even if my physical health could be restored, my mental health would never recover. I was wrong. My injuries, which were similar in scale to those of Natasha's gradually healed; and my fear about the future turned out to be unfounded. I met my husband, I fell in love, and I have been blessed with a wonderful life thereafter. I am sure the same will be true of Natasha. She is young, and clever, and beautiful. She has a great future ahead of her, of that I have no doubt. She is loved by you, and by the people who know her best. My story is not unique; thousands of young women I am sure have similar tales to tell. Give her the hope she needs and she will succeed; and please let her know that Lucy and I, and many, many other people are wishing her well.

Please Vitali hang on to this belief, because it is true. If ever you feel like wavering call me at any time. I will always be frank with you, but you must believe in a better tomorrow.

The card inside this letter has been made by Lucy for Natasha. Once upon a time children would have used crayons and watercolours to create a "Get Well" card but these days they just copy and paste; but the desire to do it was all hers, and the words inside the card are all her own. I think there is a simplicity and an honesty about them that will make Natasha laugh; and the promise of a copy of the wedding video and a piece of wedding cake may bring a smile to her lips.

As I said at the beginning of this letter we are all thinking about you. If you ever need to talk, or you think that there is anything I can do for you please don't hesitate to call me.
With all my love and best wishes,
Helena

He turned his attention to the card intended for Natasha. The envelope wasn't sealed. Carefully he opened it; she would certainly show him it when she received it so he felt that no harm could be done by glancing at it now. The picture on the front of the card was of a pretty girl in a field of Spring flowers under a brilliant blue sky with a few cotton wool clouds. When he looked at the message inside it he was filled with emotion. Lucy had written very simply:-

Dear Natasha,
I hope you are feeling better. I cried when I heard about what had happened to you. I think about you a lot. I wish you could be with me on Saturday. Mum and Dad tell me I will look lovely, and that everything will be great, but I worry that I will drop my flowers or trip over my own feet. I'm sure I wouldn't feel that way if you were watching me. Where we are going to be is a beautiful place, and according to my dad the weather is going to be brilliant. I will send you a video of the ceremony, even if I fall flat on my face, which I won't; and I will send you a little piece of wedding cake too.
Please keep getting better and better,
Love and XXXXX
Lucy

Two letters, two beautiful letters from a mother and her daughter. There was love, and compassion, and decency. These were good people who wanted to help a fellow human being. Any man who was planning to see them dead was a monster; and yet this was the outcome he had paid an unscrupulous man a fortune to bring about. A feeling of self-revulsion overwhelmed Vitali: he could not be responsible for such a tragedy. It was not too late to put an end to his grotesque plan. There had to be a better way to take revenge on Alexei. Perhaps cold-blooded murder of his enemy could suffice; it would not give him the long lifetime of misery he had wanted to secure for him, but maybe, if the terror he suffered in his final moments was extreme that could be enough. Vitali decided that in order to be able to live with his conscience, which was already tainted by guilt, he would issue new instructions to Mikel and save two people who cared about the welfare of others from a violent end.

The hunt for Josef Kosygin had begun. Officers from Greater Manchester Police had attended his home address but had discovered the house empty. He appeared to have gone away. None of his neighbours could assist; they claimed to know nothing about his movements; this might be true; but it was equally possible that someone possessed detailed knowledge of his plans, but if that was the case nobody was letting on to the police; a strict code of silence would be adhered to at all times.

A low key visit to the club where Kosygin worked as a bouncer was equally unproductive. He, it was claimed, had not been seen for two days; and other places where he was known to frequent had similar, deeply frustrating results. The man was obviously lying low. Detailed descriptions and photographs of him were passed to other police forces across the UK, with particular care being taken to ensure ports and airports were fully in the picture. The man was tagged as a violent criminal who was wanted for questioning in respect of crimes of arson and attempted murder. Unless he had already fled the country he would surface somewhere at some time; but time was a commodity that Detective Chief Inspector Mark Hobson did not have in abundance.

"We need a quick result on this one Pete" he said despondently to his long-serving detective sergeant; "once we've got the bastard in custody we can make headway, but until that time we are largely treading water. We owe it to Vitali Zalenkov and his daughter to get this case sorted quickly; what Kosygin did to Natasha is appalling. I want to see him locked up Pete; I want to see him locked up as soon as is humanly possible."

"We all do "responded Detective Sergeant Bennett; "we're all of us singing from the same hymn sheet."

CHAPTER THIRTY FIVE

Squealing like a stuck pig, turning love into loathing, thoughts of being in the limelight; and some very sensible advice

"Six puncture wounds to date, three hours of harmless fun for the lads, page after page of confessions, enough screaming to fill two horror movies, a bucket full of piss, and we haven't really started on the job yet;" Mikel was informing Vitali about the interesting conversations his hired thugs were having with the wretched Alexei.

"We've got some hilarious footage of him crying like a baby after he'd wet himself" he added; "if the movers and shakers he liked to cultivate could see him in the state that he's in now they would be appalled. He's ain't cool Mr Big who could arrange anything anymore; instead they would discover that that a man who thought himself invincible is just a pathetic cringing spineless nobody."

This was exactly what Vitali wanted to hear. It had been his intention to tell Mikel as soon as he called him, that mass murder of the innocents at a stately home was no longer on the agenda, and to risk being on the receiving end of many unflattering comments, but for the moment that could wait; he was agog to learn all about Alexei's ordeal. There would be time soon enough to announce the change of plan, and risk a lashing from Mikel's acerbic tongue, although he supposed that having received a shed load of money to carry out a dangerous task which was no longer required; would sweeten the pill as all that cash would now be pocketed without him having to do anything at all at the wedding venue. For the moment though all that mattered was listening to a description of Alexei's disintegration.

"So what has the clown admitted so far" he asked?

"Tons and tons of stuff" laughed Mikel. He's told the lads exactly what he thinks of you, and it ain't complimentary; he's used words like "cretin" and "arsehole", and a "total waste of space". He claims that you and he go back a very long way and his hatred for you is deep rooted. He blames you for the untimely death of a young woman who was living under his roof until she went missing. He thinks you may have arranged to have her killed. You didn't pay someone a few quid to have her bumped off did you?" and Mikel laughed out loud clearly regarding this suggestion as ridiculous.

"No I fucking didn't "retorted Vitali angrily; "but if the prat chooses to think that it's fine by me; but he'll pay for his stupidity; but rather than repeating his deluded rants, tell me instead what he has admitted about his own unsavoury activities."

"Well when the drill pricked his abdomen for the first time he squealed like a stuck pig. My "honest labourers" thought it was a fucking hoot; they couldn't wait to tickle him again with the bit; but by this time, he was spouting out so much stuff about himself they were hard pushed to note down everything he said; so while the flood of information spewed from his lips they restrained for the moment the urge they had to titivate him further; although every time they hit an arid interlude they gleefully tormented him again "

"So what precisely did he reveal about himself" asked Vitali; "I need details not wishy washy generalisations. I need to hear about evidence that could stand up in court if ever there was a criminal trial; so stop pussyfooting about; give me chapter and verse so that if I choose to I can hang the bastard in the court of public opinion if I elect to go down that route."

"Well he told us about a nasty little cunt called Petrov. He was found dead in a back alley in Manchester less than two days ago; he'd been shot a close range; and it couldn't have happened to a nicer bloke. Well the police have evidence that this man was present at your house on the night it was set on fire; and they believe he was the person who organised the attack. Don't ask me how I know that; let's just say I have my sources. Alexei has already confirmed to us that he paid Petrov to do what he did; and he has given us details of how and when that payment was made. If he ever comes to court charged with masterminding the whole venture these details will be sufficient to convict him out of hand; even if any confession he has made is ruled inadmissible because of coercion."

"I knew it, I fucking knew it" snarled Vitali; "he'll suffer for what he did to my daughter; I swear to God that that will be the case; but for now has he said anything else about his activities that I need to know?"

"Enough to fill a three volume novel that would make *War and Peace* look like a short story" responded Mikel; "you'll see it all down on paper when we've done with him. There's a lot more still to come out; but here's one little titbit of information that you might find interesting at this stage."

"And what is that" asked Vitali.

"Well we already knew that his wife had access to some of his E-mails" said Mikel; "but what we didn't know until an hour or so ago was that he knew that too. She thought he'd mistakenly dropped a notebook with his passwords in it, but it seems that was a deliberate ploy on his part. He wanted her to see some of the stuff he'd written about her; it was all part of a plan to unsettle her. If she thought some sort of nasty surprise was in the pipeline then she might just piss of back home to Daddy, which was exactly what he wanted. All his sensitive stuff was password protected on another computer which she didn't know he had; she had no chance of discovering any really damaging stuff about him: but there was another thing she didn't know too. He had access to her computer and could read the E-mails that she had been sending out. In particular he read some pretty horrible stuff she had sending to someone in Belarus pretending to be the woman who was his house guest; gloating over a tragedy that had hit his family; the thing is though, he thought that by his standard these E-mails were pretty tame so he sent follow up e-mails pretending to be the same female; and some of these were quite brutal. If the poor sod who received them had ever had any feelings for this girl they would have been obliterated. The power of the written word eh Vitali? Love turned to loathing; passion to unbearable pain. He is a devious bastard is Alexei; a fucking Grade A, top of the pile, devious bastard.

"So only two more days to go before you and Lucy strut your stuff in front of the world's media, or perhaps just a few dozen people with Smart phones and digital cameras; are you both ready for your moment of fame;" Jackie Nadin was teasing her friend about the posh wedding in which both Helena and her daughter had important roles to play?

"We're both going to "seize the day" laughed her best mate; "we will no doubt both be worn out by the time bedtime comes; all those autographs to sign, all those pictures to pose for; we can't wait to see the headlines in *Hello;* and then overcome by a fit of giggles she poked Jackie in the ribs and called her an "idiot."

"But we are ready" she added "Lucy is really excited about the prospect; it's a bit like Christmas Eve in our house at the moment; she can't wait for Saturday to come: I just hope she won't be disappointed."

"She won't" said Jackie; "trust me it will be great; you'll both be sensational; but what about Mark and the boys, how do they feel at the moment?"

"Well I think Christopher believes it's a lot of fuss over nothing; but he's hoping that there will be lots of girls at the disco, and that the music won't all be "golden oldies"; and he's told his mates that he's going to get rat-arsed; which we won't let him do of course; although a glass of champagne and a half of shandy might be on the cards if he behaves himself. David will be David and will play on his I-Pad for as long as we allow him to do so; which won't be for that long let me add."

"What about Mark" inquired Jackie, "how does he feel at the moment?"

"Well all his focus is on this wretched attempted murder case which he's investigating at the moment" answered Helena, "but I think for twenty four hours or so it will be a release for him to be caught up in the razzmatazz of a joyous wedding rather than wading through a swamp which is the nature of his everyday work. Nice food, a gorgeous bedchamber, and maybe even a bit of Hollywood romance for one night might make him feel like a new man; I hope it will Jackie because just at the moment he looks so tired, and so burdened down by events."

"It will do Helena, it will do; he'll be prancing round like a peacock so proud of you and the kids; he'll be grinning from ear to ear the whole time while he's at the hotel; and why wouldn't he? He's got a fabulous wife, three fabulous children, lots of happy, normal people to relate to; and for one weekend at least not a villain to be seen. He'll be in his element Kid, I've no doubt about that; his absolute Utopian element."

"Not much good news on Kosygin yet Gov", Detective Sergeant Peter Bennett was updating Mark Hobson on the limited progress that had been made in trying to locate the man Natasha Zalenkov had identified as her attacker. "He was picked up on a CCTV camera at Manchester Piccadilly, and we think he probably got on the train to London, but that's by no means certain; there is no clear evidence that in fact he did so; he could just as well boarded another train waiting to depart the station. It was rush hour at the time and the station was jam packed with people; Kosygin disappeared into the crowd; I think he's good at doing that. He'll break cover at some time; I've no doubt about that; but when and where it will be only time will tell."

"And time is something as I have said many times before that we haven't got Pete" said Hobson morosely. We can't just sit around waiting for him to make a mistake; we have to force the issue; there must be something we can do to ferret him out of hiding."

"Like what Gov?" replied the DS "If you've got a plan that's brilliant; but I've no idea at all what might work."

"I haven't Pete, well not yet. I think I might have the germ of an idea but that's all, and the more I try to rationalise it the more I struggle to put flesh upon the bone. I could do with time on my own to clarify my thoughts without any distractions, but I'm not going to get any of that over the next few days. I have seriously thought about staying at home this weekend, but if I do I'll be letting Helena and the kids down; and I don't want to do that; it wouldn't be fair on them."

"It wouldn't" agreed Peter Bennett; "and it wouldn't work either. You'd be thinking about them the whole time and feeling that you'd spoiled everything for them. You need a break Gov; and you never know; if you unwind and let yourself go over the weekend, at a moment when you, least expect it, a flash of inspiration may come. Taking a step back is probably the best thing you can do. Don't think about work while you're away then come back refreshed. Make the most of being at a swanky hotel; let your hair hang down; be self-indulgent; and then return on Monday a new man. Make it a weekend to remember; that's my advice. Weddings like the one you're going to don't come round very often. Make the most of it; create some happy memories for Helena and the kids. They'll do you proud; make sure you do the same for them; you'll think about this weekend for years to come, so commit yourself fully to the tasks of eating, drinking, and being merry."

"I will Pete" responded Hobson; "and you're right of course, but I'm glad you didn't use the whole quotation when advising me."

"How do you mean" asked Detective Sergeant Bennett looking perplexed?

"The full quotation is "eat, drink, and be merry, for tomorrow we die" laughed Hobson, "but I can assure you that isn't going to happen, although a bad head and an overstuffed belly can't be ruled out of the equation.

CHAPTER THIRTY SIX

Rage boiling like molten metal, a re-instated plan, creating a piece of misleading evidence, and what to do with a broken man

So now he knew: straight from the lips of the man he hated most in the world: Alexei Andropov had been responsible for the destruction of two of the only three women he had ever loved. The fact that he had paid a butcher to wreak havoc at his home and heap terror and pain onto his daughter was old news, but to hear it confirmed; albeit second hand; from Alexei's own mouth in his mind now totally vindicated the savage reprisal he had already initiated against his enemy. What was new: what was terrible; was the discovery that Andropov had sent out vile, cruel, taunting e-mails which purported to come from the sweetest of girls. Nobody could have received those e-mails without being filled with an overwhelming hatred for the sender, and a desire for savage redress. An innocent young woman who he had once loved long ago in another life time had suffered as a result; destroyed by the malign words of a cunning, malevolent snake. The rage inside Vitali now boiled like molten metal in an iron foundry. These lies, these terrible, potent, despicable lies had led to homicide; a few hours of torture was no penalty for such an outrage: a lifetime of anguish had to be the only answer: why should Alexei escape with any less punishment, particularly as he also now had a lifetime of regret to cope with. In the course of just one conversation the world had changed again; the terrible plan he had devised to incriminate Alexei in the grotesque murder of an innocent, and intensely likeable family was back on the table. The words he had planned to say Mikel to explain his change of heart would remain unspoken; instead he would interrogate him forcefully to ensure everything was indeed ready for carnage to be unleashed, and that there would be an irrefutable body of evidence to prove that Alexei Andropov had been the puppet master who had pulled the strings of the ruthless hired assassin who had actually fired the bullets.

For some inexplicable reason, at this moment the face of his long dead wife, the mother Natasha had never known, appeared before his eyes. With her he could have been happy, but Fate had decreed that that was not to be. He could see sadness in her eyes, and sensed her strong disapproval, but she did not know the man he was dealing with. He imagined how different his life might have been if she had not died in childbirth; but then irrationally he started to believe that at some time, in some way, Andropov would have injured her too. He was a carnivore, a pitiless destroyer of happiness; he would never have allowed her to lead a good life with him. Reality and imagination melded together into a nightmare vision of what the future might have held for his wife if she had lived. Alexei the predator had to be destroyed, and if he had to become a monster to achieve that end then that was the way it had to be.

The dialogue he had just had with Vitali had surprised him. Despite the fact that he had been paid a fortune in cash to bring about an appalling and horrific finale to a joyous event he had thought it likely that at the eleventh hour the man who had instructed him to unleash terror at a time of happiness as part of his grotesque plan to destroy his Nemesis would get cold feet and bring the whole sick scheme to a juddering halt. That hadn't happened. Mikel believed that at the beginning of the telephone conversation he had detected signs of hesitancy, but as it had continued these had faded, and by the time it had come to an end all doubt had disappeared. His "client" he could tell was totally committed to his despicable venture and his only interest now was to go over every detail of the plan to ensure its success. The reason for this change of mood seemed obvious. The more he had learned about Alexei Andropov's unsavoury antics the more incensed he had become.

And a good thing too thought Mikel. His testosterone levels were already on the rise. He thrived on the danger of an assignment; the thought of the havoc he would soon unleash was giving him an orgasmic buzz. To steal into the lion's den, to commit terrible acts of slaughter in front of a large crowd of onlookers, then to slip away unseen was mind blowing. Things didn't get much better than that; and when a successful outcome was obtained his reputation would soar. In his particular field nobody in the world would be ranked more highly. He would be the person the incredibly rich would seek out if they wanted rid of somebody they viewed as an encumbrance, or a rival, or an obstacle to future wealth and power.

What needed to be done now was to fit the final pieces of the jigsaw into place. The very next, and most important, task he had to complete was to pay a visit to the hired muscle who were having such a good time extracting information from the wretched Alexei. When he was with them, and face to face with the shipwreck of a man they had created, he would instruct his henchmen to unbind their prisoner's right arm, and when they had done this he would order the pitiful specimen of humanity to pick up, and handle a small piece of white card, and then, a few seconds later, to take up a pen, and in his own hand write upon it his mobile phone number, and below that the following few words:-

Call me when it is done

That was all that was required. This small, insignificant piece of cardboard would be fundamental to the success of Vitali Zalenkov's deranged plan to see Alexei Andropov framed for murder. It would be the foundation stone upon which the prosecution case would be constructed. Taken at face value as a genuine document, and with Andropov's fingerprints all over it; and with words of instruction written upon it in his own hand there could surely be no doubt that he was the man who had incited a cold-blooded killer to carry out an unspeakable crime. Mikel had taken care at all times when he handled the card to wear gloves, and this would continue to be the case; he would make damn sure his bare hand never grasped the card; there would be zero chance that his fingerprints would be found upon it; but as for Alexei's fingerprints, that would be another matter. Microscopic examination would show he had held it in his hands. Irrefutable evidence would be obtained by the police to establish that the mobile phone number scrawled upon it related to his cell phone; and no doubt handwriting experts would confidently assert that it was his hand that had written the cryptic message that it bore. All Mikel had to do was to ensure this card was found in the bedroom from within which a deadly attack had been staged. It had to look as if it had been inadvertently dropped by the assassin before he departed the bedchamber which meant that it shouldn't be so obvious that it couldn't have been overlooked by the murderer but not so well concealed that it might be missed by the police. Mikel knew it would need careful thought to select the right spot; he also knew that he would take as long as was necessary to work out where that spot was.

Another thing he now needed to do was get rid of the monogrammed water glass and the fliers and leaflets he had removed from Summerford Hall on the occasion of his one and only visit there. He had taken these things so that if need be they too could have been handled by Alexei and then, if returned to the hotel, they could be taken as evidence that he had actually been in the bedroom at the time of the shooting, but he had thought better of this plan. Although the hotel would be packed with guests, so any individual might easily pass unnoticed it would not help the prosecution case if not a single member of the hotel staff could identify Alexei as being present; the police might also think it bizarre that having paid a hit man to do his dirty work he had risked all by wanting to witness firsthand the actions of his despicable killer. The more likely thing anyone who had initiated Armageddon would want to do would be to be as far away as possible from the scene of the crime, and to ensure he was with people who could give him an absolute watertight alibi.

There was one more thing Mikel needed to ponder upon. After the murders had been committed Vitali wanted Andropov to be dumped somewhere where the police would easily find him. A telephone tip off to direct them to the place where Britain's most wanted man; for surely in the eyes of the police and the general public that is what he would have become; could be found would be all that was needed; but the man they discovered would be quite unlike the person they had dealt with before. It would be obvious from his physical and mental state that he had been tortured; and much as he would be reviled, the police would certainly try to discover at whose hands he had suffered. Alexei would be asked to describe his assailants, and be questioned about why he thought he had been mistreated in the way that he had. He would certainly name Vitali, and the police would no doubt want to question him about this allegation. Mikel figured that this could be a problem. Vitali would deny all knowledge of course; and his denials would probably be accepted at face value; but might it be preferable if Andropov simply disappeared without trace. Mikel thought this would be a better outcome. He decided that he would try to convince Vitali that this was the safer bet; if he failed to do this he might have to take into his own hands the decision as to what happened next; a long unhappy life for Alexei might not be on the cards after all.

CHAPTER THIRTY SEVEN

Planning a journey, visiting a prisoner, uncovering depravity, and a life hanging by a thread

"So when are you actually setting off Gov?" Detective Sergeant Peter Bennett was chatting with his boss about his plans for the weekend.

"Well, we plan to leave home soon after nine o'clock but that depends on getting Christopher out of bed, chivvying David to get his skates on, and bringing Lucy down from Cloud Nine and back onto Planet Earth; but if all goes well we should be on the road shortly after ten. It will only take about an hour to get to the venue. The wedding isn't until three o'clock so we will have plenty of time to grab some lunch and get changed before it starts. Helena and Lucy are fully prepared; there was a proper wedding rehearsal a week ago; the weather looks set fair, and providing the groom condescends to turn up, and the bride doesn't have a hissy fit it should be all systems go; if everything runs according to plan it will be a right good do."

"And does Helena agree with your timetable? My wife would be up at 5am and prodding me with a cattle prod to be out of the house by six. She's paranoid about being late for anything; it drives me bloody batty. Most of the time it doesn't make a scrap of difference if you're a few minutes late. I keep telling her take your time and calm down, but does she listen to me; she runs around like a headless chicken; I could be talking to a brick wall for all the attention she gives me."

"That's the story of your life Pete" laughed Hobson, "but no Helena's fine with the plan. She'll keep everything on track, and do so with a smile upon her face."

"I guessed as much" replied Bennett; "you're a lucky guy Gov. They broke the mould when they made Helena; beauty and brains, a rare combination; how a gnarled old copper like you could drop so lucky simply beggars belief."

"Less of the old Pete" responded Hobson, "but I take your point; there isn't a day goes by that I don't ask myself the same question."

It was a good job that the walls of Alexei's underground prison were thick otherwise his cries of pain and pleas for mercy might have reached the ears of passers-by on the street but they were strong and robust, so not a sound could be heard outside the house. Mikel had chosen well; clear thought and careful planning that was the key. Do your homework: think before you act: never be complacent: these were the maxims of Mikel, and so far they had always held him in good stead.

When he descended the stairway to the cellar it was a different story. The door to Alexei's cell although well made and in good condition could not confine the prisoner's moans and weeping to the interior of the room. Mikel smiled; good work was being done; his henchmen deserved a bonus for their dedication to the task in hand; Mikel decided that he would give them one.

When he entered the room the sight that met his eyes gladdened his heart. Alexei's shirt was in tatters, and his upper body was pock-marked with lots of small circular superficial wounds, and some of these were still seeping a little blood. It was clear he had been put through the wringer; he was whimpering like an abused animal, and his trousers were wet with urine and stained with faeces. A photograph to record his sorry state was very definitely required; and Mikel would see to it that one was taken; *a valuable keepsake for Vitali* he thought, *and one that he will happily pay good money for.*

The moment he stepped into the cell his chief lieutenant switched off his cordless drill and immediately began to update his employer.

"We're just about done" he said with a degree of satisfaction. " I'll give you a full run down of everything this clown has admitted when we go upstairs , but let me tell you now he has been a busy little bunny:- fraud, prostitution, drugs, incitement to murder; he's had his grubby paws in all sorts of nasty smelling little pies. He was Mr Fixit for all his overpaid footballing clients; he's told us a great deal about what he used to do for them. Some household names had some very kinky habits. We've got a long list of what he did for whom; the popular press would pay millions for some of the stories we've unearthed; and some of the Premier League footballers would pay just as much, or even more, to keep their nasty little habits secret.

"Good work" murmured Mikel, "very good work." Give me chapter and verse when we're done down here, but you've mentioned just now an admission of incitement to murder; tell me briefly now, what exactly did that entail.

"Well he paid a couple of Manchester villains to kidnap his wife" responded the chief inquisitor; "and the plan only failed because the police had a stroke of luck. Our little friend here is head over heels in hock to his father-in law. He hates his wife, which given her personality is not an unreasonable way to feel, but he couldn't divorce her because of a pre-nup agreement so he came up with plan B. The villains he employed were stopped en route to bring an end to her existence so it all came to nothing, although one word of this to her dad about this would bring about his financial ruin; there could be some benefit to be had in initiating a conversation with him at some stage."

"There might be" agreed Mikel, "there very well might be." He then turned to face the snivelling Alexei.

"Shut the fuck up and listen to me" he said fiercely. "In a moment or so I'm going to instruct your new best friend here to untie your arms, and when he has done that I'm going to pass you a small piece of card to hold tightly in your hand. After you have clung onto it for a bit I will give you a pen, and you my friend will then write upon it exactly what I instruct you to write. Not one word more, not one word less; and if you mess up in any way in carrying out that simple task let me warn you that what has happened to you so far will seem like a kiddies tea party compared with what happens next. Do I make myself clear? One move out of place and I'll personally tip you out of that chair and order your little playmates here to kick the crap out of you. Do you understand what I am saying toe rag?" Alexei nodded his head; he clearly understood that he was in the presence of evil, and that everything that had happened to him so far would be as nothing if he failed to comply with the orders his sadistic gaoler had just given him.

And the threat worked. Mikel took out from his pocket a pair of surgical gloves, pulled them onto his hands, and then he reached inside his jacket to remove a piece of white card. Had he been in a state of mind to think clearly Alexei would certainly have wondered why he had done this; but in his present state of mind the significance of this action was lost to him. He was however able to take the card when it was thrust at him, and even though his hand was shaking, he managed to write upon it everything he was ordered to jot down.

After he had done this Mikel mockingly thanked him for his cooperation and patted him on the head like a grandfather praising a favourite grandchild; and for the moment his torment was over. The Spanish Inquisition trooped out of the room, laughing and joking as they went leaving Alexei alone to fret about what the future might be, or even if he had any future at all.

A Premier League footballer, earning as much in a week as the Prime Minister earned in a year, had a perverted obsession with pre-pubescent girls, preferably ones with naturally blonde hair and wide staring eyes. He didn't have intercourse with them; that would have been too straight forward; he got his kicks out of them rubbing his naked body with richly scented lotions and then masturbating him until he came. When he did he would wipe his sperm onto their innocent cheeks, and then suck his fingers until they were no longer sticky. The tabloid press would love that story; Mikel decided that the readers of these worthy newspapers should not be denied their titillation.

Another household name from the sports pages, deified by his adoring fans for his goal scoring prowess snorted Cocaine by the ton; and a third sporting icon took sadistic pleasure in heaping humiliation and mid-level violence on "ladies of the night." All of this and more Alexei had disclosed under robust cross-examination. A lot of money was there for the taking; and Mikel and his henchmen were not about to spurn a golden opportunity.

And there was more too that had been uncovered. Details of payments received from clients for services rendered were now known; and payments made to other people by Alexei to do his dirty work for him had also been revealed. The amount he had handed over to two thugs to commit arson and attempted murder at Moor Top Grange was mind blowing, but it was still much less than the price Mikel had demanded for his professional help: this transaction he decided had better remain a closely guarded secret. If Vitali learned he could have saved a six figure sum had he looked elsewhere he might become disgruntled; and a disgruntled person might voice his discontent, which would not be to anyone's benefit: it was better; far far better; for him to be kept totally in the dark about this discovery.

Another thing that was strictly off limits so far as Vitali was concerned was the option Mikel was considering of going against one of the key elements of his plan. A long, miserable lifetime of being mistreated and reviled, that was the outcome Vitali wanted for Alexei; no relief from constant abuse, no respite from fear; no escape from universal contempt: if instead he simply slipped into an unmarked grave, even if a stack of "evidence" was left behind to prove that he was a monster whose name would be forever synonymous with evil; it would defeat the fundamental raison d'etre of the enterprise. Vitali would be incandescent, and would do everything in his power to brand his chosen Lord High Executioner as a charlatan and a rogue. He might be cowed into silence by threats of exposure, or more potently by a fear that his daughter would pay a heavy price for his anger, but he might not be. It could all become very messy and horrible, and necessitate extreme measures to bring the issue to a final end. Mikel did not like mess. Unusually for him he was still, undecided about what to do for the best. Perhaps after he had completed his task at Summerford Hall the answer would become clearer. For the moment he would put the final decision on hold, but at the same time he would prepare a contingency plan that could be used at once if circumstances decreed that the immediate eradication of Alexei was the best solution to this ethical dilemma.

One thing that was not a dilemma however was the knowledge that as soon as he left the dungeon where Alexei's life hung by a thread he had to visit the talented and morally bankrupt expert who was making for him the master card he needed to enter any bedroom he might select on the second floor of Summerford Hall. When he had this card all the nuts and bolts would be in place; he would have everything to hand he needed to summarily end the lives of five members of a loving family; and by doing so make headline news around the entire world.

CHAPTER THIRTY EIGHT

Two suitcases are packed, a villain is sighted, a bad movie causes a hysterical response, and keeping cool under difficult circumstances

It was late in the afternoon and in two very different bedrooms two very different people who had never met but whose lives were inextricably linked were packing suitcases. One was blissfully unaware of the connection, completely ignorant of the malign thread that drew them close together; the other knew every minute detail of a scheme that would end in tragedy; both were smiling as they busied themselves with their tasks.

Helena Hobson was carefully placing into a case the clothes that she and her daughter would wear the following day. Expertly she folded the dresses she and Lucy would reveal at the wedding. They were lovely; Jackie Nadin had been right when she called them "gorgeous;" it was imperative that she treated them with the utmost care. She had already partly filled the case with the other garments she and Lucy would need for their weekend away. Mark would sort out his own clothes. His new jacket and trousers were on a suit hanger; this would be placed on top of the other luggage in the boot of the car immediately before they set off. She had also packed overnight bags for Christopher and David, ensuring that nothing essential was left behind; given the very relaxed, not to say cavalier, attitude of her two sons towards the coming weekend this was a very sensible precaution.

The man currently using the name Mikel was also taking great care, although in his case he had only himself to think about. His suitcase was smaller than Helena's, but it was big enough to contain all the tools of his trade- the disassembled rifle, the telescopic sight, and the ammunition that would make the weapon become an implement of death. There was also a small handgun that he always took with him on every job he undertook, just in case things went badly wrong and he had to fight his way out of a building to avoid capture. So far he had never needed to use this; all of these things were concealed under a false bottom in the case. Into the main body of the case he tossed a pair of jeans, two pullovers and a shirt, as well as socks, pants and a few toiletries so that in the unlikely event of anybody demanding to see inside the case it would look at first glance like the luggage of a man planning a short break away from home. Secreted inside his jacket was the small piece of card Alexei had written on; this worthless scrap of paper had a value that was incalculable; without it nothing would connect Alexei to the ghastly murders soon to take place; with it, if he chose to stick to Vitali's plan, a dramatic arrest, a Crown Court trial, and a guilty verdict were assured. If Mikel had been a philosopher he might have mused upon the ironies of life, but he was not Plato or Aristotle, he was instead a demi-god, a being who whilst he couldn't create life could extinguish it with one tiny movement of his finger. He might never be loved but he would always be feared, and that was good enough for him. The knowledge that his very presence in a room could cause terror was a powerful aphrodisiac; he lived for the moment other people cringed; he thrilled for the moment other people died. Should that ever not be the case what would the point of existence be? He had already decided that if age or infirmity threatened to destroy his ability to cause fear he would bring a dramatic end to his own life, but he would ensure that he took many people with him on that fateful day.

"We've had a bit of a development so far as Josef Kosygin is concerned Gov", Peter Bennett was acquainting DCI Hobson with some news hot off the press. "He was picked up on a CCTV camera in Coventry last night, which means he's definitely still in the UK and that he isn't hunkering down. He wandered into an Indian takeaway shortly after 8 pm, large as life, and apparently not worried about being seen out on the street. The local police are now on high alert. The next time our elusive friend is in need of sustenance there is a good chance he might be seen going about his business, and one of Lady

Godiva's merry bunch of law enforcers may get to lift a much sought after collar."

"That's good news" replied Hobson, "But until that happens we're still struggling to make progress. Let me know the minute we hear anything concrete Pete, apart from an hour or so tomorrow when the happy couple will be exchanging their vows, my mobile will always be on; I want to be kept up to speed on this one. If need be I'll gladly cut short my stay at the hotel tomorrow night if that gives me the opportunity to question Kosygin face to face."

"And leave your ravishing wife totally neglected for the whole of the evening" retorted DS Bennett; "you must be mad Gov; a few hours here or there isn't vital. We've had this conversation before. Take twenty four hours off; we can cope; the world won't stop turning if you're not here, but the shine will be taken off tomorrow for Helena and Lucy and the lads if you suddenly up sticks and disappear "

"I suppose you're right" replied Hobson somewhat chastened; "maybe it is better if that for this weekend I stop being a copper for a few hours and just go with the flow."

"It is Gov" agreed DS Bennett; "Let your hair down, have a good time, weddings like the one you are going to don't come along very often."

Chloe Andropov was relaxing in a comfy chair watching daytime television: on the table next to her were a half eaten box of Lindor chocolates and two small bottles of sparkling wine, one of which was now empty. She was enjoying being alone in the house; she was glad Alexei was nowhere to be seen. For the last couple of days she had had the freedom to wander where she pleased and to do what she wanted to do, which had included entry into his inner sanctum and prying into his personal possessions. In the back of her mind she had hoped perhaps to find another notebook, or gain some other insight into his off-limits private life, but in that she had been unsuccessful; never-the-less to do things which he would have profoundly disapproved of had been fun. She wished he would stay away for a long time.

The only fly in the ointment was that she had no idea when he would chose to return, so while she had been doing those things he would not have allowed her to do she had been on tenterhooks, ready to drop everything at a moment's notice and scurry back to her own room to keep out of harm's way. She also did have some concerns about what he was actually doing while he was away, and whether in some way or another it might affect her; she didn't think this was likely, but it was possible; and if Alexei was thinking about her she was sure that his thoughts would not be well motivated.

The low budget soap opera she was watching about the fictional lives of doctors and nurses came to an end. Lazily Chloe flicked through the channels to find something else to her taste. She settled upon an American crime drama in which all the leading actors had bronzed well-toned bodies and glittering white teeth; and if truth be told; very limited acting ability; weirdly though Chloe found herself being dragged into the movie.

The plot was a simple one. It involved a man who unbeknown to his wife had a mistress with whom he had become infatuated. Early into the story he tenderly kissed his wife as if she was the most precious person on the planet and then he left for work after telling her that he had to go away for a few days on a business trip. As soon as he has left the house he begins to plan for himself an alibi so that if he was ever required to account for his movements at a particular time he could call upon several honest witnesses to confirm his presence at an event many miles away from the family home. With all the pieces in place, when the time is right, he plans to slip away from the event unnoticed and return to his abode; and with cold-blooded ferocity murder his wife with a carving knife.

Despite the hackneyed nature of the plot Chloe was engrossed. At the moment when the victim was stabbed to death she screamed out in terror. In her mind the figures on the TV screen had become real; the victim now had her face, and the knife wielding psychopath was Alexei. The glass of wine she was holding fell from her grasp. She started to shake uncontrollably. Was this an omen? Was this a warning about what her future life might be? She needed help. Frantically she searched through her handbag to find the piece of card detective Chief Inspector Hobson had given her with a phone number written on it, and in a state of blind panic telephoned Derbyshire Constabulary.

She seemed brighter and not as tense, possibly because her injuries were beginning to heal and she felt less pain, but perhaps also because for the first time she could sense a better tomorrow. Vitali was pleased to see the improvement. He wondered why her mood had changed; everything about her treatment remained the same, there was no new medication, no difference in the hospital regime, no change of doctors or nurses to account for Natasha's new found sense of optimism.
Tenderly he held her hand and asked her how she was, and when she smiled at him and said that she felt a little better, gently he inquired why that might be.
"It's this Dad" she replied, reaching into the drawer of her bedside cabinet and removing a pretty get well card. It came today. It's from Lucy. You remember her Dad she came to see the foal with her mum. She's sent me a few nice cards since I've been here, but this one is the nicest, and there was quite a long note included with it. She's so excited about this wedding that she's going to, and she wants to share some of that joy with me, which is lovely. The thought that a young girl who I hardly know really cares about me enough to include me in her happiness is wonderful. It makes me realize that the world isn't all bad, and that the men who came to our home and tried to end my life aren't representative of it. They're evil Dad, and there is a lot of evil in the world, but there is so much love there too. I'm so pleased Lucy and her family are going to have such a wonderful day tomorrow. She's promised to come and visit me next week to tell me all about it, and to tell the truth I can't wait for that day to come.

The telephone on Detective Sergeant Bennett's desk rang with the stridency of a toddler having a tantrum; it would not be ignored. The DS had been on the point of slipping out of the office to grab a bite to eat so he was not best pleased by the interruption. In less than high good humour he picked up the receiver. It was the switchboard. "Could he take a call for DCI Hobson" they inquired; "he's engaged on another call, and the woman who wants to speak to him says that it's mega urgent. She sounds half cut and verging on the hysterical. She keeps rabbiting on about seeing her own face on the television, and she's got some wild idea into her head that somebody is plotting to kill her"; so it was Peter Bennett was landed with a twenty minutes conversation with the ever affable Chloe Andropov. She was at her most infuriating. It was all Bennett could do not to be rude to her, but somehow he kept his cool and listened to the rambling saga Chloe related to him. He noted down what she said, and promised he would acquaint DCI Hobson of the fact just as soon as he was able to do so; he also counselled her to be on her guard, and to ring 999 if at any time she felt physically threatened.

After the call was over he made his way to the DCI's office.

"You owe me a pint Gov, if not a bottle of whiskey. I just come off the phone with Chloe Andropov. She was pixilated as per usual and spouting a lot of mumbo jumbo about a plot to kill her, which I think is bullshit; but amidst all the crap something interesting slipped out."

"And what was that?" asked Hobson.

"Well she said that Alexei ducked out under the radar a couple of days ago and she thinks he's up to something really bad; she's got no proof of course, but I think there may be something in what she fears."

"I do too Pete "murmured his boss, "I really, really do."

CHAPTER THIRTY NINE

A perfect day to celebrate and to kill, the wrong time to wish "happy birthday", a change of heart, and a possible three options

For once in a blue moon the Met Office's mid-range forecast had turned out to be correct. Mark Hobson's assertion that the weather for the big day would be great, based on their prediction, and which he had expressed more in hope than in expectation, was turning out to be entirely accurate. It was unseasonably warm; the sky was the colour of a South Sea lagoon, with just a few cotton wool clouds to add contrast to the picture. The air was fresh and clean; had the bride and groom been able to pick the weather for their perfect day they could not have chosen better: the lawns at Summerford Hall were lush and green; the deciduous trees still retained their leaves, although the first hues of autumn were now visible adding colour and beauty to the landscape. There were many places in the world where the scenery was more dramatic *but none* thought Mark *that has a more benign, more gentle feeling than here* .Being with his beautiful wife and his three kids made his spirits soar. Just for today and tomorrow he was resolved first and foremost to be a husband and father; the demands of his day job were locked away in the deepest recesses of his mind.

Helena felt the same emotions too.

"It's a beautiful day Mark" she said. "I'm so glad; Lizzie and Richard will be so pleased; it would have been such a pity if everything had had to take place indoors. If it keeps like this the photographs will be amazing. What a day it's going to be; what memories are going to be created; what smiles there will be on everyone's faces."

"And the biggest smile of all will be on Lucy's face when she walks with you behind the bride; and the second biggest smile will be on your face when you look at your beautiful daughter."

"No, no, that's not right Dad" interrupted Lucy with a grin. "The biggest smile will be on your face when you look at Mum and me. You won't be able to help yourself; you'll be like a cat with a barrel full of cream."

"Which he'll probably drizzle all down his chin" interjected Christopher. "You're turning this into a fairy tale Lucy. You ain't Cinderella, Mum ain't the Fairy God Mother, and Dad ain't Baron Hardup, even if sometimes he tries to look like he is. It's a bog standard wedding Lucy, it ain't that special; I can't see what you're getting so excited about."

"It is to me" hissed Lucy, "you're just cheesed off because you're not out playing football today."

"Ssshh both of you" said Helena gently; "it is special Christopher; it's special to Lucy and to me. It's going to be so much fun, so no more bickering, let's all just enjoy the moment and have a really great time. I guarantee that if we all just relax and go with the flow we will all of us have a weekend to remember."

Unknown to Helena, roughly forty miles away there was another person who was sure he was about to experience an unforgettable weekend. He was ready. His case was packed. Every action he intended to commit was firmly implanted in his brain. Fate could not have been kinder; there was nothing on the horizon that could cause him the slightest difficulty. The day was set fair, there was zero chance of rain, or mist, or fog; the breeze was gentle and embracing; no disruptive gust of wind might cause sudden and disruptive movement. It could be the easiest job he would ever do. That made him smile. There would be no slip ups, no elements to battle against, no hidden difficulties. For a man of his expertise it would be a walk in the park, a piece of cake, a doddle. Mikel reached into his pocket and took out his mobile phone. He switched it off. For the next few hours he needed to be uncontactable. Many years ago he had heard of an occasion when a killer with his finger on the trigger, and his intended victim firmly in his sights had been disturbed at the crucial moment by his mobile ringing. Not only had he missed his shot, he also for a split second revealed his position; the biter was bit, the hunter at that moment became the prey; the body guard who fired the fatal shot was not distracted by any electronic device. A murder attempt had been thwarted, a would-be assassin was no more, and all because he forgot to switch off his mobile phone, and his mother chose the most inopportune moment possible to ring her son to wish him a happy birthday.

"I can't wait for that moment to come;" the words of his daughter ricocheted around his brain like shrapnel lacerating forever his peace of mind. She was looking forward towards an event that would never happen; the joy of anticipation would be replaced by grief; and if she ever found out that the tragedy that had occurred had been procured by him Vitali knew from that moment he would be forever reviled. He might try to persuade her that a heinous crime had been born out of eternal love, and that if he had cared less he might not have been overwhelmed by an all-embracing, irresistible desire for revenge.

"But Lucy was innocent Dad" he could hear Natasha saying, "as were her mum and dad and her two brothers. You're a lunatic Dad, a psychopath, a monster. Get out of my sight. You've ruined my life. I will forever be tainted by your guilt. I never want to look at you, or talk to you or think of you again." He could try to convince himself that she would never find out, but no matter how deeply it was suppressed Truth generally found a way. *What had he been thinking of?* He had to stop the slaughter before it commenced. Alexei would have to be punished in another way. He could insist that he died a slow and grotesquely painful death, that would have to suffice; and maybe reports of his anguish as every bone in his body was smashed to fragments, and acid and boiling water turned his skin to pulp would one day be enough to make him believe that justice had been done.

All that was in the future however; right now it was imperative to let Mikel know that the plan had been irrevocably scrapped, that the innocent must live, and that only the wretched Alexei should feel the full power of his rage. He looked at his watch. Mikel might well be en-route to the venue;

he could even already be concealed in his hideaway with his weapon poised. There was not a moment to lose. He pulled out his mobile and dialled the number he had for Mikel; it was unattainable. Over the next twenty minutes he tried a dozen times to get a connection; the result was always the same; on every occasion he failed to do so.

His mind was in a whirl. If he could have thought clearly he would have told himself to get a grip, that he only had three possible choices and that he must select one of them.

Option one was to do nothing. Option one was to close his eyes, put his fingers in his ears, and repeat over and over to himself the lyrics of some banal pop song in the hope that this would dull his senses and drive the fear that terrified him from his mind. He knew this would fail; option one was in reality not an option at all.

Option two was much more realistic: an anonymous telephone call to the police to inform them that some sort of terrorist action would take place today at Summerford Hall. This might well work but it was fraught with hidden dangers. He knew that sometimes terrorists would use a key word known to the police to prove that a phone call was not a hoax. He had no such word to rely upon. Without it he might not be taken seriously; his call could be dismissed as the ravings of an antisocial moron intent on wasting police time. He would also almost certainly be quizzed about where his information had come from, and the call-handler would surely want to glean as much personal information as he or she could possibly ascertain. He would stay silent on that score, of course he would, but the police would without doubt try to trace the call, and with the technology they had at their disposal they could well be successful; and if they were that spelt disaster.

Even if everything was accepted at face value, and the police ordered the abandonment of the wedding ceremony because of a terrorist threat, that outcome was not necessarily the end of the affair. If they arrived at the hotel they might just get lucky and arrest and detain Mikel. What would he do once he was in their custody; that was anybody's guess? He might well conclude that he had been betrayed by the man who had been his employer; and if he did that there was every possibility that he would reveal to detectives every last detail he knew about him, including providing them with evidence of the vast sums of money that had been paid to him. The only way Vitali could not envisage any of this happening would be if police marksmen abruptly ended Mikel's life on Earth; that was a possible outcome, but not one that could be counted upon. Vitali therefore concluded that Option Two, just like Option One, was not a choice he could possibly make.

This left Option Three, which was to climb into his car and make the journey himself to Summerford Hall. This was not something he wanted to do. If he was seen by Helena or Mark Hobson, or their daughter Lucy they would want to know why he was there, and although he could pretend somehow he was acting on Natasha's behalf, possibly by wanting to capture on his mobile phone some early photographs of the ceremony to please an impatient girl, he was not sure how his gate crashing of a private party might be viewed, particularly by the hotel management, and also by the bride and groom.

And the Hobson family were not the only people he wanted to avoid. If the hotel staff saw him prowling around the corridors looking for Mikel he might be confronted and asked to leave; and even if he wasn't his presence could be captured on the hotel's security cameras; but despite these risks this had to be his best option. If he could find Mikel and speak to him face to face before anything dramatic occurred, and if he could assuage any anger he felt by offering him additional money, and the added bonus of doing whatever he wanted to do to the wretched Alexei, it might just be enough to enable him to extricate himself from the mess he was currently in. There was no time to lose; without a moment's further hesitation Vitali leapt into his car, switched on the ignition, and with a squeal of tyres commenced his journey into the heart of rural Cheshire.

CHAPTER FORTY

A radiant wife, a beautiful daughter, a race against time, an ice-cold killer, and a motorway pile up

They had all had lunch; only really a snack because in a couple of hours time after the marriage ceremony there would be a lavish meal of five courses and nobody wanted to spoil their appetite. Christopher, David and Mark had wolfed down their sandwiches, Helena had been more gentile, and Lucy had picked absent-mindedly at her food, too excited to do it justice. Christopher had snaffled what was left on her plate. "It's a shame to see it go to waste Dad" he had said when his father gave him a disapproving look, "you always say things like "waste not, want not" I'm just following your advice" and everybody had laughed.

They were all now dressed for the wedding too. Christopher and David had taken no time at all to change into their smart clothes, and Mark had only taken a few moments longer; for Helena and Lucy however it had been a different story, but they had starring roles in the forthcoming celebration which the male members of the Hobson family didn't have.

When they emerged from their respective bedroom prior to joining the bride to assist her with her preparations they looked amazing. Mark felt so proud. Lucy was right; the biggest smile in the hotel was on her dad's face; to be the husband of such a stunning beauty as Helena, and the father of such a pretty daughter as Lucy would fill any man with pride. Even Christopher was prepared to announce that his mother and his sister looked "fab."

Inside the hotel was a hive of activity. Chairs were being wheeled outside and arranged on the lawn near to the temple. Speakers were being set up and tested to ensure that the words of the vicar conducting the ceremony and of the bride and groom would be heard by all. Many of the invited guests were now filling the lounge bar and the foyer enjoying a pre-nuptial drink, or simply chatting with long lost friends or relatives. Everybody appeared to be in high good humour; people were laughing and joking and shaking hands, and slapping each other on the back; and in some cases there were long and passionate embraces. Nobody noticed unremarkable man with a small suitcase pass through the crowded rooms and disappear up the main hotel staircase.

He was in a hurry to get there but he knew that he must do nothing rash. Speed limits needed to be adhered to, traffic lights needed to be obeyed, and when he got to the motorway lane closures and all other temporary traffic flow measures had to be complied with. To be caught on camera committing an offence might be disastrous; to be pulled over by traffic cops might be even worse. Although he was desperate to meet with Mikel he forced himself to have iron self-control; at all times his driving had to be exemplary.

This was not the case with the Polish driver of the 42 tonne articulated lorry as he bullied his way along the M56 towards Chester. He had slept badly the night before; he was knackered; he had also had a blazing row with his girlfriend in Krakov and he was eager to make amends. On the seat beside him was his mobile phone which he kept glancing at; he was desperate for her to call him so he could apologise but his phone remained depressingly silent. As he passed junction 10 he could stand the silence no longer. Traffic ahead of him had thinned; in desperation he picked up the phone and dialled her number: at almost exactly the same moment Vitali joined the motorway. The sight of traffic moving freely re-assured him; just two junctions more and he would be in striking distance of Summerford Hall; it was not yet midday, he would have enough time.

He could hear her phone ringing but his call remained unanswered; his girlfriend was obviously still furious with him. Ahead traffic was starting to build again. In frustration the Polish driver tossed his phone back onto his seat and for a few moments concentrated on the road ahead; then miracle upon miracle his phone rang; in just a second he would tell her that he had been such a fool, and that he absolutely adored her. He seized his mobile, his brain searched for the right words to say; it failed to register that traffic ahead of him had slowed to a pedestrian pace. Too late he realised the error of his ways. At 60 mph he ploughed into the back of a Transit van ramming it into the car that preceded it before it overturned and burst into flames. His trailer jack-knifed and shed its load across the carriageway. All three lanes of the motorway were now blocked. A few seconds of distraction had caused carnage, but none of this mattered to the lorry driver; he was already well beyond any place where human voices could reach him.

The master key card had worked like a dream, but he had expected nothing less. People who did jobs for Mikel knew that they had to do them right; you didn't mess up; poor or shoddy work would not be tolerated: there would be unpleasant, maybe very unpleasant consequences if you did. The man whom had cloned the card for Mikel had taken infinite care to carry out the task to the best of his considerable ability; for that he had been well rewarded, and he had the added bonus of knowing that he need not sleep uneasily in his bed overnight.

Mikel had tried out the card on the door to one of the main bedrooms; the lock had responded to it, but although he was now able to enter he did not go in; it was too early in the day to be sure that the room would be empty; a late lie-in by the room's occupant could not yet be discounted; instead he used the card to gain entry to a small bedroom at the very end of the corridor. This wasn't the room from which he planned to carry out his assignment, it offered him only a very poor view of the lake and the temple but it was currently not let as it was awaiting refurbishment following a problem with the en-suite shower; it was however an ideal place to lie low until the main events of the day were in full swing. Looking as though he did not have a care in the world Mikel settled into an armchair and closed his eyes. Now was the time to take a short nap; not one person in a thousand aware of the drama that lay ahead would have dared to have done this; but Mikel, in very many ways, was no ordinary human being.

Thirty minutes later he awoke. Now he was alert, now was the time for him to change location and move to a better vantage point. He glanced out of the bedroom window; people were beginning to stream across the lawn to make their way to their allocated seats near to the temple. Picking up his suitcase he tiptoed to the bedroom door and carefully opened it a few centimetres. He listened intently for any sign of life on the corridor, there was none, so he opened the door wider and peered outside. It was as he had thought, there was nobody about. Quickly and silently he strode down the corridor to his bedroom of choice, and without hesitation inserted the key card in the lock. The door opened immediately. Within seconds he was inside, and the door was closed behind him.He placed the suitcase containing the rifle on the bed, but before he opened it up to assemble and make ready the weapon for use he pulled from his back pocket a surgical glove which he put on before he removed the small piece of card Alexei had handled from inside his jacket. It was better to strategically place this now rather than wait until his gruesome task was complete. Once the shots were fired he would have to leave immediately; seconds could be vital; a few moments hesitation deciding where to put the card could be the difference between escape and capture. He settled on a spot a few feet away from the window through which the fatal shootings would take place and let the card fall to the floor making sure it was half hidden from view under a coffee table, but that some of it remained exposed. It would look like the card had been accidentally dropped by the assassin, and overlooked by him in his hurry to leave, but without doubt it would be noticed by eagle-eyed police officers searching the scene of a crime to find any clue that might help to uncover the identity of the perpetrator.

Now he had more important business to attend to.He checked the time on his wrist watch; it was nearly five minutes to three. The congregation were in place; every chair at the lakeside was filled. He could hear the distant babble of conversation as he unpacked, re-assembled, and loaded the rifle; at the very moment this was complete the crowd hushed and the sound of the Wedding March surged from the speakers on the lawn. He opened the sash window a few inches. He could clearly see the groom and the best man seated in front of the vicar, and glancing to his left, he saw the bride and her attendants slowly processing to the spot where the marriage ceremony would take place. She looked amazing, but not as stunning as her chief bridesmaid. Had Mikel had a soul he might have been moved; had he had a heart it might have melted, but inside was just a cash register which was already filled with tainted gold.

The groom and the best man stood up, the bride and her father took their places in front of the priest, and the ceremony commenced; before long it was complete. As it was announced that the couple were now man and wife six white doves were released into the azure sky, and the new husband leaned forward to kiss his wife. All this Mikel could see through the sight on his rifle. He was sure Vitali was wrong. If he fired a fatal shot at this moment, and blood flowed from her head the moment their lips met it would be an act of murder which would shock the whole world. His finger tightened on the trigger; then he relented. It wasn't his promise to Vitali that he would obey his instructions that held him back; he was sure he knew more about dramatic impact than his tunnel-visioned employer; it was the fact that Alexei would have no credible motive to see this woman killed whereas he did have a proven connection with Detective Chief Inspector Mark Hobson; and perhaps reasons for wanting to punish him and his family in the most terrible of ways.

For nearly three hours the motorway was at a standstill. The westbound carriageway of the M56 had been closed between Junction 10 and Junction 12. Emergency crews had dealt with the dead and injured; so far there were three fatalities and nine other people had been rushed to hospital; it was suspected that at least two of that number would not survive. The wreckage of the van and four cars had been pulled off the carriage and left on the hard shoulder. The overturned HGV still blocked the two outside lanes of the motorway but it was now cordoned off from other traffic. Debris from the lorry had been swept up; and at long last, at a snail's pace, traffic was being allowed to filter into the slow lane and continue with its journey. The accident would make national news that night. What had happened was tragic; and deeply traumatic for the people who had witnessed the event; and it could have been much worse. If the traffic ahead of the HGV had been stationary and bumper to bumper when it struck the death toll would have been much higher. One man's attempt to speak to the girl of his dreams had caused carnage, but not quite on the scale of the worst case scenario.

Throughout the period of the hold-up Vitali had kept trying to telephone Mikel, but always without success. He was tormented by his failure to do so. Several times he had started to dial 999 to warn the police of the monster loose at Summerford Hall but each time his culpability prevented him from completing the call. Now at last he was moving and he still had a tight window of time. He was only a few minutes away from the hall. If he could get there while the wedding ceremony was still in progress he could rush to the spot where the detective chief inspector and his family were grouped together and superimpose himself as a human shield. His behaviour would be seen as odd certainly, and perhaps the product of a disturbed mind, but not criminal; and it might have the desired effect. Surely Mikel would not open fire while he was present? He had to realise the dramatic intervention signalled an end to the unholy plan didn't he?

And maybe things might not come to this. It was possible that the best man might lose the ring, or the bride might have last minute nerves, or the vicar develop severe laryngitis needing a replacement to be found , in which case he would have time to search the hotel for Mikel and tell him face to face that the venture was at an end. Clinging to this hope he put his foot down and sped as quickly as he could to the wedding venue.

CHAPTER FORTY ONE

A happy bride and groom, a "frustrated" photographer, unkind jokes and games, running to save a life, blood and fear, and the arrest of a suspect

The knot had been tied, the vows had been spoken; the bride and groom were now hitched; the legal formalities had been completed; soon everyone would troop into the hotel's plush restaurant to enjoy a mouth-watering five course meal and listen to formal speeches. Mark Hobson hoped that these would not be tedious; overlong boring monologues in flat, inexpressive voices would certainly take the edge of the proceedings: fortunately, although he didn't know this, the best man was an experienced raconteur with a well-developed sense of humour, and a good number of very amusing, if somewhat risqué jokes in his repertoire: however before all this the wedding photographs needed to be taken.

Clucking like a mother hen the photographer positioned the bride and groom in front of the temple placing them exactly where he wanted them to be. He demanded so many poses. He had them side by side holding hands, then looking soulfully into each other's eyes, then laughing, and kissing, and embracing. He was good at putting people at their ease. Very few of the shots that he took would look stilted, or wooden, or excessively composed; and of course if there was the odd failure it would never see the light of day. Others were then brought into the picture, the best man, the matron of honour, the bridesmaids; and then parents, and relatives, and close friends joined the happy couple; and when these photographs had been completed an invitation was made to family groups to come and have their pictures taken on the spot where the bride and groom had stood.

"It's our turn now" Helena said to a slightly reluctant Mark; "it will only take a few minutes and then we can all go and get some food."

"About time too" murmured Christopher, but he dutifully joined his parents and his brother and sister to have his picture taken. On the second floor of the hotel a window opened silently, and a supremely confident man picked up a rifle. The hour had come; he would soon shock the world with the accuracy of his shooting.

The men "baby-sitting" Alexei were having a whale of a time. He was no longer capable of rational thought so questioning him further about his illicit activities was a pointless exercise so instead they devised little games to pass the time. When their prisoner showed signs of lapsing into a catatonic state they used different ways to shock him back into reality. A dustbin lid was banged with an iron bar just inches away from his head; and when this was done he would try to leap from the chair to which he was bound; or ice cold water was thrown into his face which made him scream. One of his tormentors called him Bear Grylls and gave him the choice of drinking his own urine, or having his testacies roasted over an open fire. They joked about castration, and gleefully listed the many acts of mutilation they could perform upon him; and they had laughed like hysterical schoolboys as the last vestiges of colour drained from his face which took on the appearance of a medieval death mask.

They did other things too. They opened a bottle of fine wine and pretended to offer him a glass, which they then poured it over his head and sniggered at his discomfort. Alexei did not think that things could get any worse than this; had he known the extremes Vitali now demanded should be his fate his brain would have imploded thinking of the brutality that was soon to be unleashed upon him.

The last five miles had been without incident. At one point it had looked as if a very large tractor towing an enormous spreader filled to the gunnels with bovine slurry was about to pull onto the road in front of him, which would have been a nightmare, but at the last moment the driver decided to do the decent thing and let him pass before it emerged onto the narrow country lane Vitali was now travelling. The clock on the dashboard of his car showed 3-15pm; the ceremony should still be in progress; if nothing now impeded his progress he might still be able to achieve the outcome he so fervently desired.

Two minutes later and he had arrived at the ornate entrance gates to Summerford Hall. Another quarter of a mile and he would be at the large car park where most of the wedding guests would have left their vehicles. From here, although he didn't know this, the lake, the island, and the temple would be clearly visible, although it would be a similar distance on foot before he would be at the spot where marriages were solemnized. Frustratingly this car park appeared to be full: Vitali squandered precious moments trying to find somewhere where he could leave his vehicle before finally spotting a place just big enough to accommodate his motor car. He pulled into the space, and breathing in deeply to make himself thinner than a Maze prisoner on hunger strike he emerged from his car and looked towards the hotel. He could see from his vantage point that the wedding was now over and that people were milling about near to the temple waiting to be photographed. He half closed his eyes to cut out the glare from the sun; although it was a long way in the distance he was sure he could see Helena: nobody else could look so stunning. He started to run; in less than one minute he could be standing next to her; and then his ears caught the faintest of sounds emerging from the hotel.

The photographer was getting a little frustrated. The first family portrait he attempted was ruined by David yawning at just the wrong moment; the second was rejected because the expression on Christopher's face suggested terminal boredom; it was now his third attempt to capture a happy family group. This time everything seemed perfect. Through the viewfinder of his camera Helena and Lucy looked radiant, and the boys and their father were relaxed and attentive too. He was just about to take the picture when Lucy screamed "It's a wasp, a wasp" as a winged insect landed on her hair. Helena moved quickly to bat the offending creature away but she never made it. Instead the photographer saw her tumble forward clutching her chest; blood was seeping through her hands as she fell to the ground; and then a second later her husband suffered a similar traumatic collapse. The three children looked shell-shocked; members of the congregation who were nearby fled, grabbing the children as they ran to take them to safety. The photographer could not believe what he had just witnessed; a mad man with a rifle was on the loose; who knew who his next target might be. It was a scene of complete pandemonium. Terrified guests were running for their lives, many of them dialling 999 on their mobiles as they raced towards the safety of the hotel. In his hideaway Mikel was frustrated; the sudden movement of Helena towards her daughter had wrecked his overall plan. Two people had been shot as he had agreed would be the case, but the three children had escaped. He had not done everything that Vitali wanted him to do, but it was probably enough. Now was not the time to ponder; now was the time to be gone. Quickly he packed away his gun and, after checking that the piece of card he had strategically placed on the floor was still there, he left the bedroom and made his escape. The corridors and the public rooms of the hotel were now filled with confused and frightened people trying to come to terms with what they had just seen. He slipped through the crowd unnoticed; nobody spared a glance for the stranger in their midst; as he reached his car he turned back to have one last look at the chaos he had left behind him.

Two out of five wasn't bad he thought *particularly if it was the two most important members of the group; five out of five would have been better*; but given the circumstances he told himself *two out of five was a decent achievement; nobody* he thought *could have done better.*

Vitali was still over one hundred yards away when he saw Helena fall. His first impulse was to keep running towards her, maybe she had only suffered a flesh wound, maybe Mikel could yet be deterred from further action, and then he saw Mark Hobson fall. He was too late; the hold-up on the motorway had thwarted his bid to stop the slaughter. There was nothing he could do now. He stopped running; his legs turned to jelly; the enormity of his guilt knocked him for six. His attempt to save a beautiful woman from the cruel fate he had planned for her had failed. His world collapsed around him, he felt numb, and appalled, and destroyed. He turned away from the carnage he had directly caused, and like a man in a trance stumbled back to his car. He had to get away; he had to put distance between himself and this place of horror. What he would do next he didn't know. Self-loathing welled up inside him. How could he have been so heartless, so callous, so cruel, so insane?

His eyes were full of tears by the time he reached his vehicle; he was almost blinded by them. He scraped the side of a parked Mercedes as he tried to exit the car park and smashed the rear lights of a brand new BMW as he manoeuvred his car in haste to leave Summerford Hall. These two acts of carelessness would leave the owners of these vehicles feeling enraged, but their likely reaction never even registered with him. He had signed the death warrant of two innocent people; he could never be forgiven for that; and although he had repented it had been too late. If Hell existed he was sure to find a place there; he had done evil, unforgivable things; now he would have to pay the price.

The telephone call from the police at Coventry surely signalled a breakthrough. Josef Kosygin was now in their custody. He had been spotted by a plain clothes officer leaving a massage parlour in the red light area of the city early in the evening. The detective had followed him on foot at a discreet distance in the hope that he would lead him to the place where he was staying. At some point Kosygin seemed to have realised he was being tailed and had started to run. The officer had given chase, a brave but foolhardy thing to do when dealing with a man who had been flagged up as violent, and a known carrier of weapons. In order to try and evade capture Kosygin had darted into a busy road to try to shake off the pursuing detective. Cars had swerved, cars had screeched to a halt, horns had angrily sounded registering drivers' anger; but his bid to lose his pursuer might well have succeeded had he not looked back, and in doing so failed to see a pothole which threw him completely off balance and sent him hurtling to the ground. The officer had pounced; an almighty struggle had followed, but eventually Kosygin had been overpowered. He was now, as DS Bennett had been told, in police custody and available for interview: he had already been charged with resisting arrest, and two counts of police assault.

That's good news thought Detective Sergeant Bennett; *the boss will be over the moon when he gets in on Monday.*

It was a little less than half an hour after this that Derbyshire Constabulary received news about the shooting at Summerford Hall. Instantly DS Bennett's mood changed. Whether DCI Hobson and his beloved wife were dead or alive as yet he didn't know but there was a very real possibility that both their lives had been ended by an assassin. Bennett felt shell-shocked; his brain was filled with fury; if his Governor and his beautiful wife had been killed somebody would have to pay the price for that crime; somebody would well and truly pay the price.

CHAPTER FORTY TWO

The weight of guilt, hatred and self-loathing, an uncertain future, a question asked in fear, and a "very interesting" discovery

He had driven like a zombie; a blind man. Twice he had nearly strayed into the path of approaching vehicles only to be alerted to the danger by angry flashing headlights and the strident blaring of horns, and once he had failed to appreciate the severity of a bend and nearly ploughed through somebody's immaculately clipped garden hedge so desperate was he to be far away from the tragedy he had caused; but now he realised he could go on no longer. A sign told him that a mile further down the road was a lay-by; he might not want to but Vitali understood that he had to stop and compose himself otherwise he could very soon be responsible for the loss of other innocent lives by his appalling driving. He pulled into the lay-by, switched off the engine, and slumped forward onto the steering wheel, his head in his hands. The misery that crushed him weighed more than a thousand juggernauts; he could not bear to live with such a burden pressing down on him; and all of this could have been avoided if he hadn't dreamt up a terrible plan to punish Alexei ; and if Mikel the Jackal, had not switched off his mobile phone. Angrily he pulled his phone from his pocket and tried again to telephone Mikel. This time his phone rang, this time his call was answered, this time within seconds he could hear the clear cold tones of the hired assassin.

"I tried to telephone you" he blurted out, "your phone was always switched off. Why the fucking hell was that? We could have stopped everything if you had only picked up your fucking phone."

"Exactly for that reason" said Mikel frostily. "You hired me to do a job Vitali. I always deliver. If anyone had telephoned me it would have distracted me from my main purpose; and your whining could have put me at risk of serious harm. This was a job you begged me to undertake, never forget that you sought me out; your hatred of Alexi drove you on. If the plan has not turned out the way you wanted then it was not thought through properly. I had my reservations from the very start but you would not listen."

"But you took my money" snapped Vitali, "you took my sodding money."

"And every pound you gave me signifies your guilt" retorted Mikel; "but look upon the bright side, circumstances beyond both our control saved you from total anguish. For some reason the woman moved as I squeezed the trigger, but I adjusted and my aim was true; the man reacted to his wife being shot marginally quicker than I would have thought possible; again a less able man than myself would have missed him, but when you hired me you hired the best; never forget that Vitali; you hired the very best."

And I will regret it for the rest of my life thought Vitali, *I will regret it for the rest of my life.*

"I think we are almost done Vitali" continued Mikel, I have just one final question, and this time let me have total clarity. What do you want me to do with Alexei. The best solution would be for me simply to slit his throat and dump his body in a canal or a reservoir except, if he is as bad as you claim he is, his rotting corpse might pollute a whole city's water supply" and Mikel laughed out loud at this ludicrous suggestion."

"No, no!" cried out Vitali; "he must suffer for years, and years, and years. Do what you want to him; leave him in agony; but don't put his life at risk. He has to be arrested; he has to be locked up forever; at least let this part of my plan proceed without a hitch."

"It shall be so" responded Mikel. "I have met with hatred before, but seldom on such a scale. What did he do to you to earn your undying detestation?"

"He made me seek out a man like you" replied Vitali. "He turned me into a monster. Because of him I have innocent blood on my hands; and because of that my life is now unbearable. We were teenagers together; I thought he was my friend. He used me and laughed at my naivety. He turned a sweet girl against me with his lies. She believed him; her family spread the word far and wide that I was a liar and a thief. My family disowned me; I had to leave the land of my birth because of his untruths. I spent three wretched years living in squalor in a foreign land then by chance I saw a pretty girl being tormented by thugs. I saved her from harm. Her family took me in. Gradually we fell in love; and her love; and the support of her family, and my own hard work redeemed me. I made a new life for myself. I got married; I was happy; I thought the future looked secure then tragically my wife died in childbirth. I was devastated, and so unhappy, you could never understand this Mikel; then I started to receive e-mails from the girl I had first loved saying vile things about me and about my dead wife; and gloating that she was now an item with Alexei. She enjoyed tormenting me, she laughed at my pain; the love that I had once had for her turned into intense hatred. I wanted to destroy her, and also to hitout at Alexei. I moved to this country to give my daughter a better future. I discovered purely by chance that Alexei, his wife, and his mistress, which is what I thought my childhood sweet heart now to be, lived less than thirty miles away from me. There was another incredibly cruel e-mail which really hurt me. I wasn't thinking straight. I decided that I must have revenge. I kidnapped and later killed the family pet; I persuaded my one time girl friend to meet with me; and I took her to a remote spot under a pretext which I will not bore you with; and there I strangled her. I also stole his car and put that to the torch. Only later did I discover that it was Alexei who wrote those e-mails not Sasha. I had killed an innocent woman in cold blood because I believed she was responsible for so many hurtful lies. He created the monster I have become; can you now understand why I hate him with every fibre of my being?"

"I can" responded Mikel; "but you were a fool to allow yourself to be tricked. I will do as you say. Alexei will be suitably punished by my men then abandoned at a place where the police will find him. I think this now concludes everything Vitali; I must be on my way; I doubt if we will ever talk again."

"Maybe not" replied Vitali, "I have one last job for you to do for which you will be handsomely paid" and he then outlined the matter that he wanted to see him undertake.

At first it was just ill-defined noise, a jumble of meaningless sounds that seemed to ebb and flow and conflict with his desire to sleep. Then he started to detect human voices talking in whispers, and he became aware of brilliant white light. A hand gently patted his cheek, and a female voice then urged him to wake up. He was confused, not knowing where he was, unaware of what had happened, then it all came flooding back. He remembered a shot; he remembered his wife, his soul mate, his clever and beautiful companion falling forward to the floor blood pouring from her chest; and he remembered a moment of blind panic, a second shot, and then nothing else. Now it was clear however, now he knew he was laid upon a hospital bed, now he knew that the person trying to bring him back into the land of the living was a nurse. He had survived a murderous attack; he was still alive; but what the future might be was anything but clear; but none of this mattered to Detective Chief Inspector Hobson; what mattered was the fate of Helena, and the safety and well-being of his kids. If she had died then his life was over; if the kids had been cut down by an assassin's bullet how could he go on? He knew with absolute certainty that he could not: the question he had to ask was obvious; it was also the question he was terrified of putting for fear of what the answer might be.

He remembered a murder investigation that he had been involved in many years ago when a young mother had been forcibly removed from her home and then raped by a psychopathic killer. He had been admitted into the dwelling in the guise of a water Board employee, then he had pulled a knife and shepherded her two small children and her elderly and infirm parents into a rear sitting room and barricaded the door so they could not escape. He had terrified the girl into going with him by making threats to injure his other prisoners if she did not. She had felt that she had no choice but to accompany him. He had taken her to his van and locked her inside the back of the vehicle; then, unbeknown to her, he had returned to the back of the house and thrown a petrol bomb through the rear window. The house had gone up in flames. Police officers had later saved her life although they had been unable to prevent the killer from stabbing her before their bullets struck home. Much later, on her hospital bed, she had asked about her family. The lead detective had had to tell her that they were all dead. The look of anguish on her face when she had learned the sad news had haunted him for decades. He dared not ask about his wife and family for fear he would re-live that moment and be given news he could not bear to hear; but not knowing was also agony. Gripping tightly the side rail of his bed he forced his lips to speak the words he was terrified of saying.

"Helena", he stuttered, his voice cracking with emotion; "for the love of God please tell me that Helena is going to be alright."

The nurse who had awoken him from his sleep placed her hand on his.

"She came as near to death as anybody ever could" she said; "but thankfully she is still alive, and the doctors treating her think that she will make a full recovery; they will tell you more in a little while when you are fully wide awake; but for now take comfort from the fact that she is in this hospital, and receiving the very best care any person could hope for."

"And the kids" asked Hobson "are they ok too?"

"They are" replied the nurse; "hopefully they will be able to visit you later this afternoon."

"I'm going to see the boss later on today after I've had another crack at getting information out of Josef Kosygin. He's not said anything so far, but by God he bloody well will do" and Detective Chief Superintendent Hardy could sense the fury seeping through every cell of Detective Sergeant Peter Bennett's body.

"But stay cool Pete, and keep your hands to yourself, I don't want to see you suspended on an assault charge; and any confession Kosygin makes being thrown out by a judge on the grounds of duress.

"I won't lose control Sir" said Bennett, "I promise you that; but the bastard will talk to me, you have my word on that."

"Good" responded Hardy: "I will want a full update from you about the state of the investigation after the interview is concluded, but for the moment what can you tell me about the condition of DCI Hobson and his wife Helena?"

"Well she came about as near to death as anyone ever could do, but ironically she is actually less badly hurt than the boss. The bullet that struck her passed between two of her ribs without hitting either of them; it missed her heart by the thickness of a cigarette paper, and it exited her body without touching any of her vital organs. She has lost quite a lot of blood, but her condition is stable; the hope is that she may only have to spend a few days in hospital before she is allowed to go home. The boss wasn't so lucky; he's got two broken ribs and the bullet lodge in his lower back; he needed an operation to have it removed but, given time, he should make a full recovery."

"Now that is good news" said a relieved Detective Chief Superintendent Hardy; "is there anything else you wish to add at this time Peter?"

"Only this Sir," replied Bennett. " The whereabouts of Alexei Andropov is currently unknown, and that is relevant because when the search teams examined a bedroom at Summerford Hall which they think the sniper operated out of they found a piece of card on the floor; it must have been dropped by the assassin. It had written upon it a telephone number and an instruction to "Call me when it is done" and here's the interesting thing Sir; the mobile phone number jotted down upon it is the number of Alexei Andropov's mobile phone."

"Interesting" remarked Hardy, "very, very interesting indeed."

CHAPTER FORTY THREE

A suspect is interviewed, a crime is admitted, a report is delivered, and important questions are considered

Josef Kosygin was a big man. Natasha Zalenkov had been absolutely correct when she likened him in stature to Detective Chief Inspector Hobson, but there the similarities ended. Kosygin was arrogant, self-opinionated, and contemptuous of authority. He looked at Detective Sergeant Peter Bennett as if he was dog shit.

I'm going to have my work cut out here thought Bennett, *but I'll wipe that supercilious sneer from your face; pride comes before a fall my friend; I'm going to enjoy bringing you back down to Earth with an almighty bump.*

He introduced himself to Kosygin and, very carefully, explained to him his rights. Kosygin was supremely disinterested; he crossed his legs, folded his arms, and stared into space: if the long lanky British detective was hoping to have a meaningful conversation then he would soon be profoundly disappointed. No reply followed no reply. For thirty minutes the suspect did not utter a single word; it was only when Bennett told him that the police had numerous witness statements that named him as an associate of Leonid Petrov, and that they possessed irrefutable evidence that Petrov was present at Moor Top Grange that he started to have self doubts, which became more pronounced when the tall detective told him that the victim of the alleged assault had positively identified him as the man who had locked her inside a burning stable, and that she was regarded as a five star witness who was guaranteed to appeal to a jury.

"You could get life for doing what you did" said Bennett; "life without parole. If you ever want to walk free again then I suggest you start co-operating with me in the hope that by doing do you might lop a year or two off your ultimate sentence" and as he said this DS Bennett noticed that a little of Kosygin's colour faded from his cheeks.

He had struck a nerve, and now was the time to turn the knife. By the end of the interview a self-confessed hard man had become "Mr Plasticine", he was putty in the Derbyshire detective's hands. The police had obtained straight from the horse's mouth, a detailed account of how two villains had become involved in a serious criminal venture; and more importantly a clear picture of who had recruited them to be foot-soldiers.

The boss will be over the moon when I tell him thought the detective sergeant; *maybe a bit of good news will aid him along the road to recovery.*

She was alive, that was all that mattered; and she would recover from her injuries much quicker than him even though she had been nearer to a fatal end; if the bullet that had entered her body had been a millimetre or two nearer to her heart it could have been a very different story. The fact that Helena was still alive filled him with emotion; the fact that she had been so close to death made him weep. He wanted nothing more than to hold her in his arms and tell her how much he loved her; he yearned to draw his wife and his children close to him and promise them that nothing like this would ever happen again. He dared not think how traumatised the children might be; the events of yesterday would have terrified then; they would need support and counselling; and an unlimited amount of re-assurance and affection. All this was clear. The thing that Mark Hobson could not begin to understand was why this had all happened. He had made enemies during his years on the force; no copper worth his salt had not done so; and it was not unheard of for criminals to seek to take revenge. He knew of two separate incidents in which retired police officers had been physically attacked by family members of men they had put away for a long time; and he had read about cases where shots had been fired at former detectives as they made their way home from a night on the town. In one of these cases the wife of the officer who had arrived in her car to give him a lift had been badly injured by a bullet, but that had been an accident; what had happened at Summerford Hall was very different.

Hobson believed, with total conviction, that his wife was not somebody who made enemies. He could understand how she could have become "collateral damage" in a targeted attack upon himself; but that hadn't happened here. The sniper had deliberately chosen to aim at Helena first; that made no sense; it wasn't a blunder on his part; he had selected Helena as his prime target and seen him as only his number two victim. This was inexplicable. There was another thing about this attack which was extremely odd. The ex-bobbies whom were beaten up by thugs had been attacked in back alleys; the drive by shooting had happened late at night. This attack upon himself and his family had been purposely staged to happen before a large crowd of on-lookers; there had to be a reason for that: the trouble was Mark Hobson had no idea what that reason might be.

So he would receive an extra 20K in his bank account for carrying out the simplest of jobs. He understood exactly what was required of him, and that nothing would cause him a moment of anxiety. He knew the "why", the only question was the "when", and even this was set in a limited period of time. In no more than three days time Mikel would leave the United Kingdom to return to mainland Europe; a place he was more familiar with.

Great Britain is OK he thought, *and there are rich pickings to be had but the British think they are superior to all other nations, and that is profoundly irritating.*

There were still a few things he needed to attend to. He needed to book a flight to his next destination; he needed to remove all traces of himself from the place where he had been staying. This would take time; he would have to be thorough; he had seen on too many occasions in his lifetime the problems other people had had by cutting corners and by being slapdash.

Then of course there was the question of what to do with Alexei. He decided that he would, as he had promised, respect

Vitali's wishes. He would leave the finer details to the men who now guarded him, but he might suggest injuries; a broken leg, and some facial disfigurement caused by corrosive liquid being thrown into his face from close range could fit the bill. Neither of these injuries would be life-threatening, but they would be life-changing; and his hired hands would have fun carrying out such actions. He would also stress that when their harsh treatment of Alexei was complete the wretch must be dumped by the roadside near to a fully manned police station, and that a telephone call should be made to it as soon as their prisoner was abandoned. At last, satisfied that all his boxes were now ticked, Mikel allowed himself a rare smile. He had enjoyed his work; and his stay in England had certainly had its moments; he hoped that his next job would be as rewarding, but he very much doubted if that would be the case.

"I'm just off to visit the boss Sir" said Detective Sergeant Bennett, "but I thought I had better explain to you what stage we're at before I go. You requested an update and it seemed better to come and see you now rather than later in the day so you can have a clear picture as to where things stand at present."

"Quite right" replied Detective Chief Superintendent Hardy, "so tell me all that we know to date."

"We'll I'll start with the piece of card found in the bedroom. Not only has that got Alexei Andropov's mobile phone number written on it, we now know for definite that he has handled it, his prints are all over it."

"Excellent" responded Hardy.", "excellent. He'll have a lot of explaining to do when he's brought in for questioning."

"Which may not be for any time soon" commented Bennett; "his current whereabouts are still unknown; it could be some time before he surfaces again."

"Shit and derision" snorted Hardy; "I hoped we might have made some progress in locating him; nothing is ever straightforward is it Peter?"

"No Sir" agreed DS Bennett "but he will reappear at some stage; and in the meantime there have been one or two new developments which I think may be more to your liking."

"And what are those "Peter asked DCS Hardy? "I'm all ears; what bits of good news have you got for me?"

"Kosygin has confessed to being with Petrov at Moor Top Grange and to starting the fire there; he also accepts that he did lock Natasha inside the burning stable although he denies trying to kill or injure her. He claims he thought that there was another exit from the building that she could have used, and that his intention was only to frighten her, but that explanation won't wash with a jury. We've got him bang to rights; he'll be going away for a long, long time."

"Superb" murmured Hardy, "truly superb. You've done well Pete, very, very well."

"And there's still more to please you" continued Bennett; "We now know who commissioned Petrov and Kosygin to attack the Grange; and also exactly how much he was prepared to shell out to get the job done."

"And who was that "asked Hardy agog?

"Alexei Andropov" replied the detective sergeant, "and the price he paid for the task was £20,000 to each individual."

"Better and better exclaimed Hardy; "so there is a history between Andropov and Vitali Zalenkov; has Kosygin said what that history is?"

"No Sir, he claims he was never told, but he is in no doubt that there was one; and this is really interesting. Do you recall seeing on the news that there had been a nasty pile-up on the M56 only a few hours before the boss was shot; well Vitali Zalenkov's car was caught up in the massive traffic jam that followed that accident. It was captured on an overhead speed camera, there's no doubt about it. Well that accident happened less than ten miles from Summerford hall, but here's the really significant bit. Eye witnesses at Summerford Hall immediately after the attempt on the boss's and his wife's lives recall seeing a vehicle matching the description of Zalenkov's car struggling to manoeuvre its way out of a crowded car park; it actually bumped two other parked cars causing minor damage to both of them. Mr Zalenkov hasn't been seen at all since that time. I'd love to take a look at his car. My bet is that when it is examined it will have dents and scratches consistent with a minor road traffic accident; and if we're lucky, paint samples taken from it and from the other vehicles involved will prove a full match. He has a lot of explaining to do Sir, a hell of a lot of explaining."

"Absolutely he has, but what all this has to do with Detective Chief Inspector Hobson I have no idea. Both he and his wife treated Zalenkov with the upmost care and compassion. I believe he is on record saying how grateful he feels for the treatment he and his daughter received from them. He would have no motive whatsoever to attack them in any way."

"Maybe he wasn't trying to attack them Sir; maybe he was trying to prevent an attack; could that be a possible explanation?"

"It could" conceded Detective Chief Superintendent Hardy, "but that raises many more questions. If Alexei Andropov masterminded this attack, and the concrete evidence that we have suggests that was the case, then how could Vitali Zalenkov have known about it? He definitely isn't a man Andropov would have shared secrets with, so there would have to have been another way. I suppose somebody might have betrayed him and talked to Zalenkov, but my gut feeling is that is unlikely. It is also possible that a computer could have been hacked, but again I feel that didn't happen. And all of this leaves unanswered the biggest question of all. If Zalenkov knew a vicious attack upon a police officer and his family was about to take place, and he was well-motivated and desperate to do everything he could to prevent the attack from happening why the hell didn't he not just contact us? It makes no sense whatsoever. Only he can explain his actions. He needs to be brought in for questioning. Circulate him as a person of interest; I want to know the moment he re-surfaces."

"I'll do that immediately Sir" said Bennett. "Like you I believe his actions are pivotal to this case. So far he has been assiduous in visiting his injured daughter. I'll have a bobby placed at the hospital; I'm sure that's a good place to start. With a bit of luck he could be in our hands in just a few hours time."

"I hope so" said Hardy, "I fervently hope so."

CHAPTER FORTY FOUR

A time for big decisions, a time for sorrow, a time to confess and to conceal, a time to make an exit, and a time of terror and of pain

The kids had only been permitted to stay for a few minutes. They were obviously still shaken by the events which had occurred so he had tried to lessen their anxiety by being as upbeat as possible. It had been an effort to appear cheerful, but for their sake he had made light of his injuries. He had assured them that he felt fine and that he would soon be back on his feet; and he had promised them that nothing like this would ever happen again. They had taken comfort from his words, and left his bedside a little less tense than when they first arrived.

Jackie Nadin was allowed a little more time.

"The children will be staying with Alan and me" she said; "we'll look after them for the time being and they will be fine. I've already told them that you and Helena will soon be well enough to come home; and in Helena's case that may be sooner than anybody expects. She was sitting in a chair by the side of her bed when I left her. I think that there is a good chance that she may be able to visit you later this evening, although she'll probably be pushed here in a wheelchair to be on the safe side; she looks surprisingly well Mark; I am so, so relieved."

"I am too Jackie" replied Mark. "I've given the kids my word that everything is going to be OK from now on, and that nothing like this will ever happen to us as a family again. I've got a lot of thinking to do while I'm in here; but one thing I do know is that Helena's and their safety is more important than anything else on Earth. I've got some big decisions to make Jackie, and it's vital that I get them right."

He had slept that night in a grotty two star hotel someway inside the realm of Desperation close to the land of Decaying Dreams; and in truth the word "slept" was entirely the wrong word. He had spent most of his time in the drab uncomfortable room he for the moment was occupying sat at a dusty coffee stained table composing two very different letters.

The first letter was to be addressed to his solicitor. He had already made a will leaving all of his property, apart from one or two specific bequests, to his daughter Natasha, but now he wanted to add further instructions to protect and safeguard her interests in his estate. She would very soon become a wealthy young woman in her own right. He trusted her common sense, he did not doubt her innate ability, but the world was full of cheats, and chancers, and ne'er-do-wells; and he wanted her to be shielded as much as was humanly possible from the dross of society. He fervently wished that she could be happy but he feared that his actions had rendered that impossible. He prayed that the second letter he intended to pen might make her understand how much he adored her, and how love and hate were two sides of the same coin, and how quickly one might morph into the other; but he doubted if he could ever find the right words to convince her of this truth. The floor became littered with screwed up sheets of paper, failed attempts to express his thoughts and feelings adequately, but finally he held in his hand something he thought might do. It wasn't perfect but it was the best he could achieve. The words he wrote were as follows:-

My dear sweet Natasha,

I am so desperately sorry for the pain and hurt I have caused you. You are the most wonderful daughter a father could wish for, and across the years you have brought me so much joy. I have done wicked and horrible things that I now bitterly regret, and I know when it becomes common knowledge, which I fear must be the case, the world will see me as a monster; but please never doubt the love that I had for you and for your mother. She gave me hope when I thought all hope was lost; and when she died giving birth to you I thought my world would fall apart. You gave me a reason for living, *and your unconditional love healed me and made me whole again. But always in the background was a person who I had once believed to be a friend, but who turned out to be a deceiver. He ruined my early life with his lies; yet if that had been all he had done I would have been grateful to him, for without him the circumstances would not have come about that allowed me to meet your mother. But he did far more than that. He sent me e-mails saying vile things about your mum, and even accusing me of behaving unnaturally towards you. My anger was intense; how dare he suggest such obscene and depraved conduct. He took me for a fool. He sent me more e-mails, this time in the name of Anastasia, my childhood sweetheart. She was the first girl I ever loved, and his words, which I thought were hers, revolted me and created within me an unquenchable desire for revenge. I now know I should not have allowed myself to be goaded into anger; I should simply have deleted the e-mails from my computer; and then sought counselling to overcome my rage; but I did not do this.*

After I have finished writing this letter I intend to write to the police admitting that I killed an innocent woman in cold blood. When I realised, far too late, what I had done I thought of suicide. You were the only person who stayed my hand. My love for you, and your unwavering love for me, stopped me from taking the coward's way out. Then the man who had destroyed my sanity and caused me to embrace evil went even further. Because I destroyed his car he tried to destroy our home; because I had killed Anastasia, who he regarded as his personal property, he hired men to destroy you. I have never known such fury as that which I felt when I discovered that he had plotted to injure the most beautiful and precious person on the planet. I wanted to punish him in a way that would guarantee he would die a reviled and detested outcast in an English gaol. I devised a plan to frame him for the murder of an innocent and decent English family; and I paid a ruthless villain with a heart of stone a fortune to carry out my wishes.

In the end my darling I did see sense, and I tried to undo the harm I had initiated, but a terrible road traffic accident delayed my progress, and I was too late. I don't think I can live with myself for what I have done, so this is probably the last time I

shall ever write to you. Try to forgive my anger and my stupidity, try to forget everything about me except my love for you.
  Against all odds look to the future and have a happy life;
  Your ever loving father,
  Vitali

    He folded the letter up and placed it into an envelope which he started to address to Natasha at the hospital then an awful realisation struck him. This farewell letter would be seen as a suicide note. There was not the remotest chance that it would not be read by the police and it would be key evidence at any inquest into his death. If he sent it as it was it would totally undermine his plan to see Alexei imprisoned for a crime he had not committed. He couldn't tell Natasha anything about his involvement with the events that had taken place at Summerford Hall. If he wanted to let her know how much he regretted his insane scheme it could not be now, and it couldn't be in this letter. He decided that he must rip out in its entirety the last sections of this missive. He would, he decided, write a separate letter which he would entrust to his solicitors addressed to Natasha, but only to be opened after the death of Alexei Andropov, whenever that might be. Much therefore needed to be done. In the silence of his drab and demoralising bedroom, in the early hours of the morning he re-penned his original letter, then he composed two more letters. The one to the police admitting responsibility for the murder of Anastasia was short, factual and to the point; the one that he hoped Natasha would receive one day long into the future was emotional, rambling, and filled with sadness. He hoped this letter might cause her to forgive him, but he was far from convinced that that would be the case.

    His seats on the flight were booked, all his possessions were packed away, no trace of him was left inside the small bedroom which had been his home for the last couple of weeks. Mikel no longer existed, a new country beckoned; a new identity would soon fit him like a glove. His rifle, which he valued above all else was already on its way out of the United Kingdom concealed in the back of a lorry chartered by a Christian Aid charity to take food, medical supplies and donated clothing to displaced people in Eastern Europe, Afghanistan, and South Sudan. Once the HGV had crossed the Channel the small suitcase containing the prized tools of his trade would be delivered to a secret address to await collection at a later date. It had cost surprisingly little to see this plan come to fruition, but people who valued their own safety did not hold out for greater reward against a person like himself. The man formerly known as Mikel allowed himself a little smile. The irony of humanitarian aid concealing the stock in trade of an assassin amused him. Life was seldom as it appeared to be. A Christian God unwittingly aiding a cold-blooded killer; it was a good joke, and one worthy of a round of applause.

There remained of course the last job he had been commissioned to undertake. He did not need his trusty rifle for that task: a gun borrowed from the "lending Library" of illegal weapons which members of Manchester's underworld had access to, was all that was required. Indeed it had one obvious plus. When he used the pistol to carry out his final instructions there was a good chance that the police would match any bullet recovered from the body of the deceased with other crimes committed in and around Greater Manchester. It would be the simplest of jobs. All he had to do was to fire a bullet, at point blank range into the victim at a time when death was least expected. It wasn't rocket science; a delinquent teenage thug could probably do the job just as well; but a clean kill was demanded; and a clean kill was something he could guarantee, which a delinquent teenager could not.

"You look like shit." The goon who was prodding Alexei was grinning like a Barbary ape;" I think you need some fresh air Pal, so later on today you and me are going to take a ride; that'll be nice won't it Mate?" The look on his face made Alexei shake with fear; even in his befuddled, semi-comatose state he could tell this wasn't good news. What was planned for him he could only guess; but whatever it was it was likely to cause him pain. He wanted to protest, or to plead for mercy, or to beg to be released, but experience had taught him that if he did any of these things he would incur the anger of his gaolers; so he said nothing. Maybe he was just postponing the inevitable; but for the moment his silence put on hold any act of violence against him.

"We're not venturing out until after dark" continued his talkative prison warder; "if we went out in daylight you'd probably try and do something daft, but I ain't going to allow that to happen; but one thing I can promise you my friend is that you're going to have a night to remember;" and with those words he was gone leaving Alexei to stew in his own fear. Something bad was going to happen to him tonight, something very bad indeed. How his world had changed from a place of power and plenty into a place of misery and pain in such a short time he could not begin to compute. He had descended into a hellish twilight world in the twinkling of an eye. He tugged frantically at the bonds that tied him to his chair; and when they held firm he wept.

Time ceased to mean anything. Minutes seemed like hours, hours seemed like minutes, but eventually the sound of footsteps descending the stairway into the cellar indicated to Alexei that the moment had come. His chief tormenter and his appalling sidekick entered the room. One was carrying a long handled hammer, the other a glass jug half filled with a clear liquid which had a chemical smell which reminded Alexei of recently cleaned public toilets. "Are you ready Mate" asked the man carrying the long handled hammer? I'll just get you untied and stood up"; and then he glanced at Alexei's right leg.

"What the hell have you got on your trousers? Jesus! I think it's a fucking cockroach; but don't worry; I'll soon shift it for you" and he swung the hammer and smashed it hard into Alexei's kneecap. The pain was excruciating; Alexei let out a scream of anguish; both of Mikel's men let out squeals of hysterical laughter.

"I think he's crying because he's cold" his assailant commented; "can you do something to warm him up?"

"Without doubt" his companion replied, throwing the strong alkaline liquid contained in the jug directly into Alexei's face; "that should do the trick."

The pain was unbearable: Alexei howled in agony.

"Good job Mate" said the first man to the second; "now let's get the cunt into the van and then dump him at the roadside for the police to come and clear up the mess."

CHAPTER FORTY FIVE

A compliment is paid, "dead meat" is dumped, a longing is fulfilled, and a clean kill is hoped for.

"I'm not stopping long Gov, but I wanted to see for myself how you were getting on and to bring you good wishes from everyone back at the nick. I thought as well that you might like to have a quick update on how the investigation is progressing and to let you know that we're all rooting for you and that we're not going to rest until every person involved in the attack on you and Helena has been locked away forever in a high security gaol."

"That's kind of you Pete" replied DCI Hobson; "you're a good copper and an even better friend."

"Oh shut up Boss" said DS Bennett blushing, then eager to avoid further compliments he divulged to Mark all the stuff he had already imparted to DCS Stanley Hardy.

"It's a puzzler Peter" said Hobson to his detective sergeant after he had heard all the details. "I'm not surprised at all that Alexei Andropov's fingerprints are all over this case, but how Vitali Zalenkov fits into the picture I can't begin to imagine."

"Nor can we as yet" responded Bennett, "but we will; and when we have figured out the connection I believe we will be well on the way to cracking the whole case."

He wasn't tied up or restrained in any way, but he could no more run than could a double amputee. His face burned with the intensity of a blast furnace; the pain he felt was off the Richter Scale; all Alexei knew was that he had been manhandled out of the house and tossed like a piece of stinking trash into the rear of a smelly Transit van. He felt like dead meat on the back of a knackers truck. If he wanted anything it was for his life to end; death would have been a blessed relief; but he was sure that escape route would be denied to him.

The van bounced along the road; if it had ever had springs they had long since succumbed to metal fatigue; every speed bump, every minute change in the thickness of the tarmac sent spasms throughout his body; all he prayed for was for the journey to end; yet every brain cell he still had left told him to be fearful of what would happen when it did.

In less than fifteen minutes he had his answer. The Transit braked to an abrupt halt. In next to no time the rear doors of the vehicle were flung open, and rough, uncaring, hands dragged him from the vehicle and let him fall onto the carriageway;" and with deep rumbling, unsympathetic laughter the van and the men who had caused him so much dread were gone.

"It was only after DS Bennett had left the hospital and the children had long gone that Mark Hobson felt truly alone. He should have been at home, he should have been relaxing on the sofa watching a good film with Helena, but instead he was lying on a hard bed in an overheated room a million miles emotionally from where he wanted to be. He longed to be with Helena, to hear her voice, to smell her perfume, to touch her skin and kiss her lips. Some deluded maniac had done his best to ensure that everything he loved was taken from him. He wanted so badly to see that person in a prison cell; he knew he would never feel safe until every individual who had played a part in the attack upon himself and his beloved wife was serving a lengthy prison sentence with no possibility of parole. But more than this, at this moment all he wanted to do was to see Helena. He had been told that she might be brought to him in a wheelchair; the very thought of that made him cry. The fact that she had to be treated like an invalid appalled him. She was so full of life, and hope, and joy; and yet she had nearly died at the hands of a professional killer.

A noise just outside the door to his room interrupted his thoughts. Could it be Helena? Was she about to be wheeled in to visit him? He hoped for all the world that that was the case; and then, with some difficulty, the door opened. It was Helena: she was by herself, and walking without any means of support. She looked pale, but oh so beautiful. He couldn't help himself; tears welled up inside him. He struggled to speak; she entered the room, and bent down to kiss him where he lay. He held her hands; the floodgates opened; and the tallest and stockiest Detective Chief Inspector in the whole of Derbyshire broke down and cried like a baby.

The only certainty after birth was death; that was perhaps the one universal truth. Every man, woman and child; every creature that lived on land, or water, or in the air; every plant, every tree, every shrub would one day perish; he was no different from any other member of the human race. The only thing that set him apart from most other people (except those wretches awaiting execution on a given date) was that he knew his life would be taken from him at an unspecified time less than forty eight hours hence.

It was an intensely sobering thought, yet at the same time, a strangely reassuring one. He knew that if he had left his demise in his own hands he might have at the last minute stepped back from the brink, afraid to do the dreadful deed. Fear might have stayed his hand; fear the ingestion of a vast quantity of pills might have led to a slow, lingering death; fear that a leap from a high cliff or tall building might not prove fatal, and that a bent and twisted body would survive the fall; fear that when the moment came he could not force himself to slash his wrists or slit his throat; fear that a rope around his neck would not give him the quick exit that he hoped for; that was why he had instructed a third party to end his life. He knew he was right to have done this. Mikel had been well paid; he would complete the task. Sometime within the next minute, or the next hour he might pounce, and then he would be no more. Feelings of love, and loss, and regret battled to take control of his mind; but the victor in this battle to be the dominant emotion was relief.

He hadn't known what his actions might be while he waited for the fateful hour to come, and he had changed his mind many times; but now he had an idea about what his final itinerary should be. He needed to show one last gesture of love to the person he cherished more than anyone else on Earth. He would have to act fast; Mikel might have monitored his every move since they last talked and might strike at any time. The professional killer would pick his moment and the place of execution; his aim would be true; a clean kill would follow; although not a clean conscience; but this was the best outcome he could legitimately hope for.

CHAPTER FORTY SIX

An embittered wife, a relieved husband, a life-changing decision, a daytime killing, a new identity, and an unexpected confession

It wasn't the news that Chloe Andropov had been hoping for; Detective Sergeant Peter Bennett was sure about that. If the body of Alexei had been found riddled with bullets the DS was convinced that bottles of Prosecco would have been cracked open, and the bunting would have been hung out in celebration, but sadly from Chloe's point of view, the role of grieving widow had been denied her. Her unloved and unwanted husband had been found alive; in a bad condition that was true; but nowhere near at death's door. The Greater Manchester Police were saying that the man DCI Hobson was desperate to see interviewed was in a confused, demented state, apparently suffering from Post Traumatic Stress Disorder, and that he also had significant physical injuries viz a completely shattered kneecap, and a badly burned face caused by a corrosive substance being thrown over him.

"He's currently in hospital receiving treatment" the detective who telephoned Derbyshire Police to inform them of the arrest had said; "he isn't in a fit state to be released into our custody; so it is likely to be some time before he can be formally questioned."

"It's frustrating" Bennett later commented to Detective Chief Superintendent Hardy, "but he's going nowhere; the boss will be pleased when he gets the news."

"And how was DCI Hobson when you saw him last night" asked Hardy?

"Better than he could have been" replied the detective sergeant; "but I felt he was putting on a brave face for my benefit; underneath the public show I felt he was in turmoil; but I gather he is feeling more like himself this morning."

"How do you know that?"

"I telephoned the hospital before I came to see you" responded DS Bennett; "Helena was allowed to visit him last night. She's back on her feet and she is going to make a full recovery; and that cheered him up no end. I think he'll be a very different man when I meet with him today; and the news about Andropov will be the icing on the cake. We're entering the end game Sir, I'm sure of that; it won't be long now before the last pieces of the jigsaw slot into place."

"I hope you're right Peter" murmured Hardy; I sincerely hope you're right.

The news of a shooting outside a florist's shop in Stockport was initially of very little interest to the police officers at Buxton nick. It was unexpected. Daytime incidents involving firearms were fortunately rare; and the fact that murder could take place on a busy street filled with early morning shoppers was concerning; it was just that this crime seemed unrelated to anything High Peak officers were investigating.

Eye witnesses to the crime were clearly shocked.

"He came out of the shop carrying a large bunch of flowers" said one stunned onlooker, "and then, without warning, a man walked up behind him and shot him in the head at point blank range. Then he just strolled away as if nothing had happened. I couldn't believe my eyes. One second he was alive, the next second he was dead; and it was all so casual; God knows what the world is coming to."

There were other accounts too which repeated this version of events. The common thread that ran through all of them was the suddenness of the attack, and the ice-cold nerve of the attacker.

"He just wandered off as if nothing had happened. One minute he was there, the next minute he was gone. Things like this don't happen in England", but then again they just had.

Derbyshire police only started to pay real attention to this story when more details were released. It soon became clear that the man who had died was a person of interest so far as they were concerned. A name started to be bandied about; soon it was clear, without a shadow of a doubt, that the dead man was none other than Vitali Zalenkov.

The decision had been an easy one. She had put him under no pressure, and although they had talked about the future it had been in the sense of looking forward to being back home, and how relieved they were that the children had not been harmed, and tentatively planning the holiday of a lifetime to help them forget the traumas of Summerford Hall. A Caribbean cruise; a trip to Disney Land Florida; a visit to the temples of South East Asia; or experiencing firsthand the wonders of Japan; all of these had been highlighted as possibilities; and they had thrilled to the thoughts of travel. It was only after Helena had left to return to her ward that Mark Hobson started to consider seriously what his next move should be. He had been a policeman for over 30 years; it was the only life he knew. He loved his job; but in his eyes his job had nearly cost Helena her life; and it wasn't the first time that she had faced danger because of who he was and what he did. It was unlikely that there would ever again be a serious threat posed to himself or his family, but another attack on himself or his loved ones could not be totally ruled out. To Mark's mind the chances of this happening if he was no longer a policeman would be considerably reduced. He had put the years in. He could retire on full pension if he wanted to and seek other, less dangerous work. Although he would be walking away from his friends and colleagues in the familiar world of law enforcement it was a no-brainer, He resolved that he would tell Detective Chief Superintendent Stanley Hardy of his decision to hang up his police boots and seek out a more peaceful way of life at the first available opportunity.

CCTV cameras near to the place where Vitali Zalenkov perished had been checked. An image of a man had been discovered, but as yet nothing that was clear cut had been found. Descriptions of the gunman had been obtained from eye witnesses and the police now knew he was white, of average height, with hair that had been variously described as "dark", "mousey" or "nut brown." In time, with luck, a clearer picture of the murderer might emerge, but that did not bother the smartly dressed man who was waiting to check in at Manchester International Airport. There was nothing remarkable about Mr Novikov; he had been in the United Kingdom on a short holiday and was now returning home. Many passengers display signs of anxiety when they board a flight, but he did not. Had he seemed at all uncomfortable he might have drawn attention to himself; and that was the last thing Mr Novikov wanted; even if inside his stomach had churned and his pulse had raced he would not have shown his unease; years of living dangerously had taught him iron self-control.

His passport was checked; it passed the test; his boarding card was in order; his flight was due to depart on time; and the forecast was for good weather for the whole of the journey. He took his seat by the window. Very soon he would be flying at over 30,000 feet; and in no time at all the plane would leave UK airspace and he would be travelling east across mainland Europe. Mr Novokov closed his eyes and contemplated the future. Momentarily he thought about Mikel and then he laughed. Mikel was dead, God rest his soul, now it was time to embrace "Nikita". He smiled at the thought of his new incarnation. "Nikita" in Russian folklore meant "winner. What could be more apt? That of course was exactly what he was.

"The poor kid must be devastated. In less than two weeks she has lost her dreams, her home and now her father" DS Peter Bennett was meeting with Detective Chief superintendent Hardy to explain significant developments that had taken place since they last talked. "I'm just glad it wasn't me who had to break the news of her father's death. I can't imagine the pain she must be feeling right now. The boss will be gutted when he hears what has happened. I know if he was fit he'd want to visit her; maybe I should go and see her in his stead. There are questions we need to put to her to assist us with our enquiries in any event."

"And what are those Peter? I doubt if she was privy to all her father's thoughts and plans."

"I don't think she was Sir" responded Bennett; "but in view of a letter we have received today, and I understand that she may have received one too, there are matters that we do need to raise with her."

"Tell me more" said Hardy; "what is the significance of these letters?"

"Take a look at this Sir" replied DS Bennett; "it arrived this morning addressed to the boss" and he handed the document in question to the DCS.

The letter was brief and to the point; the words used were crystal clear.

Dear Detective Chief Inspector Hobson it read; *this is my full confession to the crime of murder. I make this admission of my own free will knowing that it will be used as evidence in a court of law. Although I am burdened by guilt and now bitterly regret what I have done I am of sound mind; I want nothing more than to set the record straight,*

I am the person who killed Anastasia Karpovich. I acted in rage because I believed she had mocked my intense grief at the death of my wife and that she had posted on-line vile and disgusting lies about my daughter and myself. I lured her to a remote spot, and there I killed her. I placed my hands around her neck and squeezed the life out of her. I did other things too which I now think touched upon my sanity at the time of the murder, but I am not prepared to share with you my reasons for doing so. It was only later that I discovered that she was innocent, and entirely without malice. An obnoxious, unprincipled wretch had spread malicious lies in her name. You have met the man Chief Inspector, you are no fool; you know how untrustworthy he truly is.

I hope that one day he will die in prison. But I will not be here to see that day. I am a good man who was corrupted and contaminated by another's lies. I should not have succumbed to rage; he killed my future; please God you will destroy his.

The letter was then signed by Vitali Zalenkov; DS Bennett did not doubt for a second that the signature was genuine.

"So what do you make of it Sir" said Bennett?

"It's a confession" answered Hardy; "and it also reads like a suicide note; and if Zalenkov had taken his own life I would have no difficulty in accepting it as such, but that didn't happen Pete, dozens of people saw him gunned down in the street."

"Well maybe that was his intention Sir, maybe he was buying flowers for Natasha as a final goodbye gift; perhaps her letter from her dad when we read it may explain things further; but here's a thought. Suppose a killer intervened before Zalenkov could act. We know because of Kosygin's admission to the attack on Moor Top Grange that that crime was bought and paid for by Alexei Andropov. Anastasia had lived with him for several years. The hatred between Andropov and Zalenkov was extreme. I think Andropov saw Anastasia as his property. If he thought her death was down to Vitali, it is certainly conceivable that he might have paid a hit man to put an end to Zalenkov's life. It could be that Vitali was murdered before he could commit suicide; might that explain the events that have just occurred?"

"It might Peter" conceded Hardy; "It very well might. Certainly Andropov needs to be questioned about Zalenkov's death; I'm sure it will turn out that he has a lot of explaining to do."

"So let us hope he is in a fit state to be interviewed soon" murmured Bennett; a thought with which DCS Hardy thoroughly agreed.

CHAPTER FORTY SEVEN

Ten days, three weeks, a lifetime, another violent death, a case solved, and a final persuasive theory

The good news so far as everyone at Buxton nick was concerned was that Detective Chief Inspector Hobson was now back at home with his family. His wife Helena had been discharged from hospital a week earlier than he had and was now well on the road to recovery. When she first arrived home Jackie Nadin had fussed over her like a mother hen. Helena was grateful to her friend for her kindness and had appreciated her help, but now she was adamant that she was fine and that nobody needed to worry about her. She was very confident that she could look after her husband and the kids without having to seek outside support.

Mark's state of health when he was released from hospital had been a bit less advanced. When DS Bennett visited him at the house on the day after his homecoming he confessed to feeling only about eighty per cent fit. Bennett had told him that this was only natural, and that full recovery would take time; and suggested that he just took things easy and didn't worry about the state of things at work. He had however promised that he would keep him fully appraised as to how the criminal investigation into the crimes at Moor Top Grange and Summmerford Hall were progressing; and it was for that purpose that he had now dropped in on his boss.

"It is good news Gov, but it's also a bit perplexing. Alexei Andropov was discharged from hospital yesterday and has been declared fit to be interviewed, he's a shadow of the man he once was, his face will be permanently scarred, and like as not he will always walk with a limp. When we put to him Kosygin's allegations about Moor Top Grange he admitted he was the paymaster; he also confessed to a number of serious cases of fraud; and is looking at an extended period of imprisonment. He denied completely having anything to do with the shooting of you and Helena, even when we told him about the message on the card found at Summerford Hall, and even though the handwriting on it is a perfect match to his handwriting; and despite the fact that his fingerprints are all over it. He claims he was forced to write and sign the card; and I can't deny he has been put through the wringer by somebody. The CPS aren't 100% convinced that we have a case which will stick; but for now they have agreed that he can be charged as an accessory to the attempted murder of you and of Helena as well as all the events at Moor Top Grange. However they want us to continue investigating the attacks upon you both, and I'm not entirely confident that they won't pull the plug on the Summerford Hall offences before they come to trial if we don't find some further persuasive evidence."

"They may have a point Peter" replied Hobson; "and one thing is certain this isn't going to be a case which is wrapped up and put to bed before I retire in just two months from now."

"Perhaps not" agreed Bennett; "but it would be nice if we could have a definite answer by that date. It would be the best leaving present we could give you if we could get everything done and dusted by then; and all the guilty parties locked up behind iron bars."

"I think you are just a little bit pissed Sweetheart." Helena Hobson ruffled her husband's hair and bent down to give him a peck on the cheek."

"Who me" exclaimed Mark "never", then he added grinning "well maybe just a tiny, wee bit."

The room was full of well-wishers; the great and the good were all there. Detective Chief Superintendent Hardy was prominent; and senior officers from all of the police divisions in Derbyshire could be spotted. The highest ranking officer in the room was the Deputy Chief Constable; the Chief himself would have been there but for a prior engagement in London. Several local magistrates were in attendance; and a couple of senior solicitors from the CPS were also at the celebration, but mainly it was lower ranking officers:- inspectors, sergeants and constables who filled the venue. Present too was a good smattering of former colleagues who had already retired from the force; one of these was Alan Nadin. There had been speeches, and reminiscences, and funny stories, and during the course of the evening there had been a presentation. Mark's friends and colleagues had bought him an engraved pewter tankard, a beautiful cut glass decanter, and a luxury weekend for two at a five star hotel in the Lake District. It was the end of an era, a momentous day, happening just three months after the events at Summerford Hall.

"A bit pissed ain't good enough Gov" interjected Peter Bennett who had been sat alongside his DCI for most of the evening; "keep up the traditions of leaving do's; take you shirt off; flex your biceps; down a pint in less than fifteen seconds; and then slide indecorously under the table. You have a lot to live up to Gov, you need to make this the most memorable send off the force has ever seen."

"You're incorrigible Pete" laughed Helena; "It's a good job that I know you're just winding Mark up; this is a night he'll always want to remember; so slow and steady from now on has to be the order of the night."

"She's right of course" agreed Bennett; "It is a momentous day. I don't know if you realise it, but the presence of all these people here is a testament as to how much you will be missed. How do you feel about things on this your last ever day as a copper?"

"I'm not sure" answered Mark. "I know I have made the right decision, but not being with you and with familiar faces in familiar places will feel strange at first. I will miss the camaraderie, and I will miss seeing your ugly mug every day; you're a good detective Peter, and an even better friend."

"Less of the "ugly mug" laughed Pete, "but on a serious note do you have any regrets?"

"Only this "replied the soon to be ex-detective chief inspector. "I would love to have seen my case resolved before I quit the job, but sadly that was not to be, but who knows maybe tomorrow Alexei Andropov will finally open up and give you the answers that we have all been seeking."

"Maybe so Gov" responded DS Bennett; "Let's just keep our fingers crossed" then he added "my phone has just pinged; excuse me for a moment while I just slip out and take this call." Ten minutes later the detective sergeant returned; he looked shocked."

"Bad news Gov" he announced. Alexei Andropov isn't going to be opening up any time soon. He got involved today in an argument with another remand prisoner at HMP Strangeways; that prisoner had somehow got hold of a knife; Andropov is dead; he's not going to be talking to anyone ever again.

His first day as a retiree, an ex-copper; an ordinary member of Joe Public had been spent drinking coffee, dozing in an armchair; flicking through the TV channels; and looking at all the "Good Luck" and "Happy Retirement" cards he had received. Mark deliberately had tried not to think about work, which hadn't been easy; he wanted to know more about the death of Alexei Andropov, but he no longer had the status to be involved in the investigating process. He hoped Pete Bennett would keep him apprised of developments as he had promised he would do; and he was sure he would keep his word.

On day two of his new life, late in the afternoon he received an update. DS Bennett was buzzing with excitement.

"Even though we've done virtually bugger all since we last spoke Gov" he said: "the case has been cracked; we now know for sure who planned the Summerford Hall attack."

"And who was that" asked Mark agog?"

"Vitali Zalenkov" replied Bennett; "He wrote a long letter to his daughter in which explains everything. He had sent that to his solicitors along with instructions that it should only be handed to Natasha after the death of Alexei Andropov. Nobody expected that would happen as soon as it has. In the letter he describes how he devised a plan to frame Andropov for the murder of you and Helena and the kids. He says he relented at the last moment, and tried to prevent the harm he had commissioned but a car crash prevented him from doing this. Everything is neatly tied up in bows, except paradoxically Zalenkov's own death."

Mark Hobson thought for a moment. "I might have a theory on that Pete" he said. "I remember watching a film a long time back in which a man who lacked the courage to take his own life paid a hit man to end it for him. That film was pure hokum of course, but could it be that Vitali paid somebody to do an act he could not bring himself to do?"

"It could Gov" agreed the detective sergeant; "we may never know for sure; but it ticks quite a few boxes; unless and until contrary evidence emerges I suspect DCS Hardy will be quite happy to run with that."

EPILOGUE

The view across the lake to the wooded hillside beyond was stunning, a picture postcard scene, breathtaking in its beauty. It might not have had the grandeur of the Himalayas, or the drama of the Rocky Mountains, but it tugged at the heartstrings in a way that many of the world's scenic landscapes failed to do. Here was a place to sit, and look, and linger, and wait for the sun slowly to sink beyond the western horizon.

Mark and Helena were seated on a balcony; soon it would be time to go downstairs and dine in their hotel's renowned restaurant; but for now being with each other and drinking in the beauties of nature was all that mattered. For two nights they were on their own; their eldest son Christopher was on an Outward Bound course with his school and the two younger children were being looked after by Jackie and Alan Nadin. For once in a very long while they had time to enjoy the moment uninterrupted and ponder the future without the distraction of family. Mark looked at his beloved wife and shuddered; he could so easily have lost her; that thought was unbearable. If she had died at the hand of Vitali Zalenkov's gunman then his life would have ended at that moment even if the assassin's bullet intended for him had missed him by a country mile. How it was that somebody so lovely, so caring, and so sensible had accepted him as a husband he did not know. Once in a millennium perhaps undeserving people got lucky; maybe he was just one of those incredibly fortunate people.

Helena turned towards him and smiled a smile that could have melted the Polar ice-cap.

"This is lovely Darling" she said; "but I worry that Paradise comes at a price. I think that for my sake you have dragged yourself from a world you loved, and abandoned a job you adored, and were very, very good at."

Gently Mark put his finger to her lips.

"Don't ever think like that Sweetheart" he said; "I enjoyed my time on the force, but that chapter of my life I have willingly brought to an end. I have you; I have the kids; that is all I need to be happy. You are my conscience; my guide; my icon and my best friend. If we want to think about the future let's look forward to me getting a new job without stress, and both of us slowly growing old together. I don't regret retiring for an instant. We have a whole new life in front of us. Let's go downstairs and drink to that. A new era is beginning for both of us; let's just sit back and enjoy the ride.

THE END

About the author

Tony Read is a retired Principal Crown Prosecutor with over 35 years experience working within the Criminal Justice system. He has degrees in English and in Law granted by the universities of Cardiff and Aberystwyth, and he qualified as a solicitor in 1974. Most of his professional life was spent prosecuting offenders in Magistrates Courts throughout Derbyshire, and later in South Yorkshire, and preparing serious cases for Crown Court trial.

He started writing while still a teenager, and has maintained his passion for literature throughout his life. His field of interest is unsurprisingly crime fiction, and he has to date written eight full length novels which feature Detective Chief Inspector Mark Hobson (as he eventually becomes), all of which are set wholly or in part within the stunning scenery of the Peak District National Park. In addition to these books, he has also written a novel entitled "Insatiable", which is a different genre of crime fiction from his other works because it looks at the consequences of murder rather than the process of solving a crime.

Tony and his wife Shirley have been married for more than forty years and have two grown up sons. Outside of work Tony has been heavily involved in the local community. For fifteen years he was Group Scout leader at Chapel-en-le-Frith. He was also for many years a volunteer with Derbyshire Wildlife Trust, and is a past chairman of the National Trust Peak District Centre.

In addition to his detective novels, Tony has published a short book of serious and comic poems entitled "Well Versed (Or Maybe Not)". He sometimes gives talks to local groups about the pleasures and pitfalls of writing novels, and regularly participates in Spoken Word events in Chapel-en-le-Frith and further afield.

Milton Keynes UK
Ingram Content Group UK Ltd.
UKHW021320140924
448342UK00009B/128